IN ANOTHER GIRL'S SHOES:

IN ANOTHER GIRL'S SHOES:

Berta Ruck

General Books

www.General-Books.net

Publication Data:

Title: In another girl's shoes
Author: Berta Ruck
General Books publication date: 2010
Original publication date: 1916
Original Publisher: Dodd, Mead

CONTENTS

1

SECTION 1

IN ANOTHER GIRL'S SHOES

CHAPTER I

THE FATEFUL MEETING

"TTAKE your seats, there! Take your seats!" I The whistle was at the guard's lips, the green flag waving.

" Stand back there – stand back from the train – hurry up, miss," said the fatherly porter who had my shabby dressing-case in his hand. " Quick! No room in the thirds? You can change after then. Jump in here."

Moving with the train, the porter held open the door of a first-class carriage.

Hastily I tumbled in. My dressing-case was flung in after me.

The train glided out of the immense murky cavern of Euston station.

" Good-bye! Mind you write, darling," called a voice in the crowd. " Mind you let us know what happens, now!"

This was not addressed to me. I had nobody to see me off, nobody to call me " darling! " I hadn't evenany one to care " what happened " to me – the panting girl in well-worn black serge, whose small, anxious face looked out of the first-class carriage window.

The last white flash of waving handkerchiefs slid past.

We were off.

Not a good start, for me.

I was hot, flustered, and miserable. Everything, from the accident to my alarm clock this morning to the lateness of my taxi, had seemed to conspire against my getting off comfortably.

My bath at the Business Girls' Club in Chelsea had been a mere lick and a promise. My breakfast had come up with the coffee too hot for me to drink, and the egg of doubtful freshness. In my scurry I had mislaid and left behind a hatpin that I wouldn't have lost for the world – a regimental button, my only keepsake from Reggie Penmore.

And then I had had to overpay the driver because I hadn't got enough change!

Now here I sat in a first-class carriage with a third- class ticket down to Wales!

The days when I travelled first-class as a matter of course were so far behind me that even that trifle weighed on my mind.

Well, I supposed that I should be able to change into a third at the first stop. It didn't really matter.

Then with a little burst of fatalism I thought, " Nothing matters."

" Life," I once heard somebody say, " is only one dashed thing after another! "

Certainly the things which had made up my life had been very " dashed! "

And such *little* things, too! I shouldn't mind it so much if it had been one dashed *big* thing.

But from having to give up going to college to staying on at my old school as a mere pupil-teacher, from leaving the school and spending my time between a city office and a London club for business girls, then from that to answering an advertisement for a nursery-governess from some stranger in some unpronounceable part of Wales

It was all very different from life as I had imagined it would be when I was young – say eighteen and a half.

I am twenty-three now. And I may have to live forty more years even more drab and depressing than the last six have been!

Of course I didn't always feel as gloomy as that. Sometimes I thought that even at twenty-three something exciting might happen, at any moment.

Oh, my eccentric stars! Haven't I proved to be right! Exciting? Well – but to begin with this railway journey that began everything else.

As the train drew clear of the northern suburbs I began to get a little more cool and collected. Anyhow here I was. I had managed to catch the train, after all. My luggage was easily counted – just the dressing- case that the porter had flung in after me. And, untilI changed, I could at least enjoy the comfort and seclusion of an empty first-class carriage.

Empty? No. Glancing up at the rack, I saw that there was luggage there already – a dressing-case of pigskin-leather, very new and pretty, and stamped in gold with the initials " V. V." There was also a long- handled umbrella mounted with a large and realistic parrot's head in emerald-green, with red jewel eyes.

The passenger who owned these trifles was undoubtedly rich. Certainly *she* would be travelling first- class as a matter of course.

Idly I speculated about my fellow-passenger. Was she a society woman? Was she pretty, or just, smart and well-turned-out by a maid who was perhaps travelling in the " Thirds? " Was she young?

And then the light from the corridor was darkened. A figure appeared in the doorway. Enter – my travelling companion!

I ventured a glance at her as she sat down in the corner seat opposite.

She-was what I immediately described to myself with some amusement as " A Vision! "

But let me begin with what took my eye first – the Vision's boots.

They were ultra-high, glossy patent-leather boots, lacing up the sides with white eyelet holes and white laces, and finishing off at the tops by two large, coquettish tassels of a very vivid purple.

Above the boot tops came a shrubbery of grey squirrel furs. Above the fur collar I beheld a pink, effective face. Above the face, again, came the dark red gleam of henna-hair; and set upon this was a little toque that seemed composed of mammoth purple velvet pansies. Enormous and jewelled were the hatpins thereof – enormous the amethysts that dangled from this other girl's ears. There were pearls about her plump throat, and upon her wrists there were bangles of several sorts.

These clished and clashed together as the Vision rose to her feet, tottering upon her Frenchily high heels, and swaying a little as the train swayed; and she divested herself of her squirrel coat, placing it upon the rack beside the dressing-case and the parrot-headed umbrella.

Who could help watching her?

Under her coat, which was lined with heliotrope satin, the Vision wore a pansy-purple costume with a little tight, impertinently-cut jacket, and a skirt that was as springy as a Highlander's kilt; spreading out, it displayed quite an inch of purple silk stocking above those theatrical-looking boots. A large bouquet of imitation Russian violets fastened in at the waist-belt disengaged a strong perfume – not of violets, but of Phul-Nana – as the Vision moved, rather fussily. She tucked in an over-hanging corner of her fur coat; took a critical glance at herself in the strip of mirror between the photographs of Carnarvon Castle and Aberglaslyn Pass. Then she patted the pansy toque into a more rakish angle; and felt for her ticket, in the large, silver- mesh bag that she carried. She picked a piece offluff off her skirt. Finally she bounced down in her corner of the carriage with a little, noisy sigh.

" There!"

And then she glanced across at me.

She had a communicative eye, had the Vision. I saw in it the announcement that, since there was nobody else to talk to! she would be quite ready to start a conversation with the frumpily-dressed girl in the corner seat opposite.

However, a funny little quirk of pride made me decide that I would not encourage her friendliness. I could still choose whom I wouldn't talk to, even if I was only a little nursery-governess, on my way to a new situation of which I knew next to nothing

Except that the people were called Sutcliffe-Smythe, and that they wrote on paper that was like a cream-laid blanket, so thick and expensive-looking, stamped with a big scarlet crest, and that they seemed very well-off.

" It didn't follow that the nursery-governess would be well-off! " I meditated, as the train sped on.

I remembered those advertisements for governesses or servants, *seen from the other side!* – the side of the employer; I remembered hearing them talked over in a fashion that seemed, now, so cold-blooded. I remembered the rector's wife calling in my mother's drawing- room at home, and saying – " I had a stream of answers from various young women. There was one from somewhere in Cumberland "

" One! " I thought, now. A sort of object? An automaton ? Not a human being at all! And now I myself, Rose Whitelands (officer's daughter, musical certificated, fond of children), was going to be " one " from " that business-girls' place in London." How awful!

If only something could have happened to stop it!

Reggie Penmore could have stopped it; my boyfriend, the medical student who used to take me out to tea on Saturdays sometimes, and up the river on Sundays. I suppose he just thought I was a pleasant sort of little person to go about with. But I thought once . . . He let me think that he cared . . . If he had cared he could have made me not just an item in the governess market but a young, throbbing human being. Quite a pretty one too. I *know* I looked pretty, in my way, on the days when I used to go out with him. " Brown hair, blue eyes, soft voice, and a very attractive spice of mischief " – Reggie had summed me up once, long ago, to a girl friend who was generous enough to repeat it. But Reggie had joined the R. A. M. C. He had left me with the memory of a goodbye afternoon at the West End Cinema, with a military button hat-pin, and – without a single word that counted. Where he was now I didn't know!

Here, thinking of Reggie and his kind, short-sighted eyes that forbade his joining except as a medical officer, I again caught the communicative eyes upon me of the Vision opposite. Her moist, curly, made-up lips parted in a smile over two rows of large white teeth. Then it opened as the Vision accosted me.

She broke the silence with the strangest remark, in the most resonant and cheerful Cockney accent.

The ten most unexpected words were these: " You wouldn't think I was a war-widow, would you?"

Had I heard aright?

" I beg your pardon? " I returned, faltering a little as I suppressed my first wish to giggle for many a

weary week. " Did you say "

The Vision settled herself more comfortably in her corner. She spread out those short, voluminous skirts, contemplated those . coquettish boots, jingled the bangles, and replied, " I said you wouldn't think it to look at me, would you? Not that I was one of these 'ere war- widows ? "

" No, no . .. . I suppose not," I gasped, utterly flabbergasted. " No; I don't think I should."

The Vision nodded and returned: " I knew you wouldn't! Nobody would. So what's the use?"

What could I say to this ? I gazed, out of the train- window, at the flying pennon of white smoke and at the glimpses beneath it of bare hedge and green field, with the advertisements for pills and milk, and with the announcement, " *Twenty miles from London.*"

How far, I wondered, was I to travel with this gaily- dressed girl who had made that extraordinary announcement?

A war-widow! Certainly she looked like anything but that.

So frank, so cheerful ?

I could not help thinking how impossible it would have been to me to speak to a perfect stranger, in arailway-carriage, about a loss of that sort! Supposing, just *supposing,* that Reggie had said . . . anything before he went out ? And supposing I had lost him

He had never been mine to lose – yet I shivered.

Had I been his widow, the widow of a man fallen in his young prime on the field of honour, I should have hidden myself away somewhere where I need see nobody for a time, speak to nobody about it.

But evidently this beauty in mauve and purple and grey fur was simply dying for a listener!

She rattled on, " Perhaps you think I ought to have got myself up a mass of crape right from top to toe? But I don't hold with mourning. Bit of crape round the arm, perhaps; or rather like the idea of those purple bands they have with a wreath (purple's my colour, y'know). I would have got one of those, only I came away in *such* a tearin' hurry after getting that blessed letter that I had no time to look round. Pity the poor young fellow was done in. Only twenty-seven, you know. I was sorry enough. But it's no use for me pretending that I'm broken-hearted. Because, between you and I, that don't happen to be the case!" announced the Vision with a frankness that disarmed, even while one sat gasping over her extraordinary callousness.

" Killed in attack, he was." She said it just as if he had stubbed his foot in running upstairs. " I expect he was in too much of a rush as usual. Always a bit of a dare-devil. First in the fray, and *cetrer.* Does seem hard on him; out of it in one, like that. But asfor expecting me to cry me eyes out and sit down and mope for the rest of my natural – well! I can't! "

She crossed her legs, thereby giving further glimpses of purple silk stocking, also of heliotrope frills and an. edge of lace. " So there you are! "

I looked at her, thinking of a friend of mine whose fiance had been given the D. S. O. after he had died of wounds. This friend, too, had refused to wear mourning ; but with a difference. She, too, had smiled. She had said it was wrong to mourn over any hero's grave. But her eyes were deep wells of unshed tears as she said it.

How different from this other girl! What story lay behind that difference?

I was to hear it, in startling scraps.

As unexpectedly as before, the Vision broke in.

" You see, I am a film-actress, I am!"

" Oh – really ? " I murmured.

Then it dawned upon me that her vulgarly-pretty but effective face seemed familiar to me.

That last outing with Reggie! The crimson *fauteuils* and the black-frocked programme-girls and the palms and the orchestra of the West End Cinema and the draped screen with the pictures fluttering across it!

I said to the Vision: " Did you once act in a film- drama where the princess of some country takes on the job of a waitress in a railway station? "

" Yes, that's right! ' *The Princess Who Wanted to 'Know! Miss Vera Vayne as the Princess Meta.'* That's me," said the Vision with a large, pleased smile. " Lor'!

A war-widow.1 Certainly she lookea ... te anything but that

what larks I did have over the rehearsal of that piece. I once made poor Arthur Harrison (he took the Prince Consort in that) laugh fit to kill himself, right into the camera, in the middle of our love-scene! Spoilt seven yards of it. Had to put the film through again, the fun we had! "

She beamed. Then she burst out again into a sequence of remarks for which I was hardly prepared.

" George wouldn't have liked all that. Go-ey enough himself, but I don't s'pose he'd have let his missus keep on with her profesh. George was my husband; Captain George Meredith."

She checked herself to laugh again. " Well, I say ' *husband!'* Had to go straight off to duty from the registrar's office, if you call that a husband? I only aew him a fortnight, all in!"

"A fort "

" A fortnight! Lord! And now " Here for the

st time a note of real trouble crept into the loud, cheerful voice. " Now what am I going to say to 'em all? "

" To all of whom? "

" Why, to George's people. I am going there now. That's where I am going. And I ain't half in a state about it, I give you my word!" exclaimed the Vision. " I'm not *their* style. No good sayin' I am. They'll think me the limit; all ways. You don't mind me smokin' in here, do you? Have a cig. yourself? "

She handed to me her case, studded with a big " V " in turquoises.

" No ? Not shocked, I hope ? " laughed the Vision, ruefully, striking a match. " *They* will be, I expect. Shocked into an apperplecktic fit at everything I do or say or look! They're about two hundred years behind the times, what I could hear of 'em."

" You haven't seen them, then ? " I asked.

" George's people ? No; not me. They wrote to me. Look! Here's the letter."

Again rummaging in her bag, the Vision produced the letter, which she positively thrust upon me.

I merely glanced through it – this letter that I was to know so well afterward! – with suddenly misty eyes.

It was a touching letter, this one from a mother who had lost her only son. It began " My Dear!" and I gathered vaguely that the writer had only just become aware that there was such a person as the girl to whom she wrote so kindly of their joint terrible loss.

It seemed that " George " had left a letter with his people, to be opened only in case anything happened to him. That letter broke the news that he had been married just before he went off to France.

(Hastily as I read this other letter, I seemed to get transmitted from it the conviction that they were dear, sweet, and friendly – " George's people.")

And now, it said, dear George's young wife was to go to them, and make friends, and be one of them.

" One of *them'! "* broke out the Vision opposite, suddenly. " One of them! Me! All I want is to get back to my job. I tell you there was going to be big money in that American chance! I can't think whyI didn't snap at it and write and tell them – but there." She blew a smoke ring. " My kind heart always *was* my ruin! I somehow couldn't write and put off people who had just lost some one they are wrapped up in. You can see they was wrapped up in George from the things he let drop about them. I know what it will be – poor George for breakfast, poor George for every meal, me having to play up to it every minute of the day! Oh! great Gollywog! however am I to do it?"

Even I could see that it was going to be difficult for her!

" They'll expect me to wear charwoman's black," enlarged the Vision, preening herself in that gaudy coat. " They'll want me to knit me eyes out over comforts for the troops! And to address Mother's Meetings with archdeacons and whatnots in the chair! And to be Poor Dear Mrs. George! *That's* the part I'm cast for by Sir Richard and Lady Meredith! Oh, isn't it enough to drive any one to change at Shrewsbury and pop straight back to Liverpool? Why ever did I start to let myself in for it ? *Fool* that I was "

Her regret was absolutely real.

Yet how differently another girl would have felt in her position, I myself for instance.

Not that I wanted to knit and address meetings with archdeacons in chairs. But I did long for my own kind of people, for their talk, their general surroundings ! And from that letter I could see that all these were assured – to that other girl.

I began to question Miss Vera Vayne, or, rather, young Mrs. Meredith.

" Where did you meet him – your husband ? "

" Giro's; at a supper-party. I've a sort of notion he'd just been jilted, and took up with me out of devil- may-carishness," declared the Vision, frankly. " But I never found out much about George, even in a fortnight. Good-looking he was, certainly," she admitted. "Look; this is him."

Out of the breast of her impertinently-cut coat she drew a large pendant slung on a gold chain. This she handed over to me as unreservedly as she had handed her confidence.

The portrait showed an oval, boyish face, dark-eyed, dark-haired, soldierly-looking, and – yes, even in that small picture one could trace an expression of what she had called " devil-may-carishness." What one could trace even more clearly was that the portrait's original was a gentleman. Only too obviously of another world from that of the opulent beauty to whom he had given his name!

" When I think I have got to face this Sir Richard and Lady Meredith in a few hours I go all wobbly at the knees," declared the war-widow. " I say, dear, let's go and pick a bit of something. I have got a table. You are lunching with me. That's all right! I simply have got to yap to somebody."

But for a wonder she became much more silent as we " picked " in the restaurant car. She was genuinely worried. Once she said, " I should be able to make allthe money I wanted presently out of movies; but when it comes to watching every word to poor George's people, it's cutting off a bigger chunk than I can chew!"

I listened, looking meditatively at the lace antimacassars on the seat-backs, then about the car, at the other people at lunch, at the flying scenery. Every mile was bringing us nearer to our destinations – me to my nursery-governessing, the other girl to that ordeal of an unseen daughter-in-law. I saw it was going to be an impossible situation for her. I guessed what the people of that young man in the locket would think of this cheerful, honest, vulgar creature that their cherished son had married! On the whole I thought I preferred my own immediate prospects. These rich Sutcliffe-Smythes *might* be quite kind. At all events I should have nothing to play up to!

We finished the execrable coffee which they give you on that restaurant car. We returned to our own carriage.

But Miss Vera Vayne's silence still continued.

I supposed that she was thinking deeply over what she should say to her unknown " in-laws "...

At Stafford she bought *The Era,* also *The Referee.* She glanced at them. Then she went off into that curiously profound reverie.

We were only half an hour out of Shrewsbury, the gate of Wales, when my fellow-traveller turned upon me with another set of unexpected remarks. A question.

" And who may *you* be? "

" I? " I said. " Oh! my name is Whitelands – Rose Whitelands."

" That don't tell me anything," said the Vision, as usual restlessly fussing with her bag, bringing out a tiny powder pad and puff. " Where are you going? Llandedwydd? Yes, but what to do? Nursery-gover- nessing? My dear, that's rather a wash-out, isn't it? Neither nurse or governess, with the work of both to do, and all the servants looking at you through their nostrils. How long is that going to last? "

Here she began ministering to her pretty nose with the powder puff. " It's no life for a girl," she said. " Are you engaged to be married? " Here she put away the powder puff and took out a stick of carmine in a little gold case. "What! no young man? Seems a pity. You are so nice-looking, in a quiet, lady-like sort of style. It wouldn't carry much across the footlights, but I dare say there are plenty would think you were IT. I should never bite, in those quarters." Here she began emphasising with the carmine stick the cupid's bow of her upper lip.

" Nursery-governessing at twenty-three," she continued. " Never seen the people, four kids to look after. What are they giving you for that? "

" Twenty-six pounds."

" What, a month? Not twenty-six pounds per ann? " Her brows rose over her made-up eyes. " Only twenty- six pounds per ann for all that? What on earth gave you the notion of going to such a place? "

I hesitated. Part of what " gave me the notion "was so silly and sentimental. It was merely that I had heard of " Llandedwydd " from Reggie once. He had gone to a shooting-party with some people there. . . . It had seemed a link, when I saw the name stamped on that thick crested letter paper.

But all I said was, " There seemed nothing better for me to do."

" Why, it's wicked!" declared the film-actress in tones of outrage. " Means you're on your uppers, don't it?"

Spoken in that tone, one could not feel offended at the remark. Besides, wasn't it true? In many senses I *icat* on my uppers!

I smiled ruefully, admittingly.

And then came a long stare from my companion, and a long drawnout, decided, " Well! That seems to settle it"

I stared at her.

" To settle what? " I asked

" Why, all this," said the Vision, putting aside her make-up toys and closing the silver-mesh bag with a decided little click.

" Seems to me I've got what you want. You've got what 7 want. Here are you; on your own, nobody to care a tuppenny dash where you go or what you do next. Here am I; grand home waiting for me and a lot o' people starting to look after me. People that aren't my sort at all. But – *they are yours! "* declared the Vision, leaning towards me with an emphatic nod. " Tell you what made me look at you when I first saw you sittin'there. I thought you were just the sort of girl who ought to have been in *my* shoes! Just the girl who *did* ought to have been poor George's widow! Black costume, quiet hat, sweet little face, touch-me-not sort of manner, and all. Yes! "

She nodded again, hard. Then she announced: "Look here; it would be just about right – *if we swopped! "* CHAPTER II

THE WILD PLAN

"WOPPED?" I repeated, without understanding. The other girl did not answer for a moment. With brisk, decided movements she took down the smart pigskin bag from the rack. She snapped it open; taking out a packet of papers, a case for paper- money, a little jewel-box. Then, leaving the bulk of the things untouched, she fished out a violet aigrette and a mass of filmy mauve frills.

" My favourite blouse, this one. Brings me luck whenever I put it on," said the film-actress, by the way. " Can't afford to let you have that one."

" To let *me* have it ? " I echoed, while she folded the things she had unpacked into a neat parcel and stuffed it into the lining pocket of the fur coat which she now put on.

Then once again she nodded across at me, encouragingly. " I meant what I said – that about swopping. It's all right," said she. " We've only one life to live down here, haven't we? And chances don't come twice in a lifetime, do they? Well, then! What is there against your taking my chance and my taking yours? Look here. I won't get out at Llandedwydd. I'll go on to Aberystwith. I've got an old Aunt there. I can geton to Liverpool to-morrow. *You* get out at Llan- dedwydd, and say you're for Lady Meredith's. See? "

I gazed at her.

She seemed in earnest! Could it be that years of acting in those madly impossible melodramas, where Princesses take on jobs as railway waitresses and waitresses marry Princes, had put her out of all touch with real life?

I stammered something about it's being impossible that she was serious. She cut me short. She seemed to take her wild suggestion with child-like sincerity. Where was the difficulty? she insisted. She repeated that we were both unknown. Raising her voice above my remonstrance, she declared that I, and I alone, would " fill the bill" as George's wife.

" Why, you would be it, dear. IT!" she went on, irresistibly, as our train drew up at the platform of Shrewsbury station. And during the few minutes' " wait " she recapitulated her case . . . Suddenly she broke off.

She exclaimed, firmly, " Come on! All change here! "

Seizing her bag, her parrot-headed umbrella, she leaped from the train, catching me by the arm and bearing me along with her as a leaf is borne along on a noisy stream.

" Wait, wait! I don't believe I change here," I protested. " I believe my train goes right through to Llandedwydd "

" No, no. You get out "

I have only the most mixed recollections of whathappened at this most flurried juncture. I know I said, "My bag!" and "Wait; let us ask – the train's just off again! "

The train certainly was going to start.

" Llandedwydd! Yes, don't change," shouted a porter. " Get in, there! "

In jumped the Vision again. Quickly I prepared to follow her.

Then came the unexpected, the wholly unprepared- for climax!

My new acquaintance, who had thus decoyed me out of the train, positively shoved me back again on to the platform! With a triumphant laugh she banged the door of the carriage in my face!

The next thing I realised was that her – our train was moving off, and that she had hurled the pigskin-leather bag (stamped " V. V.") on to the platform at my feet.

Also a small packet done up in a handkerchief.

Breathless with helpless bewilderment, I stood there, rooted to the grimy pavement, gazing at my – her train, which was steaming on to my destination.

The last I saw of the Vision was that showy purple toque above that pink face beaming exultantly at me out of the carriage window. The last I heard of her was a piercing, joyous scream of " So long, dear! Good luck! Cheery 0! And give my fond love to George's people!"

Just imagine the situation!

Here I was held up, almost at the end of my journey; thrown out of the train, my own luggage reft from me |(It wasn't labelled or anything!) Here I stood, watching the train turn the bend, with the gleeful farewell of that other girl who had played me this trick still ringing in my ears!

Miss Vera Vayne, poor George's young war-widow, had indeed made her leap for freedom!

But what about me – Rose Whitelands – left there with Vera Vayne's dressing-bag, her mad Gilbert-and- Sullivan-like plan that I should take her place, and this – yes, this other little packet that she had thrown out after me, what was it?

Bewildered I picked it up from the platform, unwrapping the scented handkerchief in which she had rolled it up. What was it?

Ye gods! It was the little gold chain and the pearl- framed pendant that contained " poor George's" portrait!

So she really thought I was going to carry out her mad scheme? She did? For safety I clasped the chain and pendant about my own neck. Then I stood there helplessly watching the train long after there was any train left to stare at. Oh, it was too bad of that girl! To land me in this fix! To make me late with my new employers. To let them start with an unfavourable impression of me; unpunctual, careless about luggage! How should I explain things to the Sutcliffe- Smythes?

The voice of one of the railway servants broke in . upon my stupor. " May I see your ticket, please? "

I still had my shabby little black moire bag.

In a mechanical way I felt in it for my ticket, and presented it.

He – the railway man – was one of those highly conscientious persons. He said, " I think I saw you get out of a first-class, didn't I, miss? There will be eleven shillings and sixpence excess fare to pay."

" But – but I was put in by the porter at Eus- ton "

u Very sorry, miss," said the man, reproachfully. "But you could have changed at Stafford, couldn't you? "

Of course I could have. It was the fault of the Vision and her conversation that I had not done so. Unspeakable girl! Why, why had I ever set eyes on her, or she on me? Already she'd cost me

" Oh well, how much is it? " I demanded with exasperation.

" Eleven shillings and sixpence, miss," repeated the man.

" Here's a sovereign. Please bring me the change."

It was my last sovereign, too!

Now what was I to do? I took a walk along the gloomy station. At the end of it I could just catch a glimpse of that wired-in enclosure in a field, with a barricade, and a sentry and a row of sheds. I had heard what it was – a camp of German prisoners. Through the gap in some hoardings I could just catch glimpses of the motley crew, staring up at the trains. Some were in the uniform of German infantry; some were sailors.

One big, blond brute whose face impressed me by its expression of hardness and savagery was dressed in a white sweater with knickerbockers, puttees, and the blue Bavarian cap with a scarlet band. A grotesque, disquieting apparition! I had a thrill of satisfaction to think that at least he was safe behind sentries and barbed wire. Yes, there was at least one trapped wild beast whose fangs and claws could work no further ill!

Into my meditation the conscientious porter again broke, bringing my change.

Less than nine shillings represented all I had in the world until my first quarter's salary should be paid me by the Sutcliffe-Smythes!

" Would you like a cab, miss? " suggested the porter, who evidently had a suspicious eye upon me.

"A cab? Where to? I am going by train, I suppose

I turned away to where the timetables of the local trains were pasted up. There wasn't another train on until four-fifteen, which was a very slow one. All Miss Vera Vayne's fault!

Tiresome, tiresome creature who had thrown me out of the fast train and had left me here, with her dressing-bag to account for and my own (without a label), whirling on to Aberystwith!

The platform where I was walking up and down had been deserted except for that suspicious-eyed porter. Now, with a good deal of noise and stampeding and talk, a party appeared – a party of most unprepossessing looking people.

Mother, very fat, with a coarse and common face coming out of furs more bushy and important-looking than the Vision's coat. Daughter, about seventeen, beautifully dressed, with a pretty but disagreeable face.

Two little boys, very pasty-faced, with bright green coats, black velours hats, and long leather leggings, one child in tears.

Woman, evidently a maid, looking sulky.

Chauffeur in chocolate livery, looking insolent. . . .

The appearance of the whole party seemed to cry aloud of money recently come by. Yes; it was *nowoeau- riche* in the extreme, with talk to correspond. I heard scraps of it, in the grudging, grating accent of the Potteries.

" Perfectly absurd, a Rolls-Royce breaking down like that! Is this what one pays seven hundred pounds for, I should like to know? Seven 'undred!" (crescendo). " And then to go breakin' down the very first time we take a spin from the Hall into Camrys! As for you, Browne " (this to the chauffeur), " nothing'll ever persuade me again that you know your business! No; not if I did get you with a character from Lord Nantwich!"

A terrible woman, I thought, idly, with a terrible voice. It seemed scarcely fair that such a voice should be allowed to own seven-hundred-pound cars; or that its daughter should possess such an exquisitely-cut coat! A sow's ear looks so much more like what it is when really strenuous efforts have been made to convert it into a silk purse.

And the two pasty children, with their beautifulclothes and their over-fed-Iooking little faces; I couldn't help taking a sudden insane dislike to them, though as a rule I like little boys.

They were squabbling and whining by turns. " Mother, Derek's ate all my choc'lits! Mother, Derek's ate the whole box full of my choc'lits!"

" Vernon! You come away and don't get worrying Derek," ordered the furry mamma, fretfully. " Fighting and quarrelling in front of everybody, like common children! I can't think why ever you behave so badly. Give over at once! And, Robinson!" turning to the maid, whose sulkiness I could now understand, " Why you can't keep them in order better than you do do I can't make out. I don't know what servants are coming to! Seem to think they get paid good wages for doing nothing whatsoever! Well, thank goodness! after to-day I shall have somebody really responsible for the boys. If they don't get properly brought up, what with a nurse, and an under-nurse, *and* a highly-certificated nursery-governess at twenty-six pounds a year I suppose *she* will have gone on by the fast train."

Here the young girl, who had been staring rather rudely at my solitary, black-clad figure sitting on the wooden bench by Miss Vera Vayne's bag, broke in. " Mother! " – she nudged the lady with the furs. They both glanced at me again.

" Perhaps *that* is the one," I heard the daughter say, in her unabated voice. The *one?*

As I woke to a sudden chill of realisation of what allthis might mean to me, I saw the lady in the furs beckon to her the suspicious-eyed porter.

Presently he approached me. He said, in his disagreeable voice, " The lady sent me to ask if you are the governess wot's expected this evening for Mrs. Sutcliffe-Smytiie?"

She had sent a porter to ask!

I had been chilled before by the suspicion that these odious people, with their talk of money, and their insolent-looking servants, and their querulous, unlikable children, might be those same Sutcliffe-Smythes who had engaged me by letter. Fancy living with *them,* on *their* salary, in the kind of home that *they* would provide for *their* nursery-governess! Miss Vera Vayne's picture of it had not been overdrawn! Oh, no! It was no life for a girl! And now the last touch! Sending a porter to ask if I were the governess! CHAPTER in

A CHANGE OF PLAN

THE chill at my heart gave way to a flame of anger.

Before I quite knew what I was going to do I found that I had done it!

Coldly I looked the suspicious porter in the face. Coldly I replied, " Oh no! I am not 1"

No, not for me! I thought to myself. Not *those* people! Thank goodness I'd seen them in time! I allowed myself one more look at them. Then I turned away, into the refreshment room. I ordered for myself a cup of tea which I felt I badly needed. Over it I pondered what in the world I was to do next.

I had eight shillings, and my ticket on to Llanded- wydd, where those awful Sutcliffe-Smythes lived. But there lived there also those other people. Those people who had written the charming letter to their boy's young widow, the film-actress who seemed to bring film-drama with her into everyday life!

They would be waiting for her, those nice people! Expecting " Vera; " wondering why she had not come; wondering why she had not let them know anything. Presently they would be anxious, distressed.

It was a shame!

But it provided me, as I sat there stirring my tea in my thick railway cup, with the brilliant idea of what I must do.

First of all I must send off a wire to that dreadful Mrs. Sutcliffe-Smythe's address, with regrets that it was impossible for Miss Whitelands to come as arranged.

Then I must go on to those other people at Llanded- wydd.

Not to carry out Miss Vera Vayne's grotesque suggestion ; heavens, no! But to explain to " George's people." To make a clean breast of the whole story. To beg my fare back to London from them. Yes; I could do that. They were of the kind who would understand. Then I could get back to town. I'd return to the club. I'd try and find work in a factory of munitions and repay them in instalments. Anything would be better than the service of that appalling woman on the platform!

I must go on to these people, I must make a clean breast of the whole story and beg my fare back to London from " George's people."

An hour later I was in a third-class carriage of that low train of which the Sutcliffe-Smythe's odious party was occupying a first. Another hour and the train drew up by the funny little primitive railway station at Llandedwydd.

I took my – no, *her* bag, and jumped out.

It was already dark; the soft, fresh-aired gloomlighted only by a couple of flickering oil-lamps before a small shed. To right and left of me brooded the landscape of an utterly unknown place. Before me and behind me walked the few passengers who had alighted at this tiny Welsh station.

Just in front of me I heard the scolding voice of Mrs. Sutcliffe-Smythe. " I am very annoyed, I am very annoyed ! " This to the man who was taking the tickets. " Hasn't any young person come down from London to the Hall ? " Then more pleasantly, but very loudly, I heard her say to some one else who was looming up out of the dark. " Ah! Sir Richard! how do you do? How are you keeping? Have you come to meet poor, dear, young Mrs. George? That's right, that's right. Little car running all right? Ah ! you are better off with your small motor than what we are with our big ones. We have had no luck at all with the Rolls. Break-downs ever since we bought the Hall!"

Her rasping, Staffordshire voice trailed away into the gloom.

By the light of the swinging lantern which the porter carried I saw approaching me a tall, graceful, loosely- built form – the figure of a man of about sixty, still bearing evidence of his training as a boy. A charming man's voice said something in a softly-sounding language which surprised me. I had not realised for a moment that it was Welsh.

Then it went on in English, " Yes, by Jove! here we are. Here's the young lady! This must be Mrs. Meredith."

Horrors! He must mean me?

Yes! He was close to me now, dragging off his cap with an easy, charming gesture, taking my petrified hand into his own before I could open my lips.

" How d'you do, my dear? " he said. " Let me take your bag."

He took it, the expensive pigskin possession of his defaulting daughter-in-law!

" I brought the car down myself to take you up to the house. We expected you by the other train, really," said the man who had expected Miss Vera Vayne. " This way. Very dark, isn't it? Though I expect it's no worse than London nowadays, what? Hope you'd a fairly comfie journey, but it's an infernal line. Hope you aren't very tired, my dear. Come along."

I had stepped short on the platform.

" Oh – er – please wait a minute. I want to tell you something," I broke in, desperately turning my face up in the direction of the face that I could scarcely see. " I'm so sorry, but you are making a mistake, Sir Richard. You *are* Sir Richard Meredith, aren't you? But I am not – not the person you've come to meet. I am not Mrs. George Meredith, but I have come to bring you some news of her; I "

Here I became aware that the tall man was shaking his head above me, against that background of slate- grey sky, now luminous with the suffused light of an overclouded moon. I heard the charming voice say, deprecatingly, " 'Fraid it's no good, my dear. 'Fraid it's no use talking to me. Thought you'd know. Inever can make out what people say the first few times. Mother'll explain it to you. Fact is I'm stone-deaf."

" Oh! " I gasped.

Stone-deaf?

And I who can never make even a moderately deaf person hear what I have to say!

No; it was no use my attempting to explain yet. It was a pity he had begun with that embarrassing mistake of taking me for poor young Mrs. George! Still, I couldn't begin to make that clean breast of it just yet; for that I should have to wait until we got up to the house. So, resignedly, I followed the host and the bag, to neither of which I had any right! out of the white gate of the little station to where two half-hooded headlights threw moons upon the hilly, narrow Welsh road.

In a dream I got into the car beside Sir Richard Meredith, " poor George's " father.

" Not a long drive," he told me, pleasantly, as we sped along with the soft evening breeze whistling in my ears.

Not long enough for me to collect my whirling wits and assemble the words in which I was to clothe my story to these perfect strangers!

What a story it was, I thought, Hurriedly, as the motor lights fell on a gateway between two stone pillars surmounted by the two stone balls. The story that I was not their expected guest, that their expected guest was " *embusquee"* in Aberystwith at that moment! That she, Mrs. George, found so terrible the idea of meeting her husband's family that she had fled theordeal! That she'd taken a stranger into her confidence, and had even tried to thrust that stranger into her place!

Oh, what a chance George's wife had tossed away – to the girl who couldn't possibly take it!

The father-in-law at least was an enviable relation to have. His charm had made itself felt in that first second at the station. There had been something indescribably kind and courteous in his least gesture as he helped me into the car. It didn't make any difference that he was deaf. If he'd been dumb as well, the turn of his head, the clasp of his hand would have expressed him. An unadulterated *Dear!*

I wondered what he would say to the story that I should have to tell as soon as we reached the house.

We were just about a hundred yards from that house when the second motor break-down occurred which I had heard of that afternoon.

The first had been that Rolls-Royce in which, thank goodness, I should never have to take my humble seat. The second was to the Merediths' car that. Sir Richard Meredith was driving.

It slowed down – stopped. His boyish voice came out of the luminous gloom beside me.

" By Jove! now I shall have to see to this! Get it out of the way of those other people who came over motoring. George's aunts."

He leaped out; proffered a hand to me.

" Look here, my dear child, I am so awfully sorry! You will have to go on to the house by yourself, I'm'fraid," he said. " Something is bound to happen to the car whenever I try and drive visitors, bound to. You go on. You'll find my wife expecting you. You can't miss the house, can you ? "

I could not.

For at that moment the moon emerged from a heavy indigo cloud above us. Her silver light showed up the grey, oblong bulk of the house ahead, faced by a big oval sweep of gravel.

Long windows, lighted up, and curtained in red, gave the place a homely, welcoming look that sent the oddest thrill through me – unknown waif that I was!

If only I could have claimed that welcome! If only that home had been mine!

" Am I to go straight in? " I inquired of Sir Richard.

I had raised my voice. But he evidently didn't hear my scream. He was bending over the car, unscrewing one of the lights to look into the bonnet.

So, leaving my bag – or rather not my bag – in the car, I walked straight forward, across the gravel, towards those homelike red lights.

I ascended two shallow steps beside an old-fashioned mounting block that seemed to carry one back to the days of long ago meets and hunt breakfasts. In the moonlight I had a glimpse of mossy Welsh turf, of flower-beds with a gold and white gleam of early spring flowers growing close against stone walls.

I caught hold of the steel bell-chain beside the heavy oak door and pulled.

The entrance door opened. A dark red hall curtainwas pulled aside by an old butler who might have come straight out of the pages of Caldecott's picture-books.

He was pink-faced and portly and white whiskered. *Not* as alarming-looking as the maid and the chauffeur who accompanied those never-to-be-forgotten Sutcliffe-Smythes!

He looked down (he was rather tall) in quite a fatherly manner upon me.

I stood, feeling conscious that I made a forlorn little figure enough in my black serge and my chastened black hat, tired out with travelling and positively dithering with anxiety as to how I was going to explain the totally unexpected state of affairs!

Even the beginning threatened to be quite enough of a poser!

For the fatherly old man-servant asked me in a pleasant voice, " Name, madam? " j

Heavens! what was my name? I mean, what name was I to give him?

Miss Whitelands? No; my own name would convey nothing whatever. It was just possible that poor George's mother would be " not at home " to strangers at that juncture. This would make things more complicated even than they were. I decided rapidly that, for the moment, I should have to give that other girl's name. But, what *was* it?

Was I to say, bluntly, " Mrs. George Meredith? "

No, a curious superstition held me back. For a girl to call herself " Mrs. " while she is still unmarried is considered to bring her the blackest of ill-luck.

Miss Vera Vayne – was that just her – my – stage name? The name that was thrown on to the screen before the film-drama flickered on with the picture situations that were no more far-fetched than this in which I now found myself? Had she another nanje – an ordinary one? Miss Sallie Moggs, for example? Anyhow, *what* was I to say?

2

SECTION 2

CHAPTER IV

THE HERO'S MOTHER

LIGHTNING-SWIFT these thoughts dashed through my mind. I suppose it could have been only the briefest pause that followed the old butler's "Name, madam?"

Then the problem solved itself.

There was a swift rattling of curtain-rings behind the man-servant. Another portiere was drawn hastily aside. In the domed opening there stood, dark against rosy light, a woman's figure.

It came towards me with a little rush. The sweetest of women's voices cried, " Here she is, here she is! "

My hands were taken, I was warmly kissed by the lady who had come forward; and the welcoming voice hurried on " I am so glad! . . . Oh, Pritchard, how could you not remember that it must be Mrs. George? " This to the old butler. " Bring in some fresh tea for her directly! And you, child, come in, come in. I am George's mother."

She drew me through the curtained opening into a large oak-panelled hall that seemed full of people ....

Confused and at a loss, I kept my eyes on " George's mother."

She was tall, and dressed in softest grey (wof black!), with grey fur at her throat and wrists. Her hair had been fair and fluffy; it was now creamy-white and fluffy, dressed high and looking rather like a head of full-blown meadow-sweet, I thought. Her finely- chiselled, sorrowful face must have been girlishly lovely, A gracious-looking creature! It would not be difficult to confide in her, to tell her the whole of my story . . .

(So I thought, in my ignorance of what was to happen!)

Impossible, however, to blurt out the explanation of my presence before a hall full of visitors. I must wait until *they* had gone! I glanced at them . . . Three elderly ladies and a couple of girls of the typical country-neighbourhood kind. Still wearing the fashions of nineteen-fourteen, and still talking (probably) in the cliches of eighteen hundred and ninety-six. But kind, and of the same world as their delightful-looking hostess . . .

" Sit down, child, by me! " she said, smiling, but with a tender little sob in her voice.

She made room for me on a low sofa in front of the tea-table. I sat down, feeling quite incapable of doing anything more. I drank the delicious tea and ate the hot buttered scones that were handed to me. I glanced about me at the hall with its gleaming black panels, against which hung mounted heads of ibex and markhor. A huge tiger-skin was stretched before the fire of cheerily-blazing logs. (The scent of that wood-fire mingled with the scent of pot-pourri and sandal-wood that seemed to cling about George's mother, with thescent of *freesias* that were growing in lustre-bowls on the window-sills before the drawn red curtains. And over the whole place, over all these people, there brooded another atmosphere as fragrant and unmistakable.

The atmosphere of Home!

Any stranger, coming in as I had come from the jar and stress and hostility of the outside world, could tell at once that here was a place where generations of a charming family had lived and had been very happy, very fond of each other.

Homes are not to be " bought," as those Sutcliffe- Smythes had bought their " Hall." That conviction was to be borne in upon me in some odd, intangible way by everything that met my eyes here. It gleamed at me from the trophy of old swords above the door; there were stories to each blade. It shone in the lovely, smooth-worn, heirloom silver of the tea-service, bearing the initials of some bride long since dust. It glowed from the Indian draperies of the couch; it lurked in corners with pottery, and shelves of tawny books, and black-framed prints. Gradually these things had grown together to make this British home the place it was; a place of gracious customs and observances and liberties. Just *so,* layer by layer, the coral must grow up to form the Enchanted Island!

I am sensitive to the Spirit of Surroundings.

About me rippled a stream of kindly, ordinary talk, to which I did not have to reply except by monosyllables. I think it was just about the weather, themoonlight, my journey. Non-committal things, just said with the kindly intention of making me feel at ease.

I – at ease! Knowing what I should have to undertake as soon as the visitors left!

Presently ("having seen me!" I thought) they rose to go. Their car was summoned; they departed. As they went, Sir Richard Meredith came in, rubbing frozen hands, smiling at me as if we had been related for years. He was followed by a big white bull-terrier, walking delicately.

As I sat bolt upright on the couch, inwardly fidgeting, casting about for an opening for my explanations, the bull-terrier stepped up to me.

He thrust his pink satin muzzle into my hand as it lay in my lap. He heaved a deep, doggy sigh; and gazed up at me out of his jewel-bright, pink-rimmed eyes with a look that meant only one thing.

" *Let's be friends!* "

" By Jove! George's dog, handing himself over to you at once," broke in Sir Richard's slow and pleasant voice as he turned to take the last piece of buttery, congealing toast out of the dish. " Why, Straf, old boy! Did you know it was your master's wife, then ? "

Ohl

I turned quickly to the tall, loose-knit figure in leggings and country tweeds, seeing for the first time how kindly was the lean, silver-moustached face above it.

" Sir Richard!" I began desperately, fondling the dog's ears as I spoke. " I must tell you I am not "

Then I pulled up, remembering. Stone-deaf! No use talking to *him!*

So I wheeled round upon Lady Meredith, who had sunk down again on the couch beside me. Rather suddenly she put out a slim hand on which diamonds blazed in a great star of pink and green and golden fire.

"Ah! *Look,* Richard!" she said, delightedly. To my astonishment her husband responded, " Look at what, dear? "

Had he heard the soft voice?

No. His eyes had followed the movement of Lady Meredith's lips. This he could read, it seemed, as easily as print.

" Look," she said again. " I *knew* she would wear my little present!

And her ringers caught at something that hung over the front of my black voile shirt.

Another unfortunate falling-out!

Heavens! It was the pendant with the portrait of poor George! The last thing that had been flung out at me on to the platform by George's film-acting wife. I had put it round my neck for safety. I had forgotten to remove it. This added to the complication! How truly terrible! How *careless* of me, I thought. And in rating myself for my carelessness in having forgotten this detail, I lost the opportunity for breaking into the conversation with my bombshell of admission!

For the soft, rather hurried voice of George's mother, which seems to well out of her like water from a spring, went bubbling on. " I don't think you will mind ourspeaking of George always as if he were still alive and with us, will you? I cannot bear to have all thought and all mention of him put away as if it were something to be forgotten as soon as possible. To me it is much easier to bear if I speak of him – of our boy – as if he were only awayr with his regiment for a time. That is why I have all his caps and sticks and fishing rods about, and his school groups, and everything that belonged to him. That was why I was so, so delighted when the girl that he loved "

" Lady Meredith, Lady Meredith," I broke in quite desperately this time. " There is something I must say – I want to speak to you about "

" Presently, dear, presently," she said. " I hope we shall have plenty of long talks together. , But I am going to take you to your room, now. I am sure you are longing to take off your hat and change."

Certainly I was longing to change. But not in the sense that this poor dear lady meant!

She said again. " I'll show you your room, Vivie "

Here was another surprise.

"Vivie!"

So that was the pet name by which Master George had introduced his wife in the letter that he had left behind? I wondered what else he had told his people about her? Did they know, for instance, that the new daughter-in-law was on the stage? I felt sure, somehow, that they never suspected what the Vision had described as " the movies." Probably they had beenallowed to think that I – she – was in Mr. Benson's Company. Any " nice " girl could do that! Playing Cordelia, perhaps in King Lear. . . .

Ha, ha!

But it was no laughing matter.

Inwardly rehearsing the phrases which I meant to " spring " upon my hostess as soon as we were in my room, I let Lady Meredith lead me up the shallow, uneven oaken stairs, polished as a piano-lid. I let her take me down a red-carpeted corridor of which the walls were hung with old sporting prints. Then she opened a white door.

Inside was the cosiest vista of firelight and creamy walls and a chintz-curtained bay.

" George's room as a little boy," said George's mother. She came in and touched the white bookshelf, full of Hentys and bound red volumes of the *Boy's Own Paper*. She made a little gesture towards a glass- fronted corner-cupboard full of silver cups.

" His pots; won at the school sports," she told me with pride. " This he got at Sandhurst for throwing the cricket-ball. Oh, my dear, that reminds me ... I must tell you what he said once when he was a little boy of "

How would it have been possible to interrupt her in the full flow of some anecdote about the Beloved? On she went; softly, volubly. I hardly heard what the story was, at the moment.

Probably every woman has heard it – or told it. For I am sure it belonged to that class of story whichonly mothers tell, imagining that it stamps their George or Billy or Ted as standing alone among the Geniuses, the Titans, the Originals.

Oh, those absurd, delicious, heartbreaking little stories of the childhood of the Gods!

Still talking, George's mother smiled down at me.

There was a moist sparkle in her gaze. But, as well as those withheld tears, I saw something else in her eyes. Something that would have pleased me so, under any other circumstances! Under these circumstances, it appalled me. It was going to make my task far more difficult even than I had feared.

For – George's *mother* liked me!

Unmistakably she liked me. She was pleased with me – that is, with the daughter-in-law that she fondly imagined I was ! She was delighted with the choice that her soldier son had made of a war-bride!

An irrepressible thought arose.

What, what would she have thought if she had seen *the real one?* The Vision? The authentic " Vivie! "

Imagine *her* slang and her scent and her cigarette- case, here! Imagine those boots of hers – in this house of theirs!

Even as the flame of this illuminating thought died down, I heard the door gently closed from outside.

George's mother had slipped out just as a rosy- cheeked Welsh maid brought in the hot water.

Again I'd missed the opportunity of breaking the news of my identity! CHAPTER V

A TEBROB BY NIGHT

MY chance was not yet come. I should have to tell them before dinner, as soon as I went down to the drawing-room.

Now, I supposed, I had better wash. It was a deliciously large copper pot full of hot water that reposed in the Mason basin on a delightfully substantial-looking washstand. And the maid had already unpacked for me.

In front of the looking-glass were laid out brushes and combs, and scent, and powder-things, all bearing the monogram V. V.

Of course her bag had been brought up to my room. I had better see what all the things were.

I turned to the chest-of-drawers; beside the tall pier-glass that, I suppose, had not been there in " George's " day.

In the first long drawer lay a pile of what I can only describe as extremely Leicester-Squarish " undies." Pale mauve batiste patterned over with little pink hearts and trimmed with much machine lace.

Terrible!

And on the bed with its pretty eiderdown there was laid out my – that is her dress for to-night atdinner. A frillsome petticoat, a purple silk skirt (very full and looking short enough for a little girl) and a flesh-pink chiffon blouse, entirely transparent. There were also filmy black silk stockings and a pair of evening slippers that seemed to consist of soles, ultra-high heels, and a criss-cross of beaded straps.

Terrible!

And, of course, quite impossible for me to wear; any of this garish finery!

I should have to go downstairs again as I was, wearing the dusty worn black serge that I stood up in.

I could at least do my hair, though.

With a deep and worried sigh I turned to the glass to take the hat-pins out of my crushed-looking little velvet hat.

As I did this, the worst shock of all that day of shocks assailed inc.

A draught of cold night-air poured unexpectedly in upon me, and I looked up to see if the window had been left very wide-open. . . .

Then came the horror!

For, even as I glanced above the mirror of the toilette-table set in the bow-window, I suddenly beheld a nightmare sight. Appearing between the flowery chintz folds of the curtains was what seemed like a ghostly mask; white-cheeked, dabbled with blood. Could it be a man's face, glaring in at me ? Yes! It was no delusion. It was the face of a man; haggard, scratched, bleeding, as if he had made his way likesome hunted animal through furze and thicket. A man ? Here ?

" A burglar! " was my first thought. " A burglar who's climbed up the ivy and got in through the window!"

Then the curtains parted. With one lurching movement the man stepped into my room. With an added rush of terror I realised that this was no burglar. Burglars don't wear uniform . . . And this big blond ruffian had on a torn and disreputable coat that still showed it was uniform, of field-grey, and trench boots coated with soil. ... In a bewildered flash I knew why this get-up seemed familiar. I had seen it lately. I'd seen it in the prisoners' camp near the station at Camrys.

Horrified beyond expression, I thought – " A German? "

The German, his brutal face ghostly under the mask of scratches, stood staring at me for an awful second. I was too horrified to cry out, to open my lips. Then, hoarsely, he spoke.

What he said I don't know. I believe I caught something about " clothes; " " money." Then the big figure in the battered grey uniform took another step towards me.

It was quite the most terrifying moment of my life. Still dumb with horror, I put out my hands.

I was going to faint; I felt it. I felt myself clutch at something, the thing nearest to me. (I did not know then that it was the side of the tall pier glass that stoodto the right of the toilette-table.) I saw the savage face change, spring suddenly nearer . . . Then darkness shut out everything else. There was a crash. I felt myself falling, falling . . . and then I knew no more.

3

SECTION 3

CHAPTER VI

A STBANGE AWAKENING

I WOKE out of what seemed a sleep of ages. In unconsciousness I have heard it is sight that is the first of the senses to go. The first of the senses to return is hearing. So before I opened my eyes, my ears were opened. I heard a man's voice saying close to me. " Oh! yes, I think so. She will be all right now." And my first feeling was one of drowsy, dreamy astonishment – recognition! Surely I knew that voice?

It came to me as it were out of some dim and distant previous existence.

Vaguely I remembered hearing it long ago as I sat back against the cushions of an up-river punt. . . ,: The boat had swayed gently on the water under the arbour of over-hanging willows. And that voice had said " Jolly here, isn't it, Rose ? "

It was the voice of my boy-friend, the medical student; Reggie Penmore!

And it sounded now in my ears as I lay back, scarcely awake, against pillows.

That settled it. This was a dream, of course! It must be a dream. For Reggie was now somewhere in France, with the R. A. M. C. He hadn't even bothered to write to me.

The Reggie of our Sunday outings who (I thought) cared for me! How realistically his voice had come back to me in this dream!

And then I thought that I should open my eyes from it to find myself in my dreary little club bedroom, in London, with the card of printed rules hanging just under the gas bracket on the green distempered wall opposite to me.

Ruefully I wondered if it was very late? I had a vague impression that I had to be off early to put my name down at some agency in the Strand? I knew there was something hanging over me that I had got to do. But my mind was still all in a blur as to what this might be. Perhaps if I opened my eyes I should remember.

I opened my eyes, dazed and drowsy. . . .

Here was a fresh surprise!

For I was not confronted by the green distemper and the drab linoleum and the yellow painted furniture of my well-known London quarters, after all!

My eyes fell

First, on a rose-pink satin eiderdown quilt, and on the shiny rail of a bedstead which were quite strange to me.

Secondly, upon the glimpse of a room with creamy wall paper and flowery chintzes which I didn't know at all!

Thirdly, upon a pair of khaki-clad shoulders and upon a face that I did know; a grave young face withkind eyes that regarded me steadily from behind glasses.

Reggie? Yes! It *was* Reggie Penmore! Was this still part of the dream? Or was it reality? If reality how had it all happened?

" Reggie, what are you doing here ?" Then I thought " ' Here '? Where *is* ' here '? "

" What is the meaning of all this ? " I asked.

My voice sounded strangely feeble in my own ears.

I tried to struggle up into a sitting position, but was stopped by an almost blinding pain in my head.

I put my hand up to it. I found I could not move my right arm. It hung in a sling! And my head, too, I now felt, was bandaged. . . .

" What's the matter?" I asked, utterly petrified. " What have I done to myself? Am I hurt? "

u Not too badly," said the well-known voice of the phantom Reggie – or was it the real Reggie?

The face at the sight of which I had been so surprised smiled encouragingly down into mine.

" Just a cut on the forehead, and your arm a little wrenched; nothing serious," said the well-known voice, in a tone that was not as well-known to me. It was Reggie speaking, but speaking as if to a stranger. " You will have to keep quite quiet for a bit. That is all. Good morning. . . . Thank you, Nurse. ..." He disappeared from my range of vision. Had he gone out? Yes. I heard a door shut. I heard his voice again outside it, some way downstairs, I shouldthink, speaking very loudly as if to a deaf man. (" Oh, yes, sir. Quite all right.")

Then some one else rose up from beside my bed.

I saw a woman's shape between me and the window. A gleam of sunlight fell in a white shaft upon a woman's piled-up hair. And a gentle woman's voice, known and yet strange to me said, " It is all right! It is all right now, Vivie dear."

And who was Vivie?

Wildly I said again. "Where am I?"

" My dear child, you are with us " said the gentle soothing voice.

I " Us ? "

; " You are with George's people."

George's people ? Ah! That brought it back to me. . . . All in a flood it rushed into my mind again. I remembered yesterday. The journey in the train! The showily-dressed film-actress, with her wild, comic- opera proposition that she and I should change roles! Her thrusting of me out at Camrys station! Yes, now I remembered! The Sutcliffe-Smythes, and my refusal' to go on with them! My meeting at Llandedwydd station with Sir Richard Meredith. . . . (Yes, that was the name! Meredith) the kind deaf man to whom I was not able to tell my story. I remembered my arrival at the house – " George's" house . . . My sweet reception by " George's " mother. I remembered everything, up to the shock of last night.

" That dreadful man!" I exclaimed suddenly, shuddering violently as I remembered the threatening facethat had stared at me through the curtains. " That man that was in here! I was so terrified. Oh! He came right into this room! I thought "

A soft hand, scented with sandal-wood and potpourri, was laid upon my lips.

" Hush, child. You are not to talk and excite yourself," Lady Meredith ordered me. " You had a bad fright, poor darling, but it is all over now. The man was one of the German prisoners, escaped from the camp at Camrys. They think he managed to hide himself in one of the transport motors at the bottom of a heap of sacks. He must have got a lift quite a long way down the Llandedwydd road before he made his way here across country."

" Oh! He looked so awful "

" Ssh! He was taken in the grounds here. Straf found him; pinned him till the guard came. He's gone. Now be quite quiet, Vivie. The doctor says that the great thing is for you to be kept quite quiet for some days. I am not going to talk to you any more now, dear."

" But – but I want to talk to you, Lady Meredith," I began, as I saw the graceful figure in the grey frock with the chinchilla trimming moving towards the door again. " Please "

And I stretched out my unwounded arm.

A minor pang of horror went through me as I noticed the sleeve of the garment in which that arm was encased.

It was of that pale mauve batiste, patterned withthose little pink hearts, and trimmed with a quantity of cheap lace.

Also it reeked of alien sachet powder. The perfumes that clung about Miss Vera Vayne (young Mrs. George, I should say) in the train!

Not only was I metaphorically wearing that other girl's shoes, but I was actually wearing that other girl's nightie!

And not only that – but the third finger of my left hand was wearing a plain gold ring!

Horrors ! How had that happened? Who had done that to me?

It was only a little later that I realised that they had taken my mother's ring from the right-hand finger where I wore it

I suppose they thought by mistake?

" Lady Meredith," I appealed again. " I am "

Shall I never be allowed to finish a sentence in this house ? Again I was cut off!

" If you are a naughty child and *will* talk to me," said the voice of George's mother, tenderly rebukeful, " I shall have to go away."

And she went.

Just before the door closed on her, she said, " I will send Nurse Phyllis to look after you." CHAPTER VII

PEISON DE LUXE

I AM a prisoner! I have been a prisoner now for nearly two whole days.

Yes. To all intents and purposes, I, Rose Whitelands, am as much of a prisoner in Lady Meredith's beautiful guest-chamber as that recaptured German is in the camp at Camrys.

I cannot take one step towards freedom! I cannot get any one to listen to the wild but perfectly true tale which I have to tell – of how, by a series of grotesque accidents, I have been substituted for a young woman on whom I never set eyes until that evil hour when I was flung into the first-class carriage – where I had no more lawful right than I have here! in this deliciously comfortable bedroom with the daintiest invalid meals brought up to me four times a day and with a hospital nurse in blue and white entirely to myself.

This nurse, who is the only other human being I have seen since the morning of my accident will be the death of me, I know she will.

Let me describe her.

She is a quiet young woman of about twenty-six, well- named Phyllis! For she is not only "neat-handed,"but neat-footed, neat-figured, neat-featured, and, I imagine! neat-minded.

In the neatest, most efficient manner she attends to my every need – except one, the need to get my story told – and believed. And while she massages my wrenched arm and plaits my hair and dresses the gash on my forehead which I got by pulling that mirror over on to the top of me, she utters neatly cheerful remarks; generally the same ones every day.

A favourite one of hers is, " Such a mercy it is that you didn't break that glass, isn't it? That would have meant that you were going to have seven years of misfortune!"

" Oh, I don't know," I said at last, impatiently, the last time that this remark was proffered. " I don't know, Nurse, that *any* worse things could have happened to me than what have happened already! "

" Things are never so bad but they might be worse," said Nurse Phyllis in her professionally matter-of-fact tones.

" Aren't they!" I said, lying back while her neat hands sponged my neck and shoulders with warm, scented water. " Do you know what I've felt like, all these days that I've been kept in bed here, without even going out of the room? A lunatic! One of those in old-fashioned novels. One of those poor dears with relations who lock them up somewhere for the rest of their natural lives and refuse to listen to what they say, even if they – the ' lunatics ' – *Tcnow* that they are as sane as anybody else "

You needn't move," said Nurse Phyllis. " I'll lift your arm."

" I am locked up here, just like that! " I complained, while she gently soaped the arm. " You, Nurse, are the lunatic's keeper! "

Nurse Phyllis smiled pleasantly. " Oh, don't say that, Mrs. Meredith."

This was *too* much!

In a frenzy of exasperation I thumped my un- wounded hand against the pillows and cried out, " Don't call me Mrs. Meredith! "

Nurse, without turning a hair, squeezed the sponge into the basin and then took it away. She was folding my towels on the washing-stand-rail as she amended cheerfully. " I beg your pardon. I will remember that you prefer to be called Mrs. George."

At this I could have screamed aloud. I could, really. However, I knew that when one is very angry, it ia effective to lower the voice instead of raising it.

So I said with unnatural softness, " Nurse, will you please come here? Close to me, so that I can see your face."

Nurse moved noiselessly away from the washing- stand and came and stood beside my bed. I looked up into the neat, expressionless face under the tidy brown hair and the cap, crisp and white as the petal of a gardenia. I felt, myself, very rumpled and flushed and towseled and feverish with impatience as I lay back on the lavender-scented frilled pillows with the big " M " on one corner; I must have looked like an excitedlittle girl beside this cool young woman with the " nothing-surprises-me " manner.

But I had the upper hand over her. I was going to surprise her now!

" Nurse," I said, softly but impressively. " I want to tell you something. You must not say ' Mrs. Meredith,' nor must you say ' Mrs. George.' You must never use *either* of those names in speaking to me!" I looked for the impression to be made by this mysterious announcement. None!

" Oh, certainly not, if you prefer it," said Nurse, pleasantly. " I know a great many professional ladies prefer to be known by their stage names only. I have had quite a number of patients theatrical people. Let me see. You wish me to call you Vayne – Miss Vera Vayne?

" No, I don't wish it! Of course I don't wish it!" I said, feverishly. " That isn't my name either. None of those are my names. I will tell you what my real name is," I said earnestly. " It is Whitelands – Rose Whitelands."

" Oh, certainly, Miss Whitelands. I will remember," said the imperturbable nurse. Not a shadow of surprise either on her neat face or in her matter-of-fact young voice. She went on, " Don't you think you'd like to have a little nap now? "

" No, I do not," said I still more urgently. " Not until I have got something off my mind! "

Nurse said, comfortably, " You mustn't worry about it now."

"Mustn't worry? What's the sense of telling me that?" I protested, hotly. "I can't possibly stop worrying!"

" Then I shall really have to go out of the room "

" And I shall have to lie here and worry much worse!" I cried, almost in tears. " I can't fret and fret over it like this. It's driving me distracted. It – it's bad nursing to let me! " I told Nurse Phyllis as she stood there. " Listen. You must listen. If I mayn't talk to Lady Meredith, I must talk to you!"

" Not if you excite yourself," stipulated Nurse, shaking the white-capped head at me. " You know it's because you excited yourself talking to Lady Meredith that she doesn't come near you."

" I'll talk calmly, then," I promised, trembling. " To begin with "

Check after check!

The next of them was a tap at the bedroom door. Quickly Nurse went to see who was there.

" Only the maid," she said, " with a post-card that came by the second post for you."

" For me ? " I said, incredulously. " How can it be for me, when nobody knows I'm here, except "

Nurse handed me the card.

In a large, splashing hand it was addressed " To Mrs. George Meredith."

I turned the card over.

It showed the coloured picture of an Atlantic liner at sea. Across this was splashed in the same hand'writing: *"How are you getting on, kiddie? I'm top- hole. Just off. Yours to a cinder, the Princess Meta."*

Too well I knew who had written this cheerily defiant message!

The post-mark was Liverpool.

This was Miss Vera Vayne's farewell, was it, to the country whose dust she had shaken off her high boots ?

In a sudden spasm of anger I crumpled that card of hers into a ball and tossed it into the heart of the wood-fire. It blazed and was gone.

" Oh, why did I do that? " I cried, the moment after. " I ought to have kept it, to show. " That card,

Nurse " I turned to her again " *was from the real*

Mrs. George."

" Oh, yes? " said Nurse, without a flicker. " Was it, really? "

I caught hold of a corner of her apron, stiff as a sheet of white notepaper. I clutched it as I went on.

" Never mind the card, then, but I must tell you the story "

I took a long breath. Then, beginning of course at the wrong end of the story instead of at the right, I burst out with " I'm sure it ought to be a lesson to everybody never to have any secret marriages in the family!"

" Oh, well, all sorts of odd things are bound to happen in everybody's family, sometimes," chirped Nurse, brightly. " I often think, if we could only have a peep behind the scenes at some of the real history of familieswe think we know, how surprised we should be. I once nursed a lady myself who "

" Yes, I dare say," I broke in (knowing some of those interminable " nurse" stories that begin with these words), "but you listen to me first. Lady Meredith *won't.* I expect she was fearfully anxious, though, when she heard that her son was married, and she didn't know what sort of a girl it was *to! "*

" Oh, well, naturally," said Nurse, standing there like a cheerful blue-and-white monument to the matter-of- fact. " I always think of that saying, ' *My son's my son tUl he gets him a wife.' "*

Nurse has the type of mind that can *think* in these sayings. It must save her a great deal of trouble. I went on " I dare say Lady Meredith thought the girl might be quite impossible "

" I suppose no mother thinks anybody could be quite good enough for her son," commented Nurse. " Particularly if he is the only boy. I think only children are a mistake."

I said, " Perhaps she imagined her dropping her aitches and calling a table-napkin a serviette, or being horribly fast, instead of a meek, mousey-looking sort of girl like I am "

" Oh, I don't know about ' mousey-looking,' Miss Whitelands," interrupted Nurse once more encouragingly. " With your hair parted in the middle like that and done in those two plaits, I think you look like a picture of the Madonna."

' I don't *feel* like one! " I almost snapped. " Still, you should have seen the real Mrs. George. I wonder what you would have thought *she* was like a picture of ? Look, for instance, just *look* at her nightie! The one they've put on me! *Do* you suppose I should ever have bought clothes all sprinkled over with little pink horrible hearts, for *myself?* "

" Oh, I thought those looked rather pretty," soothed Nurse, " on you. It all depends who wears things, what they look like, as Lady Meredith said herself."

" *She* thought these mauve atrocities I'm in are *mine* "

" You promised," warned Nurse, " that you would talk calmly."

" So I am. So I will," I said, gabbling as fast as I could to get it in and irretrievably crumpling that bit of apron in my hand. " But here I am under false pretences, without meaning to be! Isn't that enough to make any one excited? I never *meant* to come, and yet I don't get a chance to explain!" I clutched the apron more firmly. " She made me get out of the train at Camrys, you see, and " And in disconnected, incoherent sentences I went over the whole impossible-sounding story; journey from Euston, meeting with the film-actress, the scene at Camrys, the arrival at Llandedwydd, the checked confession

All I can say is that it seemed to have got worse with keeping!

I went over some of the incidents a second time, urging my case. " You see, if my own bag had been labelled " "If I'd only told the SutcliffeSmythes " " If only Sir Richard had not been

deaf "

Then in the middle of a sentence, I gave it up again.

I heaved a big sigh, shutting my eyes with exhaustion.

I dropped the apron-corner. In a small, desperate

voice I wound up, " What am I to do now ? If you

were in my shoes, what would you do, Nurse? "

I might have guessed? I might have known the kind of answer that I had to expect from such as Nurse Phyllis!

" I should try a little of this nice Eau-de-Cologne ice on your forehead, Miss Whitelands," she said in a quiet, " soothing " (?) voice.

She put me back among my pillows. She took the little tube of frozen perfume to rub it over the unbandaged bit of my forehead. Then, from its case on the washing-stand, she took her thermometer.

Her thermometer! Oh! What it is to have to do with people who lack one grain of imagination! Nurse thought that everything I'd just said must be due to a rise in my temperature!

I could have snatched that little hospital thermometer from her hand and hurled it into the fire to share the fate of " The Princess Meta's " post-card.

But with a great effort I restrained myself.

Fuming inwardly, I lay back gagged by that thermometer in my mouth, while Nurse sat on the foot of my bed and glanced at her wrist-watch.

When she took her instrument of refined torture outof my mouth, she gave a little nod as she looked at it, but said nothing at all.

I said, in a voice that even she must realise was perfectly calm and unfevered, " I know it all sounds the most absurd rigmarole you ever heard! "

" Oh, I don't know, Miss Whitelands," said Nurse with her back to me, rinsing the thermometer. " We nurses are quite accustomed to hearing queer things, I assure you. Nothing surprises us! I remember one patient of mine, a Captain "

" Yes, yes, but I know you think that all this could not have happened to one girl in one day! " I took up, anxiously. " It is rather a *lump* of excitement all in one place, isn't it, Nurse? It is rather more than my fair share! But I don't suppose there's anybody over fifty who couldn't look back on their lives and point to at least one day of it when things happened that were more like melodrama, like something on the stage than real life!"

Oh, I quite agree with you," said Nurse Phyllis, amiably, polishing the thermometer with a corner of the clean towel as she spoke. " I really sometimes think that truth is stranger than fiction!"

Too well, too well, I could see with which of these two things she thought I had been regaling her!

Hopeless to try and convince her, yet!

" I must see Lady Meredith again," I went on from the pillows. " I feel that I shall not be able to get a wink of sleep to-night unless I've seen Lady Meredith."

Here a brilliant thought struck me. " If I don't sleep, I'm afraid you won't either, Nurse," I said more regretfully than threateningly. " I shall keep on fidgeting and ringing for things, I am afraid."

This made its mark!

I saw the first flicker of annoyance on Nurse Phyl- lis's neat features.

Much encouraged, I went on: " Yes; I am afraid neither of us will close an eye to-night unless I see Lady Meredith to have another try to explain to her who I am – and why. You *must* ask her to come! "

Nurse paused for one moment.

Then she said, as if nothing had disturbed her placidity: "Very well, Miss Whitelands. When Lady Meredith comes in, I will say you would like to sec her."

" When she comes in ?" I repeated, dismayed. "She's out, then?"

" Yes. She and Sir Richard have gone off in the car to Camrys. Such a devoted couple, aren't they? They always remind me of Darby and Joan," said Nurse. " Perhaps Lady Meredith will be able to see you for a few minutes before dinner. But you will not be able to talk to her if you make your head ache, you know! " she added in the tone of one addressing an intractable three-year-old. " And I expect it is aching now."

It was.

I closed my eyes again, sighing, fretfully, -I dare say I am a trying patient. But, under the circumstances, wouldn't any one think that she was a trying nurse?

" Try and get a little nap, Miss Whitelands," she suggested, lowering the blind. " I will leave you."

"No! Don't leave me," I begged her. "I hate being alone with my thoughts just now."

" Very well, Miss Whitelands, I will stay," said that cheerful, obliging, capable, and utterly exasperating little nurse. " I will stay and write my letters in your room – on one condition. You must promise not to talk to me."

So I promised.

She sat close to the window, scribbling away on a writing-block on her aproned knee, while I lay silent.

Mentally I was looking over her blue-print-clad shoulder, at the letter which I could imagine she could compose. I based it on several letters which I had myself received from a young trained nurse; a girl who had stayed at my club once, between her cases. So I imagined that Nurse Phyllis would be telling her people at home or her best girl-chum or her young man (or whoever that letter was to).

" *7 am in the lap of ht-aniry here, I can tell you.*"

" *This is such a comfie house to be in, and they feed you splendidly.*"

(This was always the first thought of that other hospital nurse!)

" *My patient is the most weird sort of girl,*" I thought the letter would go on.

" *She is an actress, and the widow of a young Indian Army officer who was killed the other day, and shecame down here to stay with his people and she was so terrified by an escaped German prisoner getting into her room the night that she arrived, that what with the ihock, and the fall, and I suppose being in such awful trouble over her husband's death, it seems to have quite turned her brain, poor wretch. Every minute she insists on being called by a different name, mixing up aU the ones she has played under, I expect!* "

Yes; this is what I expect Nurse Phyllis must have been thinking behind her neat professional mask of a face! I imagined her writing about me

" *You wouldn't think she was an actress, to look at her. Quite a quiet little face, rather pretty blue eyes, and a lot of ordinary string-coloured hair. She doesn't a bit' go ' with her clothes – the loudest things in underwear I have ever nursed, since that Milanese baroness with the morphia habit. She will have it that they aren't hers. Poor thing, this afternoon she informed me that she was not ' George's wife' at all. She gabbled out some cock-and-bull story about having changed places with that other girl. She insisted that the was not Vera Vayne, and wanted me to call her Miss Rose*

Whitelands. Of course I should agree to call her Christabel Pankhurst or Mrs. Charlie Chaplin if she asked me. One has to humour them! "

Smoothly the fountain-pen scuttled on over nurse's pad.

I grew tired of concocting the hypothetical letter it wrote, and lay there fuming over the fate that had brought me there to watch it.

Yes; it had been first one kind of set-back, then another!

" One dashed thing after another," as I'd thought at the beginning of my fateful journey.

Each minute that I spent in my present false position made explanation harder. How soon, oh how soon, should I be able to have a talk with " George's " mother ?

(Later.)

I have seen Lady Meredith this evening. At last I've had my interview with her.

I have told her in so many words that I am not the girl she thinks I am. Not her daughter-in-law, not anything to do with George, but a perfect stranger who never set eyes on him in her life!

And this is as far as I have been allowed to get. With both her slim jewelled hands holding mine, and witli her cameo-like face under its white hair looking down tenderly into my own, Lady Meredith smiled and smiled, and then with the invincible obstinacy of those who are habitually gentle she refused to hear another word about the matter!

Could anything be more hopeless?

" Nurse told me something of all this," she said softly, " but we won't talk about it any more just now."

"Nurse!" I ejaculated, wriggling under the bedclothes. " Oh, but I know Nurse couldn't have told you the story one bit properly. She didn't believe me herself. I know she didn't! *Did* she? "

won't talk about it now, my dearest child,"she repeated softly, lifting one of my plaits and laying it down bn the sheet again.

" There will be time for us to discuss all that when you are quite, quite well. You are not well yet, Vivie."

I said with a gulp, " My name is Rose – Rose White- lands."

" Yes, darling. A very pretty name, too," said Lady Meredith, putting her lips down to the bit of bare arm that showed below the sleeve of my – I mean – of Mrs. George's awful nightgown. George's mother said, with the tender flattery that doesn't seem insincere in her, " You have a face like a rose! It is rather a white rose at present, though. I want to see how pretty it can be when it is pink again. But that won't be for such a long time, unless you really are a good child and obey the doctor's orders."

One word in the last sentence gave me a sudden brilliant idea. A ray of hope! How utterly foolish of me not to have seen it before!

" The doctor! "

Eagerly I said " That doctor who came! The one

who was here when I came to "

" Do you mean Captain Penmore ? "

" Yes! Yes! " I cried, delighted to have even a familiar name to support me. " He's a friend of mine! He knows me! Didn't he tell you so ? "

Lady Meredith hesitated. Then she said, " To tell the truth, he didn't say he'd met you before, Viv – Rose."

"He didn't? But he used to be such a chum ofmine," I insisted indignantly. " We've danced *miles* together! We – Oh! *He* knows who I am! He would tell you that everything I've said is true. *He* knows that I am not your son's wife! Ask him. He will explain ! Please send at once for Reggie Penmore! "

Lady Meredith looked down, half-puzzled, half- regretful.

" I am sorry, dear. So sorry! " she said. " But I'm afraid we can't possibly send for young Captain Pen- more again. He has gone back."

" Gone back ? " I echoed, dismally. That one ray of hope had to be extinguished, then? I relapsed on to my pillows once more. " Gone back to France, do you mean? "

" Yes. To – Paris, I believe he said, but I am not sure. He was only over on five days' leave," George's mother explained to me, " staying with some people on the other side of the Valley "

" Yes, yes," I put in eagerly. " He used to stay with some friends in Wales, I know. I remember he told me so. Oh, I know lots about him," I persisted, twisting restlessly on that luxurious bed. " *He* could explain to you all about me! I wonder he didn't say anything "

An unreasonable resentment against my one-time boy friend began to stir in my mind as I went on, " Surely he must have thought that the reason he was sent for when I had that accident was because he was somebody who knew me? "

" Oh, no, dear," said Lady Meredith, wonderingly."How was he to know it was for you? We sent over, post-haste, for ' some one in the house.' You see, our own old family doctor who came when George was born, happened to be attending a farmer's wife up in the mountains. So we sent to these other people because we had heard that they had this young R. A. M. C. man staying with them. But it was his last day, and of course he's gone now."

Gone! My one friend! Why, oh why, had he slipped out of the room that morning before I could even speak sensibly to him? What had he thought – Oh! Of course I knew what he'd thought! He'd been under the same delusion as all these other people! They'd told him that " young Mrs. Meredith " had met with an accident. And, of course, there seemed no shadow of a reason why he should disbelieve their word about who I was.

Reggie Pcnmore must think that, since the time of our friendship and our outings, I had got married.

Married without saying anything to him about it! Yes; he too, *he* thought that I was " George's " war- widow!

Wasn't this more than any one could *stand?*

This simply must not *be*

" I must write to Captain Penmore," I said, quiver- ingly but decidedly. " Please – if you would let me have some paper at once – a pencil – I must write "

" My dear, you certainly must *not* write," said Lady Meredith, even more firmly. " Writing isn't ' keeping quiet,' as you have been ordered to do. I ought reallynot to have let you talk so much now. I ought not to have come in, only "

Her voice grew coaxing again.

" I did so want to see you, Vivie – Rose, I mean! I'll come again, but I must go now." She glanced at her bracelet watch. " It is time you took your bromide," she declared. " Nurse! ah, here is Nurse. Goodnight, my little Rose."

A scented kiss, an encouraging little nod of the white marquise head, a wave of the slim hand, and she had fluttered out of my room like a charming grey moth.

I was left again!

And again I'd been gently but firmly and effectually checked!

Can any one imagine being in a more maddening position? Here I am, cut off from any one who has ever seen me before. I can't even remember the name on the post-card of the steamer that is carrying to America the girl who forced me into this lunatic situation ; I can't even tell them *that* as a clue to Miss Vera Vayne! Here I lie, in a bed like a warm and springy sort of snow-drift, helpless, surrounded by new magazines and hothouse flowers, by invalid dainties, and by kindness and care such as I haven't met with for many years!

They – Lady Meredith, Nurse Phyllis, and the maids – are all perfect angels to me. They'll do anything for me – except believe my story or give me anything to write with!

What can I do?

Nothing more for the present, I suppose.

Simply " stick it out" and stay here in the lap of luxury until this gash on my forehead is quite healed up and my arm is out of the sling.

Then, somehow, I shall have to manage to give the slip to Nurse and my kind, unbelieving hostess. I shall have to get a wire off, to London. Yes; I'll wire to Cynthia Deane – the girl who was so brave about her *fiiM-i'* who won the D. S. O. She will have to be begged for enough money to get me back to town again. I don't know her very well. But she's an old schoolfellow, after all. Besides, I know nobody else I could ask! As soon as I can – oh! the first minute that I can, I'll be off to the Business Girls' Club and the " daily round, the common task," as I'm sure Nurse Phyllis would call it.

Anything is bettor than the mzcommon task of feeling patient in these circumstances! CHAPTER VIII

A BID FOR LIBERTY

HURRAY!

I am so much better.

They have taken the bandage off my head. I shall only have quite a thin white scar on my forehead after all; and even that will disappear in time. My arm is no longer in a sling. And the white-haired old family doctor who came to-day says that the young lady may be allowed to get up to-morrow or the day after.

The young lady doesn't intend to wait for two more whole days, thank you.

As soon as Nurse Phyllis takes her two hours " off " this afternoon, I shall get up and dress.

I shall be reduced to *stealing* a telegraph form, and to bribing one of the maids, with my few remaining shillings, to send it off for me!

What shall I say to Cynthia? Oh, something like this: " *In great difficulties kindly send two pounds at once to Whitelands care Lady Meredith The Bryn Llandedwydd."*

Or, ought I to put " to Mrs. George Meredith " *? No, of course not.* She'll be quite bewildered enough as it is. It would only puzzle Cynthia to death. AndLady Meredith knows that " Whitelands " is the name I give myself in what she considers my delusion!

At two o'clock this afternoon Nurse Phyllis, in her dark-blue cloak and her little velvet bonnet, flitted in from the adjoining dressing-room where she sleeps.

" Is there anything more I can do for you, Miss White – Oh!"

She stopped abruptly.

For apparently Miss Whitelands was wrapped in the sweetest of after-lunch siestas. I lay motionless. I breathed regularly. With a big effort I choked back my triumphant giggles as I caught, through my eyelashes, a glimpse of Nurse putting the white cord of the electric bell well within my reach and then tiptoeing out of the room.

I waited five minutes.

" Just to allow her time," I thought, " to tell Lady Meredith that poor dear young Mrs. George is now in a nice refreshing sleep and had better not be disturbed by anybody!"

Then I got out of bed. For a minute I felt rather as if my feet were not strong enough to hold my weight, rather as if the floor beneath them were made of cottonwool ! Then, pulling myself together, I made my way, holding on by chairs, to the window. Taking cover behind the sprigged chintz curtains that had hidden the German fugitive, I peeped out of the window.

It was lovely country, now that I saw it in daylight; a mixture of wildness and appealing beauty. There, against dove-grey skies, a range of jaggedmountains were deep, indigo-blue. Next, a fringe of shaggy woods seemed to hold every shade of brown and purple in their leafless depths.

Nearer my window stretched the foreground of the drive between the bare beech-trees. The greeny-brown sea of moss beneath them had broken into a white, dancing foam of snow-drops.

And there – Ah! *There* went Nurse!

I watched her neat, precise little figure in navy-blue speeding away down the drive towards those large gates between the stone pillars.

Presently I noticed another, a smaller, figure coming up the drive towards her.

A telegraph-boy?

How is it that nine people out of ten never can pass a telegraph-boy going in the direction of their abode without stopping to ask him, "Is it for me?" It must be a deep-rooted need in human nature, I think; the need for hoping that something unexpected and out- of-the-ordinary may happen at any moment!

(I can't complain that this need hasn't been generously catered for in my own case lately!)

Be that as it may, I saw Nurse Phyllis stop the lad, pause for a minute. Now she was asking, of course, if the telegram were for her. He shook his head, and came on towards the house.

I caught myself thinking, " Supposing – just supposing the wire should happen to be for *me? "*

But that was absurd.

There were only two people in all the world whoknew that that I, Rose Whitelands, wrongly supposed to be young Mrs. Meredith, was here at all. And Reggie Penmore wouldn't have anything to wire to me about. And Miss Vera Vayne was on her way to the States.

Anyhow, Nurse Phyllis was safely out of my way by now.

Now to get dressed!

That was more easily said than done.

For after ten minutes' search in my room, its wardrobe, and its chest-of-drawers, I came to the dismayed conclusion that my clothes must have been spirited away somewhere,

The shabby black serge coat and skirt in which I had travelled down had disappeared. So had even my own underclothes.

And that reminded me of another little annoyance. If only my own clothes had been marked with my own name! But I'd been too rushed, before I left the club, to mark the tiny outfit of all-new clothes with which I was going to my new post. Now they'd been taken off to the wash without even a redeeming " W " upon them!

All that were to be found were the flimsy evening- things of Miss Vera Vayne's, and the pile of her pale- mauve-and-pink-patterned undies! She didn't seem to have a dressing-gown among them.

And I couldn't go down as I was, and prowl about the house in this flimsy, showily-coloured nightie! So, seeing no help for it, I slipped into Nurse's room. Itook from its peg her dressing-gown of coral-pink cashmere with its creamy lace ruffles.

Nurse Phyllis has quite pretty things of her own, I must say.

Her little bedroom slippers of pink quilted satin with white fur turnovers fitted me exactly.

It was not worth while doing up my hair. My arm was a little tired already from the exertion of unfastening the wardrobe-door and pulling open drawers. So I left my two thick brown plaits hanging with the two pink ribbon bows tied by the neat-handed Phyllis. Then I glanced again about her domain. . . . Why, *why* wasn't the girl a little less meticulously tidy? Why must she needs lock up all her writing things? Here, downstairs and in the distance, I heard the faint sound of that telegraph-boy's bell. The thought struck me that I might myself ring for the maid, ask her to fetch me some telegraph-forms and a pencil.

But that left me so at her mercy! She would probably go to Lady Meredith for the things. That of course would spell defeat for me again. No; I'd much better have the written telegram in my hand, ready to give the maid when I rang for her.

Allowing time for the telegraph-boy to be off again, I slipped out of the dressing-room door, listening for a moment anxiously.

Nobody seemed to be about.

The Merediths, with the dear bull-terrier Straf at their heels, were probably pottering about their gardens at that hour of a dry, early Spring afternoon. Theywould be seeing how the bulbs were getting on, or lifting up and peering into the violet-frames, or planning out the new border. Or perhaps they would be further afield, inspecting an out-house here, condemning a fence there; busy among the endless, countless country jobs that root families to the land. I supposed that most of the green and brown wilds that I could see from my window belonged to the estate. Only the heir to the estate had gone forth to defend it all, to find glory and a grave in French clay, with so many other sons of British homes like these! . . .

Softly I scuttled down the corridor, and softly and uncertainly down the shallow, uneven stairs. I thought I remembered that, in looking about the hall on that first eventful evening, I had noticed that there was a writing-table with a stationery-cabinet in a sort of little recess under the stairs.

I would make for that, loot what I wanted, and then scuttle upstairs again to write out my telegram.

Heaven send that I didn't run straight into Pritchard the butler!

The welcoming hall with its oak panels and its cheery log-fire was deserted, I thought as I came down, steadying myself by the back of the settle and by the carved arms of chairs.

No sign of Pritchard.

I was in luck at last

But, just as I was turning the corner by that recess, I suddenly realised that the Hall was not deserted after all.

I heard Lady Meredith's voice; not soft and bub- bling-over as I was accustomed to hearing it, but raised.

It rang out with a note of sharp, of poignant agitation. The words that it uttered startled me.

"Oh, Dick! If it should not be true?" George's mother was crying. " Oh, if it were not true, Dick, after all?"

I stopped, with a startled glance at the group before me.

By that writing-table in the recess of the Hall sat Lady Meredith; her grey skirts billowing wildly about her as if she had just sunk suddenly down on the nearest chair, her back towards me, her hand dropped and clenched at her side. Close to her stood Sir Richard. One brown hand of his was on his wife's shoulder. The other tugged at his moustache. His head with its thick, close-cropped grey hair was bent down. I could not see the expression on his face.

But about the whole attitude of these two people there was something that arrested me, even as I would have turned to slip away.

Something in the atmosphere was quivering . . . quivering with excitement, with the sense of something having happened.

What was it?

And what had been the meaning of Lady Meredith's poignant little cry " Oh, Dick! If it should not be true? "

Perhaps they had been talking about me – about the girl whom they considered their daughter-in-law?

Could it be that at last, at last George's mother realised that she might have been wrong about that?

" If it should not be true "

" It's true right enough, dear," said her husband's slow and charming voice; curiously shaky. " Why, of course it's "

Here he lifted his head. He saw, against the dark panels of the Hall, the apparition in the pale pink dressing-gown and slippers with her hair in two plaits.

"By Jove!" he said, quickly, almost joyously. " The little lady herself. I say! Here she is, Megan."

His wife turned quickly round in her chair.

Her fair face under the soft white hair was flushed. It was agitated as I had never seen it before. Her lashes were wet; her breast heaving.

I saw that she had been checked in the midst of a sudden storm of tears.

Poor dear! Oh, *poor* dear!

For at the sight of her face I thought I realised what had happened. After all her bravery and her cheerful talk of her lost boy, the reaction had come at last. She had broken down ... it was only too natural!

But I – a stranger – had no right even to see that mother's grief. I must not intrude.

Stammering something, some incoherent apology, I would have hurried away.

But I had not taken two steps before George's mother had risen. There was a rustling as her greyskirt brushed a crumpled envelope that had fallen to the hall-floor. Then with one of those quick, graceful movements of her she was close beside me. She had caught me by the arm.

" Vivie – Rose, wait," she interposed. Her soft, bubbling-over voice was now husky with a sob forced down. " Don't go, dear; stay "

" Oh, I can't. I didn't know you were there. I'm – so frightfully sorry," I faltered miserably. " Forgive me "

"Dear child! 'Forgive?' Don't be absurd. You – you think I'm upset – I'm not," took up George's mother, still holding me by the arm. She cleared her throat. She seemed to make an immense effort to speak in her usual voice and with her usual manner. But I felt that she was shaking all over.

" I'm not – indeed I'm *not* upset! " she persisted. " It's – not that." She smiled a rainbow smile. And then she seemed to put herself and her own trouble firmly aside. Once again she was all tender anxiety for the stranger within her gates.

" Darling Rose, what is it? You ought not to have come out of your warm room like this!" she said, hastily, with a hand on the cashmere sleeve of Nurse's dressing-gown. " You wanted something. Couldn't you make anybody hear you ? What a shame! Wouldn't the bell ring? "

" Yes – No! I didn't ring the bell," I faltered.

Then I took the bull by the horns. It was the *only* thing to do.

I said quickly: " I came down to try and steal something to write on. Nurse wouldn't let me have anything. And I had to have a telegraph form," here I turned towards the writing-table. " You see I've got to wire to a friend," I concluded, steeling myself to speak firmly, " to tell her about my coming away. Now that I'm nearly well I shall have to go away, you see."

The Merediths were looking at each other above my head as I spoke.

George's mother, without raising her voice, said to George's father whose eyes, as usual, had not left her, " She tells me that she wants to go away and leave us."

"Go away, what? Oh, no, my dear. No. No can do," said Sir Richard, turning to me with quite a merry smile. " Not a sound scheme at all! "

He gave a little laugh.

" Can't be done just now," he persisted, shaking his head at me. "Why! Dash it all! What on earth should we say to "

His wife broke in rapidly. " What should we say to the doctor, if we let you travel before you were strong? "

She put a protecting arm about my shoulders and drew me towards a low white door opposite to the writing-table.

" I wanted to have a little talk with you this afternoon. We will go and talk in my little den, shall we? " she said in her soft hurried voice. " It is warmer therefor you, poor darling, coming down in your dressing- gown and slippers "

(*"Your"* dressing-gown and slippers was good!)

" And then we shall be quite undisturbed. Come,

Richard " The charming head looked back and

nodded at him over her shoulder. " It is a family conclave!"

"Rather!" said Sir Richard, cheerfully.

He stooped to pick something off the floor by the writing-table; it looked like a note that had been dropped. He thrust it into the breast-pocket of his shaggy Norfolk. Then he followed us into his wife's own little den.

Such a pretty room! Octagonally shaped, with primrose-coloured walls and black, carved oak furniture. It was sweet with Lady Meredith's characteristic scent of sandal-wood and pot-pourri; and everything in it seemed essentially feminine, from the big knitting basket to the embroidered blotter on the writing-table.

Above that writing-table the wall was covered more closely than the walls of a picture gallery. It was hung with framed photographs. At one glance I realised they were all photographs of the same person at various ages.

They began with a round bald head and a solemn little old-mannish face looking out of the Niagara of lace and cambric of a baby's christening-robe. Then came the model of a sturdy Cupid, clad in a smile, who had flung himself face downwards on a cushion. Thenthere was a little boy in a sailor suit. Then a big boy, in " Etons." Finally the same photograph that I had first seen in the pendant that was taken for my inspection out of the bosom of Miss Vera Vayne's blouse – the pendant which was lying on my dressing-table upstairs!

The mother of the original of these studies drew me down beside her on the plump lap of the low couch before the fire, blazing merrily behind the glass screen.

George's father stood, where a man loves to stand; on the hearthrug leaning one elbow on the mantelpiece among the Chelsea china figures and the Indian cups.

Putting a booted foot on one of the logs of the fire to crush it into its place, he said to his wife, " Going to tell the little girl now, are you ? "

His voice was oddly eager! Hers was very quiet as she replied, raising her head so that he could read from her lips: " No, no. That is, yes. I shall tell her what we were discussing before lunch."

Their eyes met, and they smiled together. Ah! Even if their cherished son was killed, they still had each other, said that look. Married sweethearts of nearly thirty years' standing! I thought them darlings, these two people who were nothing to me, but who were still, still under the illusion that I – I, Rose Whitelands! I who had never seen the young man in my life! was all that remained to them of their boy George.

I loved them! What a pity that I mustn't allow myself to love them, or to do anything but disillusion . them as soon and as thoroughly as possible!

Now for my clinching attempt

As I opened my lips to it, Lady Meredith took my hand – the right hand to which I'd moved my mother's wedding-ring back again.

" Rose, dear child! What I want to say to you is "

" Forgive me for interrupting you," I broke in, pressing the white hand that still held my own. " But I've tried so hard to let you know my whole story, and always something has got in the way of it. Now I can tell you "

" It's not necessary. Dear little girl, I've heard it all," said Lady Meredith, quickly. " You did tell me, you know. You told me yourself about your – your feeling that you are not George's wife." And she glanced at my ringless left hand.

" Feeling! " I echoed, feverishly. " If it were a matter of *feeling!* But, oh dear "

From his stand on the hearthrug Sir Richard looked down at the pair of us on the sofa with infinite kindness in his eyes. I believe he adores his wife so much that he would love anybody to whom she has taken a fancy! This is what seems to have happened here.

" What is it now, honey? " he asked his wife. " What does the little girl say ? "

Evidently he cannot yet read from my lips.

In her unchanged, gentle voice his wife said, " The child still persists that she was not married to George."

" Plenty of wives left at the church door since thiawar," said Sir Richard with an encouraging boyish nod to me. Either the whole of my story has not been passed on to him! Or, more likely, he thinks it wiser to ignore it. *Oh!*

I said, desperately, " Let me write it. Oh, let me write it down."

With the air of one who gives a sick child envelopes to scribble on, Lady Meredith rose to fetch for me the embroidered blotter. She found for me paper and her own silver pencil-case. I wrote, as I sat there, on my knee. . . .

I felt them both looking down, kindly, pitifully, at my bent head.

I wrote. . . .

And, written down, I must say the story looked even madder than anything I had tried to say to them.

Lady Meredith took the closely written sheet; glanced at it, handed it to her husband. He read it; said mildly, " By Jove!" and put it into the breast of his Norfolk where he had stowed away the other note.

I said, looking helplessly from one to the other, " you won't believe me."

Here I had a surprise.

"You're wrong, Rose," said Lady Meredith, softly. w What I wanted to tell you is this. We agree to accept everything that you say."

I stared at her as she sat close to me.

"Accept ?" Ah! I saw. That didn't mean" believe." She was humouring me, as Nurse had done when she called me " Miss Whitclands!"

In desperation I wriggled my bare toes about inside the pink bedroom slippers.

I said, almost threateningly: " Then, if you ' accept,' you will allow me to go back to London again, at once."

Another surprise.

" Dear, we don't want you ever to go again," said Lady Meredith. " We are asking you to stay on with us, ' for keeps,' as my husband says."

"But " I stared again. "How can I? How

can I? If I've made it clear to you who I am, even if you're only pretending to believe me, you – you "

I stopped for a minute. I saw that Lady Meredith was tenderly, patiently waiting for me to stop.

She said, in the soothing voice of one comforting a child who has woke up out of a nightmare. " We won't trouble about whether I believe you or not. Let us take it that I *do* believe you, darling, every word of it. Suppose you are *not* my dear little daughter-in- law that I so much wanted to welcome here! Suppose you are a stranger, who never even met our dear George "

" Yes, that's just what I am – I am! " I persisted.

Her eyes never left my face. As for Sir Richard, he was watching her, with the same look on his face as he might have had on the day when she accepted him.

" Say that we believe you," said Lady Meredith, whilemy conviction grew that now she never, never would believe me. " But let it make no difference at all. And let me tell you what I mean."

I listened. What else could I do?

" For years after George was born I longed for a baby daughter to come," she said. " I wanted a girl to bring up, to dress prettily, to help me entertain, and to go about with me later on. Home is more hom-y with a daughter there! But none came! "

She gave a little movement of her slim hand towards that shrine of framed photographs above her writing- table. She said touchingly. " He is – he was our only child."

Those five pregnant words have summed up the tragedy of so many women's lives, nowadays! A great lump rose in my throat. Tears rushed into my eyes, causing the sweet face of George's mother to waver and become blurred before me. But when I blinked those tears away I saw that *she* was not crying. She had been serene before her breakdown. Now she was almost – yes, almost gay in her cheerfulness. A wonderful smile lighted up her face, just as the white gleam of the snow-drops lighted up the whole sweep of Welsh landscape outside the bow-window of her cosy room.

With her arm round me now, she said, " I'd hoped that George's wife, when he got one, might be really a daughter to me. Some ' in-laws' are quite as nice to one as if they were no relation at all!"

" Yes, but "

" One can't choose for one's children. One has towelcome the daughter-in-law whom one has, *not* the daughter-in-law one made up out of dreams," said George's mother. " But oh, how I hoped George would choose a girl who would 'fit in,' nicely, here! And when I thought he had "

Shade of Miss Vera Vayne, that Vision of theatrical finery and vulgarity, the girl whom George had chosen! Why had he? I thought, gazing at the people and the place of what a Yorkshireman calls his " come-from." How *could* he? I should never know . . . George was out of the way of all explanations. Again I thought of Vera. ... I heard myself laugh out, wildly.

Lady Meredith's clasp tightened.

" Oh, yes, dear; I know we've agreed that George *didn't* choose you! I know! " George's mother hurried on. " *But if he had,* I should have been so glad! There, Rose! You would have fitted in, you know. We should have loved to have you here!"

" Oh," I faltered. " It's too sweet of you to say so, but "

" I mean it," she persisted, softly, rapidly. " So much you could do for me, darling! Helping with my letters, my committees, and when people came . . . doing the flowers for me . . . shopping ... a thousand things! Couldn't you ? Couldn't you stay on here for the present as the girl of the house? " she suggested in a voice that might have persuaded one to stay on for ever in Siberia, or the Sahara, or among the ice-floes of the South Pole, provided that it were with her.

" Give up the idea of leaving us, Rose," she coaxed. " Stay on with us. Won't you? *Not* as George's wife, then, but as one of ourselves? As our adopted daughter? "

CHAPTER IX

AN ADOPTED DAUGHTER

IT seemed too good to be believed! I could scarcely believe it; waif that I had been for the last five years! I was to stay here, in this delightful home, with these perfect darlings of people who begged me – actually begged me to become their adopted daughter?

I turned again to George's mother, who wanted to be mine.

" Can you mean "

" But of course I can; I do! " She laughed a little, looking across the rug at her husband. " Richard! She asks if we really mean her to stay? "

Sir Richard gave a quick little toss of his grey, soldierly head. Then he put out a long, lean, brown hand and patted, very kindly, my dressing-gowned shoulder.

"Mean it, little lady? Rather so, rather so!" he said, boyishly. "Only too pleased to have you, eh? Bring a little more life and youth into the old place for her ladyship. Somebody to discuss her frocks and frills with; gossip with her when she's doing her hair. Friend of her own age. I'm too old for her, you know. She is the girl who never grows up!"

" Oh, Dick! you utter schoolboy! " scolded his wife, with soft eyes. Apparently this is always a tender little joke between them; each of them pretending that the other never gets any older, while Time marches on for the speaker.

" It's you and Rose who are the contemporaries!" declared Lady Meredith. " Strangers will think you're brother and sister, and I the Mamma of both of you, when she comes to live here! "

At this I drew back my hand. I made my last protest. I said, tremblingly but firmly, " If I do come, it is not under false pretences? It really is not as George's wife ? "

" No, no. It is as your own dear little self," insisted Lady Meredith. " It is because I should have chosen you, out of a whole crowd of other girls, for the wife George ought to have had. Now say that it is all right! Say you'll come "

" I don't deserve it. I feel that I am taking what should be another girl's right. But " I ended desperately, " but *I am coming!* "

And I let Lady Meredith take my face between her two slim jewelled hands and kiss it in token that the bargain was sealed.

" Ring, Richard, for tea," she said, then, in her soft, that-settles-it tone. " We'll have it in here. It's cosier than the Hall to-day, and we need not be disturbed by any visitors. And, Rose," she touched my pink cashmere-clad knee, " you will stay and have it with us to-day, won't you? I am sure that you're tired of having it upstairs in your bedroom! "

" I am, rather," I admitted, smiling, and still dazed, still not realising the change that I had accepted in my life. " If you don't mind my staying in this – this dormitory-party get-up!" I glanced down at the slippers, the pink cashmere. " Thank you, Lady Meredith."

She gave a quick little shake of the white, beautifully dressed head.

" You mustn't call me ' Lady Meredith,'" she said. " You are my little daughter now. We must think of a name for you to call me "

A thought came into my head. Before I knew whether or not to utter it, George's mother herself said it aloud.

" If – if I had a daughter-in-law I should not wish her to call me that. Not ' Mother.' Nobody ought to be called by that name but a child's real mother."

" Thank you," I said, and kissed her hand.

She looked very kindly at me and said " If – I only say *if* I had a daughter-in-law, I should have liked her, I think, to call me ' *Belle-mere.*' After all, it's what I should be to her, and it sounds . . . pretty."

" I should like to call you something that you thought sounded pretty! " I said, on an impulse. " I *will* call you ' *Belle-mere!' "*

And when I saw how pleased she looked, I was glad that I had said it.

After the maid had brought in the silver tea-things and the cake-stand and we were all three left aloneagain, my adopted mother-in-law told me, with a look of real and girlish glee, about the " plan " that she had mentioned.

" If you really are strong enough to think of travelling, Rose, you may have to travel; not from us, but with us," she said. " You know that we are thinking of going abroad almost at once."

"Abroad?" I echoed. I am sure my face lighted up.

"Abroad! Oh, are you?"

I hadn't been abroad since the last Christmas holidays from my school, when we all made the Winter sports in Switzerland – my people, my cousins, and I.

" Oh, it's such a long time since I saw anything but England, London!" I cried again. " It would be heavenly to go abroad! "

Here, over their tea-cups, I saw the Merediths exchange a glance of real and youthful delight.

They were living in my pleasure!

Lady Meredith, beaming all over her dear face, said: " It is not really very far abroad to begin with, wherever we may decide to go on afterwards. It's only Paris!"

But I put down my tea and clasped my hands with joy at the thought of seeing Paris again; Paris with its wide, smiling gaiety, Paris with the picture-galleries that I had loved as a schoolgirl!

"Ah! You're fond of gay Paree, are you?" said Sir Richard Meredith, nodding as he noticed my gesture. He came to the table to cut for himself an enormous wedge of Welsh plum-cake, moist and brown and rich as leaf-mould. He smiled down at me and said: "You'll like that, will you? Go about and see what's on at the theatres and what lunatic new lampshades we can get up for you in the way of frocks!"

" Richard! The wide frocks are not nearly as ' lunatic ' as the old sheaths were. It's only because it takes a Briton exactly eighteen months to get accustomed to the *least* new idea in fashions!" protested Lady Meredith. " Little Rose will look perfectly sweet in anything Jeanne makes for her. I'm longing to get her to work on her. Where are we going to put up ? "

" Oh, some nice comfie little hole in the middle of things. What's the matter with the Ritz? Show the little lady the latest things in Polish princesses and French airmen," said Sir Richard. " Talking of airmen (more tea, dear, thanks), there are the captured Taubes at the Invalides to have a look at "

" And the theatres! Oh, to see French acting again, with somebody young – I mean somebody else young," cried Lady Meredith, joyously. " We simply must take the children – I mean, you and Rose, to see that delightful dancer at the "

She bubbled on, while I, sitting beside her with a piece of untasted bread-and-butter in my hand, could only wonder and wonder at these new " people" of mine, who were George's *real* people! Here they were. the extraordinary couple, discussing clothes and hotels and theatres, for all the world as if they were planning a trip to Paris in the piping times of Peace! Nobody would have supposed for one instant that they were a stricken couple who, at the beginning of their mourning, were going to visit the land on whose soil their only son had shed his blood in the cause of Right!

And yet, an hour ago, I had seen his mother's stormy tears!

Ib my bewildered surprise I could only suppose that this other was all deliberate; a gallant struggle indeed. It was all part of their behaving as if George were not really lost to them, only away for the present.

It didn't *look* like acting, though. . . .

And I decided that part (if it was not deliberate. No; it was sympathetic unselfishness; it was delight because I was so pleased – I, the adopted daughter – at the projected trip to France. Sir Richard Meredith began pacing restlessly over the dead-rose-coloured carpet of the little room; his wife's eyes shone with excitement, her cheeks were flushed pinker than my dressing-gown, as they chatted about their preparations for this journey.

In a pause I asked, " Are you – are we to go very soon, then? "

" Oh, the sooner the better; the sooner the better!" said George's mother, with an eagerness that I suppose must have been to please me. " As you are so well – and you really do look well to-day, Rose! " – hereshe stroked my cheek – " I think we could quite well run up to London the day after to-morrow. The day after to-morrow, I said, Richard ? " turning to him.

" Oh, quite, quite! " nodded Sir Richard.

" And as soon as we have got all our passports," planned Lady Meredith, " we can just dash across the Channel, and be nicely settled in Paris before we meet "

Here she pulled herself up sharply. She went on again.

" Before we meet the person we are going to see over there. You – you know, dear Rose, I am really going over to see a – a relative of ours."

" Oh, are you? " I returned.

" Yes; it's – it's an aunt of mine," explained George's mother in that voice that always reminds me of a clear, bubbling-over brook. And then, turning her face upon the husband whose sunshine it is, she repeated for his benefit, " I have just been telling Rose that our chief reason for going over to Paris just now is to – to meet an aunt."

"A what? An aunt? Oh, by gad, yes," said Sir Richard, in an odd, almost startled sort of voice. "To meet an aunt. Quite!"

And then it was my turn again to be startled.

For I saw Sir Richard put down his third cup of tea. He put it down abruptly, precipitately, wedge of cake in the saucer and all; he *plumped* it down in the very middle of a large open bowl of pot-pourri that stood on the oaken table to his right.

And then he " plumped " himself down on the arm of the couch where his wife was sitting beside me; he opened his mouth and went off into a " Pah, ha, *ha!"* of boyish laughter, sudden, unexpected, and loud.

" Dick! " gasped his wife.

, Then, without warning, she joined in her husband's mirth. She laughed; her slender form shaking, she laughed, hiding her face as a giggling schoolgirl daughter might have done, against her husband's rough sleeve. At last she paused, for breath, I think. She lifted her head.

" Oh, Rose! Don't think me hysterical," she struggled to say. Of course it was just what I had been thinking her! But who could blame her? After the strain and agony which she had so recently been through, was it any wonder that George's mother was more or less hysterical now?

She pulled out a handkerchief to dry the tears of over-excited merriment that were running over her cheeks. Breathlessly she began to explain: " He always laughs – he always makes me laugh at – at the idea of this particular aunt. It is very wrong of us, but we can't – can't help it!"

" Is there something very odd about her? " I asked – feeling that a few more surprises in this family would be nothing to me now.

Lady Meredith, tidying her hair with her hands, looked up to repeat my question to her husband as h still sat astride of the couch-arm beside her. Hewent off into another shout of that boyish laughter.

" Oh, yes," he exclaimed through it. " Oh, by George – by gad, yes. A very odd aunt. Yes; rather so! One of the most peculiar things in aunts that you ever saw; ha, ha! "

" Oh, Dick, don't " his wife implored him. I

thought she was going off into wild hysterical shrieks once more. But she pulled herself together and wound up. " Don't alarm the child! "

" I am not going to be alarmed, *Belle-mere,"* I said, smiling gratefully upon my adopted mother. " I am sure I shall like this aunt. I seem to like everything belonging to you! "

"Richard, did you catch that? Rose thinks that she is going to like the aunt!" translated George's mother to her husband.

And once again that odd pair, that youthful Darby and Joan, burst out laughing together as if over the most thoroughly enjoyable joke that they had ever heard!

(Later.)

An idea came to me to-night as I was having my hair brushed and myself " put straight" for the last time by Nurse Phyllis.

She, by the way, was not in the least surprised to find that her dressing-gown and slippers had been down to tea in Lady Meredith's boudoir. Nor to find that I was planning to go abroad with the peoplewhom, yesterday, I had disowned. As she herself says, nothing surprises a hospital nurse. Rather a pity I never put my name down at a hospital myself! The training might have helped me during the surprises, the excursions, and the alarms with which my young life has simply been packed during the last ten days of it.

But about the suspicion that has just occurred to me.

This aunt in Paris; this aunt over whom George's father and mother were so curious, and laughed until they cried! *I don't believe in her!*

I mean, I don't believe it's an aunt at all that they are going over to France to see. I know what I *do* believe it is! I've thought over the mysteriousness of it all, and here's the solution I've come to. I believe it's a brain-specialist; yes, one of these ultra-clever Parisian specialists that they are taking me to.

They think that he may hit upon some treatment that will cure me! Me!

For I know, I *know* they still think that I (George's wife) can be cured! They still put down all my protestations to loss of memory. Yes; they think I've lost my memory of who I really am, and that it's due to shock, following upon great grief.

They think that I may yet be brought to remember that I am George's wife, and all about it!

What will they say when the specialist himself pronounces that I am a perfectly normal young woman inher sober senses – only not the young woman whom they think?

Another question that haunts me about Paris – isn't it there that Reggie Penmore may be working for the Red Cross? Shall I see Reggie in Paris?

4

SECTION 4

CHAPTER X

COMFORTABLY UNDER FALSE COLOURS

PARIS!

Such a different Paris from the one of which

I had a glimpse when I was a girl of sixteen,

eight years ago.

Then, my mother and I put up at a modest little French hotel, in the rue Notre Dame des Champs, on the " other " side of the river, where tram-bells clanged incessantly and the flocks of art-students strolled down the Boulevard St. Michel in long curls and velveteen trousers as wide as a pair of petticoats; and we used to have our meals at Garnier's in the Boulevard Mont- parnasse, dining sumptuously (or so I thought!) for two francs fifty, at a little table set out under the striped red-and-white awning above the asphalted pavement.

But now I am staying, as the adopted daughter of Sir Richard and Lady Meredith, at what Sir Richard described as " the comfie little hole in the middle of things."

The Ritz!

This huge hotel with its great rooms and its arrogant decorations and its windows that stare indifferently out on to the Place Vendome with its Napoleoncrowned column pointing a warning finger to the skies – it seems like an enchanted palace to me, even though I come to it after the cosy luxury of that Welsh country house set like a hassock at the foot of the mountains. Sitting here in my bedroom at the Ritz, I have to force myself to remember that other room that was mine a fortnight ago. That narrow London club bedroom with its grimy ceiling, its repellent linoleum, its cockling card of rules reminding me, as I dressed,

" *All lights must be out at 10:30 p. m.*

" *Members who fail to be at the breakfast table at 8 a. m. will be fined threepence.*

" *It is forbidden to bring eatables of any kind into the bedroom.*

" *Warm baths, 6d. each"*

Oh, what a world of vivid contrasts!

After all that – this!

There is only one drawback to it all.

This luxury, this beauty, this kindness by which I am surrounded are not really meant for me, Rose Whitelands. No! Not for all Lady Meredith's protestations, that she has adopted me " for myself alone." I know; I know!

This room, this deliciously comfortable French bed, this polished Empire furniture, this heavenly bath- room-all-to-myself, gleaming with white china, glass shelves, and bright taps, the smiling attentions of the

//-' /If / :. *ffl* . *sf* / 'A%A *&?&*

that perfect day when we sped over the silver waves

black-haired *femme-de-chambre,* the new fur-lined *manteau-de-voyage* that I have just thrown *off,* the whole feeling of leisure, and holiday-making, and ease – none of these things are mine by right. They belong to George's wife!

It is Vera Vayne, the film-actress who is now " somewhere in New York," who ought to be reaping the benefit of them all!

This thought has pursued me, right across the Channel on that perfect day when we sped over the sflver waves and under the silver escort of that airship that floated above us until we reached the French harbour.

And there is bitterness in the thought – and fear.

It's true that I have made every effort to let the Merediths know the real state of affairs, and that the false pretences under which I am being petted and spoiled are not my own fault. It's true that I was furiously exasperated, all those days in Wales, over the " one dashed thing after another " that prevented them from taking my story seriously.

But now – Oh, I'm beginning to think that I shall never again really want them to believe that I am not George's wife!

I'm so happy with them. I've never liked any people so much since the whole of my own family were swept away from me at once by the tragedy of a wrecked express.

I'm like a stray kitten that has wandered in, outof the cold murk of some wet London back-yard, into the warmth of a welcoming fireside.

This does sound as if I cared for nothing but my creature-comforts, doesn't it?

But, honour bright, that's not true.

It's not because " George's people " are rich, and have that beautiful house in Wales, and can afford to travel in circumstances that make everything as easy as if we sat on the magic carpet of the fairy-tale, and were simply wafted from place to place.

No! The comforting atmosphere in which I find myself enveloped is not so much a matter of material things as of a sweet and thoughtful affection that wraps me like a cloak.

And shall I have to drop it again? Must I again become a " stray," back to the wet and the cold?

Quite possibly.

For this grotesque situation *cannot* continue. The wonder is that it has gone on so long! Presently something must happen to convince the Merediths of their mistake. We shall meet somebody that knows me, or that knew George and the real Mrs. George. There's Reggie Penmore, whom I ought to see.

Or, of course! There's the impending visit to that specialist, to whom they so mysteriously referred as " the aunt."

He will persuade them. . . .

And then?

What will they have to say to me when they are at last quite sure that I am I, and not the other girl inwhose shoes I have been disporting myself all this while?

Will their feelings towards me change utterly? Only too natural to suppose that they will. . . . Most people's would. . . .

But the Merediths aren't like most people.

Even if they let me go away

But they won't!

Oh, I wish I knew if they would or not!

But I am doomed to be kept in suspense about all this a little longer, it seems.

For, as soon as we arrived at the Ritz, a telegram was handed to Sir Richard Meredith.

I saw him glance at it as we all stood by the big counter arranging for our rooms. As he read it his face fell with a look of quite extraordinary disappointment.

"This is a bit off, Megan, eh?" said he. "Look here." And he handed it to Lady Meredith. She read the wire.

" Oh, well! It can't be helped, dear," said his wife, though her own cameo-like face looked also suddenly blank. All the girlish gaiety and interest was wiped out of it for a moment. " It's – a pleasure deferred, that's all," she said, looking at him comfortingly, and then she smiled at me.

I asked, " Hasn't ' the aunt' come, then, *Belle- mere? "*

Curious how they always call this supposed relative " *the* aunt"! I should have thought that they mighthave known that this alone would have been enough to make me suspect that something was in the wind. They might at least have invented a name for this specialist – " Aunt Mary," say, or " Aunt Georgians "!

" Her leave – her visit is to be postponed for perhaps a week or ten days," Lady Meredith told me, as we went up in the lift to our floor. " Everything is so uncertain, you know, nowadays. One can't make sure of anything not being altered at the eleventh hour! It is a great disappointment to us. I'm afraid it will quite spoil Richard's pleasure for the present "

Evidently she forgot that I had seen " Richard " in fits of laughter over the idea of the aunt! And that he had said she was the oddest thing in aunts that he had ever seen! So now she pretended that he was passionately attached to this so-called aunt!

" But we must make the best of her not coming just yet," wound up George's mother as the lift stopped and we got out. In the corridor we passed a lady in a wonderful oriental tea-gown and with her hair dragged straight back off her forehead and fastened in a sort of washing-bob at the back of her head. She looked beautiful, and mischievous, and eccentric; and she stared at us, hard, as we passed on towards our rooms.

" That is a Princess of one of those curious little States," Lady Meredith told me in a low voice. " I wish she was not quite so – odd."

Feeling rather mischievous myself, I couldn't help suggesting,'

" No, dear child, no. Good gracious, no!" said Lady Meredith in a queer stifled voice, as she opened the door. She bit her lip. But I couldn't decide whether this was because she was annoyed, or because she was trying not to laugh again. In her room she said: " The aunt isn't in the least like that; the Princess Jinka is *not at all* her' sort, Rose! . . . But that is a beautiful tea-gown she wears," she added, with a meditative eye upon the blue cloth coat-and-skirt that I was wearing myself; she bought it for me in a hurry as we passed through London. " Which reminds me that there is one good thing about the aunt not being in Paris just yet. We shall be able to get some clothes – shopping done for you, childie, before she comes!"

This morning, therefore, we left Sir Richard at Cooks', while we went shopping.

Oh, the wonderful revelation that it was to me!

We walked, my adopted *Belle-miire* and I, across the streets of Paris; I revelling in the clearness and smokelessness and breadth of it all! the silvery lights, the light road, the tall pale houses. I had forgotten how smiling, after the dark dear set face of our own capital, is Paris with her many trees, her frequent grass-plots, and her sudden splash and spray of white fountains. ... I realised again how bright, in her moving crowds, is the glitter of her uniforms. As we passed down a cobbly side-street something went by in a sky-blue tunic, with a flash of gold lace 'and the glow of a scarlet stripe about him. I couldn't helpexclaiming to Lady Meredith, " *Oh,* isn't it a relief to see soldiers *coloured* again! "

"Oh, Rose! Unpatriotic!" she said, turning to me with reproach in her face. " Even by a comparison, you mustn't ever run down khaki!"

" I don't! " I protested, hotly. " Of course I should always love our own darling muddy barbed-wire torn khaki *better* than the most gorgeous "

Here I pulled myself up. For I had seen a delighted smile break over Lady Meredith's face as she walked along beside me. How awful!

Of course she imagined that at last some memory of " George" in his war-worn khaki had begun to pierce the mists that wrapped his poor young wife's distraught mind!

Why had I opened my mouth to say what I'd said?

I think I missed several of the most fascinating shops while I scolded myself for my stupidity; and I had not lost all of my scarlet blush of confusion when we reached a corner-house bearing, on a black marble shield, the gold-lettered inscription:

" JEANNE."

Lady Meredith said joyously, " Here's our woman! "

And we entered.

From the downstairs hall shallow winding stairs led to the upper temple of this French dressmaker's. The whole upper floor was cunningly divided by screens, domed openings, and walls.

Everything in these screened-off rooms was beautiful ; from the thick dust-coloured carpets to the colouring of the walls; deep peacock green down to the picture-line, then cloud-grey. There were low couches; there were cushions for hassocks. There were side cupboards, like china cabinets with glass doors, through which one saw rich pieces of hand embroideries and beaderies of every colour. A simple red rose was " painted " on to a strip of black-and-dark-green bead background, all looking indescribably sober and rich! A strip of milk white was patterned in pink and orange flowers, and hung amid a gay riot of fans, feathers, and painted lamp-shades. Truly it was a room in which all the vanities of all the centuries seemed to join hands. The walls were girdled with a belt of framed fashion-plates cut from " *Le Journal des Demoiselles,"* and " *Le Pallet* " pictures of the Thirties and Forties and Fifties, exquisitely finished and coloured with the artistic conscientiousness of a butterfly's wing.

Moving to and fro against this background were the mannequins, the vendeuses, the great Madame Jeanne herself; a tiny little woman in grey, who smiled upon Lady Meredith as she entered, and then went on talking volubly, with all her eyes and lips and hands, with her whole face and body and dress, to a knot of customers who were standing with their backs to us.

From those backs I could see that they were English. Two of them were girls; one with a thick black plaitdown her back. One about my own age. The elder lady was evidently their mother. She was rather short and stout, but a pair of very small and graceful feet and ankles showed beneath her brown fur coat, and her grey, fluffy hair was glossy and beautifully-kept- looking below an audacious feathery toque.

I was looking at her and at the way she tilted her head, rather ironically, to listen to Madame Jeanne's cascade of talk, when I felt my arm caught in a sudden and desperate clutch.

What was it?

I turned to see Lady Meredith's face looking more agitated than I had seen it since that afternoon in the hall at home (curious how I call the Welsh place "home" to myself, quite naturally!). She dragged me a little aside.

" Rose, listen to me a minute," she murmured in a flurried tone. " That woman, talking to Madame, look! She's a very old friend of mine."

" Oh, how nice for you to meet her," I was beginning. But evidently there was something about this that George's mother found the very reverse of nice. She hurried on, " I shall have to speak to them. I want you to do something for me, darling."

"Oh, yes, *Belle-mere.* Anything!" I said, gladly, thinking that there might be something that I could fetch for her from the hotel. If there were only more things that I could do for her, for her who does everything for me!

She was saying in that desperate little whisper " I'vea special reason for not wishing these people to know that – you know, darling! "

Then, still more desperately, " I can't let her – them know that you are – *are not George's wife!* I want them to think it for the present. Only for the moment! It will all be explained – afterwards, Rose! Please, *please* will you "

I don't know what reply I was going to make. But before I could think of making any whatsoever the woman with the audacious toque had suddenly swung round on her high booted heel, and had seen George's mother.

" Hul – lo!" she exclaimed. Her breezy, confident English voice rang out through the exquisite room with its artistic fittings and its populace of Frenchwomen gesticulating, smiling, uttering their little cries of *"Mais, parfaitement, Madame! ...* La *taille tera beaucoup plus serree, beaucoup, beaucoup, beau- coup! . . . C'est navrant, Mademoiselle, mais c'est wai. ... Ah, ca sera trrrrrres gentH! . .* ; *Ravisante. ...*"

" Hullo, Meg Meredith!" repeated the English customer in the brown fur coat. She had brown eyes, too, I saw; very bright and shrewd, and a clever, low-browed face with a decided chin. Very quickly she moved over the dust-grey, dust-soft carpet, and put out both hands to my adopted mother. " Jolly, seeing you! I say, I'm so frightfully bucked, I don't know what to say to you! "

"Thank you; oh, thank you, Ethel," said LadyMeredith with a little nervous catch in her voice. I wondered if she disliked all this effusiveness. People who are rather demonstrative as she is are shy of domonstrativeness in others.

" Thought we might perhaps meet you here; regular happy hunting-ground," said the other woman. Then as I stood a little behind George's mother, seeming to study a crinoline fashion-plate, I felt her bright, brown eyes fasten themselves upon me.

" Hullo," she said again, brightly. " I suppose this is the – the young lady in question? The new little daughter-in-law, eh?" CHAPTER XI

THE LITTLE DAUGHTER-IN-LAW

little daughter-in-law!"

1 There was a second's pause. I stood there,

wondering if Lady Meredith would say " Yes, it is." Of course I could not contradict whatever she meant to say; not after that breathless little appeal she had made to me before her friend turned and saw us! No, not even if she did introduce me as George's wife!

But this she didn't do in so many words.

That second's pause restored her poise. With her sweetest smile, George's mother said: " Oh, I hate the words ' in-law'! It always sounds like a family em- broglio of some sort! Don't you think so? I always call her my little daughter. Rose!" She turned to me, " this is an old schoolfellow of mine, Mrs. Tracey "

The elder lady shook hands very heartily indeed.

" and her daughters."

The grown-up one of these daughters was a strikingly handsome girl; dark, slender, and very tall. I thought she looked rather hard at me.

" We're here about Phillipa's trousseau, you know," explained Mrs. Tracey, with a nod towards her.

" We've just finished for to-day, but never mind. We'll wait with you until your vendcuse is disengaged; look at the new models together. This is delightful. When did you come over? We must see lots of each other," she went on to my adopted mother (who, I felt it in my bones, had some reason for not wishing to see "lots" of her old schoolfellow). "Let's sit down to it, shall we? "

As they turned to the low couches set against the wall I heard Lady Meredith saying something very quickly, to the other woman, that sounded like " *doesn't know anything yet."*

Could she mean me?

Then had she told some of her friends about the extraordinary " delusion " under which George's poor young wife was still labouring?

" Doesn't know anything yet "

Very mysterious!

It must have had something to do with me. For I saw Mrs. Traccy's brown shrewd eyes flash me an astonished glance before she nodded and said carelessly, " Oh, really? . . . There's room for us all here, I think."

We all five sat down on the couches that lined the room like seats set for chaperons at dances.

And presently it was indeed a dance as of butterflies that flitted past us. One by one over the thick dust-coloured carpet the mannequins stepped past us on very high-heeled, neat, snub-nosed boots. They turned, twisted about, lifted an arm, raised the insideof a coat-flap to show the gleaming lining, preened and strutted and fluttered in conscious, conscientious coquetry, showing off in all seriousness each feature, each new note of the new fashions. Then quickly they stepped back one by one towards the dressing-rooms at the other side of the shop, to emerge once more in yet other garments. The voice of the *vendeuse* gave an order, now and again, " Mademoiselle! *Vous pagserez* "

One girl came out smiling in a redingote that was still *en main:* it had a snipped-out collar and no sleeves and was patterned with white tacking-threads.

In one of the further rooms another mannequin, such a pretty girl with vermilioned lips and exquisitely-dressed hair! was revolving slowly in a bubble of dark-green silk, before two men in morning-coats and grey trousers.

Men? In such an incongruous setting? In such a shrine of femininity?

I gazed at the largest of the men, big and gross- looking, with jewel-bright, little eyes that peeped out of rolls of sallow flesh. He was apparently taking in every detail of the dress on that fresh and piquant French girl; picking up one of the little cascades of ribbon that rippled down the wide spread of her skirt, examining the set-in of the sleeve, stretching out a large, fleshy finger towards her collar, the first of the kind that I had seen; it spread a corolla of net about the flowering bud of her little face. The man nodded approvingly at it.

" He is a buyer for the foreign market," Lady Meredith explained to me as I gazed wonderingly upon this curious little scene, " and he comes here for the latest ' creations,' as he probably calls them."

" Odious fat brute," commented Mrs. Tracey in her careless, breezy voice. " No job for a man, I consider; do you? "

She turned suddenly to me. I said, without stopping to think, " I can't help feeling that there is only one job for a man, since the War."

" Perfectly right," said Mrs. Tracey, and I was conscious that her tall, handsome daughter (" Phillipa," I suppose) gave a quick look at me above her mother's shoulder. I wondered if she were going to marry a soldier.

Of course they all thought that I *had* married a soldier!

Really, if there is very much more of this, I shall begin to believe it myself!

I shall, really!

With all this talk of " George " and of " daughters- in-law " and of " Belle-mere" and the rest of it, it would not take a great deal to make me wonder " What if the Merediths are right and I am wrong? What if I *have* lost my memory from shock? What if I *were* married to ' George' just before he went away for the last time? "

That's nonsense, of course. But it would be considerably easier for me if I could believe that it were sense! I felt fearfully uncomfortable under the un-

spoken comments of the Traceys as they sat in Madame Jeanne's room. Outwardly they were watching the fashion display in that atelier of a business that is carried on with all the brains and the heart and the artistry at a Frenchwoman's command (which is saying a good deal). But, actually, I suspected that all three, the breezy mother and the silent daughters, were much more interested *in me!* They were watching Lady Meredith's " little new daughter-in-law "; the small, brown-haired, blue-eyed, bread-and-buttery little thing (yes! I am sure they thought I was a bread- and-buttery little thing) who married Captain George Meredith!

Since the Traceys are old friends of George's mother, I suppose they knew " George " himself quite well ?

At all events they must have *seen* George!

Really everybody I meet nowadays has seen George – except me, his alleged wife!

It was in the midst of this reflection that Lady Meredith's own special *vendeuse,* a smiling young woman in a dark-blue skirt and a liqueur-green satin blouse, came up to our party. She had just " seen off " an American customer with an air that seemed to imply that the dear departing one was her only friend. Now she greeted Lady Meredith in a way that would have convinced anybody that her (the *vendeuse's)* pleasure was to serve her, and her alone.

" *Bonjour,* Camille," said Lady Meredith, answering the smile. " I have brought here my daughter for you to dress."

Ecstatic gestures from Camille. Flow of French compliments.

" These daughters! My advice to any mother is, ' *Have sons! ' "* broke in Mrs. Tracey with a humorous dry glance from me to her own handsome, silent Phil- lipa. " Have sons! Then, when you marry *them,* all the trousseau you've got to pack them off with is a lounge-suit, couple of pairs of pajamas, and a safety- razor! None of this everlasting *corvee* of underthings and frocks and hats for seventy-three different occasions !"

" Oh, but, Ethel! That is half the fun," protested Lady Meredith diffidently. (She is terrified of " Ethel," I can see.) "Now, Camille!" She turned to the vendeuse, with whom she is far more at her ease. " Now to command a delicious little trousseau for . . Mademoiselle " – this last word was very much slurred over, I noticed.

There followed a conversation in French; so swift and bubbling-over on both sides that I could catch only a little of what was actually said. I did catch the general drift, however. It seemed to be that Lady Meredith was going to have every " young" model in Jeanne's copied for myself! There I sat, in the simple blue coat and skirt that I had thought looked quite new and smart in London. Here, in this Temple of Fashion, it made me feel like a provincial Cinderella over whom the wand of the fairy godmother was to wave, converting her into a real Princess.

I gasped over those half-understood orders thatLady Meredith was issuing to Mademoiselle Camille in her fluent, pretty French, helped out by copious gestures. Could it be that all these dresses were to be made for *me?* The *costume tailleur* that continued to be " for everyday and comfort," without a touch of the forbidding, utilitarian note that seems almost inseparable from the English " tailor-made!" The *taittenr habille* that made all the English " best dresses " that I had ever seen look pompous and pretentious! That afternoon frock, enough to make any woman long to take up her abode

" *in a land where it was always afternoon!* "

Those evening-frocks, as different from any other evening-frocks that I had ever seen as an orchid is different from all other flowers!

About the evening-frocks Lady Meredith was a little difficult. She shook her charming head over them. I heard her impressing upon Camille that she had not yet brought out a model that was enough exquisite, enough innocent, enough young-girl for

Here a wave of the slim hand towards me.

And here I broke in. I had something to say to this.

" *Belle-mere! " I* began, and then I blushed scarlet again, realising that the two Miss Traceys, both the plaited flapper and the one who was choosing her own trousseau, had pricked up their ears at the word I had used. So *that* was what George's wife called George's mother!

I said, fighting down my self-consciousness while the eyes of the whole party from Mrs. Tracey to Camille were fixed upon me, " If you wouldn't mind, I – I *don't* think I want a *petite robe* of cloud-white with bits of *bleu del* about it, unless you want me very much to wear it! "

" Dear child! I only want you to wear exactly what you like and what suits you," cried Lady Meredith, with a quick reassuring little touch to my arm. " But d'you really not like the little white frock ? Why ? "

" Because it would make me look so extra-innocent and young-girlish, as you said. And I do look so that, as it is! And – and I do so hate it! " I declared, half- laughing at the absurdity of my own confession. " Nurse Phyllis telling me I was Madonna-ish and all that kind of thing; I'm so tired of it! I do have to *look* so much, much more dove-like and young than I really feel or *am! "*

" Ah, my dear, and what won't you give for the power of looking that, fifteen years hence? " This, with emphasis, from the matronly Mrs. Tracey. " Still, I think I know what you mean now," she added, with her swift, shrewd glance at me. " Why not have that same model expressed in flesh-pink for her, Megan? It would look awfully sweet, and not quite so innocuously simple."

" *Exquis,* Madame," pronounced Camille; and she brought out from the back regions of the shrine bouquets of petal-soft patterns in flesh-pink, rose-pink, coral, shell-pink, hydrangea. . . . She held them upone by one against my throat. ... I noticed that one thing about me seemed to cause no surprise to Mrs. Tracey and her daughters. Namely, that George's young widow should be preparing to array herself in all the colours of the rainbow! This they took as a matter-of-course, apparently.

Perhaps they had just one trait in common with that never-to-be-forgotten girl whom George really married; perhaps they, too, " did not hold with mourning? " Evidently George's own mother doesn't. You cannot describe her soft dove-greys and oyster-colours and pearly draperies as mourning. And to-day she had tucked a big pink carnation into the belt of her chinchilla coat! The conventionality of black is dying out among many English families, I suppose. . . . There would be too much of it, alas!

The planning of my new pink frock, with a girdle of that white beadery patterned by gold-and-rosy flowers, and with a skirt to be held out above the ankles by lines of crinolining, kept us busy at Madame Jeanne's until well into the lunch-hour.

Little black-clad, neat-haired *ouvreuses* came down from some upstair work-room and slipped through the show-rooms to some way out at the back; and I could not think why Lady Meredith seemed to be reluctant to leave. Then I began to suspect that for some mysterious reason she was anxious to let Mrs. Tracey and her daughters leave first. Mrs. Tracey made no move until at last Lady Meredith rose. " And now you're coming to lunch with me. Oh, yes, you must!" saidmy adopted mother's old schoolfellow in her confident, rather dictatorial voice that carries all before it. " Come along; I want you to see my funny little French house."

" Oh? You've taken a house in Paris now, Ethel, have you?" asked Lady Meredith as we stood at the glass-doored entrance to Jeanne's, looking up and down the street for a *voiture.*

" Yes," said Mrs. Tracey. " We're living in a villa-ey sort of thing at Passy. Convenient for while we're doing all this shopping for Phillipa. Then there are drawing-lessons for Maude. And it's nearer for Tom to come when he gets leave. You know what a model wife I always was. . . . Ah! A taxi-auto at last. Good. You get in, Meg."

I knew quite well that Lady Meredith did not want to get in. She wanted – why, I could not guess – to leave these friends of hers as soon as possible!

But she could not break away. On the gale of Mrs. Tracey's ironical breeziness she was borne along much as I had been borne along that afternoon at Camrys station by George's wife.

Before George's mother could say she was afraid we had an engagement, we were all five wedged into that queer little red pillbox of a taxi-auto. We were jolting breathlessly over the cobbled Paris streets, lurching wildly from side to side, tearing round corners at the angle of boats in a stormy sea and after a fashion unknown to the British taxi.

One desperate leap of the vehicle flung meon to the lap of the speechless, handsome Phillipa Tracey.

"French cabs are the limit," she laughed – almost the first thing that I had heard her say that morning. But as she spoke, settling herself in her seat, I caught her eyes full upon me. And those dark searching eyes seemed – or did I imagine that they seemed? – to be full of a message to me.

They seemed to tell me, " I want to talk to you, presently. There's something I want to say to you! " Then we drew up at the Traceys' house.

5

SECTION 5

CHAPTER XII

THAT OTHER GIRL

I LIKED what Mrs. Tracey called "the little villa-ey sort of place at Passy."

It stood at a street corner where five roads met and was one of a row of houses, all tall and high and white, all with green shutters and with evergreens in front, and with plaster Cupids and the heads of Sphinxes decorating the outside of it.

Inside, everything was very French; the warm, even temperature, the absence of any English fireplace or equally English " litter," the walls covered in yellow brocade instead of wall-paper, the oval luncheon-table with its pink table-cloth, pink table napkins, and the bowl of gold-fish that was the only table-decoration.

I enjoyed all these little unfamiliar details as much as I enjoyed the French cookery of the lunch; a dish of casserole chicken smothered in delicious thick rich brown sauce with *cepes.*

Even this lunch was only one more of the things that ought by rights to have been enjoyed by Miss Vera Vayne!

But as I sat there (in the place of George's wife!) I noticed once more that George's mother was not enjoying anything; not the exquisite French meal, notthe dainty, un-

English arrangements, not the society of her old friend who was apparently bent on making us both welcome!

I could see that even as she sat at table Lady Meredith was, for some reason, *on thorns the whole time!*

Was she afraid that I, sitting next to the handsome, silent Phillipa, was going to " come out with " something about my " unfortunate delusion " as she considers it?

No! For hadn't she appealed to me about that in Jeanne's showroom? And hadn't I tacitly agreed to say nothing to these people about my real relationship to her? Hadn't I called her *Belle-mere* two or three times in their hearing already?

It is not " her little new daughter-in-law " that she was uncomfortable about.

I could only put it down to the idea that perhaps Mrs. Tracey herself managed a little to shock Lady Meredith by her breezy, ironical frankness. For it was our hostess who did all the talking, her daughters making a half-amused, half-critical audience, after the fashion of children who are less popular than their parents. I suspected that the Tracey girls did not confide in their mother. And their mother retorted by discussing daughters in general as if they were one of the plagues of Egypt.

Then she turned the talk on to Phillipa's coming marriage.

Phillipa is engaged, it seems, to a gunner-major witha huge house in Shropshire. I could not help wondering if it was the house she had accepted rather than the husband?

" All daughters ought to be packed off to homes of their own as soon as they're too big to be packed off to their schools," decreed Mrs. Tracey as the sweet came in; a wonderful cream of *marrons.* " No woman wants to have a great grown-up girl hanging about the house and reminding her how much better her own figure used to be – no, thanks; cream is death to me – after a daughter has been out six months one's either jealous or ashamed of her."

Lady Meredith said, gently and uneasily, " I should never have felt that about a daughter." She smiled at me. " But I'm old-fashioned, Ethel."

" There's no such things as being ' old-fashioned' or ' modern,' really," pronounced Mrs. Tracey, crumbling her roll. " There's only being this kind of woman or that." I felt that she said always a little more than she meant. " Plenty of women to-day would seem *vieux jeu* beside some of those dead-and-gone people, Cleopatra, Phryne, Saint Theresa. At all events there's one job for most of us – getting husbands. You'll agree with me there, Meg."

Lady Meredith, sipping the very sweet white wine, actually took up this challenge. " I thought you were more of a feminist than that, Ethel? I thought you considered that nowadays a girl ought to have other interests in her life besides marriage? "

" Such as love, for instance? " retorted Mrs. Tracey, outrageously.

She gave a quick, defiant twinkle towards me; she wanted me to realise that she was " trailing a coat" for her old schoolfellow.

But I would not smile.

Poor Lady Meredith! What a shame! She flushed and rose to the bait like a slim grey fish.

" Surely you don't consider there's any difference! " she cried in her soft, hurried voice. " Love and marriage are *surely* the same thing! One means the other!"

" Glad you've found it so, my dear," said Mrs. Tracey, drily. " Certainly you and Richard seem to have. But are you and he the exception, or the rule? The exception."

" The rule!" protested my adopted mother; and her voice sounded argumentative and very young. I had a sudden, swift vision of her and Mrs. Tracey with their hair down, wrangling together in some Victorian class-room years and years ago.

I couldn't help smiling at the picture.

" There! Your little daughter-in-law doesn't agree with you, Megan," Mrs. Tracey teased her. And again I felt that Phillipa Tracey, sitting beside me at the table, turned her dark glance upon me as if there were something she wanted to say to me.

I protested, " Oh, but – but I wasn't smiling because I don't believe what *Belle-m* – what Lady Meredith said!"

And even while I said it I wondered what part her real daughter-in-law would have taken in that discussion. I seemed to see the wraith of her pansy toque and made-up face above the pink tablecloth; I seemed to hear her loud, blatantly truthful Cockney voice trumpeting out: " *Oh, well! S'no use me pretending I was madly in love with the man I married, because, between you and I, that didn't happen to be the case!* " Or some other kindred sentiment!

Poor Lady Meredith! Surely, *then* she would have been more uncomfortable than she seemed to be now!

Coffee was brought in!

" Coffee as it should be; as black as night, as sweet as love, and as hot as hell," quoted our hostess, nonchalantly. " I think we'll take it into the drawing- room, Celeste " this in French to the trim young

bonne. " Funny little room with six sides and a window in each. Makes one feel as if one were the amorous gold-fish, gaping round and round a globe."

We had our coffee in the little parquet-floored salon that she described – coffee with a *petit verre de cassis* that tasted just as if one had picked those blackcurrants, of which it was made, warm from their sunny bush. Then Mrs. Tracey said she wanted to show " that model housekeeper, Megan," the rest of the house. Maude, the flapper-daughter, had departed, chaperoned by her French governess, to her drawing-class on the other side of the Seine. So at last Phil- lipa, the silent girl with the eyes, would be left alonewith me. I felt that she would be less silent as soon as her mother had gone out of the room.

Lady Meredith turned, as if she did not wish this to be.

" I think Rose would like to see the house too," she suggested, in her quick, diffident voice. But without further beating about the bush, Mrs. Tracey laughed and said: " Oh, I dare say! I'll show her another time; kitchen and all. But now I want a little talk with *you,* Meg! "

Lady Meredith gave me one last reluctant glance. Then the two mothers went out together.

I and the other girl remained sitting in that goldfish globe of a drawing-room.

Phillipa Tracey stretched her long arms over her head with a tiny sigh of relief. Then she rose and picked up a long, inlaid box of cigarettes.

" Will you smoke? " she said, handing it to me.

" No, thank you. I don't smoke," I said, smiling a little ruefully as I remembered that the real Mrs. George (had she been there in her proper place) would have accepted what she had called " a cig."

The other girl took a cigarette, lighted up slowly, and as slowly dropped into a chair facing mine. I looked at her. She was certainly good to look at with her tall slenderness and her proud, perfect features that were almost classical. But – she was hard, I felt.

She smoked for a moment in silence; and I thought it must have been my imagination that had promptedme to think, in the cab and at lunch, that she wanted to speak to me.

Then she turned to me again and I saw that it had not been my imagination. This girl did want to say something to me.

She blew a smoke-ring, and watched it, not me, as she spoke. She began with what was, under the circumstances, rather an odd little remark.

" George will have been glad that you don't smoke," she said. " He never really liked it. Not in women, you know."

I said nothing.

What could I say? It was news to me that this unknown George didn't care for women to smoke. But then anything about him was news to me. It was these people who knew all about him.

" Do you mind my talking about him ? " asked Phil- lipa Trace)', quickly but quietly. " We were quite friends, you know."

" Oh, no! Of course I don't," I put in, as quickly. " I don't mind *at all!* "

This was so true. In fact, I wanted her to go on talking about him; this young man who lies quietly in a hero's grave " Somewhere in France," rid of all the troubles and complications big and little that beset those he has left behind him. I am beginning to feel a growing curiosity about this George as he was " in his habit when he lived." His character, his likes and dislikes, everything he used to do and say. I feel as if I had begun to read his story two chapters or sofrom the end. I wished I could go back to the beginning of that book and find out how things started. It's a mystery to me that a man with a mother like Lady Meredith should have chosen for his bride a girl like that flamboyant film-actress Miss Vera Vayne. (" Vivie! ") It's so odd

Or isn't it really odd? Is it the sort of thing that might be expected to happen? Does a man always choose his wife in a fit of reaction against the type of woman he's been accustomed to see in his own house?

Perhaps this other girl, who evidently knew something about George's tastes, would throw some light for me on the whole of *I"affaire* George generally?

Leaning forward to draw nearer to herself an ashtray upheld by three bear-cubs in Copenhagen ware, Phillipa Tracey said, more gently, " I was very fond of him myself, in a way."

" Oh, were you? " I said, rather stupidly.

But what else was there to say?

" All the same," she went on, " I always thought him rather a mermaidy sort of young man."

" Rather a ? "

" Mermaidy sort," she repeated. " I mean ' two- kinded,' half of him very go-ahead and the other half submerged and trailing away in a flood of prejudices, like that against women smoking."

I thought, still more bewildered, " And wasn't he prejudiced against the *way* that other woman smoked? For there are ways and ways. Hers were – *so* veryfilm-actressy! " Miss Tracey went on. " We always fought like cat and dog, you know, George and I."

" Oh, did you " I began. And then I sat up

against my chair and broke off with a little laugh. " You must think I can say nothing except ' Oh, were you,' and ' Oh, did you '! " I protested. " I am not really an idiot! But I don't know what else to say, and I do want very much to hear what you – what you thought of him, and – and all about him that you can tell me!"

She looked down at her own long, slender hand. Her engagement-ring was a beautiful emerald, I noticed.

She said, as drily as her mother could have done, " Of course you know him very much better than anybody else! " And her tone added " *Or think you do!* "

" Oh, but no! I don't think so," I protested. " You see, I didn't really know him at all!"

(Literally true.)

She blew another smoke-ring and said " I suppose you mean because it was such a frantically short engagement ? Well! " She glanced at her own ring. " I don't believe the length or shorth of an engagement need make any difference. Some people you don't know any better if you're engaged to them for seven years, like Jacob and Rachel."

" I suppose not," I said, a little impatiently.

I didn't want Miss Phillipa Tracey to go on theorising about engagements, thrilling as that subject may be. Her mother and Lady Meredith might come back from their own little talk at any moment. And Iwanted to have improved the shining hour by hearing something more about George.

The queer, unexpected girl before me was watching my face. Suddenly she smiled. And she said, in a much more approachable voice, " Forgive me if I ask you something that sounds the *limit* of impertinence ? "

" What is it? " I asked, all curiosity.

"It's this," said the girl who had known George. "Were you really – did you really care very much for him? "

"What?" I nearly said. I crossed my feet, fidgeting on the parquet floor. I was utterly at a loss. How I longed to be away, anywhere but where I was, in that evenly-warmed, Frenchily-furnished *salon,* faced with that question by that strange girl! Oh, if only the real Mrs. George had been there in my shoes – in her own shoes, I mean. She would have known what to say. She wouldn't have cared, in fact, *what* she said. An echo came back to me of her talk about her lost husband. " *Pity the pore young feller was done in. Expect he was in a bit too much of a rush, as per usual!* " She might have thrown off the very same comment now.

But I had my adopted mother to consider.

She had begged me to accept my false position, for the moment, and I had accepted it. I had even slipped that ring of my mother's on to my left hand, so that the Tra. ceys might not notice at the luncheon-table that " George's young widow " was without a wedding- ring. I could not let Lady Meredith down by tellingher friends, or even by letting them suspect, that I had not cared deeply – for that unknown young man.

Yet I could not, could not say " Of course I cared; why else should I have married him? " So how was I to answer?

" Ah, you needn't say anything," the other girl took up, looking at me quite gently. " You are pretty; you are a sweet, warm-hearted little thing that any man might like "

I blushed with pleasure and surprise.

" But," she said, quietly, " you have never been in love with anybody."

"Not?" I said, lifting my head, startled; opening my eyes.

For what about my one-sided, unrequited, sad little love-affair? What about those dreamy Sundays, last Summer, up the river? What about Reggie Penmore? He hadn't cared for me, after all; but hadn't I cared for him, cried over the thought of him at night?

Yet here was this odd girl who had met me for the first time this morning telling me calmly, " Oh, no. You could be very much in love, I think. But it hasn't happened – yet."

" What makes you think so ? " I demanded, rather indignantly.

" I can see it," said Phillipa Tracey. " You see, *I know the* difference! "

And for the moment I saw a great change come over the handsome face that I had thought hard. It flushed and sparkled. Then we heard Mrs. Tracey's breezycareless laugh upon the stairs. And her daughter said, hastily, " Quick, before they come in. There's just one thing I want to ask you." I made sure it would be " Was George very much in love with *you? "* A worse poser even than the other!

But it wasn't that. Leaning towards me as she tossed the end of her cigarette away, Phillipa began " Did George never "

She hesitated, laughed a little.

" Never what ? " I asked.

Then at last it came out in a rush; the question that I had suspected in this girl's eyes ever since I had seen her this morning; the question that she had been saving up, for I don't know how long, to ask George's wife.

" Did George never speak to you of me ? " CHAPTER XIII

APPARITION OF AN OLD FRIEND

THERE was not time for me to answer this leading, this startling question of Phillipa's.

For at that moment the door opened and the two mothers came back into the little *salon;* Mrs. Tracey with her short, firm-chinned face well up as if she'd " just come out on top " in some argument. She probably had! Lady Meredith looked flurried but unconvinced.

I expect this is as it was in the beginning and as it ever will be with this oddly-assorted pair! Antipathetic ! As the poles apart in type! Yet I expect they will never cease to be " such old friends." I believe that plenty of these " old friendships " have that basis. Two old-time antagonists meet; they squabble as they did in their youth.

And as they spar or gibe, the years drop from them. They forget their crow's-feet and their responsibilities; they ignore "double-chins and disillusionments; their grown-up children (listening) cease to exist, for them. Even in the act of contradicting each other they give back to one another girlhood and the dearest of the days that are no more. Yes; I think that must be the secret.

Phillipa Tracey had only a moment in which to sayhastily to me " I'll see you again. We must have a talk. Let's have tea somewhere. I'll write and make an appointment," when her mother's voice broke in, overbearing all else as usual.

" Yes, I'll come on with you two, Meg. That will be great fun," she was saying, half-kindly, half- maliciously. " How *thoughtful* of you to have a friend's French chauffeur wounded in that very hospital, and to want to visit him this afternoon! " (I suppose this was some excuse of poor Lady Meredith's.) " It's the place where I go and do dispensing, three afternoons a week, for the Croix Rouge. I shall be able to show you everything. Come along! "

So again my adopted mother found herself pursued by this relentless friend. Again she bore us off; this time without Phillipa, whom we left behind with a million notes to write, she said, to thank for wedding-presents.

We drove, in an open horse-cab this time, through the narrower cobbled streets into that queen of all the thoroughfares, the Avenue of the Champs-Elysees.

To my eyes it seemed as if the width of our Trafalgar Square stretched from the towering houses and hotels on the one hand to those on the other; I was not yet acclimatised to this spaciousness, emphasised by the lines of chestnut-trees beside the pavements.

Here crowds went by; shopping ladies, *blesses* with bandages and crutches; beautifully-dressed French children with English nurses – and yet there seemed more than room to spare. Space, space! Air, freedom, and light! These, I suppose are things that giveits air of gaiety and wealth to the Ville Lumiere, whether in war-time or peace.

I glanced at the shops past which we drove. There, too, was space and light. Guerlain's parfumerie, with its show-window that " shows " little but artistically-designed emptiness, decorated by a couple of slim tables upholding perhaps three priceless vases of scent and a giant powder-puff. The Rolls-Royce palace of plate-glass and insolently reserved advertisement. A florist's, with just one lovely careless cluster of mauve- and-lemon orchids flung down on a velvet cushion.

" How these French shopkeepers study human nature! What they aim at is making everything they sell look as if there could be only one of it in the world!" commented Mrs. Tracey, following my glance at the line of shops.

" Now, the motto for our English windows seems to be ' *Plenty more where this came from!'* No wonder that it's here that the millionaires rush for their shopping! There's an object-lesson for the *jeune-flle a wiir/i. i.* If you wish to attract, never go about in droves with other girls. Quite sound, isn't it, Mrs. George ? "

I think I smiled politely enough, but I was really not thinking very much what she said. I was thinking about that daughter of hers – that mysterious and disconcerting Phillipa.

" *Did George say anything to you about me?* "

Now what could have been the meaning of her asking *that,* I should like to know?

What could George have had to say about MissTracey to his wife? *Why* did Miss Tracey put that question to the girl that she imagined was his wife? Did she mean to tell me, if we did make an appointment to meet again?

I wondered, and wondered, as we progressed down the noble avenue, where every make of car flashed by, swift humming-birds of shining green and grey and buff and hedge-sparrow's-egg blue. Beside these our obsolete-looking cab was like some dingy tortoise crawling along.

At last, however, we arrived.

We drew up before the tall white fa9ade of one of the many hotels that have been converted into hospitals, flying, at the entrance, the banner of the Croix Rouge.

Little did I dream of what awaited me within! As if with some presentiment my adopted mother glanced anxiously towards me. We were ascending the broad steps that had once been thronged by globe-trotting millionaires and their suites, that were now trodden only by doctors, nurses, wounded Allies and their visitors.

" I hope this won't be a little too much for Rose, perhaps," hesitated Lady Meredith.

" Oh, bless your dear heart! What could be ' too much' for a girl at that age?" pooh-poohed Mrs. Tracey as we entered the museum-like vestibule. Two years before it had resounded to the clatter of all the tongues of Babel. It was quiet enough now, in possession of a single white-moustached French orderly.

" Don't you remember you and me, Meg, before we were married or anything?" persisted Mrs. Tracey. " How we'd be out all day otter-hunting, and then tear home fifteen miles in the rain on our bicycles? Feet on the handlebar for the last three downhill, so as to be in time to dress for some dance? And then we'd keep it up until morning without turning a hair. Youth's *got* to work off the overcharge," she said. " And overcharged a girl must be, if she's to last out for what she'll have to stick, afterwards."

" Yes," murmured George's mother, a little nervously, as we passed on to the lift, " but you see, Rose *has* been ill "

" Soon be in the pink, now," said Mrs. Tracey, with an emphasis on the " now." What could she have meant by that, I wondered?

My wonder at anything of the kind was switched off as soon as we stepped out of that lift on to the corridor on the first landing. For coming down that corridor, in the full light of the big windows, I beheld a figure so familiar that I thought I must have made some ridiculous mistake.

In fact, I let the unmistakably English young man in khaki, with his absent-minded look and his eyeglasses, go past us unseeing before I found breath to gasp " Reggie. . . . That looked like Reggie Pen- more !"

Quickly our hostess turned to me. " Why! D'you know him? A friend of yours? "

" Yes; oh, *yes"* I said, eagerly. " It *-was* him, then?"

" It is Captain Penmore. Yes; he's working here now. Lent to the French, I believe, for something to do with the X-rays," explained Mrs. Tracey. " A nice boy. He'll never set the Seine on fire, of course; but I'll call him up."

Her slim feet carried her rather stout figure quickly down the corridor towards Reggie's departing back.

" Captain Penmore! Friend of yours "

He turned; came up.

Greetings and explanations. . . . There we stood, the four of us. I felt my " nothing-matters " mood creeping over me again. Reggie Penmore looked (naturally!) rather flustered and taken aback. Lady Meredith looked wildly uncomfortable.

Poor, greatly-tried dear! I saw she thought that all her precautions for that day were going to be brought to nought. Though, up to then, her " little new daughter-in-law" had been good and amenable and had said nothing about her " delusion " to the Traceys, still now she was *bound* to break out! Now that she was confronted by somebody whom she knew, or thought she knew! Now (before the merciless brown eyes of " Ethel " Tracey and all) the said daughter-in- law would be certain to burst out again with the announcement: *"Captain Penmore knows! He knows that I am not George's wife!* "

All this I read in poor Lady Meredith's horrified eyes.

I nodded reassuringly to her. I murmured " It's all right, *Belle-mere."*

For it would be all right. Now that I knew where Reggie Penmore was to be found, I could write to him; I could let him know how matters stood. I could explain everything!

It was not to be expected, I was afraid, that I should get a chance to speak to him alone, here in the hotel hospital. He was passing on. . . .

But Mrs. Tracey bore him along with us in her inevitable manner. " You're not on duty, Captain Penmore? No. I know you aren't. Then come along and see us through. I'm helpless without a man to back me. They'll turn us out, and I want my friend Jjady Meredith and her daughter-in-law " (!!!)

" to see all over this place."

A curious place it was, that volunteer and amateur Parisian hospital; a little haphazard to the eyes of any one used to a pukka military hospital on English lines. Yet what effort, what good-will was shown in all the arrangements! It was a picture of the transformation of France; luxurious rooms, gilded and moulded and sculptured, given over so gladly to harbour the stricken fighters, with their rough night-shirts and with their shaggy hair. What a change, from the frivolities of the frock-fairies' show-room of this morning to the grim reality of the Croix Rouge hospital this afternoon! A vivid contrast, too, between the women and their art which they took so seriously, the men and their suffering which they took so lightly!

One mere boy, with crutches at the head of his bed, was plaiting a straw basket. He smiled and nodded cheerily as the three Englishwomen and the young doctor peeped into the room.

In a bed at the further end of the room lay a patient whom we could not see for bandages.

" That poor fellow can't speak; he is a bad case of lockjaw," explained Reggie Penmore. " You see, the Boches came up to him where he was lying wounded, and cut him about so with their knives when he was lying on the ground ..."

" Oh! no, no! I can't believe that that *can* be true," protested Lady Meredith. " I *can't* believe that the Germans would do such terrible things as that!"

" Can't you? " said Mrs. Tracey, drily, turning her shrewd eyes from the poor bandaged wreck to the gentle, incredulous face of my adopted mother. " Well, Meg, I am afraid that there are quite a number of our people who share your incapacity to believe any evil of the Hun! "

And turning to the *poilu* with the basket-making, she said, in French, " Madame imagines to herself that the gentle Germans would not torture one of the enemy wounded."

The French soldier from the Front threw back his dark head against the pillow, showing all his white pointed teeth in a short laugh. He exclaimed: *"A – ah! Les crapauds! Les chasser, les ecraser* "

And with a look of purpose in his bright eyes he went on plaiting his straw – to fill in time.

Near the next ward we passed a startling apparition in all white; she was powdered, she was perfumed, and the little Red Cross upon the veil that bound her brow was less scarlet than her made-up lips.

They bestowed a smile and an effusive " *Bonjour, Madame! "* upon Mrs. Tracey as we passed. I saw my adopted mother shrink a little.

Mrs. Tracey chuckled.

" The Countess is a thundering good nurse, Meg," she said. " A really efficient woman."

" Then why," protested Lady Meredith, " does she "

" Touch herself up a bit? Why shouldn't she? " argued Mrs. Tracey. " She'd look horribly washed- out without a trace of rouge, now that she works such hours."

" Better than looking unnatural, theatrical," said Lady Meredith, almost sharply. " I *hate* that."

And again the thought came to me, the thought that's haunted me intermittently ever since I first set eyes on the gentle, fastidious face of George's mother.

" *What, what, WHAT would she have said to the real Mrs. George? "*

Mrs. Tracey laughed.

(This last wrangle, by the way, took place as we inspected a ward-kitchen.)

Mrs. Tracey said: " The men prefer a little makeup, I believe. The *blessh.* They think it means that *ma sceur soigners* herself to please them, and it cheers them up, poor fellows!"

" But why pander to what the men like if they like all the wrong kind of things?" suggested Lady Meredith. " Ought one not to try and *influence* them "

" Oh, yes, Meg. One ought! " agreed Mrs. Tracey with that destructive twinkle of hers. " The only thing is that while one's busy doing it one looks up and finds that the men aren't there. They've flocked off to be ' influenced ' by somebody with a more popular method. Now," she broke off, " what did you say your wounded chauffeur's name was? . . . Yes; that's the man. He's on the second floor. I'll take you up. But it's scarcely worth while our all trampling up there; in fact the Countess, who's looking after those wards, doesn't like more than one visitor there at a time. Little Mrs. George," with a nod at me, " had better stay down here. And – Captain Penmore! " She turned to poor Reggie, who had been following us about with an air of longing to go and hating not to stay. " Perhaps you'll take charge of her "

I could have jumped with relief.

Reggie was to take charge of me!

I might have the chance of coming to an explanation with him at once!

Over her shoulder Mrs. Tracey said, kindly, " Show her some of the common and garden objects of interest,

et cetera " I believe it was Reggie who suggested

that "Mrs. Meredith" (Heavens! He, too, called me that!) might care to come and see the apparatus in the X-ray room.

Next, I heard myself say eagerly: "Oh, yes! I should love to see it! Do show me the room "

The others had disappeared into the lift again. Reggie said " Will you come this way? "

A moment later we two stood alone together in the X-ray room.

Yes; the chance of a clean breast was coming now.

For Reggie Penmore did not attempt to explain any of the mysterious-looking apparatus about me.

He just turned straight to me. And he said, in a voice that was a little astonished, but a good deal more reproachful, and hurt:

" Rose! Why did you never tell me that you were married? " CHAPTER XIV

AN IMPROMFTU PROPOSAL

'"lyTEVER tell you?" I repeated, with real anger

ly vibrating in *my* voice and blazing out of my

eyes at the young R. A. M. C. man with the

quiet, sensitive, rather hurt face. "Never tell you?

Well, why do you suppose, Reggie? Because there was

nothing *to* tell, of course! "

" I suppose you mean because you weren't going to be married the last time I saw you," took up Reggie, still reproachfully. " You might have written, afterwards."

" *You* never wrote," I said, voicing a very old grievance. " *You* ought to have written to me, at the club, I think. I'd nothing to write to you about. *Nothing! " I* insisted, coming back to the point again as he opened his lips. " I – I never *was* married, you see."

" I don't see," said Reggie, staring down at me. "What about when I was called over to that place in Wales, that time during my last leave! When I was told that ' George's wife' had met with an accident, and I came and found you – *you,* lying there. That was a nasty knock, Rose, to get without being prepared for it!"

'- I should think it was, if you mean *my* side of it," I said, with some bitterness. " Considering I wasn't married at all! " " What ? " Amazement began to grow through the reproach of Reggie's face. " Not married at all? " he repeated, leaning a hand on the table and looking down at me. " Not married to this young Meredith? "

" Not to young Anybody!" I announced, with a shake of the head that made me drop my curly tor- toiseshell pin.

Reggie picked it up and held it, absently.

He said " They both called you ' our son's wife' "

" I know. They would, of course! " I said, furiously. " Not *my* fault. They can't say I haven't let them know I wasn't the creature's wife!"

"Where did you meet him?" said Reggie, with a quick odd stare.

" Meet him? ' George? ' Nowhere! "

"What?"

" I've never seen him! I've never set eyes on "

" But if you've never seen him," interrupted Reggie Penmore in the voice of one suddenly awakened out of sleep, " his people can't possibly imagine "

" They can! They do! " I insisted. " Oh, it's been awful! Reggie, don't think I am mad, will you ? " I went on, hastily, putting my hand on his sleeve. " That's what *they* all thought; Lady Meredith and Sir Richard and Nurse Phyllis and all of them! "

" Thought you were mad ? "

" Well, next door to it," I amended, feeling reallycomforted to see how utterly taken aback Reggie looked. " They think I just don't *remember* being married to George." . . .

Reggie's blank face made me stop to laugh.

" And even when they pretend to believe I'm Rose Whitelands and the rest of my story," I went on, " they are only marking time about it. Why d'you suppose they've brought me to Paris? To consult a specialist about me. That is, *they* call it an aunt. But I knew from the very start exactly what sort of an aunt *that* would turn out to be; a "

" Stop, stop," Reggie said, shaking his head, be- wilderedly. " I can't take all this in. What the – why – what induced these people to – that is, d'you mind beginning *at* the beginning, Rose, and telling me exactly what happened? "

I drew a long breath. " Yes," I said. And I did – but I needn't go over it again here. I seem to have told that same wild story so often already; film-actress, scene on platform, Sutcliffe-Smythes, escaped prisoner, check after check to what I wanted to say

What I'd "stuck out" to the Merediths and to Nurse Phyllis in Wales I had all over again with Reggie Penmore, in the X-ray room at the French hospital. Only with this difference. Told as I told it to an old friend who already knew so much about me, it did not sound nearly so improbable. Why, why couldn't I have told it in that way to George's people ?

Breathless, I stopped at last with the words " And here I am!" And I waited to see how Reggie wouldtake it. I wish men were not always so much *calmer,* outwardly, than we women are. It's so disconcerting, when one of *us* has worked herself up over a story into a state of flushed and gesticulatory excitement, to see one of *them* receive the climax with a noncommittal "H'm!"

That was the first remark that Reggie made at the end of it all. Then he took off his pince-nez and polished it on the khaki handkerchief he drew from his cuff. I remembered that little trick of his; it always used to annoy me, vaguely, for no reason. After all, it was *his* pince-nez. Only I was waiting for what he was going to *say!*

Presently he said, rather slowly, " I don't see why you shouldn't have asked those other people to bear out your story."

" Which other people? " I asked, quickly.

" Why, those people who'd engaged you. The Sut- cliffe-Smythes, or whoever they are, could have told the Merediths that you were their governess."

" No, they couldn't – they couldn't," I said. " You see, they *wouldn't!* Not after I had deliberately told the porter the Sutcliffe-Smythes sent to ask, that I *wasn't their governess!* That complicates matters, you see."

" Yes; it does," said Reggie, doubtfully.

Then he added something that surprised me.

He said, much more briskly, " Well! you can't stay on with *these* people, can you? "

A sort of reaction, a chill, took me at this. Not stayon with the Merediths? Leave them, with whom I was so happy?

" I don't see, Reggie, why I should do *that,"* I argued, forgetting, for the moment, how hard I had tried to do it. " It's not as if I was *pretending to* be Mrs. George, is it? I am here, now, as their adopted daughter."

" Yes, but you said yourself that they don't mean it for that. They're taking you because they still believe the other. And, in that case, I don't see how you can very well stay where you are," protested Reggie Penmore, frowning a little through those glasses. I wished he wouldn't frown. It looked so unfriendly, and we *had* been such friends. I had always looked forward to seeing him each time. This time was so . . . different!

" You'll certainly have to go," he said.

I know it was frightfully inconsistent of me. But I suddenly felt that nothing on earth would make me go; not until I was *sent!*

Rather defensively, and quite absurdly, I said "Where ought I to go?"

Reggie Penmore didn't answer that question.

At least, I suppose that what he said next was meant to be taken as the answer.

He was suddenly in the middle of it all before I began to take in what he was saying. Something about " Dearest, darling little Rose," and " I've simply got to tell you," and " It's been going on for such ages now!"

" *What* has ? " I asked, scarcely believing what it all seemed to be about.

He said " Surely you must have known, before I joined, how much – Oh, Rose! How much I cared! "

" How could I know? " I said, breathlessly.

" What? Not those times up the river, when we took sandwiches and moored behind that island and I read Stevenson aloud to you ? You must have known ! "

" I didn't. I didn't! " And at that moment I really was speaking the truth. For, however much a girl may think the man cares, the *certainty* of it when he tells her so makes everything else seem so very vague, so undecided. She feels " No! I didn't *know* before." And as I stood there facing Reggie I actually forgot what I had felt before. I forgot the nights in my club bedroom when I'd made sure that " to-morrow " he would say something. Then, however, I remembered the night after he'd gone away to France, when I'd cried because he'd left me without a word that counted.

And a little resentfully I said to him now " Why didn't you say so, *then? "*

" I didn't think it would be right, Rose," said Reggie, gravely. " I thought it scarcely fair to you."

" Men's ideas of what is ' right' and ' fair' to girls seem to me the funniest thing in the world," said I.

Reggie went on, " I didn't think I ought to bind you in any way."

" Yet you were frightfully annoyed when you thought I was married," I said.

" That had nothing to do with it."

"Oh," said I.

He said: " I'd so little to offer you, Rose! And I might be going to – well, who's to know what is going to happen to any of us when we get our orders, nowadays? I never did approve of these rushed engagements, with the man, perhaps, going off to stop a bullet the day after he had proposed to the girl," said Reggie. He spoke very quietly and very sensibly. (There are times when sensibleness makes one feel a little cold.) "And as for these war-marriages, I think they are absolute madness."

" So do I. Oh! So do I," I said earnestly.

To *think* of what George's rushed war-marriage had let *me* in for!

But Reggie was saying: "As it's turned out, however, this settles it. Give me your address, Rose; the Ritz? Very well; I'll call to-morrow. I'll explain things to Lady Meredith. I'll tell her that we are going to be married "

It sounded simple enough. It sounded so taken-for- granted. All difficulties seemed to be ignored by this young man who had – yes! He had made me very unhappy once.

" Going to be married," I said, still scarcely taking it in. " Well! But *are* we? "

" Of course we are, darling little girl," said Reggie, smiling. " I shall pack you off home to my married sister at Winchester at once. You can stay with her until my next leave is due. I shall get some more next month. And then I'll come home – to you, Rose."

He moved, to put his arm round me.

Once I should have been breathless with delight to see him make that movement. And now – I moved aside. I was as surprised at my own involuntary action as he looked himself.

"Why?" he said. "Mustn't I touch you? You do care for me, don't you, darling? "

On any of those Sundays I should have felt that it was too good to be believed in, Reggie's voice, saying those words – to me!

And now – we", I can only think of a rather un- romantic image that expresses my sentiments exactly. Sometimes at the club, when I've got home tired from the city on a clammy wet evéning, I have thought " Now for a lovely boiling hot bath before I go to bed!" And then I've discovered that it is too late; that they've let the kitchen-fire go down, and that the bath-water is just moderately tepid, without either the caressing comfort of warmth or the tingle and thrill of cold!

It was this same dismal, Laodicean feeling that invaded the whole of me as I listened to the love-making of the young man for whom I had once cried my pillow- sopping wet!

Perhaps one is brought up to expect too much of love-making? Is that it? Perhaps it's *never* as good as one imagines that it's going to be before it happens ?

" You can't mean," Reggie's voice was saying tenderly, " that you don't *want* to get married ? "

" Oh, Reggie, I believe I've had quite enough of getting married," I said, ruefully. " Being married by mistake, I mean "

" Our marriage wouldn't be any mistake," he said.

" Wouldn't it," I said, rather uncomfortably. " Are you – so sure? "

" Of course I am, Rose. So are you," said Reggie, with an encouraging little nod. " Only, poor little darling, you've been so worried and badgered and bothered over this business that you really don't know what you are sure of or not."

" Do you think that's it?" I said, hesitatingly. " Of course I have been worried "

" And you're not going to be worried any more. I'm going to take care of *that,"* said Reggie. " Once I let these Meredith people know that you and I are engaged, as I shall to-morrow – or, I'll come back with you this afternoon, if I may? "

"No! No!" I said hastily.

"Why not? The sooner the better."

" Oh, no," I objected. I added something that might have come from the lips of Nurse Phyllis herself.

" It's so *sudden! "*

" Sudden ?" said my boy friend, incredulously. " You asked yourself why didn't I tell you before! And it's been going on for – what? Two years or more now."

" The – the end bit has been rather sudden," I protested, lamely. " I – I must *think* about it."

" Oh! Very well," said Reggie Penmore, unwillingly. " How long d'you want to take over it? "

It sounded rather as if we were talking about getting some typewriting done.

I sighed for just one minute of feeling as I should have felt if all this had been . . . months ago up the river!

Turning to the door I said " Give me ten days, Reggie!"

" Thundering long time," said he, reluctantly. "Why ten days?"

" Because in ten days' time the Merediths will have seen ' the aunt,' " said I.

" What on *earth's* it got to do with their old aunt?"

" It isn't an aunt. I explained it to you!" I told him. " It's this brain-specialist that they are going to see – about me. You had better come afterwards," I told him just as we went out. " *He* had better be the one to tell them the truth!" CHAPTER XV

THAT OTHER GIRL AGAIN

OF all the surprises and unexpectednesses that have been buzzing about me like a swarm of bees ever since I left Euston station on my way to Wales, I must say that almost the greatest has been to discover *how I myself have changed.*

I seem to have quite a different identity. ... Is it because for weeks I've had a different name forced upon me?

Does that make a difference?

Anyhow, the difference is there. Just think how I took Reggie Penmore's proposal – and how I thought I should have taken it!

In my " previous existence," while I was at the club, working for my living and associating with scarcely anybody but girls who were doing the same thing, my friendship with Reggie Penmore was quite the most interesting thing in my life.

Sunday, with his visit, was a green oasis in the desert of the workday week! Reggie, and what he would say or do, was the one bright spot in all my thoughts. Reggie was the peg on which I hung all my imaginings about men, and love, and life!

When he came and the club maid, with an understanding little smile, announced " A gentleman to see Miss Whitelands," it made the whole world different. When he went, with a " Good-night, Rose! It has been jolly!" the rosy glow faded from my horizon. My week's work (that " work " which is supposed to satisfy and exalt the modern girl) was just a bridge to carry me over to the next holiday when he should call for me.

Then came the break. His departure. My wretchedness that I feared I should never, never " get over." Then the gradual " getting accustomed" to every day life without sugar, so to speak. But still the thought of him had remained at the back of my mind.

Even the morning that I started for Wales I was distressed beyond words because I had lost the keepsake hat-pin Reggie gave me before he went away. Even in the train I had given a shiver over the idea that anything might happen to him at the Front. Even in that glimpse of him that morning at the Bryn I'd sensed again the glamour and the glitter of the river under the willows, where he had said " Jolly, here, isn't it, Rose? "

What is the meaning of this change of front, now that I meet him again, here in Paris?

Puzzled, I have been trying to figure it out to myself.

It would all be easy enough to understand if I had met somebody else! I mean somebody with whom I'd fallen in love. That would explain it, of course.

But there isn't even that. There's been nobody. No rival to my one-time best boy-friend. No questionof falling in love. No sort or kind of other young man whatsoever!

Then what *is* the explanation?

In the lonely hours of the night (that black screen on which one flings the coloured moving-pictures of one's thoughts) I have tossed on my delightful bed and wondered, speculated. Watching the lighted dial of the electric clock set into my bedroom wall, I have at last come to some sort of conclusion about the matter.

In those old days Reggie Penmore was the high light in the darkness, the only amusing thing that ever happened in my life.

Now – well! What crowds of exciting and amusing things happen to me every hour of the day!

All around me are these stimulating things to see, to listen to, to do. Even my new frocks from Jeanne's give me as much of a thrill as I used to feel only at the sight of a note from Reggie on the criss-cross letter- board of our club when I got back from work. Then, instead of the too-well-known groups of business-girls, there are all these new, entertaining people. Lady Meredith and Sir Richard, who spoil me so. Mrs. Tracey, with her generous heart and her annihilating tongue. That perplexing Phillipa, who is going to write to me about something.

Then there are all the new people who are working for Lady Meredith. There are the crowds to watch in the streets. The come-and-go of the life in this hotel. There are the shops. The *etampes de la Guerre,* in which artists of France reflect the mood of Francetowards her unworthy foe. There are the hosts of fresh and arresting impressions.

And every single one of these things seems to have made itself into a rival to that young man whom I should once have been overjoyed to marry.

How many girls could bear witness to the probability of this sort of check to a love-story? It isn't always another young man who comes between, is it? It isn't always woman's inherent fickleness. It's simply a change of foreground that let her see the central figure from an angle in which he isn't central any more!

And again I wonder how many girls go on with the love-story, and marry the young man just because he still represents the only interesting thing that has ever happened to her?

" Hullo – hullo, yes, it's *you* I want to speak to," comes the voice across the wires. And the business- girl's office-routine is brightened by the telephone-call, the luncheon, the bunch of violets from some commonplace clerk who becomes All-Romance for her in consequence.

" Is Miss So-and-so at home?" sounds the voice at the door. And the nice home-girl flies down, all a-flutter, to entertain the only man of her generation who ever calls at the house.

And they call this " falling in love!"

I shouldn't.

If I were the young man would this be good enough for me?

No.

If I were a young man I should want to be loved for myself, individually. 7 should want the girl to thrill and flutter *because I was Arthur* (or George, or Reggie, or whoever I was). I should want to be quite sure that she would turn her back on a ball-room full of delightful partners, all clamouring to dance with her, and that she'd sit it out with me, from choice. If I were a young man I should be afraid to marry any one but the girl whose life was packed with interests and amusements and admirers. How else could I know that she wasn't (half-consciously) marrying the First Chance of Love, Life, and the Way Out?

This idea doesn't seem to worry young men. Perhaps their *amour-propre* is so deeply rooted that they think " Whatever the circumstances, this little woman couldn't possibly help truly loving ME."

And the girls?

Do they never ask themselves " If I had the refusal of even four different and attractive young men, should I still have accepted this one? Should I,' forsaking all other,' still have wished to take him ' until death us do part'?"

I suppose they don't often think this. Perhaps, as I heard Mrs. Tracey tell my adopted mother on the way back from the hospital, " Most people never, by any chance, ' think' at all. Otherwise the race could not go on."

And I suppose I myself should not be thinking ofthese things if I had been really, deeply, in love with Captain Reggie Penmore. If I had been, the thought of him would have remained with me through all the joyous, shifting scenes of my Paris trip. I should have whispered to my lover in my heart at every turn. The very sunshine, painting giant silhouettes of great French monuments on the pavements of the Place de la Concorde, would have reminded me how it cast slender, flickering shadows of willow-branches on my own white skirts as we two had sat in a boat on the English Thames.

But as it is . . .1 see that the mysterious Phil- lipa may have been right when she said " You could be very much in love, I think, but it hasn't happened yet."

(Later.)

What has happened now is that I have had my interview with Phillipa Tracey.

She wrote to me to ask me to meet her at Suzanne's hat-shop in the rue de la Paix. The note was addressed to " Mrs. George Meredith " at the Ritz. There, of course, I have put down my right name, Miss Rose Whitelands, travelling with Sir Richard and Lady Meredith.

It was she who brought me the note; and I was afraid that she was rather unwilling to let me accept Miss Tracey's invitation. Then she said she would come with me. This, of course, was not what I wanted. But I could not tell " *Belle-mere* " that I thought Phillipa had something she wished to say to me, alone.

So together we set out under the arches of the rue de la Paix.

We found Phillipa, all in dark-blue, sitting at the back of Suzanne's show-room. Next to her we beheld the furs, the audacious parrot toque of her mother.

" Ah! Thought you'd come, Meg. Capital! " said Mrs. Tracey, shaking hands with her usual heartiness. " I want you to come across with me to Beer's and look at a model that I think is more suited to my build than the ('allot; frock I told you about. Come along. We'll leave your girl and mine to gossip together over the *chapeaux."*

I saw just what Lady Meredith thought of this plan. No use! Since " Ethel " decreed, so it had to be!

Another moment and the two elder ladies had taken their way towards that dress-maker's whose business is carried on in what was once a palace; ivy-garlanded without, and within a maze of museum-like rooms, with immense staircases, with chandeliers that have blazed down upon royal levees.

As they disappeared, I took the seat next to Phillipa in Suzanne's outer shop.

It was lined with mirrors, and thickly carpeted in inignonette-colour. They are so wise, these French, in choosing dull, neutral shades for backgrounds to show up their flower-like wares in frocks and hats! There were several other customers about. A group of French ladies sat opposite to us, looking as if they were engaged upon the one aim and object of their lives. Near them sat a young American, sleek, straw-coloured hairparted in the middle, watching a little French actress buy a toque. He looked indulgently interested, as if at the antics of some pet, as the models were brought out to her. The vendeuse, very tall, in dark-blue satin and the new, tighter waist-line, poised the hats on her customer's head with an almost unconsciously perfect gesture. And the gesture arranged – *d'un trait!* – the veil. Another brought out the appropriate pearl pin, crusted with brilliants.

I watched these proceedings that would have interested me so much another time. But at the time I was only anxious to know what this girl beside me had brought me here to say to me.

" Thank goodness everybody is engaged. We can talk now," she began, quite breathlessly, turning to me. " To begin with, Mrs. George "

"Yes?" I heard myself answer to that misfit of a name. "Yes?"

" I was afraid," said Phillipa, " that you'd be certain to dislike me so."

"I?" And I opened my eyes at her. " Why should I dislike you ? "

Phillipa laughed a little absently, glancing at the group composed of the pretty actress, the tall woman displaying hats, and the young American who was exclaiming "Say! isn't that 'cute'? Take a look at yourself, Frissonette!"

Then Phillipa said ' Well! You must have noticed that Lady Meredith has a grudge against me?"

Of course I could not say that I hadn't noticed anything so obvious. I was silent.

Phillipa Vent on, " She was annoyed that you should meet me. She was afraid to leave you alone with me. I thought you would have a grudge, too, if she had told you."

"Told me what?" I asked.

She didn't answer directly. She said " I always think that the girl who has accepted a man ought to feel so grateful to the girl who – who didn't take him. But the *fiancee* usually looks upon that other girl with a mixture of pique, suspicion, anger, and contempt! "

"Does she? Well, but if – if you meant yourself, I don't think anybody could feel those things towards *you,"* I said, quite sincerely. " I like you," I said, simply.

As simply the dark girl replied " I am so glad you do. After I met you, I hoped very much that you might. I wanted us to be friends. But I was afraid you would probably have been ' put off' me, as soon as you were given to understand that I – was the girl who had treated him so shamefully. Encouraged him – thrown him over "

" Do you mean George? "

Really comical, how easily that stranger's name trips off my tongue!

Phillipa Tracey nodded. " Of course."

Here was what promised to be another side-light on the character of this George of theirs! I turned my shoulder to the interesting groups in the shop. Wonderingly, I looked at my companion. Was she going to open for me some fresh chapter of the book that I seemed to have begun to read at the wrong end?

I said " He wanted to marry you? "

" He did."

" And you refused him ? "

" Yes, I refused George," said Phillipa, quietly. " And I was afraid his people would never forgive me. In fact, his mother won't. No woman ever forgives the girl who didn't jump at the chance of marrying her boy, even if the girl herself is the last one she would like to see coming down the aisle on his arm!"

" But that is unreasonable," I said. " Even if it is Lady Meredith! Why should you marry George, if you didn't like him enough? "

" Oh, my dear!" said Phillipa with a little quick, curious laugh. " The whole truth was that "

Here, from an inner shop, another *vendeuse* came up smiling. This was a very Spanish-looking girl with red lips, black hair done to one side with a comb, and short, full skirts, showing delightful boots that seemed to have been painted on to her ankles.

" Mademoiselle desires? " she said.

" Oh! I want to see some shoes, I suppose," said Phillipa, absently. " Hats, I mean, hats. Yes, bring me out some hats, please. Some small shapes; something black-velvety and close, I don't know – anything."

And as the girl departed, Phillipa went on, " I must try and explain before my mother and your mother-in- law comes back. I would like you to know just a littlehow matters stood, and that I wasn't quite such a beast as you have perhaps heard that I was! It wasn't just that I – I flirted with him and then turned him down with a loud bump because I'm heartless, and fickle, and – all that. I was just going to tell you. The whole talk was that *he didn't like me enough."*

I gazed wonderingly at her. How graceful she was as she sat, reflected from every point of view in the show-room mirrors! How handsome, how becomingly dressed, how well-bred! I said " Why didn't he like you?"

She shrugged her slim shoulders. " He didn't approve of me. No! No more than he approves of my mother. George couldn't bear the way I look at life. Without any of these softening *couleur-de-rose* veils, that his own mother, for instance, wraps up everything in."

Here the *vendeuse,* coming up again and catching an English word that she understood, beamed upon us and said " Veil! ah, yes, they are being very much worn at the moment. More than ever, Mademoiselle, more than ever, and tied in this new way "

" Yes, they will always be worn, and they will always be liked, by most people," agreed Phillipa. " But some of us want to *see! "* And she raised her dark head a little defiantly.

Quickly the *vendeuse* set upon it a creation that looked as if a cluster of three white begonias had grown into the shape of a military cap.

" Now, Mademoiselle! Ah, but that is ravishing! That suits the type of Mademoiselle to perfec "

" Yes, that seems all right. Very well! How much? I'll take this," said Phillipa, with scarcely a second glance at the hat.

She went on, quickly, to me: " At the bottom of his heart George is intensely conservative. He divides women, for instance, so entirely into two classes. First, the wife-woman, like his mother and all the women she would meet, sweet and gentle, and without any ' whys ' to life, without any paradoxes or rebellions or frankness in their natures. Next, the well – a girl like that, say " She gave a tiny glance towards the vivacious little French actress with the geranium-lips, who was now leaning on the young American's broad shoulder, to coax a more expensive aigrette out of him.

" The girl who amuses the off-hours. And if there ever seems to be any blurring of the line between the two, between the wife-woman and the joy-girl, it upsets the notions of the young man like George," said Phillipa Tracey. " He doesn't understand a chorus-girl being an admirable, stodgy wife and sewing for her baby in the dressing-room. Such things are, but it puts him out in his reckoning. And he doesn't bargain for a girl in his own class who hasn't the illusions and prejudices that he's accustomed to! "

What the *vendeuse* did not bargain for was the lack of enthusiasm displayed by these English demoiselles in the matter of their thrilling occupation of choosing hats. She brought them now three at a time, cullingthem like giant flowers from the tall, stem-like stands. Hats soaring at the back, drooping at the front, swooping at the sides in a million scarcely different ways that will be timidly copied in London two seasons from now, perhaps. Hats by *Suzanne!* Beautiful, adventurous. Hats for the moment and silhouette of which all nature has been ransacked. In this brim lurked the fluting of a sea-shell. In that curved the turn-over of the incoming wave. Here, petals had been studied; there, fronds of fern. And all to reproduce, in velvet and silk beaver and milanese straw, the live lines of beauty that should best set off a woman's face or hair. What artistry! In other words, what French millinery!

And with what British immovability Phillipa put it all aside, to turn to her nearer preoccupation!

" Yes; I suppose I'd better have the white one. And the midnight-blue velvet thing that rakes up at the back like a fan-tail pigeon. . . . No, not the *burgogne* model. Makes me look too *married* . . . no, I won't have it copied. . . . Nothing else to-day, Mademoiselle. . . . Please send them up. . . . No, I've no time to see any others. . . . We'll wait here in the shop for Madame. ..."

Then, turning to me, again, she summarized, " No. George, at the back of his soul, had absolutely no use for a woman of my type. He thought me clever. Men always think ignorance is bliss for themselves. That's unforgivable in a girl. Short-sighted beings! He thought me hard. He was shocked."

" But, Miss Tracey," I protested, " if he had been, he wouldn't have proposed to you!"

"Oh, wouldn't he? That began it. No man can squabble and argue and fight for very long with a girl, without a chance of – of the other coming up," declared Phillipa, taking the hand-glass from the silently reproachful exhibitess of Suzanne hats. " So – there came a moment when George and I bickered and quarrelled and wrangled ourselves – rather near." She glanced at herself in the hand-glass, but she seemed to be looking at something far, far beyond the reflection of her own dark head. I seemed to guess that the " moment" had been in some way very wonderful to her.

Then she put down the glass and said, briskly, " The results of that sort of moment don't last, Mrs. George. I knew that if he didn't. He thought he wanted to marry me in spite of myself and in spite of himself. And a ghastly mistake it would have been. I told him so."

I thought suddenly of Reggie Penmore and his proposal.

I said, looking at her as she drew on her gloves again, " I wish you would tell me what – how George took that."

" He was annoyed, of course. Yes, very annoyed," said Phillipa. " He said he would go away and marry the first girl he could find who looked as if she would be ' consistent.'"

" Ah! Of course! " I said, quickly.

" You knew about that already, Mrs. George, of course," said Phillipa.

But I was thinking of another remark of the real " Mrs. George," in the train:

" *I fancy he had just been jilted ly somebody or he wouldn't 'a' looked at me!* "

Then Phillipa Tracey said " George was very lucky in his ' find ' of a consistent girl! "

" Oh! I don't know " I said, fidgeting uneasily

on my seat beside the girl whom I had to allow to take me for George's wife.

She went on, " When I heard it was somebody whom he'd only just met, somebody on the stage, I thought her ' consistency ' would be quite another sort! "

(I wondered if she had formed to herself a fancy picture that was as highly-coloured as Miss Vera Vayne?)

She said, as if by the way, " I suppose you don't – I mean, I suppose that on the stage you take what they call the *ingenue* parts ? "

" Er – I haven't taken any *others!* " was how I got out of this.

Phillipa said " Well, and I hadn't imagined that you would be a real *ingenue* yourself! The home type; the girl of veils and traditions and illusions, *plus* "

" *Plus* what? " I asked.

" *Plus* more intelligence and heart than the type usually has," said the other girl, glancing at me sweetly and generously. " Mother was so surprised (if you don't mind my saying so) to see that you were a lady. I was so pleased to see that you were a woman. Or " – she laughed a little – " or that you could be – will be one."

I began to feel very embarrassed. This conversation was getting to be all about myself – the girl in another girl's shoes. It was Miss Vera who ought to be sitting in this hat-shop, listening to these compliments – or, at any rate, to the conversation of the girl who had refused her George!

" It's George I want to hear about," I said, frankly. " Please will you tell me what he was like? "

Phillipa raised her dark brows.

" What he was *like?* But you should know! "

" Yes, of course," I said, hastily. " Of course *I've* a picture of George "

(So I have. In that pendant.)

" But other people see the same man so differently !" I explained. " I sometimes think that if one could borrow a friend's eyes for half an hour one would walk down a street without recognizing half the people that one knew. I want to know just how *you* saw George, if you don't mind telling me."

" Not a bit. I'll tell you if the two mothers don't come in," said the other girl, with a glance towards the glass doors of the shop, "*t*before I finish. How I saw George? Well, to begin with, there were his looks. Those, of course, were ' a cert.' He'd more than just good looks, though. He had plenty of what I call scent about him."

"Scent?" I echoed, rather distastefully.

She laughed, leaning back against the lounge where we sat, talking swiftly and softly together.

" I don't mean that he used to sprinkle himself with Lily-of-the-Valley, or sew a piece of *peau d'Espagne* into the top of his waistcoat! I don't mean anything you get out of a sachet or a bottle. Not that kind of scent," Phillipa explained. " I mean scent as flowers have it. Something intangible that is given out. Attraction; personality, I suppose. Either people have it or they haven't. Your husband certainly had it, Mrs. George."

I had to accept the name in silence. In silence I listened, while this girl who had known him conveyed to me her impressions of that young soldier, dead in his country's cause.

She slipped into the Merediths' own way of using the present tense about him, just as if this young officer, killed in an attack, were only away with his regiment.

" His men, of course, worship him," she said. " I've heard that they would crowd about him to shield him with their own bodies when he's out on any dangerous job. He is a mixture of a dear, good, sweet fellow – and of a young devil. Sometimes he has fits of sheer, little-boy-h'ke naughtiness. He's obstinate, and cantankerous, and charming all at once "

" That sounds more like a woman," said I.

" Ah; but George is one of these ultra masculine male men who do show that tiny touch of feminine ' finish,' " said Phillipa. " It's , like his soft voice – youknow that deadly soft and gentle voice of his, Mrs. George "

(How *should* I know it!)

" that is so much more certain and forceful than

the men who make any amount of noise!" said Phil- lipa Tracey. " Everybody – nearly everybody – does whatever he wishes them to do. Servants love him, and dogs, and children; all simple souls who go by their instincts instead of by silly, muddling-up reason. And women like him. All women, from a sophisticated creature like – like mother, to a flower-girl I saw him give his seat up to in the tube. ' Lord love your handsome face,' she said. Sometimes people who pass him in the street smile, enjoying that glimpse of his youth and freshness. He's an exasperating creature in many ways, but he does walk into people's hearts. I don't think the man is born who could be indifferent to George Meredith. Certainly not the woman! "

Except one, thought I to myself as I sat silently there; except the woman to whom he'd given his name! She had spoken of him with tolerant, indifferent pity. . . .

Another of Life's little ironies!

And something else struck me now.

This Phillipa, who had turned him down – she was not merely " not indifferent." In spite of her calm, critical, detached voice, in spite of her friendliness to " Mrs. George," in spite of her serenely cynical ways, in spite of her gunner-major and her trousseau and the big house in Buckinghamshire of which she wouldbe mistress – in spite of all these things, in spite of her refusal to marry him, she had loved the dead boy. She loved him now, and she would always love him!

The conviction came to me in a flash.

I put out my hand and gave hers, as it lay on the edge of the lounge, a quick little squeeze of sympathy. And as I did so, a wave of compunction swept over me.

This friendly, stoical girl had given me so much of herself; what was I giving her of my confidence in return? Nothing! Worse; I was wilfully misleading her. This confidence I had received under false pretences. She had talked openly and generously to me only because she imagined that I was *his* widow!

" Oh ! I can't stand it. I shall have to tell her," broke from me aloud. " I simply must tell you - "

) new friend glanced at me inquiringly. She turned her short, proud profile, silhouetted against the notice that is put up in Suzanne's shop, as in every shop, hotel, and restaurant in Paris –

" TAISEZ-VOUS ! MEFIEZ-VOUS ! DBS OREILLES ENNEMIS VOUS ECOUTENT."

That reminded me that my lips were sealed. Not because of German spies and " enemy ears." This large-hearted Phillipa was no enemy to the girl whom her rejected lover had chosen (as she thought).

But what about Lady Meredith?

I must ask her permission before I told Phillipa Tracey the story of my identity!

So when the girl beside me said " What must you tell me ? " I had to reply " I can't tell you anything yet. I must speak to – somebody else, first. Tomorrow, perhaps "

" To-morrow Mother and I are going away to stay near Versailles," said Phillipa. " We want to be near a cousin who's come over to see her wounded husband at the hospital there. We shall be away for some days."

" Very well. Then, when you come back! " I arranged, just as Mrs. Tracey and Lady Meredith came back to the shop to take us off to tea at Rumpel- mayer's. " When you come back, Phillipa, I'll tell you all about myself! "

And I meant it.

Never suspecting what fresh avalanches of surprise were preparing to hurl them-selves into the landscape of my life before Phillipa and I met once more! CHAPTER XVI

BELLE-MERE BREAKS THE NEWS

THERE was no time that evening to ask Lady Meredith for her permission to confide my " delusions " to Phillipa. But ask her I certainly must, later. Sir Richard and she and I dined early, and went to the theatre. The gay and moving pictures both on the stage and in the audience crowded out of my mind that question, as it in turn crowded out the rather uncomfortable thought that had been pricking my conscience – Reggie Penmore's proposal.

Anyhow that was held up until I had seen " the aunt"; the mysterious " aunt" who, I guessed, was really nothing of the kind.

The next day was given up entirely to dressmakers and fittings. Some of my clothes are done already; the blue-grey cloth tailor-made costume, just the colour of a French soldier's overcoat, and the evening frock that has been " expressed," as Mrs. Tracey calls it, in pink, scarcely flesh-pink, but *rose tendre.*

That came home late this afternoon, with various hats and with parcels of gloves and silk stockings and shoes. My bedroom at the Ritz looked more a little enchanted island of luxury than ever with this rising tide of pretty things billowing about it. All day I hadbeen looking forward to trying on the pink frock which I should wear to-night at dinner.

I took ages putting it on. Lady Meredith had been teaching me what a difference is made by learning to do this carefully! I started up from the very beginning with a warm bath with a packet of Russian violet bath- salts in it. Half an hour to do my hair, which had been newly washed and waved. Ten minutes for polishing my finger-nails. Then came all-new under things, white as mist, no patterned hearts about *them!* Then the silk stockings, from which I cut the etiquette. The pink brocaded shoes, and the petticoat that looked as if it had been made out of all the convolvulus-blossoms in the world. Oh, how did we women ever harden our hearts against that so-feminine item of our attire: Her- rick's " tempestuous petticoat " ? A million thanks to the fashion that has restored it to us; *bouffant,* coquettish, to hold out the spread butterfly wings of our pretty, new frocks! I had just fastened the last tiny gilded snap of the *rose-tendre,* when there was a tap at my door. Lady Meredith entered, still in her outdoor things, with a paper in her hand.

"Ah, *Belle-mere!* I was just coming to you!" I told her, preening myself delightedly above the spread crinolined skirts that swayed, letting me feel that I had trod on air. " I was coming to show you this. Are you pleased with it ? "

I swung round with my hands at my waist; I took a few little dancing steps, as I had seen the mannequindo at Jeanne's; I twirled about again, smiling over my shoulder at my fairy god-mother.

" Oh, Rose! You little beauty! " cried Lady Meredith, impetuously. Oh, my lovely little Rose! How

fortunate that that frock One would think that

you had guessed "

" Guessed what? " I asked, pausing as I pirouetted.

" Nothing, darling child," said George's mother. " I only mean, it's – it's a frock for a very special occasion, isn't it? "

" Oh! D'you mean I mustn't wear it to-night at dinner? " I asked, a little disappointedly. Reluctantly my hands went up to the hidden snaps of the bodice.

" But of course you must wear it! " Lady Meredith cried, quickly, putting out her hand. " Keep it on; keep it on. You are all ready for dinner as you are, aren't you? And it's quite early. Quite. I was just coming in to – to have a little talk, dearest child. I'll sit on the bed here." She moved aside a cascade of lingerie from the *Mille et Une Nuits* shop, and sat down on the edge of my bed. " You sit down in the armchair. Yes, there. What lovely shapes those flounces take as you sit," she said with the little excited gasp in her voice that helps to make it so girlish. " Now, we'll talk "

" Yes; I did want to talk to you! " I said, making up my mind that here was my opportunity for telling her my great wish about Phillipa Tracey. Surely she would not deny me! I said " Of course *after* you've finished telling me what you have to say."

Lady Meredith laughed.

Several times I've noticed that curious, involuntary little laugh of hers when she had been made rather nervous by something; as, for instance, the remarks of her old friend and antagonist, Mrs. Tracey.

But what could she have to be nervous about here? Alone with me? Nothing. Yet her slim hands shook as they held that paper, a folded sheet of *La Patrie.*

" There is a very curious story in this paper to-night, Rose," she said, also shakily, " about an officer, a young French officer, whose people received the official notification of his death – oh! ever so long ago – just after the battle of the Marne. And now, now after more than a year! they have discovered that he is alive and well, though a prisoner of war at Doberitz. He was wounded in the head, and he was unconscious for a long time. When he came to, they think he must have lost his memory. This does happen to lots of people, you know, Rose. Lots of people," said Lady Meredith, emphatically. I made a little hopeless gesture where I sat. Then I lifted my head suddenly. I saw what she was doing, I thought. She was breaking the news, I thought! Breaking the news that I was to meet some wonderful brain specialist, who knew all about these curious cases, and who would be able to restore me to myself!

She went on. " But this young French officer is now entirely recovered. At last he has been able to get tidings of himself through to his people – think of their joy!"

" Musn't it be splendid for them," I said, with a pang of sorrow for these other people who had lost their son.

" Yes, Rose, think! His people! His mother! You know what these French mothers are. Compared with them even the most devoted English parents seem cold and casual. Only outwardly, of course. We *feel* just the same. All mothers must," said George's mother, huskily. " To think what that woman must have suffered! Do you know that terrible little poem of New- bolt's, Rose, about the casualty lists? I forget its name. It describes how the father of some young soldier who has been killed in action can hear the news with pride because his boy has died gallantly. But his mother, dear "

She cleared her throat.

" The mother sits apart. . . . And the $oem ends:

' *Within Tier heart she rocks a dead child, crying,*

My son! My little son! '

That is how the young French officer's mother felt, Rose. You are too young to know that. But I – I!"

" *Belle-mere* – dearest! Please don't distress yourself like this – please?" I faltered, horribly distressed myself. I got up from my chair. I moved quickly across to the bed. I sat down beside her, taking her hand. I would have given the world to bring her any comfort. But what could I do? What comfort canany one bring to Rachel mourning over her children – because they are not ? "

An instant's silence. Then I felt that George's mother was pulling herself together. Her hand answered the pressure of mine. She turned her dear face.

Her eyes were bright, wide with the tears she would not allow to drop. She had bitten her lip in the effort; I saw a tiny thread of blood running down her chin She drew her handkerchief out of her grey satin, silver- clasped bag that she always carries. After a moment she spoke.

" Now all that Frenchwoman's tears are turned to joy. And not only hers. That young officer " – she tapped the paper in her hand – " had left a young wife, newly married. Think – when he meets her again! What they will have to say to each other!"

I nodded. It was terrible to see how she put herself in the place of these other, happier women to whom their beloved had been restored, or was to be restored.

In a firmer voice George's mother added, " All wars must be full of such stories, Rose."

"Do you think so?"

" Why, but one hears of them so often," she said. " In this war, too. Think of some of the refugee stories at the beginning! Think of the young airman who was picked up at sea by that trawler, when he had been reported missing after a raid." She held my hand, tightly. " Think of the families who were mourning, only the other day, over people they thought they had lost in the Appam! They thought there was no hopeleft. But so often – so often – long after one has given up hoping "

She stopped as if she didn't know how to go on.

And then, suddenly, her voice changed, utterly. It rose to a note of laughing triumph.

" Child! " she cried; " haven't you guessed, *yet?* "

" Guessed "

It was the second time since she had come in that she had used that word.

" Guessed? What am I to – ah! "

For in a flash I had seen what she might mean. Could she mean *that?* Was it possible? Oh, no! Surely not

I leaned nearer, gazing into her face, now quivering again with agitation, but not unhappy agitation. The tears, so long suppressed, welled out. Tears of joy?

Doubt changed in my mind to a certainty. . . .

It leaped to my lips.

" *Belle-mere," I* gasped, catching George's mother by the arm as I sat close to her. " *Belle-mere* . . . George isn't killed after all?"

She, George's mother, shook with sobs, but her face answered me. It was radiant.

" George is alive? " I cried. " Is he? Tell me. *Is* he? "

" Yes! Yes! " she answered me in a quivering voice. " George is alive! "

" Oh! " I gasped. " Oh, how – *lovely!* "

And a wave of great gladness seemed to carry me off my feet for the moment. For that moment I couldonly take in one idea – George's mother, who had been through such agony, was to know this joy that the Frenchwoman of the story in to-night's *La Patrie* had known. " This *my son which was lost."* This adored George, the centre of her world and of Sir Richard's, not dead after all! They had *not* looked their last on that handsome face of his, they were not to be left with that aching hunger for the sound of his voice, of his footstep across the Hall! George was alive!

I am sure my face lighted up – I felt it do so – as if I had been this unknown young man's friend from childhood up.

" How lovely – how *too* lovely! " I heard myself falter again. I flung my arms round his mother where she sat. I forgot for the moment everything but what this meant to her. I asked quickly, " It's quite certain?"

She laughed, tremulously, girlishly, against my neck. " It was certain weeks ago! Weeks! We had the telegram " Then she lifted her head, took out her

handkerchief again, dried her eyes. She cried out suddenly, " Don't you see, Rose? This was what we were talking about, Richard and I, that afternoon at the Bryn. This is – ' the aunt'! "

I gasped, speechless. " The aunt! " The mysterious aunt of so many jokes. Lady Meredith took me by the shoulders and kissed me, murmuring something incoherent about " knowing that it would come all right, as soon as the child was told "

" The child "

That suddenly brought me to myself again. That suddenly reminded me of my own position. It reminded me in whose shoes I found myself!

Why, of course, it was Vera Vayne who ought by rights to have been sitting in that bedroom at the Ritz, listening to the glad news that she was not a war-widow after all!

Now! What more would all this mean – for me, for the *imposter-malgre-lui?*

George's mother made one of those irrelevant little remarks that sometimes break from one's lips in moments of stress; the bubble on the tidal-wave.

" You oughtn't to have let me crush your pretty frock," she said, and she rose lightly to her feet.

I still sat, quite dazed. George – alive! And I – supposed to be George's wife!

I said, "Was he taken prisoner?"

"Prisoner? Oh, no!" she laughed, gladly. "He was almost buried alive though, you know, in the explosion of one of our own mines. That's how he was reported killed, and it was overlooked – not corrected –

for two days he lay there under the heap Oh,

you'll have to ask *him* about it. He was wounded "

"Wounded?"

" Oh, only slightly. In the leg. He managed to crawl out "

" And you'll be able to see him," I asked breathlessly, " soon, perhaps ? "

" Sooner than we had thought. We – we *have* seenhim!" George's mother told me, radiant. " We saw him – this afternoon, Rose."

" You saw him? " I cried, springing up from the bed and facing her as she turned to the door. " He's in Paris already, then ? "

" He's in Paris," said George's mother with her hand upon the door. She opened it. " He's in the hotel," she added. Then she turned her creamy head and girlish face, laughing, over her shoulder. Triumphantly she cried, " He's here! "

Then, while I stood there as if turned into an image of stone, she slipped out.

I just heard her call " *George!* "

There was a strange step, firm yet light, in the little corridor that leads from the big corridor to my room.

A strange young man in khaki entered suddenly, almost as if he had been pushed in. The door was closed behind him. . . .

There we were . . . staring at each other.

6

SECTION 6

CHAPTER XVII

THE CONFRONTATION

IF that room at the Ritz could have had one wall knocked out and the rest of it removed bodily on to the stage of a London theatre, it would have looked exactly like " the much-discussed bedroom scene" in some Pinero-ic play, which a London girl would be doubtful about taking her mamma to see.

There he stood – the dark young hero, tall and gracefully built, in his khaki and his riding-breeches, and the brown boots lacing up the front almost to the knee. And there was the young heroine (myself) confronting him, with her light-brown hair as beautifully dressed as that of Miss Billy Burke or Miss Gladys Cooper, newly emerged from their dressing-rooms and with the exquisite pink Paris frock that seemed – as Lady Meredith has said – to be for a " special" occasion. Poor dear, little had she dreamed what this " special occasion " was to be! All around me the room was strewn with my newly-bought possessions – undies, hats, boots, and shoes. It looked for all the world as if the young husband had just returned unexpectedly from the Front, and had surprised the young wife in the very act of packing up to elope.

If the scene had been photographed for an illustration in *The Playgoer,* the legend underneath might hat run, "Mr. So-and-So (as Captain Meredith) – *'Ml God! Were you going to leave me? You? ' "*

But what Captain George Meredith actually did hastily and in quite an ordinary and pleasantly sofl voice, was something perfectly undramatic and matter! of-fact.

" Oh! I am so sorry – I beg your pardon. I made a mistake." He whisked round to the door again.

Another second and he would have been in the corridor, I could imagine his scolding Lady Meredith side, " Mother, how careless of you! "

I took a swift step after him.

" Captain Meredith," I cried, in a little voice than sounded terrified enough.

With one hand on the door-handle, he turned round again. His head made a dead-black blot against the white panels of the door; the clear oval of his face, withr the dark eyes and brows and the little dark moustache, which looked as if some one had touched with two inky,, fingers his upper lip, was one astonished question.

"What is all this?"

" Captain Meredith," I faltered again.

Then I stopped. We both stared at each other forl an awful second.

Then he spoke.

" Er – I came to see my wife "

" Yes ? " I said, clenching my hands nervously atl the sides of my pink butterfly skirts. " Oh, yes! Ofl course "

Ixith stared at each other for an awful second

He said again, " Er – as a matter of fact, it's my I wife I came to see."

Yes," I said, adding, in a flurried little rush, " she [isn't here."

The young soldier's very bright dark eyes were fixed I upon me. " But you called me back."

" Yes, I know I did. I've got such a lot to tell

I you- – "

His dark brows lifted.

Then they drew together as if in sudden anxiety.

" Has anything happened? " he asked, sharply.

" No, oh, no!" I said, quickly; and then again, " Only there's *such* a lot I've got to tell you, Captain Meredith. Your wife "

" Yes ? " he said. I saw him look once towards the white door of the cupboard, and then towards the door , of my bathroom, as if he imagined that Miss Vera Vayne must be lurking there.

He said, " I expected to see her ... I suppose

you're No, no, of course you're not!" he broke

off. (Probably he was going to say that he thought I was her maid.) "I suppose you're here with her? You are a friend of my wife's ? "

" No, not exactly," I faltered. I put my hand out to the brass rail of the bed, clutching it so as to have something to hold on to during this impossible interview. j The young, astonished voice took up, " You *know* fcer, though?" I " Yes, oh, yes – slightly."

" Then will you tell me where she is, please? "

" I don't know, Captain Meredith."

" You don't know? – but "

" She isn't here," I said, firmly shaking my head.

" You mean, not in the hotel, or not in Paris? "

" Not in Paris," I said. " I – I think she has gone to America!"

" America! " he echoed in tones of the greatest astonishment yet. " But that can't be. What makes you ? " Then, as if suddenly remembering something, he added, in a more ordinary voice, " But, I say, my people have just told me that she is here with them."

" Yes, I know," I said, clenching the shiny bed-rail that clouded in my hot hand, " they think so. Of course *they* think so. They think that your wife is here because "

"Well, because what?" asked the mystified young soldier, still frowning a little. " What do they think?"

With one hand on that bed-rail, the other clenching its nails into my palm, I looked up at him, and told him the mad, unbelievable, preposterous thing that they did think.

" You see, they think that I am your wife! "

" What ?" rapped out Captain Meredith, like a pistol shot.

Then, taking a step nearer to me, he said, in a quieter voice, " What did you say? "

I moistened my lips for this impending catastrophe of explanation. As a start, I blurted out the firstwords that came into my head. Few, but scarcely well- chosen words.

" You see, Captain Meredith, I am not your wife."

He gave a curious little gasp (I am sure he well might, poor man), and I had to go on, " No, of course, I am not your wife! Of course, you can see that for yourself; but then they think – they all think that 7 am your wife – that I am married to you. ..."

" That you arc ? " And at this the whole of

him seemed to become concentrated into a pair of young, very dark, bright eyes that scanned the whole of me, my hair, my frock, my hands, my shoes. Then he said, " Who said it? "

" Your people! " I answered, desperately. " Sir Richard and Belle – I mean, Lady Meredith."

" Why do you call my mother ' Belle'? " he asked, sharply.

Again I moistened my lips to reply, but he took up, " Did you tell them you were my wife? "

" No, no! " I cried, fervently. " Of *course* not! "

"Who did tell them?"

" Nobody!"

"Nobody?"

" No, they seemed to have – have "

" Seemed to have what? "

" They seemed to have just *decided* it!"

" Really ? " said Captain Meredith, slowly, and looking at me hard. " That was a funny thing for them to do, what? Seems rather curious! "

And then he suddenly moved and shut the door; andI felt as if every friend I had in the world had been shut outside!

He moved away from the door and took hold of the nearest chair as if he wanted to have somewhere to sit at once. (I remembered that he had been wounded.)

That chair was piled with the mist-white heap of my new *cache-corsets.* The laciest of them fell across the young man's brown boot as he moved. Stonily he looked down upon them.

Glad of an excuse to have something to do, I rushed across hastily, with my rose-pink corolla of flounces fluttering all about me. I picked up the heap of pretties and cast them on to the mauve satin eiderdown quilt of my bed.

Then Captain Meredith sat down, rather suddenly; and said to me, abruptly, as I stood there, " Well, I must get to the bottom of this. Will you tell me who you are, please? "

I began, shaking.

" My name is Whitelands – Rose Whitelands "

"Miss Rose Whitelands?"

"Of course!" I said.

" I'm sorry, but there doesn't seem to me to be anything particularly ' of course' about all this," he retorted. "Where do you come from?"

" Shropshire – that is, London."

" Well, which? " he demanded, looking sternly at me.

" I mean I come from London just lately, but my – my people come from Shropshire, when I had any peopie. They are all dead. M – my father was a soldier, too."

" Go on," he ordered.

His voice sounded for all the world as if he were conducting a court martial and I were " the accused person named in the margin."

That suddenly infuriated me.

Up till then I had been breathless, falteringly embarrassed, and nervous to the verge of tears.

But his manner (and his want of manners) seemed to bring me back some of my self-possession.

I let go the bed-rail. I lifted my head and stared at him.

So this was the much-talked-of George, was it? Well, I thought very little of him and his ways. Plumping himself down in a chair like that, in my room, without thinking of asking me if he might! Far less waiting until I had sat down! I would just show him what I thought of that. So now, feeling completely mistress of myself, I said, quite witheringly:

" Thank you; I will sit down."

And I dragged forward the chair that was by the toilet-table.

This was covered with all my new silk stockings that I had taken out of their boxes to gloat over.

I seized them, the gleaming strips of filmy black, horizon-blue, pink, and *tete de negre,* and I tossed them down on to the bed with the other things.

Then down I sat, with another up-lift of my *rose- tendre* flounces all about me. Down I sat, with my littlepink brocaded shoes set squarely on the thick carpet in front of me, with my hands clenched in my lap and my eyes glaring, defiantly, at this odious young man opposite.

" Now," I began, and at the same moment he began, " Now! "

He didn't seem to be at all impressed by my annoyance!

And he went on, " Now having told me *who* you are, will you please tell me what you are? "

" I was in the city to begin with, as a girl clerk," I said, very stifly. " Then I was a nursery-governess – at least I was going to be a nursery-governess."

"And now?" he said, with a glance like a kind of dark searchlight about my pretty and expensive-looking room. " Now you have *no* occupation ? "

I gave a tiny stamp with my pink shoe on the carpet.

" I told you I was with your mother, Captain Meredith!"

" Yes," he said, drily, " In what capacity? "

I gave another little stamp. " I told you that, too! " I retorted, looking at him. " She thinks I am your *wife!* I'm getting quite tired of telling you this, but that's what she thinks! "

He continued to look at me, hard.

" Of course," I took up, angrily, " It's the most extraordinary mistake that ever was made. *You* know I am not your wife; 7 know I am not, but "

" And how sopn have you come to know it? " he asked, very drily. " I mean, how soon did you realise that you had better give up the pretence? "

For a moment I hadn't understood him.

Then I said, " What pretence ? " Then it began to dawn on me.

" *Oh!* " I said, with a gasp.

(I might well gasp!)

" You think," I challenged him, " that I have done this thing on purpose! You think that I – I have smuggled myself in! That I am an impostor! An adventuress !"

" Well," he returned, with a short laugh and another black searchlight of a glance, " what does it look like; what?"

Now, here the most extraordinary thing happened.

Perhaps it will hardly be believed, but in the mixture of my feelings at this moment, among the mingled horror, confusion, and agitation, there crept in – yes, there really did creep in – a tiny glow of *satisfaction* over the glaring mistake that this young man had just made!

An adventuress!

I, who had *suffered from* looking so much more bread- and-buttery and prunes-and-prismy than I really am! I, whom Nurse Phyllis had said looked like a little Madonna! I, for whom Camille had wished to make a little innocent robe of cloud-white with sky-blue ribbons like a baby! I, whom Phillipa had supposed would pnly play the *ingenue* roles at a theatre!

Here, at last, was somebody who actually credited me with being the *villain* of the piece!

An adventuress?

Ha!

But all these thoughts, of course, came afterwards. At the time the fury was uppermost.

" An adventuress! " I echoed, hotly. " You had better ask your people about that. Ask them if I haven't tried to explain. Ask *them* if I haven't told them over and over again that I am not your wife! That I am not Vera Vayne – that I have never seen you in my life! Go and ask them! Lady Meredith is in her room." I pointed, imperiously, to the white door. " Go and ask her at once, please! Or fetch them; fetch them!"

" Wait a minute," said Captain Meredith, drily, and without taking his eyes from me. " I could ask my people at once, as you say, but I'm just wondering whether they are exactly the people to fetch."

" What do you mean? " I snapped, staring at him. " What other people could you ask about it? "

" Well," he said, slowly and deliberately, " this might possibly be a case for fetching the police."

" *The police? "*

I felt myself opening my eyes to four times their normal size as I gazed at him in furious amazement.

A young man like this, who had married a young woman like *that* with that accent and those hearts all over her underclothes! He, if you please, threatened me with the police?

Didn't it show that he didn't know one kind of person from the other?

" Do send for the police!" I heard myself saying with an angry little laugh, as soon as I could find breath and words. " Send for them. Do. I would like you to! I suppose they will think that you imagine I am a German spy! But do send for them! "

I laughed again, furiously.

" I hope they will send somebody who knows English, because I don't think I *could* tell them what I thought of you in French! But send for them now! " I tossed my head back and looked challengingly towards the door. " Send, send at once!"

Again Captain Meredith, covering me with his eyes as with the muzzle of a pistol, said, " Wait a minute. I want to ask you a few ques "

" I am not going to answer any questions of yours until you send for the police!" I told him, defiantly sitting there. " I sha'n't say another single word until you have sent for them!"

And there, while the minute hand of the clock might have gone round once, we sat in angry silence confronting each other. He, with his eyes steadily on my face, I giving him back his look with more defiance.

Yes, this was George. This was the adored apple of his mother's eye!

This was the young man about whom even a nice, sensible girl like Phillipa Tracey had spoken with such yearning enthusiasm. This, this, THIS *wnspeakable* was the man that everybody thought I had married!

Oh! I wasn't going to stand this for another minute!

Up I skipped again, like a pink-dressed Jack-in-the- box, preparing to make a dash across the room to the bell.

But he was before me. He was too quick. He rose at the same instant; he stood with his belted back to that bell. And I stood, too, for a moment, with my hand stretched out towards it.

" Please let me pass," I said, imperiously.

He said, " What are you going to do ? What do you want to do?"

"Can't you sec?" I said (very rudely, I hoped). " If *you* are not going to send for the police, 7 am! "

Well, of course, it ended in neither of us ringing the bell.

As he stood there, Captain Meredith said, in rather . an altered tone of voice, " Look here, I say. You know you do owe me some sort of an explanation."

" Yes, if you would listen to it! " I flashed. " But you won't."

" Perhaps I have been a little too precipitate," he said, slowly, and his fingers went up to those two smutty finger-marks of a moustache on his upper lip.

A memory came back to me of his wife – his real wife's talk, " Expect he was in a bit too much of a rush as per usual! " . I answered in my most forbidding tone, " I think' precipitate ' is a very kind way of putting it." But I let my hand fall to my side again.

" Yes, well now, look here," he said. " Don't you realise I have had a bit of a shock? I come round to this hotel; my mother meets me, she tells me that my wife is here with them. Says my wife's been very ill, and will have to be prepared for my coming. My mother says she will go and prepare her, and that I can come in in half an hour or so. She then comes up here, leaving me in her room. Says she will call me. I wait. Well, then I see her coming out of this room; *this* room, mind you! She calls me in; leaves me. I expect to find my wife. And I find *you!* You, an absolutely strange girl that I have never set eyes on! "

" Well, you were a strange man, that 7 had never set eyes on!" I argued, indignantly, wishing to show him that all the grievance was not on his side. Indeed, no! " You were just as much of a shock to me. Or more! For I thought you were at least killed! "

" Ah, yes," he put in, quickly. " You thought I was out of the way "

" And 3'ou think that I played this trick on a dead man," I cried, angrily again, again making a movement towards that bell. But he said, quietly: " Will you tell me the whole story quite frankly just as it happened? "

" Will you leave out threats of calling in the police, then? And will you not interrupt me," I stipulated, severely, " and will you stop being so *frightfully* rude? "

" Rude? " he said. Then, rather more thoughtfully,"Perhaps I didn't go about it quite the right way, Miss Whitelands." I was going to tell him that he couldn't have gone about it in a way more utterly wrong, when he added, " Perhaps I might have begun by asking you if you would sit down ? "

" Yes, you might have done that," I snapped.

He said, quite mildly now, " Will you sit down ? "

" Thank you," I said, with what I hoped he saw was irony.

And down I sat once more in the same chair from which I had skipped up to ring the bell.

He added, " May I sit down? "

" Yes," I said, and then he too sat opposite to me as we had sat before, but with an intangible something quite different now.

He began, " I shall have to cross-question you, you know."

But it was no longer his court-martial voice, so I nodded, in a half-resigned, half-mollified way.

He said, " Well, you say you know my wife, slightly. [When did you first meet her? "

" I first met your wife about a month ago," I said, briskly, " in the ten-thirty train from Euston going down to Llandedwydd via Camrys."

What a business-like opening, I thought to myself!

Captain Meredith nodded his dark head; so, quite encouraged, I went on.

" There was no room for me in the Thirds "

Here he interrupted.

" What were you doing travelling third? "

" I always travel third," I told him, impatiently. " I mean I *did* always travel third. You don't suppose I had any money to waste on travelling first-class, do you? Why, I "

Here I pulled up rather embarrassed. He hadn't said, " Well! This doesn't look the kind of room of a girl who usually travels third class." Nor did he glance at my thirty-five guinea frock, and at all the other hallmarks of luxury by which I was surrounded. But I felt that the comment was made, if not by him, then in silence by *them!*

I went on, hastily. " So the porter pushed me into a first-class carriage. And there sat "

Here I pulled myself up. I had so very nearly said " The Vision." In the nick of time I altered it to " Your wife."

" Yes ? " said Captain Meredith, with his little nod. " And you entered into conversation? "

" No, 7 didn't! *She* did. She turned round and said to me "

Here I had to make an effort to keep from reproducing the remark in its original Cockney. " She said to me,' *You wouldn't think* 7 *was one of these war-widows, would you?* "

" Here – hold on, hold on! " put in Captain Meredith. " Begin at the beginning, please. What did she say to you to begin with; before she said that?"

" Nothing! " I answered. " That was how she *did* begin!"

Captain Meredith said " H'm." He said it exactly as Reggie Penmore himself might have done. Perhaps all men have several of these maddening little tricks in common ?

Then he commented, " Rather an extraordinary way to start a conversation with a person whom one ha never seen before."

" Yes; wasn't it? " I said. " Of course it was! But then, if you come to that, everything "

Here again I had to pull myself up. I was just *going* to say, " Everything about the Vision was so extraordinary!"

This, I knew, would not have been allowed. However " extraordinary" and showy and vulgar the" Vision might be, she was his wife, and I should have been told to remember it. This is one of the ways, 1 think, in which men are more particular than we are. I'm sure that if I had been unlucky enough to marry a male Vision, with hearts sprinkled all over his pyjamas I shouldn't have minded *who* had said *what* about him, afterwards!

However, I went on to the dark and silent young man before me. " She told me all about you, Captain Meredith."

" Oh? " he said in an absolutely expressionless voice. " May I ask what she told you? "

" Well, she told me that you had met her at Giro's and had married her after only knowing her a fortnight, and that it was at a Registry Office," I hastened on, quite glibly. " And that you had to go back againto duty before you could see her again; and that then you were reported killed."

" Yes? " he said. " But, if you will allow me to say so, there is nothing in all this that might not have been common property among other people."

" You mean that some of her friends might have told me that? I might never have seen her at all? " I took up, angrily. " Is that what you mean ? Why! Do you know that I have got heaps of her *things* to prove that I met her? Her dressing-bag with V. V. all over it! And her pearl pendant with your portrait; and her "

" She gave you those ? " said Captain Meredith, evenly.

I brought my fist down angrily upon my knee.

"You think I stole them?"

" I am waiting to form my opinion," said Captain Meredith, quietly, " until I have heard the whole of the story. Please go on with it, Miss White- lands."

" I am, I mean, I'm trying to "

" Well, then she told me about your people. She said that they had written to her, and asked her to go there (to the Bryn) and be one of themselves. She showed me that letter. She told me how awfully much she didn't want to go."

He gave a little quick movement.

"She didn't want to go to the Bryn?" he said, sharply. " Why on earth – why not? "

" Because she had the chance of such an awfullygood engagement in the States," I explained. " And besides – because – oh, because she was shy! "

" Shy!" he exclaimed; and there was a note of incredulity just appearing through the blankness of his tone.

" She said she would be shy," I told him; " she said they were ' not her sort.' And then " – I cleared my throat. It was a difficult part that I'd come to! – " then she asked me all about myself, and what 7 was going to do. And it was then, when we had lunched and got very nearly to Camrys, that she said we ought to 'swop.'"

" Swop. She said *that? "* he took up.

" Yes; she said that I must go on to your people, and give out that I was her, that I was your widow! She said that I was to take her place "

" Indeed. And she was to take *your* place, as a nursery-governess ? "

" No, no!" I said, impatiently shaking my head. " She was to go back to Liverpool and take this cinema- film's offer in America. That was her plan! "

There was a brief pause. I looked at his face. " I don't believe you believe a word of it!" I said, desperately.

Quite mildly he admitted, " I must say that, up to now, it all strikes me as extraordinarily farfetched."

" Yes. But that's nothing, nothing, to what it gets later on!" I answered lugubriously, shaking my head. " It gets *far* more far-fetched, afterwards "

" Well, let's have it, anyhow. You were just up to where you agreed to change places with my wife "

" Agreed!" I broke in almost frenzied, drumming with my toes on the carpet. " I never agreed, never! Why, I wouldn't hear of it. I *told* her so. Then we got to Camrys, and what do you think? Lo and behold, she pushed me out on to the platform, and left me there!"

" She pushed you out? How?" (drily). "Through the window? "

" No, no! Of course not. She opened the door like this " – I imitated, violently, the gesture of opening the door. " She told me that we changed. She got out with me. Then she hopped in again at the very last moment, leaving me, and the bag, on the platform. There! Do you understand ? "

He said nothing.

" And there I waited," I went on, " and presently I saw these people, these that I was going to at Llandedwydd as a nursery-governess, come into the station."

Captain Meredith interrupted again. " May I ask why you didn't appeal to them, and tell *them* the whole story? "

" May I ask if you know the people? " I retorted. " Sutcliffe-Smythe their name is, and they live at the Hall."

" Ah – the new tenants," said Captain Meredith, with a subtle something in his tone that showed me he had met those awful people.

" Well, perhaps you now understand why I couldn't possibly have told them anything," I said to him, impressively. " So I went on, by the next train, to Llandedwydd."

" Ah! It was then you decided to accept my wife's offer that you should step into her shoes ? "

" No; it wasn't. It *never* was! I never, never wanted her shoes or *anything*. I went on, partly because she had disappeared and I was going to explain everything to your father and mother "

" Well? " he said, with a little lift of his dark head. " And why didn't you? "

"And why hadn't I? Because of – oh, dear! Because of ' one dashed thing after another '! " I quoted with a little exhausted sigh. " To begin with, Sir Richard met me, and you know he is deaf. Then, when I got to the house, there were people there with your mother. And then there was an escaped German prisoner, of all things! in my room "

" Yes, I heard about that, and how you fainted and fell and hurt yourself, and were very seedy for some time. My mother told me *that,"* said Captain Meredith, in a voice that showed me that this was the only part of the story which he found himself able to believe. " But when you got well again, Miss White- lands," he added, " why didn't you explain to them *then? "*

"I did – I tried to. I wrote it all down!" I told him. " I did everything! They thought it was loss ofmemory! I couldn't get them to believe a word I said!"

" Did you try your hardest, Miss Whitelands ? " said the young man in a tone half-whimsical, half-contemptuous. " Come, come; you know! Surely there were a dozen things that would have borne you out! What about your own luggage? "

" That went on to Aberystwith with your wife. I only had a little. I had come down to so few things. It was only a suitcase that I could take in the carriage with me, and even that wasn't labelled! "

" Pity," said Captain Meredith, quietly. " And you were at the Bryn, how long? – a fortnight? And still you didn't manage to get them to see what had happened? Oh, come, Miss Whitelands, come, come!"

The calm reasonableness of his tone began to madden me again. I jumped to my feet. I cried, " Well, at all events, there's one way to settle things now."

He looked at me as I stood ready.

" What way do you mean? "

" I mean that now, at all events, your people will believe what I say! They may not think I know who I am, but they will know you know whether I am your wife or not! " I cried. " They can't think you've had loss of memory too! When you tell them that everything I have been saying about never having seen you before is the truth, the whole truth, and nothing but the truth, then, then, then they are bound to believe! Aren't they ? " I couldn't help clapping my hands, and giving a little skip of relief to think that all this tangledweb could now be torn aside. " Let's go and tell your people now! " I suggested, eagerly. " Please come along! Lady Meredith will be in her room " (as I had said once before that evening). " Come along now and tell her."

But he seemed in no hurry, as I was.

"Wait a bit, do you mind?" he said, slowly. "I want to think about something, first."

He got up rather slowly from his chair. Fingering that little moustache of his, he began to move about my room.

I, leaning against the bed on the other side, watched him, and could not help noticing how lightly, in spite of a slight limp that he had, he moved.

He was a tall young man, and those brown boots of of his would have looked immense indeed by the side of any of those little high-heeled shoes of mine, yet he moved noiselessly, unlike the small-footed *femme-de- chambre* who brings me in my *petit dejeuner* in the morning. I suppose that lightness of tread is not so much a matter of size and weight as it is of build and proportion and having " the use of " one's figure?

This Captain Meredith certainly has. In that limited, littered, girly-girly room he walked, easily and lightly. I suppose that freedom and grace comes of being good at games? That he is, too. I remembered the silver pots that his mother had shown me with such pride.

He didn't upset or even touch anything, until he passed by the toilette-table where there was a greatgrey-green crock filled with feathery sprays of mimosa, scented and yellow and fluffy as a duckling's back. Lady Meredith put that in there for me this morning.

Her son bent his black head over the golden mass to sniff at it luxuriously; for a second he seemed to have forgotten me. Then he turned round, stood, and said to me, quietly:

" I'm afraid it's going to be no go for the present. No can do! "

" What do you mean? " I asked, startled. " *What's* ' no go '? "

" All this. I mean I can't spring this thing on my mother like this, at a minute's notice."

" You mean you aren't going to tell her that I am not your wife, that your wife "

" No! " He spoke quietly but very firmly. " I can't."

I gazed at him more aghast than I had been at anything else.

" Why not? " I asked, sharply.

He said, very gently but unexpectedly, " I don't want to kill her!"

I stared.

" But why on earth should it kill her? " I asked. " Just to hear that my story is true, that I am not her daughter-in-law? "

Then came a fresh surprise.

He said, " You didn't happen to know that my mother has got a weak heart?"

" Has she ? " I asked, suddenly aghast. " A weak heart? Lady Meredith? No, I didn't know anything about that."

" Nobody does except me," said her son, gravely. " About a year ago I took her to be overhauled by a doctor-man of mine. (She thought it was only about a rather troublesome little cough that she had just then. I made him give me a confidential report. This was it, you see. Heart – and any shock that could possibly be avoided to be kept from her."

I said, quickly, " What about the shock of your – of her thinking that you had been killed? "

" By jove, yes," he said, almost as if to himself. " It's rather a wonder nothing happened when she heard that I had been outed. Dare say it didn't do her any good. . . . Still, you see," he added, turning to me again, " that was a thing for which she was prepared, in a way. She knew when she said good-bye to me that

it might be It was rather with the idea of taking

her thoughts off if anything did happen to me that I left her that letter to say – about my marriage. But

now ! This ! " He frowned gloomily down

at his feet.

"Now she's to have this shock? To be told this about the girl she thinks is her daughter-in-law, and that she is so delighted with? For she said – no end of things to me just now, about" – he glanced at me again, resentfully – " about you! You should have heard them, Miss Whitelands."

" I – I have heard them," I said, miserably, hangingmy head. " I'm afraid, I'm dreadfully afraid that your mother is really fond of me."

" Most unfortunate!" muttered the young man, morosely. " Tell her that *you're* nothing to her! That her real daughter-in-law has bolted! Rather a nasty jar for a woman who ' ought to be spared any shocks,' Miss Whitelands! Don't you think so ? "

Confused, helpless, distressed, I stood there.

" Well " I faltered. " What do you think I – what

do you think we shall have to do? "

Crisp and concise as an order came Captain Meredith's reply.

" We shall have to carry on!" CHAPTER XVIII

I

ARRY on,'" I repeated, dazed. "You

mean "

" I mean that for the present we shall simply have to go on as we are," said the young soldier. He drew down his upper lip between his very white teeth as if to try and bite that tiny moustache of his. He said, " My mother thinks you are my wife. Very well." I He reddened, slightly. " You will have to be my wife, I that's all. I mean – I mean – of course I mean as far I as saying you *aren't* is concerned," he erplained, I rapidly, " and *only* for the present. Later on every- I thing can be explained "

" But – your wife – "

" I shall have to find her, of course, at once; bring her back. But," he said, " there isn't much point in saying she's disappeared before I can say she's here again – or, at any rate, on her way back to me; is there? One can let people down gently, you know."

I looked at him. How " gently " did he imagine that *any* sight of the Vision was going to let his mother down?

As for myself, I certainly did not want to fall in with his plan. What? Just when all this bother wascoming to an end ? Start *new* bothers ? Goodness only knew how many and of what kind these might be. ...

My reluctance must have shown in my face. He turned away from me. He touched, quite mechanically, the yellow ribbon of a box of sweets that Sir Richard had given me, and which lay beside my hand-mirror. It was then that I noticed Captain Meredith's hands – scarred and scratched, with nails that looked as if they had been broken or bitten down to the quick. I supposed he had worn them with digging himself out of that heap of earth by the mine. . . . He seemed to feel my glance upon them, for suddenly he put them behind him, and then wheeled round to speak again.

" Don't agree, Miss Whitelands, if you would hate it; and, of course, I can't make you. Still, will you ? "

It was said almost casually, but with an intensity behind it. (How British that was!)

I looked at him. I thought of *Belle-mere,* who has been so exquisite to me in all the little ways as well as so generous in all the big things. I thought of Sir Richard, that lover who never grows old. I thought of the doctor's verdict and I made up my mind again. I said " Very well." I gave a little nod. " I will."

" Sounds like the marriage service," I thought. Could it possibly be that the same thought had crossed his mind? At the back of his eyes I surprised a look that might mean laughter – helpless, half-amused, half- defiant laughter.

And I smiled. He did not smile at me.

He said, not quite certainly, " Well, thank you verymuch." Then he glanced at the clock and said " It's getting late. What time do they – do you dine? "

" It is past the usual time," I said. " We had better go."

" And pick up these people of mine – ours," amended Captain Meredith.

" Oh, yes; do let's go at once," I said, whisking up a little lace handkerchief from my dressing-table and holding it in my hand like a flag of truce. " I don't know what effect this sort of thing has upon you, but / am absolutely starving, Captain Meredith."

He looked at me as he held the door open.

In that look I read that, though he was perhaps not quite so sure now about the adventuress theory, he was still keeping an open mind about me. f

" An open mind " is what men call it when they mean . that they don't want you to know that they don't know what to think.

Then he said " By the way, you do know my Chris- J tian name, don't you ? "

" Do I know it? " I exclaimed, almost with a groan. " I should think the name George must be stamped on *f.* my heart like the name of Calais must be on the Ger-
KL-

’.

man Emperor's!"

" And your name, I think, is Rose? Or at least I suppose my mother and everybody call you Viv – call you by my wife's name? "

" No, indeed they don't! I never would let them! " I assured him just as we stood outside Lady Meredith's door.

As I tapped I pulled myself together for an ordeal. The ordeal of witnessing Lady Meredith's delight at seeing us (" us! ") together!

No doubt she had been imagining a blissful reunion between the two young people. A rapturous love- scene! (How perfectly awful!)

No wonder I set my teeth as I knocked at the door.

But it wasn't opened by Lady Meredith.

The black-haired, smiling *femme-de-chambre* informed me that " M'Lady and the Lord Sir Meredith had gone down to dinner, it was half an hour ago, in the restaurant."

" Gone down without me – without us, I mean ? " I said.

Captain Meredith said " Yes " as if he hardly heard what I was saying.

Indeed, his whole voice and bearing now reminded me of a person who is answering questions while, at the same time, he is absorbed in reading some book. And what a book it was, poor fellow! I expect he was busily going over in his mind tags of the things that I had just been saying to him, as well as who knows what scenes out of the chapters that I have never read. The chapters that have to do with his marriage! His relations to that other girl whose shoes I have been wearing!

He went on, " Yes; my father always likes his dinner pretty early. I expect he thought we should be sure to be late."

; I'm never late," I told him, rather hastily, as we

U ’

went down in the lift. " I'm always a most punctual person. Sir Richard said so."

" Yes ? Well, I expect they thought there would be an exception this evening," said Captain Meredith in his blankest tone. " I expect they both thought that we should have such a lot to talk to each other about. So we had, of course."

Certainly it was late. As we passed down the long red-carpeted corridor that leads to the restaurant at the Ritz, there were several people who had already dined, sitting in the red chairs by the little round tables.

We passed the Princess Jinka sitting by herself in that wondrous tea-gown of hers. To add to my astonishment she turned large, friendly eyes upon Captain Meredith. She gave him a sweet smile, a little wave of her jewelled hand.

He bowed, very unsmilingly. I wondered if he could ever really laugh.

We passed a group of three young British officers. One was in khaki, still muddy from the trenches. One was in trim blue with the curly braid about his sleeve that meant that he belonged to the Royal Naval Reserve. And the youngest was in the Kit of the Royal Flying Corps. His face was something between a hawk's and a baby's. It was as pink and smooth as my own. As we went by I heard him say, " Finest rag I've been in since I got my wings – "

And then, as we passed, all three broke off laughing and talking; and I could feel them trying to disguisethe fact that they were staring hard at those new pink flutterations, and those little rose brocade shoes of mine.

How glad, oh! how glad I was that I had got them on for this very special occasion!

People think that new and beautiful clothes make one self-conscious. Perhaps they may have this effect on men, the eccentric creatures! But it is the *want* of new and beautiful clothes that makes a woman conscious of herself and her shortcomings. The possession of a faultless frock is so much more helpful, protecting, stimulating than that of the cleverest conscience.

At all events, I had both! We entered the restaurant, that big, long room with its right-hand wall all looking-glasses and with the clustering wall-lights that bathe everything in a kind of milky radiance.

The subdued sound of chatter and laughter rose up from the tables; tables for twos and fours, for larger parties.

I glanced about. I saw a good many heads turn towards us.

Yes, I suppose they thought we were another example of the touching and decorative " war-couple." The bride in the trousseau frock, the young husband snatching what may be his last taste of life and love and laughter!

" Ah! There they are! " I said, looking towards a table on the right. " There are your people."

For I had just caught sight of a glimpse of Sir Richard's black coat and of his wife's meadow-sweet

coloured cone of hair above the pink lights of a table for two.

For two, only?

They not only had begun without us, but they were having a tete-a-tete dinner.

Did they think, then, that we should have so much to say to each other upstairs that we shouldn't want anything to eat at all ?

And I, that couldn't have been more ravenous!

" Hullo! " said Captain Meredith into his mother's hair.

And she turned with a beaming smile and a soft, delighted little flurry of explanations.

" Oh, George darling! We didn't think that you were dining here to-night. We thought that you would be taking the child out to Henry's for your first dinner together, the first evening and all. Still, now you have come it's delightful. . . . Richard, tell the waiter to move us to a table for four. We will all dine together !"

We did all dine together.

Ye gods! What an awful meal it was!

Not the food; of course that was lovely. (Soup of the white velvety kind, sole, bird, and a wonderful pear as big as a football with a tall jar of rich cream to which one helped oneself with a ladle.) But the conversation.

I noticed, out of the muddle of my own embarrassment of the first few minutes, how Captain Meredith roused himself with an effort from that engrossingreverie of his, and tried to keep the conversation strictly neutral and matter-of-fact. He clung to details of what the food was like, at his particular mess; and how those last socks had worn which Lady Meredith had knitted for him. He gave news of so-and-so and so-and- so in such-and-such a battalion. He told a story of some youth in the mess who had returned beaming from leave, and who, when asked after his people, returned, mildly, " You don't suppose I was such an ass as to let my people know I had leave, do you? "

(I saw Lady Meredith's dear face looking so puzzled over this story!) Then he went on to ask for news of some cousin on a torpedo-boat. All this was as though he had taken trouble to keep me well out of tr. e conversation.

But at every opening dear Lady Meredith, radiant as a girl in the pink-shaded candlelight, brought the conversation back to me, as if she could not impress it sufficiently upon her son how very much one of themselves I was already, and how delighted she was that 7 – 7 should be the fourth at that happy (?) little family dinner-party!

It was nothing but appeals to me, " Rose, darling, you know So-and-so ? " Also plans for the Summer. " If Rose cares for London in May," and " Won't your cousins be delighted to see Rose at Laurel Grove? " and " Of course she hasn't seen anything of the family yet, but when we go back we shall take Rose to "

I should think Captain Meredith must have got almost as dead sick of that name as I had been tiredto death of the name of George! As for me, I was presently *past* feeling embarrassed, past feeling annoyed with him for having insisted on keeping me in this position. I found myself taking a mildly malicious amusement in seeing himself force himself to smile at his mother across the table, and to answer, more or less absently, still out of that book of his thoughts!

Presently he took refuge in some inquiry about an aunt of his.

His mother bubbled out again into delighted laughter.

" Talking about aunts, did Rose tell you how we had teased her? " she said, moving the silver candlestick aside a little so as to see her darling's face more clearly. " We told her, you know, that we were coming over to Paris to meet an aunt! "

" Did you ? " returned her son, absently again, bending his dark head over the champagne in its bucket of ice by his side. " And did you meet her, Mam? " (He uses the Welsh word, I noticed, for mother.) There was another soft bubbling of explanations from Lady Meredith.

" *Wasn't* it a joke, George!" I really began to feel very sorry for that young man.

He turned off into a conversational by-path that I am sure he thought could have nothing to do with his wife.

He asked, " And how is old Straf, Mother? "

" Oh, Straf is quite all right, dear, but what do you think, George?" took up his mother, pleased at this opening. " Your nose is out of joint with your owndog by your own wife! Richard," she turned to her husband, " you tell George about Straf the very first evening that Rose came home to the Bryn."

" Oh, by Jove! yes," took up George's father. " The old fellow went up to your little girl here wagging his tail for all he was worth! Talking to her like a Christian ! And he will follow her about everywhere now, won't he, Rose? He knows well enough whose little Rose she is!"

Yes; it was roses, roses all the way!

Suddenly and quite loudly George Meredith exclaimed, violently, " Oh, dash! " For his strong fingers had snapped the stem of his finely-chased French wineglass. It fell from his hand on to a fork and sent a shower of tinkling glass fragments and of whispering wine-bubbles over the cloth.

In a softer voice, but one that seemed to have much more annoyance than any amount of bad language, Captain Meredith said, " Oh, bother the thing!"

" Oh, but that is supposed to be so lucky," I put in as the *garfon* hurried up, smiling, to repair matters. I felt I must say something, for up to then I had scarcely opened my lips. " Haven't the French got a proverb of ' *un verre blanc casse, fa porte bonheur* '? "

" Ah, Rose! " said Lady Meredith, in her soft, emotional voice, gazing fondly from her restored son to her adopted daughter; " I think George would tell you that he had already been brought all happiness in the world!"

This was embarrassing enough, wasn't it, under the circumstances ?

However, worse was to come after dinner.

We were the last of the diners. As we strolled, slowly, back through that long, red-carpeted aisle of a corridor I walked behind with Sir Richard, who is already beginning to learn to read from my lips as he does from those of his wife.

Captain Meredith went on ahead with his mother.

I saw her slip her slim hand inside the khaki-sleeved arm of the son whom she thought she had lost. I heard her say, gently, " George, dear, I suppose you are arranging about the room for yourselves ? "

" Oh, no, Mam! I am not putting up here, you know," her son's voice took up, precipitately. " I am round at the Grand; got my traps there and everything."

" Have you, dear boy? " said Lady Meredith, just as we had reached the end of the corridor. " But I thought all of you came home on leave with only just as much as you could cram into those funny little haversacks of yours."

" Oh, yes; but I have got them all there," said the young man, still more hastily. " And I think, do you know, that I had better be getting back there now and turn in. I am still just a bit tuckered out, you know. I think I will be off."

" Do, dearest," said Lady Meredith, smiling up at him. Then she added, " But you will have to waitjust for a minute or two while Rose gets her cloak and things to go round with you."

Now, just imagine it!

Just please imagine it! They imagined that I – I was going round to the Grand with him – with Captain Meredith! That is what they thought.

Well, I suppose it was natural.

But I hadn't thought of it. I'd never imagined their taking such a thing into their heads.

I wasn't prepared for it.

There I stood, amazement widening my eyes and part- jng my lips. Precipitately, I said " Oh! But I am not going to "

And here Captain Meredith rose, rather ably, to the situation. Not precipitately, but just deliberately and blessedly matter-of-fact, he broke in, " Oh, but you know, Mam, I am going to leave Rose here with you tonight. I am not taking her round with me, of course! "

The last two words were a stroke of genius. I realised this in the middle of my flurry.

For if somebody only says " of course " in a sufficiently convinced tone of voice on the spur of the moment, the unprepared persons to whom the words are addressed are hypnotised into thinking that he is stating some obvious fact.

" Oh, of course," echoed poor Lady Meredith, mechanically, and utterly taken aback.

She didn't say another word while her son turned off to fetch his soft peaked khaki cap and his " British warm " and the little stitched leather-covered cane.

" Good-night, everybody," he said, pleasantly, without looking at anybody in particular. And he made a swift but unfussy exit through the revolving glass doors of the Ritz with a little parting nod and the words " See you in the morning! " CHAPTER XIX

ONE TETE-A-TETE AFTER ANOTHER

EVERYBODY knows the kind of play or book or music-hall joke that is based on the situation of two young people who long to be together alone, but who are always foiled in their wish.

Always there is a crowd with them; always they are pursued by some chaperon. Or there is a little brother who, gnat-like, buzzes about them at every turn. Or some unconscious stranger is for ever breaking in upon them and destroying the yearned for tete-a-tete.

Well, it now seems as if Miss Vera Vayne's husband and I would have to live for the present in the middle of this situation – *reversed.* We simply are not allowed to get out of seeing each other alone!

It has been a case of " one dashed tete-a-tete " after the other.

And it is all poor dear Lady Meredith's doing.

This is pathetic as well as exasperating.

I know that every moment of her son's leave – whether it is spent here in Paris or in Wales – is precious to her.

Unselfishly, she thinks that the mother ought to retire into the background now. " My son's my son till he gets him a wife," and all that kind of thing. She has made excuse after excuse to enable herselfand Sir Richard to go off, leaving " the two dear young things to see a little more of each other without us!"

This morning – the first morning after that adored son's arrival in Paris, she was truly worried because George did not turn up at the Ritz until half-past ten o'clock.

I thought her worry was because the days would not be long enough for her to spend with him.

No; it was not that kept her gently fuming with her outdoor things on while the young man delayed to make his appearance.

I guessed, of course, that he might have plenty of private business on his hands on his first morning after he had discovered that that wife of his had elected to leave him in the lurch with a reluctant substitute and a couple of unconscious parents!

However, poor Lady Meredith could hardly be expected to realise this, just yet.

It was " Darling Rose, if George doesn't come in five minutes I'm afraid we shall have to be off without him." This was as Williams, her indispensable Welsh maid, was fastening her cloud-grey veil above the violets in her toque. " I made sure he would be round here as soon as we had finished our coffee. You will have to explain "

" But surely you are going to wait to see him, or go round to the Grand ? " I suggested, startled.

" Oh no, darling. We, Richard and I, have some old friends we simply must go and see."

(Neighbourhood of " old friends' " abode not specified.)

" As it is such a heavenly morning, you and George ought to go for a stroll all down the Boulevards. You *won't* let him walk too fast on his poor dear leg? " said his mother, a little wistfully. " But of *course* you won't."

She rose from her chair before the looking-glass, and took the grey-satin bag from her maid's hand. " Now good-bye. I shall telephone to the Grand on my way

down to ask if he has started Ah! There he is,"

as a tap at the door was followed by the entrance of the young soldier. His worn khaki had been brushed within an inch of its life, by the *valet-de-chambre,* I suppose, at the Grand. His black head was as glossy as the toe of my own little new patent-leather boot; but I thought he was paler than he had been.

" George, darling, you haven't slept!" cried his mother, with sudden concern as he bent to kiss her, after a curious little burlesqued nod and greeting to me. " You are dark under the eyes, George."

" Oh, nonsense, Mam! One never sleeps the first night on leave. It takes some little time getting accustomed to sheets and comfortable, stuffy rooms, and things," said her son, briefly. " Are you ready to come out?"

Here Lady Meredith made her little explanation again. " Oh, you know, George, father and I are ' shaking ' you and Rose. We have some old friends," et cetera, et cetera.

So George and Rose were practically pushed out into the bright February sunshine of the Place Ven- dome.

" Topping morning, isn't it ? " said the restrained voice of the young soldier, as our feet led us up towards the arches of the rue de Rivoli past the shops of glittering jewelry laid out on trays, so enticingly, that one is almost persuaded to believe in it. Past the shops of fine under-linen, men's shirts exquisitely bemono- grammed upon the sleeve. Past shops of prints and yet more prints: Steinlin's, Mordant drawings, the furious comments of Raemaekars, and Kirchn's refreshing frivolities.

I could have lingered to look at these, but Captain Meredith, in spite of his slight limp, hurried past them. " Topping morning," he said again; but I was thinking of what I should have to say to him, presently.

We turned to the right and walked into the Tuileries Gardens, with the formal spaces and the huge sphinxes and the great stone flower-vases and the bench where that immortal old man sits feeding the sparrows.

They hovered about his head as thick as a swarm of gnats; they caught in mid-air the crumbs that were tossed to them.

That old Frenchman must have been a young soldier in 1870.

To-day France was engaged in a struggle beyond comparison, more desperate than that disastrous com- paign of a few months. But the Gardens in their gracious formality seemed to recognise nothing of it. The sphinxes stared down, blankly, upon us – the small English girl in the *militaire-blcue* costume and the young British officer who had just come from fighting, beside his French Allies, for the cause of civilization.

" Topping morning," he said as monotonously and mechanically as if he had been the talking Myner at the Zoo.

I felt that behind the sphinx-like mask of my companion's face another war – a war of sentiments and complications – was raging.

I knew that he must have gone through positive *years* of thinking since the moment that he had bolted from " our " hotel to his own last night.

Well, I knew why he looked as if he hadn't slept. He, probably, had spent the whole night cogitating over the extraordinary complications he had come back to after the comparatively simple conditions of existence in the firing-line.

At the foot of one of the great stone monsters I turned to him.

I spoke as if I were carrying on, uninterrupted, the conversation from last night.

" Captain Meredith, I have thought of something," I told him, looking up at him.

With a start he seemed to come back out of I don't know what meditations.

" Well? " he said.

" There is somebody in Paris," I told him, " who knows all about me, who knows who I was, and what – what I am and all that."

" Rather a change," said Captain Meredith, looking at me, gravely.

He tapped with the leather-covered cane he carried at one of the chains bordering the flower-bed near the pavement where we were seated; then he said, in a voice less absent, " Who is she, if I may ask? "

" He – it's a man," I exclaimed, quickly. " An R. A. M. C. man who is at one of the French Red Cross hospitals here. We – your mother and I saw him the other day. Then I saw him alone, and I told him the whole story as I told it to you! Only, *he* believed me! " I wound up, bitterly. " I would like you to meet him." I made a little quick movement, turning to the road by which we had come. " Shall we go and see him, now? "

Captain Meredith looked down at me with a curious, searching look. I reddened a little and I wondered whether the said " confidante " was in his thoughts. He spoke, slowly.

" Should you mind," he asked, " if I went and saw him by myself? "

" Mind! I would much rather you did," I cried, more than a little defiantly. " Why, I *want* you to! I don't want to see him again yet."

And I didn't.

I had still the uncomfortable feeling that I had behaved rather badly about Reggie Penmore's proposal. I should have to answer it, of course, among the other complications that lay before me now.

And for the life of me I didn't know how to explain that I didn't want to marry him.

" Perhaps it might be a good thing if I went," returned Captain Meredith, again with that curious look. " Please tell me the name and the address."

I wrote them down for him on the back of a bill from the Printemps that I had in my bag.

I wrote, sitting on one of the Tuileries benches.

Then I said, philosophically matter-of-fact, " I suppose I couldn't go back and wai for you at the Ritz alone? Williams might know and tell your mother; and she might think we had quarrelled. Am I to wait for you here? "

" Too near home, don't you think? " suggested the young man, with the ghost of a twinkle in his dark eyes. He looked towards the grey pile of the Louvre, sombre and solid against the gay skies, and said " I don't like leaving you like this, but it must be done, I suppose? Suppose you go and look at some pictures in there," pointing with his cane. " When I have called on this Captain Penmore I could pick you up at that Winged Victory thing on the stairs, you know it? "

But who would not draw the line at art galleries on a morning when Paris smiled in the sunshine, spreading gay and coloured in real pictures before one's eyes? I suggested our meeting again in the Luxembourg Gardens, close to the merry-go-round, an old haunt of mine when I was here before – before the war; and he departed.

Presently I was there again, finding everything in the big grounds under the trees almost exactly as it was before. Almost, not quite. One of the differences wasa sad one. So many wounded French tommies in the come-and-go of the moving crowd, among the laughing, romping children (whom they had fought to protect), so many brave-faced *poilus* with arms in slings and legs helped on by crutches.

Quite half of the mothers, too, who wheeled perambulators or who sat on the benches watching their children bowl hoops and fly balloons, were shrouded in widow's weeds. These sights had not been there in my day. For this was Paris in war-time.

But there, just the same, was the small brick Mus6e with its guard of stone Bacchantes; and there, just the same, were the low stone balustrades and the wide circle below about the fountain where bare-legged French children sailed their boats. And there, quite unchanged (how unlike the towns of North-eastern France!) was the *carrousel,* the well-known canopy under which other children rode astride heraldic lions and elephants.

Round and round they sped, while the hurdy-gurdy played the same gay little tunes that it had played when I was here before. Only a few more notes were dumb in the treble, as some of the notes of France's sons are dumb. The bass kept excellent time, as even France herself, that is so much more than any of her sons, is keeping excellent time. I watched and listened, half attending, half wondering what was going on at that moment at the Red Cross hospital. What Captain Meredith would say to Reggie Penmore? What Reggie would tell him?

For at present, I could not help feeling more concerned in my own part of this story than I was about the part that had only to do with Miss Vera Vayne and her husband; interesting as that, too, promised to be. ...

Then suddenly I saw, emerging from the surrounding crowd of nurses in black gowns and white Brittany caps, the tall figure of a Briton at his best – namely, in uniform – Captain Meredith himself.

" Already! " I said, discomfited. He nodded, tightening his lips under those two little black finger-prints of a moustache. Without speaking for a moment, he came and stood beside me watching the merry-go-round. From his face, as I watched, I saw that he was one of the few quite young men who really love little children.

He watched them whirling past on the merry-go- round; sturdy French boys of ten years still wearing socks only just above the ankle, and girls all black curls and navy-blue capes.

They still play the same game that they played when I was here – a kind of quintain. Perhaps they played it in my mother's time. To each child the *patron* of the *carrousel* hands a wand; and while they tilt past at full speed each child tries to pass the wand through a wooden ring that dangles from the stand. Above it hangs the notice in French, " *Three rounds without winning will give you the right for one turn without pay.* "

" That's fair enough, isn't it? " said Captain Meredith, suddenly, with a curious little twisted smile. Heseemed to be speaking to himself rather than to me. " We don't have things arranged for us like that when we are grown-up. If we don't win, we don't win; and we aren't given another chance to try."

This was all very true; but why wouldn't he tell me at once what Reggie had said? Just as I was going to ask him straight out, a diversion was caused by three tiny boys, obviously French in feature and speech but dressed in complete imitation of a Scotch soldier – bonnet, kilt, sporran, shoes. As they passed, these midgets saluted the British officer, saluted with the gravest cor- rectitude and smartness (" one, two! " taking their time from the left).

Captain Meredith acknowledged the salute almost as ceremoniously and without a flicker on his face, although to the salutes of some French tommies whom we had passed he had responded with a smile for each. I thought it nice of the young man to understand that the saluting babies must not see a suspicion of laughter. But he could be simply horrid to grown-ups, I thought!

Impatiently I turned to him above the heads of the children awaiting their *tour.*

" Well," I said. " Did Captain Penmore tell you I was not an impostor? "

" No," said my companion's soft voice. " He did not."

"He didn't?" I cried, incredulously. "He didn't tell you all about me? "

" No. You see, I didn't see Captain Penmore," said this other maddening young man, digging little holeswith his cane in the gravel of the Luxembourg Gardens. " I didn't see him."

"You didn't see him? He was busy, I suppose?"

" I suppose so," agreed Captain Meredith. " They keep those fellows " (prod) " fairly busy."

" Oh, well; I hope he said when he would see you ? "

The curious look again from Captain Meredith. " Oh? Why do you hope that? "

Really it is terrible, the obtuseness of men!

"Why?" I cried, hotly. *"Why?* So that you should at *least* know that there is such a person as Captain Penmore! So that you should at least see that *one* thing I told you was true, whatever you think! "

" As to there being such a person as Captain Pen- more, well, it would be easy enough to look him up in the Army List, wouldn't it? " said the young man, quite mildly regarding me. " And as for what I think – well! that is a thing you don't know, Miss White- lands."

This was so true. Consequently it made me so furious that I didn't know what to do.

I turned scarlet with resentment. I glared at the dancing plaster statues outside the gallery. They really danced, through the tears in my eyes.

Then I heard the young man beside me say, steadily, " I was rather rude to you last evening, I think."

" I told you so," I said, without turning my head.

" Yes," he said, simply. " Well, this is my apology, you see."

" What is? " I said.

" *What* is ? " He broke off to clap his hands and smile as a little girl passed her wand through the wooden circle for the seventh time. Then " Why," he said, " do you actually suppose I went to see that Captain Penmore of yours ? "

" You didn't go? " I said, blinking my eyes.

" To discuss you with him! Oh, no! " he said, quietly. " I hd it all out with *you* last night. I don't think there is the slightest need, now, to drag in any third person."

" He would have convinced you," I cried, angrily, disappointed.

At that he smiled a little.

Then I saw what he meant. He meant it as a sort of compliment. . . . Perhaps he meant that he didn't need another witness for the defence. That he had come round to thinking that Rose Whitelands (Miss) might have been telling the truth after all!

I was mollified, of course.

But I was still rather vexed. I said " You will have to see him some time! If not to satisfy yourself, well, then, to satisfy me! Because when your wife does turn up I shall have to explain to her – oh, dear! What a lot of people I shall have to explain to! " I put in, ruefully. " I shall have to explain to Miss Vera Vayne that I *did* try to show you by every means in my power that I hadn't fallen in with her plan! By the way," *J.* took up, quickly, " what *are* you doing about your wife? How soon do you suppose you will be able to get to know where she is, Captain Meredith? "

He took a deep breath, as though after some exertion that I hadn't realised.

" It depends," he said, shortly. " Of course being war-time makes it so much more complicated than it would have been before. I tried to get them to let me telephone through to my solicitors in London. Found that was stopped to-day. Everything held up; couldn't get them. I wired, of course."

"What did you wire?" I asked as we began to walk away from the *carrousel* towards the entrance to the Gardens.

"I wired," he said, " I wired to them to search sailing-lists for the last three months and find out by which boat Miss Vera Vayne was supposed to have gone over to New York. You did say she had gone to America, Miss Whitelands, didn't you?"

" Well, that is where she told me she was going," I informed him. " She told me she would be off there, directly."

" Yes. Well, *now* I have got to wait for the answer to that blessed telegram," he said, slowly, as we turned down the rue Buonaparte, that narrow little studio of a thoroughfare, all picture-shops. " As a matter of fact I went back to the Grand when I left you, to see whether an answer could possibly have come yet. It hadn't. I dare say I sha'n't hear until one or two o'clock. We might lunch there," he said. " Do you mind if we do ? "

" Oh, no," I said, resignedly.

" Do you mean you would rather lunch at the Ritz ? "

" Oh, no! I mean I don't mind where we lunch," Isaid. " I sha'n't mind anything – I sha'n't be satisfied about anything until the answer has come, and until we know exactly how soon we should be able to have this thing straight."

He said, " By Jove! You can't wish that any more devoutly than I do! "

" Oh, no! I know I can't," I agreed, and I almost laughed.

For the natural thing is to suppose that this young man, who has come back from the front to find the wrong wife waiting for him, should be consumed with impatience until the right wife turns up.

In the meantime he looked tired, I thought. It was for his sake more than my own that I suggested that we should drive instead of walk to the Grand.

We took an open cab.

It was nearly at the door of the Grand that we passed, in the street, another British officer who looked up, quickly, at my companion and seemed about to give him a friendly hail. Then an odd change came over his face. He passed on.

I said, just before we stopped, " Somebody who knew you? "

" By Jove! yes," said Captain Meredith. " That is Thornton – that is Major Thornton. Rather awkward, that."

"Why, what is the mat ?" I began.

He explained, quickly, " That fellow was my – my sort of best man. He was the only one of my friends I had there when I was married. I didn't know he had gotleave just now. I only hope to goodness he won't come round inquiring for. . . . Oh, no, of course he won't do that. . . . Wish we hadn't met him!" he said, gloomily.

I expect it was because he hoped we should meet nobody else he knew that Captain Meredith selected a table for lunch in the furthest and most secluded corner of the restaurant. Of course I knew from the very look on the waiter's face that he imagined it was because the young British officer wanted to have me – ME! all to himself!

I do hope he is an English-speaking waiter. If he overheard even a few scraps of our conversation, he must have known that we couldn't have been anything approaching a couple in love!

For Captain Meredith, becoming a little less gloomy and a little more confidential after the soup and the fish, began to talk quite a lot to me. The subject that he selected was, naturally enough, his wife.

" I say, Miss Whitelands, do you mind," he began in quite a friendly voice – " do you mind if I ask you a few questions about Vera – about my wife, you know? "

Very different from the tone in which he claimed, last night, the right to ask me questions!

And I, also in quite a different tone, said, over the table, " Oh, of *course,* I will tell you anything I can."

I didn't realise at the time quite how little this would be.

" You see, you saw her last," he said, with his eyes, meditatively, upon my face. I don't think he saw me. I think what he saw were the thoughts in his own mind, whatever these may have been. " You saw her – well, it must have been just after I was supposed to have been outed," he went on. " Do you mind telling me exactly how she seemed to take it? "

This sounded an easy question, didn't it? I suppose it might have been easy, applied to almost any other woman who has been made a widow by this terrible war. But applied to the Vision – to the garishly cheerful creature with whom I had had that one bewildering meeting! The highly-coloured film-actress of whom every look and tone seemed to be stamped ineradicably upon my memory! Her young husband, opposite to me,

now asked " Can you remember how she ? Well,

what she said, for instance, about the affair? "

I could have told him, I think, in Miss Vera Vayne's very accents.

(" *Oh, well, 's no use me pretending to be heartbroken! "* Only I couldn't tell *him* that, could I? Could *anybody?)*

" I suppose she seemed sorry, and all that ? " suggested the young man, to help me out.

" Oh, yes! " I fibbed, feverishly drinking claret that I hoped would put some sort of heart into me for this cross-examination. It was far, far more difficult even than the one I had stood up to last time.

For I had only been telling the truth then, and only fighting for myself. Now I should have to tell fibs – or at least to soften the truth; and all to spare him.

He said, encouragingly, " I suppose she had gone intomourning for me, and all that sort of thing? I suppose she was wearing black ? "

" N-n-not exactly black," I faltered, thinking of that kaleidoscope of strident purples, like a parterre of cinerarias, in which the Vision had arrayed herself in all her glory. " She was wearing – I – I – I suppose it was – "

I gulped.

" – AflZ/-mourning. But I think she told me she didn't hold – I mean, approve of mourning."

"Oh? She said that?" he said, quietly. "And then, what? "

He helped himself to a spoonful of green velvet spinach, and seemed to be waiting, waiting anxiously for me to say something.

But I found it too difficult!

There I sat, silent, the girl who was supposed to be his wife, facing, over that cosy luncheon-table, a young man full of inquiries about the girl who was really his wife. Inquiries that of course I ought to be able to answer! And of course I should have been able to answer them. Only – only Think if I *had!*

As I still hesitated to give him a verbatim account of Miss Vera's conduct as his " widow " that I *might* have given him, he prompted me.

" For instance, did my wife seem at all keen – well,

not' keen ' exactly But did she take it in the way

that seems to have bucked my mother up about it, that I was supposed to have been killed in action? The " *'era's death'* touch, don't you know? " he said, withthe typical British flippancy that our men use as a glove wherewith to touch something too sacred to be approached with the heavy hand. " Did she take the sort of – er – the ' Pro Patria ' view of it? "

Anxiously he looked at me. It seemed to mean a good deal to him that his wife should have felt – as his *own.* women-folk would all have felt.

I helped myself to salt – which I had taken already – with my omelette.

Then I said, in a rather forced voice, " Oh! She – she did mention that you'd been killed in an attack."

I heard again the tone in which she'd said it; loud, gaily callous, matter-of-fact.

(" *Killed in an attack, he was!* ")

" That was all, what? " he said. And I could catch the disappointment behind his quiet tone.

Quickly, I took up, " Oh, but she thought you – you must have been very *brave!* "

" She said that? " also quickly, from him.

" N-not in those *words,"* I answered, " but "

My brain was a-buzz during the whole of this dialogue with the words that the " war-widow " had used in the train.

" *Always a bit of a dare-devil! . . . First in the fray, and cetrer! . . . Expect he was in a bit too much of a rush, as per usual! . . . Pity! ...*"

I tried to paraphrase them into suitability.

I said " She said you were always first when there was anything daring and dangerous to be done."

" Oh? " he said. " I – er – I can't imagine her say-' ing that, somehow. . . ." Then, quickly, " I don't mean I don't know that was what she gave you to

understand, Miss Whitelands. But – the exact *words* were

" I'm – I'm afraid I'm n-not very good at remembering exact words "

Here the waiter came again with something. I was so worried I didn't know what we were eating now. The next thing that Captain Meredith said was in a lower, more confidential voice; almost appealing, indeed, as he leaned a little forward over the table towards me.

" You see – you are a girl yourself," he said, " and – if I may say so – quick at things. I wish "

He stopped.

"What do you wish?"

" I wish," he answered, " that I could manage to get out of you some sort of clear *impression* of my wife."

This amazed me. I nearly upset my glass, as he had upset his last night at dinner.

" Impression of your wife? Mine? " I repeated, but he gave a little hasty shake of the head. No; certainly he hadn't meant to pump me about what I thought of her!

He explained, " I should like to find out just how it struck *you,* the way my wife seemed to be thinking about – about me, and my being outed before she saw me again."

Here I suppressed a little sigh of thankfulness that he couldn't. It would have been too, too cruel to " lethim in " to *any* of the true inwardness of that scene in the railway-carriage!

He went on, " You see, Miss Whitelands, it doesn't matter my telling you that I hadn't seen – hadn't known very much of my wife before we were married, because you know that already, from her. She told you it was a rushed sort of business, didn't she? I dare say she said – said it took her by surprise, and that she accepted me on the spur of the moment, sort of? Just because " – he laughed a little, but his eyes were still anxious – " because she hadn't anything else to do at the moment, and because she was a – a good-natured sort of girl, what? and "

There was something rather dreadful to me in his flippancy now; something horribly touching.

To think that he – the son of people like the Merediths – should know that he had been married out of good-nature by a loud-voiced, showy Cockney! To think that he should have to cross-examine a stranger for details that he wanted wherewith to remind himself that his wife was a good-natured and womanly creature under all her garishness . . . for this, I suspected, was at the bottom of his questions.

Oh, *dear!* This was not the part of the story that concerned me, Miss Vera Vayne's reluctant understudy, at all. But at that moment I began to feel as if I were concerned in it – and for him.

Poor boy!

I looked up straight into his intent face. I spoke, quite impetuously. " Captain Meredith! She – yourwife never said that. She *never* said she'd married you because she hadn't anything better to do. Your – your wife did speak of you quite – quite "

" Well, how? " he demanded, fixing his eyes upon mine as if he meant to read out of them all that they had ever seen in that wife of his. " She spoke of me how? "

" Affectionately," I said, desperately; turning my eyes away.

They fell upon an empty coffee-cup that stood before me.

I rose.

I said, with an instinct for flight, " Let us go, shall we, and see if that telegram has come for you yet? "

We passed the entrance hall.

It had not come.

We sat down to wait in the large hall of the Grand, with its enormous counters for " *renseignments,"* and the hot air blowing up through the gratings in its floor. There was a stir of people coming and going through the big swing glass doors that are worked so much more quickly than those in our own leisurely island; there was the *obligato* of the shrill-pitched French " *allo, atto,"* at the telephone, to our talk. But our talk had to go on, it seemed; Captain Meredith was not going to let me off the rest of my cross-examination.

" You say she spoke of me ' affectionately,' " he took up, turning to me as we sat side by side now on a padded leather seat. " What do you mean by that? "

" Oh, well! What *does* one mean by that? "

" Lots of different things," he said, drily. " Now, in this instance "

(" *Allo! Allo!* " from that clerk at the telephone. " *Insistez, Mademoiselle; in-sist-tez, done!* ")

" ' Affectionately,' " insisted Captain Meredith, beside me; " now, in the case of my wife, what did it amount to? "

" That she spoke – nicely of you, of course," I said, staring hard at some colossal framed photographs, on the opposite wall, of the Riviera, of the waves of Biarritz. How I wished I were there! How I wished I were *anywhere* but here, driven into these corners!

" How,' nicely '? " went on the inquisitor. I think he realised that this was what he seemed to me. Red crept faintly up his cheek through the clear, pale, *mat* skin that is characteristic of the black-haired Welshman, as he pursued, " I'm afraid I'm not able to give you much peace, Miss Whitelands, until you tell me one or two things that my wife said, giving you the impression that they were ' nice ' and ' affectionate.' "

So I turned upon him, blurting out one of the few redeeming " things " that the Vision had uttered; the remark with which she had handed to me the portrait pendant that still lay in my dressing-table drawer at the Ritz. It was a remark that would certainly have gone far to gladden the heart of any *woman* deserted by a husband.

" Your wife said – she said you were very good-looking; *that* she couldn't deny! "

I wasn't prepared for the young man's reception of this compliment.

" Ah – *rot!* " he said, shortly, and – yes, irritably. The deepened red on his cheek was now a signal of real annoyance, I saw, just before he turned his head away from me and began drumming his fingers impatiently on the leather padding of the seat.

I remembered something another girl had told me; a girl who'd known lots of men of different kinds.

" A man has to be fond of a woman before he allows her to mention his good looks," she'd said. " Until then, he is down on her like a sledge-hammer for any allusion to his personal appearance. Why, I don't know. He seems to imagine that if she calls him handsome she thinks he's vain. ... Or that he's effeminate (as if that had anything to do with looks). He will allow her to praise the *strength* of his arms, and even lets her feel those great hard bulbs of muscle hobbling all up and down them – but she mustn't say anything about the *shapeliness* of them. That's the kind of grotesquely-minded baby Man is! "

So it seemed, as I glanced at the averted head of the man beside me. And yet I'd only quoted what his wife had said – and he'd *asked* for it.

" *Allol Allot* " screeched the shrill telephone voice again.

Suddenly he turned. " I expect you think that was rude, too," he said, brusquely, " but you see, I was trying to get at something she said that *counted* "

" And you think that what – people think about yourlooks don't count. *Oh"* I said, shaking my head over the utter hopelessness of this sex. " As if it wasn't the most important – well, one of the most important things in the world! "

" To you, of course. Girls *have* to be attractive," said Captain Meredith, simply. " But, look here, Miss Whitelands. What *else* did my wife say about me? Please? "

CHAPTER XX

IN THE OTHER WIFE'S SHOES

I FELT as if I'd been " in court" for the last eight hours. What else *had* the widow said about this young soldier of hers who was then supposed to be dead? Oh! Why *hadn't* she said something *really* nice, something that he had *deserved?* If it had only been Phillipa Tracey, Phillipa who ought to have married him, about whom he was making these inquiries! *She* had said plenty of things that it would have been pleasing to quote, heartening to hear.

"His men adored him. ..."

" *A mixture of a perfect young devil and of a dear, sweet fellow"* ..." *He'd personality – attraction – the woman wasn't born who could be indifferent to George."*

Yet – here he had to beg to be told if his wife – his own wife – had said anything " affectionate " about him! It was all his own fault because he hadn't had the sense to care for Phillipa enough! And still

Still the impulsive feeling took me that it was a black shame that things were so, for him! A sudden wild desire came into my mind to invent things, to pretend that I had suddenly remembered expressions of endearment, of violent grief from the widowed Mrs. George. I think I even opened my lips to say something of the kind. ... I don't know what stopped me. . . . But, as suddenly, I felt I couldn't fib about this. I cleared my throat.

And the words that came from my lips sounded tame and flat and dull and un-" affectionate " enough!

" She said, Captain Meredith, that it was hard lines on you to be out of all the fun at twenty-seven. ' Poor young fellow,' she said."

Rather blankly, he repeated, " ' Poor young fellow.' That was all, what?"

I said, rather shakily, " I'm afraid that's all – all I can remember to tell you just now. ..."

" Oh. . . . Thanks. . . ." he said, and now he spoke again in that absent, absorbed voice of his.

And I had a horrible feeling that now he *had* got what he'd been asking for all this time. The " clear impression " that his wife hadn't cared so much as one of the jingly charms on her bracelet that he had been killed. " Pore young fellow! " Another item of one of those saddening casualty lists – it was all " such a pity. ..." But she hadn't grieved for him more than for another stranger. And he knew it.

Into the quite painful silence that ensued there broke the voice of a youth in livery asking for Captain Meredith.

Ah – a telegram!

The telegram at last, perhaps ? The answer from his lawyers?

Yes. For after he had read it, he handed it to me.

And, as I read it, I almost wished that this eagerly- awaited message hadn't come.

Instead of simplifying matters at all, it had complicated them.

It was signed by a strange name. I suppose the name of Captain Meredith's lawyers.

And it said:

" Miss Vera Vayne has not sailed for America."

I stared at Miss Vera Vayne's husband.

" Not sailed! " I repeated. " Why hasn't she gone to America, then? "

He gave a little half-humorous shrug of his shoulders; and I began to feel as if I didn't know what he was thinking of again.

" How should I know, Miss Whitelands ? " he said with that kind of mild patience which is far beyond any expression of ill-temper. " It is all your idea that she had gone to America."

" Well, she said so," I repeated. " She said that was where she was off to, and . . . besides! I have just remembered "

" Remembered what? "

" I have just remembered that she sent me a picture post-card," I said, " with a picture of the ship on it – a White Star Liner."

" Ah!" he said with a lift in his voice. " Do you mind letting me have a look at that card? "

" I can't," I said. And I could have groaned.

" Why can't you? " he asked, surprised.

" Because I tore it up," I told him. " That is, Ithrew it into the fire the minute I got it at the Bryn. I was sorry directly afterwards. But just when I got it I was so angry that that is what I did, Captain Meredith!"

He was biting his lip and looking right away from me at some of the huge framed Riviera photographs. I noticed a change come over his face. The gravity and friendliness were waning again, and I saw a hint of the expression that he had worn last night in the bedroom.

I said, at once, " You are beginning not to believe me again. Very well. I can't help it. I am doing what I can to help you. I am making myself fearfully uncomfortable, now, by falling in with your plan not to explain to your mother for the present. But by the time you do," I went on, ominously, turning to him as we rose, " there will be so very much more. Every hour that we are together now, pretending it is quite all right, will make it ever so much more complicated when we come to owning up that it was quite all wrong!"

" You think so ? " he said, slowly, as we passed the circular doors. " At all events I shall do my level best to see that we don't have any more hours of it than is absolutely necessary."

" The fewer the better," I retorted, severely.

I felt I ought to get a little of my own back.

I straightened my shoulders as we walked along the street, taking the narrower side-turning as a short cut.

I wouldn't say another word.

As my companion lapsed into silence also, I began toassume more and more dignity. Once one begins this one never knows when to stop and it becomes so uncomfortable.

Presently I thought, ruefully, " Oh, dear! will neither of us say anything more until we get back to the Ritz? "

And then Captain Meredith pulled up in front of a flower-shop.

It was a small place, but cleverly dressed, showing great boughs of eucalyptus with grey-green leaves and bobbles of yellow, also huge bottes of orange marigolds set beside vivid pink carnations. It takes the French florists to recognise the beauty of these two shades set together. The English eye would have been too timid.

" I think I will get some flowers," Captain Meredith was saying.

Now, as every one knows, there is nothing in the world that any woman likes better than having flowers given to her by some man. It is a pity that men don't realise more how much pure delight can be bought for fourpence and fastened into our waistbelts with a bunch of violets.

It's an emblem of the homage of all his sex, paid to all of ours!

But, just at this particular moment, before this particular flower-shop, I drew back, stiffly.

" Oh, no, thanks! " I said, coldly.

Captain Meredith smiled, drily.

" Mayn't I buy some for my mother? " he asked.

His score, wasn't it?

I bit my lip.

What could I do but go with him into the shop?

Here we found the usual neat-haired Frenchwoman who is now at the head of every little French business, with the usual look of anxiety in her eyes that means the usual husband at the Front.

She came to serve us from buttoning the red-check overall on the usual little black-eyed French boy.

Captain Meredith seems very fond of little boys. He smiled, very nicely, at this one, I noticed, as he said " That's a fine *petiot* that you have there, madame."

" Ah! Monsieur! How much I regret always that he is not a little girl!" complained the florist-woman (quite insincerely, I am sure). " This *gosse* of mine, it is my tragedy! He – he loves nothing but bricklayers. Give him mortar wherewith to smear himself to the eyes and he is happy. *Tandis qu'une petite fills* – a little girl would sit there with her doll – tranquil, pretty to dress "

She sketched the whole scene with a gesture as she turned to me. " Does not madame agree with me? "

And she added the paralysing suggestion, " Fortunately for her the *belie* of madame is perhaps a little girl?"

Well, there was only one way to face this situation. I took it.

I gave one wild glance at my supposed husband, then we both dashed out of the place with what our Allies call " *un fou rire.*"

We laughed and laughed as we almost staggered together down the rest of that rather narrow little backstreet with its shops that hung up half the goods outside the doors thereof, and which lighted up dark corners with huge orange-coloured pumpkins that looked like enormous Japanese lanterns with a slice out. Outside a print-shop full of eighteenth-century engravings we had to stop and laugh helplessly into the window. The owner of the shop raised a bald head and an amazed face above a sheaf of etchings.

I suppose he thought we were the very maddest of all the many English " mads " who had ever passed that way! Then Captain Meredith pulled himself together and spoke as we walked on.

" That's broken the ice, anyhow," he said. He laughed again as we came into the Place Vendome, and said, as if gay with reaction after all the strain of the morning, " Well, it's the rummest show altogether, isn't it, Miss Whitelands?"

" Yes; and you've only had an evening and morning of it," I reminded him. " I've had nearly two months of – of "

" I know you've had a rotten time," he said, simply. And look here, I – I "

" You what? "

" I'm sure you burned that post-card," he said.

" That is very penetrating of you," I said, defiantly, but still in quite a friendly manner as we reached the Hitz. " I know men are supposed to have such an eye for character!"

He gave a funny little ironic bow that was quite friendly, too.

Then he said:

" I say, you will let us make the best of things as they stand, won't you? We won't complicate them any worse by squabbling and snapping with each other? Let's call a truce. Let's make it as easy as we can for each other until my wife turns up."

" If only it is fairly soon," I said, fervently, as we stood once more in the great entrance of the Ritz.

" It shall be as soon as I can possibly make it," the young soldier promised me, giving over to me the armful of flowers for his mother. " Look here; I am going back to my hotel, now, to write a long letter to my lawyers to put it all down exactly what has happened and how they are to take steps, instantly. I shall tell them we are coming back to England in about a week or ten days. My mother said a week or ten days, didn't she ?" he lowered his voice as he glanced about the lounge, which was deserted.

" Yes, I think Lady Meredith wants us to stay here another ten days for shopping and things," I said.

" Very well. While we are here, we are here, so to speak," he said, whimsically. " I will go and write now. Take the rest of the afternoon to it." He gave a little nod and then saluted. " My people are out? I suppose – I suppose I had better – I mean, will you let me call for you and take you out somewhere to tea afterwards, say at half-past four? "

I promised to be ready.

The other Merediths were still out.

So was Williams, the Welsh maid.

I put the flowers in water for *Belle-mere.* Then, I passed a solitary afternoon among my new pretties. Trying on my new hats again, running pink ribbons into some of the *cache* corsets which had blue. It isn't my colour.

As I pottered about my room the burthen of my thoughts was still: " When my wife turns up." Yes. When Vivie turned up – the Vision, the real Mrs. George. When she was in my shoes, as I had been for all those weeks in hers, what would happen? *How* would it happen?

I went through half a dozen imaginary scenes.

I called up for myself Miss Vera Vayne as I had seen her in just those clothes. I expect she had other even louder ones. I pictured for myself Lady Meredith's fastidious cameo-like face as she passed her in the lounge. I saw the look of delicate, aloof disapproval. The look which I had seen her bestow upon the Princess Jinka.

And the Princess Jinka is nothing compared to the film-drama princess!

Then I reproduced for myself the soft, masculine voice that has been in my ears all the morning; the voice in which he would perform the introduction.

" Mam – Mother, *this* is my wife! " And his mother's tone, *V* Your wife? "

She would look round for *me.*

I gave a little shiver and put away that picture. It was too harrowing! I must not think of *Belle-mire.* I began to think instead of myself and what it wouldmean to me when I lost, so to speak, my present job as the Merediths' daughter-in-law and adopted child.

It would mean going back again to face the world of cheap clubs and business girls and the search for work.

Apparently there is plenty of work going now in England of one sort and another. I might make munitions, or punch tickets at the gate of a Tube-lift, or take round letters.

Anything I did would be unutterably dreary after all this.

Still there was one thing I wouldn't do. I'd be a female plumber and spend the rest of my *life* in " going back " for various tools rather than marry Reggie Pen- more, *now*

" Now " – why " now " ? Why, because I'd seen what happened to young men who were married out of goodnature. They were made miserable, disappointed, disillusioned – as I am pretty certain Captain Meredith has been made (already) by that wretched, defecting " Vivie." And I'd rather be miserable alone than with a miserable husband – two in one house, no thanks!

Miserable I shall have to be at first, of course.

How I shall miss the Merediths, *Belle-mere* and Sir Richard!

How extraordinary it will seem to have been so much to them, to have been so intimate, to have known them for every hour of the day. To have been let in to a million of absurd little bits of family secrets and gossip, and then to become – less than nothing to them!Something like " a maid who was here," " an adopted daughter who was with us once "!

But no; I am sure *Belle-mere* will always remember me a little, if she can forgive me for the deceit of these days in Paris. Perhaps she will write to me at first, then her letters will dwindle down, becoming fewer and fewer. Then she will just remember to send me a card at Christmas or something of that sort.

Oh, dear! it is very depressing being left alone by oneself!

I used to spend most of my life alone and not to mind it. I suppose these last few weeks have unsettled and spoiled me.

Well, I must get unaccustomed again to the luxury of companionship.

In the meantime it is nearly four. Captain Meredith will soon be coming to take me out to tea.

I wondered if Captain Meredith were going to continue that cross-examination of me about what his wife had said; continue it into the afternoon.

But he didn't.

He merely said, pleasantly, when he called for me at the appointed hour, " I've just got off to my lawyers ithe very longest letter I've ever written in my life, or that I ever shall have to write, I hope. D'you loathe writing letters, Miss Whitelands? And now I expect you're a bit fed with my business-affairs. . . . We'll drop that subject for the present, shall we? "

We did.

We walked into the Gardens of the Champs-Elysees. And, suddenly, I found we were talking just as easily and naturally as if he had been any young man who had been introduced to me by his people, and as if I'd been any other girl whom his mother was chaperoning in Paris. We laughed together at " Guignol" – the French version of Punch-and-Judy in which all the French children delight; we watched the old woman with the black shoulder-cape selling every-coloured balloons. She, too, was here in peace-time. But she had a new- toy to sell, now: mimic Zeppelins, that floated, long and light and gaily-coloured, above the heads of the children at play. She also showed medals of France's idol, the Seventy-Five.

We had tea, we two, in a *patisserie* where one takes fork and plate from the counter, and selects exquisite sandwiches and *choux a la creme* before one settles down to one's place. And Captain Meredith entertained me as if there were no " part to play" an longer. We talked and talked. . . . Not about the war. directly; he seemed to avoid that war with its booirH ing of big guns and its rippling crackle of rifle-fire, it tragedy and comedy, its squalour and magnificence that was all going on beyond this smiling stoicism of Parisl in war-time.

I tried to get in one or two questions on a subject i that interested me, naturally – the blowing up of that I mine that had so nearly killed him, his escape, and just what *had* happened. . . .

But here he was tantalisingly silent, as men so often

are about the things of which women really wish to hear. He muttered something about " *Luck* " and " *Not my show at all; the subaltern's* " and " *First thing I knew was that I was glad I hadn't been wounded in the back; I've always hoped I shouldn't ever be that.* "

Even from these snatches, even from his aloof, " shut" expression, I seemed to get a glimpse of another Captain Meredith whom I had not seen and whom I should not see. This was the Captain Meredith known to his own mess. The man who, as Phillipa Tracey had told me, was adored by his men.

He'd asked *me* plenty of questions to-day; but he didn't seem to want to answer any of mine: at least, not about the events, the places, and the things that he seems to have summed up in a vague jerk of his dark head and the two pregnant words " *Over there.* "

I know he said " One can hardly believe, when one's back here" – a glance round the *patisserie* with its dainty wares and smiling waitresses, its flowers and prettiness – " what one's just come from, over there."

I asked no more questions about that.

But he told me lots of other things; about his time in India; about his school. We talked of books.

Oh, yes; I know the popular idea is that young soldiers of his type have never read anything, and that they haven't an idea in their heads beyond polo and racing.

Perhaps Captain Meredith would be considered " not commonplace enough for a soldier " by the sort of person who still clings to that funny old idea! . . . Wediscussed him too; the anti-militarist, the person who looks upon the army as " a plague-spot in time of peace and in time of war an infamy."

(I noticed again what an " enjoying " kind of laugh Captain Meredith has.) Then, turning to more amusing topics, we talked of swimming and tennis and dancing. Of the new songs at the Palace. Of Kipling's articles; of " The First Hundred Thousand," which I haven't yet read. Of the jokes in this week's *Punch.* He was as easy to talk to, I found, as a brother who was also a great chum. Just like that, I should think. I haven't ever had a brother. But Captain Meredith seemed so much more sociable, in a way, than the young man whom I had known best in the world. I remembered that Reggie would always rather read Stevenson aloud to me than go on chatting, aimlessly, for a whole afternoon.

Curious to think that I had now spent almost as many consecutive hours with this reputed " husband " of mine, as I had spent hours, spread over a Summer, with Reggie Penmore! Besides, I could talk less freely to Reggie, because in his case there was always the possibility that he might think I was trying to flirt with him.

So I really enjoyed this afternoon, with this young man about whom that question could not possibly arise, since Captain Meredith was married.

It was only after we came out again into the starry twilight and the stir of the boulevard thai: Miss Vera Vayne's husband reminded me again ofthat fantastic and for-the-present-unbreakable bond between us.

" I say, there's something else that's just struck me," he said, as we walked along – we seem to have spent our time walking along together for several weeks now; odd to think that it's only just one day! " You know when you didn't want to let me buy you any flowers? Well, I'just remembered that my mother will think it fearfully queer if I hang about Paris all day with – with my wife " – he said it in the only possible way, lightly and raggingly – " and don't get her any little souvenir or thingummy jig to celebrate the joyful what's-its- name!"

" Oh, Lady Meredith won't notice," I said, hastily. " Won't she? " said he. " You know better. Father mightn't notice. *She* would. And she's been wondering quite a lot already! Why should I have said ' Vivie ' in my letter, and ' Rose' now. Why I didn't introduce you to her at once. Why – oh, plenty of that! "

" Then a little more won't matter," I said, shaking my head. " Even if your mother is surprised at your not buying me things in Paris, it – it'll have to take its chance. As I'm only a woman, I don't have to try and be logical. So I can only tell you that, somehow, I – I don't want to take any more presents for your wife! " We crossed the road here. I saw him looking a trifle puzzled. Then he suggested, " Well, look here ... I

say . . . could you take some potty little thing for
yourself, then?"

" No," I said, brusquely.

We had been loitering, rather, along the broad pavement. Now I felt myself quicken my pace.

Over my shoulder he said, in an altered voice, " I say, Miss Whitelands! You don't – quite understand. I only meant – I say, don't walk quite so fast, if you don't mind. No! That's all right, but I can't tear along like that, just yet. I was only going to say, isn't there any little thing that we could show off before my mother with, and yet the kind of thing that you could have let me give you if I'd been just a friend of yours, introduced to you, say, by Captain Penmore?"

I felt confused, and a little pleased, and puzzled, all at once.

I felt that he was trying, by the way he said things now, to make up for the manner in which he had spoken to me last night. (Only last night? Centuries seemed to have elapsed since then!)

Towering tall above me as he walked beside me, he said, in the lightest, most friendly way, " I hope I haven't shocked your sense of Etiquette and What to do When? But look here." He twirled his cane.

" Even the most Victorian survival of a girl – well, even my mother when she was a girl – was allowed to take some presents from men. Aren't there lines laid down something in this way ? A man can give books to a girl who isn't – well, who hasn't exactly anything to do with him. Or he may give things that don't last, something that can be cut down and cast into the oven, so to speak. What about chocolates ? "

" Sir Richard showers them upon me!"

"Cigarettes, then? – you don't smoke? I thought, somehow, that you wouldn't. What else is there that doesn't last? Ah! Scent! That's purely ephemeral stuff, what? D'you care for scent? "

It seemed ungracious to refuse everything that he offered so lightly, so tactfully!

In another moment we had entered one of those palaces of perfume where enormous bottles, square and oblong, crystal-stoppered and beribboned, were displayed in caskets or stood on ebony tables.

" What shall we have? " said my companion, glancing at a case of these.

They bore the somewhat odd titles "*L'heure bleue,*" "*Pour Troubler,*" and "*Vertige.*"

" Yes – I think perhaps we'll have something with a more ordinary sort of *name* for my mother," said Captain Meredith quickly and blandly. And he ordered a square vase of perfume marked " *Quand l'ete vient.*" To my horror I overheard that it cost seventy francs, and my only comfort was to remember that it was bought not on my account but on Lady Meredith's.

I meant to display it to her as soon as we got back to the Ritz.

Here we found that Sir Richard and his wife had come in – and had gone out again, leaving a message that they were going on to a theatre and that we were not to wait for them.

Again? Captain Meredith had certainly been as nice and as tactful as one could expect of any sorely-tried young man with a real wife to be tracked and a makebelieve wife to be entertained at the same time. But – except for the afternoon " interval" – I had been with him from shortly after 10 A. m. to seven in the evening!

Was the whole evening to be consecrated to another endless duologue between Vera Vayne's husband and myself?

Apparently, yes.

We two dined out at an enormous and palmy restaurant, where I was just thinking how wonderful everything was when I heard a white-moustached Englishman at the next table growling, angrily, over his coffee, " Food execrable. Execrable! You see, the whole place caters for English and Americans. They just demand comfortable *surroundings* for their meals. Light, air, nicely-padded sofas. Don't understand the cooking of anything. Not anything! Everything here too salt. And the *crepes!* The *crepes* that ought to be made at the table! Just brought to be heated over a little grill and to have the rum sauce added. You can't call that a *crepe!* Why! It ought to be a new *sensation!* "

For the rest I remember only a huge turkey that was wheeled round beneath an enormous cover, and wheeled out, after the *maitre d'hotel* had finished carving it, a perfect scaffolding of bone; I remember a party of rollicking French airmen who came in accompanied by curious French dogs, based on the- fox-terrier; I remember a pretty American blonde, sitting with a man in mufti at an opposite table and sipping through a straw a *creme-de-menthe frappe.* The violent green of her drink, the scarlet of her lips, and the gold of herhair made a picture like that of a magazine cover. I remember, too, Captain Meredith's regret that there was no band here in war-time.

" I used to stand Bubbley to the band, and get them to play all the maddest tunes. Rag-time, catchy revue things – the sort that sets everybody's foot tapping and makes them want to yell choruses," he told me with a reminiscently wicked twinkle in his eye that seemed to show me yet another Captain Meredith whom I hadn't met. The one who supped at Giro's with film-actresses. " And then I'd order those fellows to slow *off* into ' *Mon cœur s'ouvre a ta voix.*' You know, that fearfully droopy one out of ' Samson and Delilah ' ? "

Here he hummed a bar or two –

("'Ah, verse moi – verse moi l'ivress-e!'") and I was astonished at the sweetness and truth of his singing-voice, pleasanter even than the soft speaking- voice in which he continued:

" That blessed old song makes every soul in the place, no matter how battered or fat or old they've got, begin to hang out a sentimental look to the music. Always gets 'em. Every man jack of them thinks it's ' *the tune that means so much to him alone'* Then one gazes round and grins."

" Very horrid of ' one,' then," said I, but laughing a little. " It probably *did* mean. . . ... Well, I don't

think "

" What don't you think? "

" I don't think any one ought to laugh at – at people's sentimentalities."

" Why, no. Perhaps I don't think they need," said Captain Meredith, finishing his coffee. " I suppose you think *I'm* "

He broke off and went on, more briskly, " Well, are we going on to a theatre? "

We went on to the *Souffles Franfaises* to see that striking French version of a play that must have seemed to a French audience so curious in its essence – " *The Man Who Stayed at Home* " – for what France must have thought of any country at war in which any of the men were allowed to stay at home.

I enjoyed the evening, I think, as much as I had enjoyed the afternoon.

And when we arrived back at my hotel I had forgotten all the consternation and *gene* with which I had begun the day.

Everything would be smoothed out presently; it would all come right, I felt – perhaps I should only have a very few more days of treading gingerly, for the sake of another girl's mother-in-law, in that other girl's shoes!

" Good-night, Captain Meredith," I said at the entrance with a friendly ease that was half of gratitude, half of relief that his people were not there, this time, to see us.

"Thanks so much!"

" Oh! I – I'm sure there's nothing to thank *me* for," said the young man, taking the hand I held out. " Er – good-night. Say good-night to my people for me, will you?"

"Yes; I will."

"Thank you. Er "

"Yes?" I said, turning. I had been just going to pass the circling doors.

" Tell my people I shall come round early in the morning, do you mind? And that they've simply *got* to come out with us somewhere, to-morrow."

" Yes; oh, yes, I'll tell them. I *meant* to," I said.

He said " Yes, so did I. They – they *must,* you know. Good-night!"

" Good-night," said I, and went in.

Certainly I was *very* glad that his mother wasn't there to be amazed at our (from her point of view) inexplicable " goings-on," as she had been last night.

True, she had said " of course."

But it's obvious that she thinks it anything but " of course" that I (the presumed Mrs. George) should stay on here with my parents-in-law at the Ritz, while " George" himself sticks to his room at the Grand! Why, I expect she and Sir Richard have talked and *talked* over our eccentric behaviour already! In fact, their attitude of mind is probably summed up in that verse from John Gilpin:

– " *all the world would stare If wife should dine at Edmonton And I should dine at Warel"* CHAPTER XXI

THE WHITE VIOLET

I AM sure *Belle-mere* had hoped that after the theatre last night, and after having been left carefully alone together for a whole day, her " two dear young things " might have gone " home " together. Yes, I am sure there was a look of disappointed surprise on her face when I came into her room this morning, early, in my indoor things, and without my supposed husband.

But she suppressed the surprise, and turned to me at once with her little order for the day.

Her plan was that, since it was such a beautiful February morning, all golden sunshine, and blue-and-white skies, and a laughing breeze, we should go out of Paris, into the country woods, and see how the buds were all bursting and the birds carolling a welcome to Spring.

" Oh, yes ! that will be lovely! " I exclaimed.

" So glad you like it, darling," said Lady Meredith, beaming at me over a little purple leather *attache* case scented with her characteristic perfume of sandal-wood and *pot-pourri.*

She seemed to have been busily arranging some papers. All our passports were on the chair beside her.

" Are we going somewhere where we shall need our passports ? " I asked, surprised.

Those passports are a bugbear to me; such a nuisance !

In the old days before the war no English people bothered about having such things just to go across the Channel!

" Oh, no, dear. You won't want those. At least, perhaps you'd like to keep your own," said Lady Meredith, hastily locking the little case. " I only thought that you would like perhaps to spend the day at Saint- Cloud. You could have lunch at that jolly little inn there "

" ' You'? " I repeated, surprised, looking down at the creamy head bent over the purple case. " But surely Sir Richard and you are coming, too ? "

" Oh, no! dear Rose; just you and George."

(Again?)

I protested. " But you see nothing of him, *Belle- mere!* Besides – I am sure he – George – would like to see some more of you."

The smile which she turned up to me was tender, and rueful, and whimsical all at once.

I knew that George's mother meant " This is not my turn just now."

But I went on, " I am thinking of George – *George* doesn't want always to be just alone with me!"

" You absurd child," said George's mother, laughing. And then, with a sudden trace of anxiety, " Why not? You haven't had any sort of little – little breeze with George, have you, my dear, about anything? ... I thought for a minute that perhaps "

" Oh, no! " I floundered; " certainly not! "

" No? But I know that sometimes, even when people are very much in love with each other, . . . it's difficult, at first, to adapt oneself," said George's mother, with a wistful appeal for confidence in her face. " There can be all sorts of ... misunderstandings. You are quite sure, childie, that there hasn't been anything? "

" Nothing, nothing, nothing at all!" I said, quite violently.

I went on, " Only, I hate to seem so – selfish about him. I am sure George would think it nicer if we *all four* went to the woods together to-day."

And I was preparing to go on arguing this when George himself appeared.

But even his quietly insistent " Oh, yes, Mam! you had better come, too; you and Father. Much jollier, all together," were of no avail. His mother entrenched herself behind having " rather a headache," and his father, quite naturally of course, refused to leave her side.

So *again* Captain Meredith and I found ourselves packed off, to spend more enforced hours, as we had spent them yesterday, in each other's society.

This time the background to our walk and talk was not the bright come-and-go of the Paris streets and restaurants, but the solitude of the woods, the dead- leaf-carpeted paths under trees. Their lacework against the blue sky was patterned every here and there by the tangled blot of a bush of mistletoe. Down belowwas the Seine, sparkling in the morning sunlight, and all about us there was the sense of Spring. Of grass, and young leaves that were growing. Flowers that were budding. Everywhere there seemed the feeling of something that was presently to burst out into full and joyous life.

I should have enjoyed that morning of Spring in the country but for one thing.

It was not only the scene that was different from yesterday, but the temper of my companion.

Yesterday after he had written that letter, he had come to me in real friendliness. He had made an ally of me. He had realised that none of this was my fault. I had, yes, I really had enjoyed being with him.

But, to-day, at Saint-Cloud I did not enjoy it.

At once I felt the difference; I knew what had happened.

He was cross because Lady Meredith had insisted upon our going out together. He had wanted his mother and father to come. That was all very well, but I don't think he need have shown me that he was annoyed by it. After all, *I* had done my best to bring *Belle-mere* and Sir Richard out! I don't think their son need have relapsed into that really sulky silence as we walked.

With me the whole time (and with him I suppose) was the *sot to voce* memory of how I came to be there at all, and whose shoes ought by rights to have been treading the crisp oak leaves and the moss of Saint-Cloud, beside the brown military boots of her young husband!I could almost hear the flick-flack, flick-flack of those purple tassels against the patent leather of her theatrical footgear.

" By Jove! yes," said Captain Meredith, at last, absently, as he walked along.

" What did you say ? " I asked him, quite politely.

" What ? " he said, as if startled at my voice. He turned to me. "I didn't say anything, did I? – I'm afraid you find me very stupid to-day. As a matter of fact I didn't sleep well," he excused himself, rather lamely. " I don't seem able to sleep in Paris . . . what was I saying? "

" You said ' By Jove, yes!' " I said, patiently, for I was rather tired of his speechlessness. " And I didn't know what you meant."

" Oh! I don't suppose I meant anything," said Captain Meredith, gazing away from me through the still, bare aisles of branches which would in the Summer be leafy depths that the eye could not penetrate. " I was just thinking."

" Have you ever been here in the Summer ? " I asked, in the sort of tone people use at tea-parties. " It would be rather a nice place to come to, I should think."

"Do you think so?" said Captain Meredith, suddenly, rather violently. " Once this war is over (if it ever is!) I don't think I shall ever want to see any part of France again, as long as I live!"

This was not very encouraging to my amiable little effort to make small talk. So, as we sauntered along, I relapsed again into silence.

I think it was that silence that was broken by a sudden whirring of wings in the thicket close beside us. From out of the dark-green *touffle* of ivy there came a vivid flash of black-and-white against the blue sky.

" Oh, look! A magpie! " I cried, quickly.

" Superstitious, aren't you?" said Captain Meredith in his expressionless voice. " Isn't there a superstition that one magpie is the sign of ill-luck? ' *One for sorrow.'* "

" Yes, but ' two for joy,'" I took up with a little skip of elation as I saw a second flash of black and white just ahead of us. "And three! Look! ' *Three for a wedding!* ' "

Captain Meredith said nothing.

Funny, moody creature that he is!

Ah, well! it's a good thing perhaps that he is married to somebody who, I expect, will not be unduly elated or depressed by his moods. I should think Miss Vera Vayne will probably take it all as it comes, whether her husband is cheery and companionable (as he was yesterday), or morose (as he was to-day).

We seemed to meet no one. So near Paris, and such primal solitude!

Suddenly we came upon one of those surprises that await walkers in the woods. We had been going along a thicketed aisle but now we came to a clearing. A little glade, with a moss-covered trunk of a tree lying across it, with a dip below it, over which we could see a smiling countryside of gardens, of cheery little red roofs and white house-sides. Paris was a dove-greypatch in the distance. Here, everything was bathed and irradiated with that light, that living promise of Spring just hidden, Spring only just round the corner; tiptoe and waiting for her cue to make the whole world a garden of roses!

I heard the voice of Captain Meredith just above me saying again, absently, " By Jove, yes!" and then,

" No, dash it all " And then, with more feeling in
his voice he said, " Some things do seem a horrible waste."

" What things ? " I asked him, looking down at the fairy-tale village of red roofs, at the veil of light-blue smoke curling upwards above them. " How do you mean a ' waste,' Captain Meredith? "

" Oh, I don't know," he said. " I mean," he spoke, more slowly, " I mean – I suppose I must have meant afl the numbers of jolly little French villages, just like those, that have been smashed up and spoilt like a child's house of bricks, over there." Then he pointed with his cane to the overturned log, and said, " Shall we sit down there a bit? I have something to tell you." In his unexpected way he turned to me and told me, quickly, " I'm off, you know."

I didn't understand him. I looked at him, inquiringly-

" I am off," he said again. " I'm going to cut! "

" What can you mean ? " I asked, quickly.

" I mean I am going to leave Paris. I am going to get over to England to-morrow. You see, I have got to. I can't manage this business any longer here."

"This business? You mean of finding your wife?"

" Yes. Of course it's – it can't be done – not by letters and all that kind of thing. I shall go over to Blighty to-morrow."

I looked at him in astonishment.

I had been forgetting my companion as one sometimes does when one is in the middle of beautiful or touching scenery. But now the stirring woods, the rollicking skies, and the nestling villages at my feet seemed to fade away from my consciousness.

I became aware more distinctly of that young man in khaki sitting beside me on that log, his clear, pale face rather set.

" Going over to England ? " I repeated. " But it was arranged that we were to stay another ten days in Paris before we went back. What about your people, Captain Meredith? "

" Nothing to do with them. They needn't trek. You will stay with them," he explained. " But 7 am going to get off to-morrow. I have got to see my lawyers. I have got to – " (prod, prod, prod, with his cane into the dead leaves in front of him). He wound up, energetically, " I have got to *do* something, you know. By Jove, yes! "

" When do you think you are going? " I asked him, blank with surprise. " To-morrow? "

" Yes, oh, yes! to-morrow, I should think. To-morrow is a fairly good day, since I can't possibly get a boat to-day," he said, now digging with his heel into the leaves. " Yes, I shall be off to-morrow."

" But," I objected, " but you haven't got the letter from your lawyers yet. You know you thought that might come, if they answered at once, by to-morrow. Oughtn't you to see that first? "

" I ought to see them," he said, slowly, discontentedly. " Anyhow, I ought to get away at once. If not to-morrow, then the day after." (Prod.) " I shall tell my people, anyhow, that I am going off, I shall tell them that as soon as I get back."

A sudden fright took me. I said, rather falteringly, " Captain Meredith, are you sure that – that "

"Sure that what?"

" Sure that they won't make *me* go back too?" I suggested, forlornly. " I am so afraid they think that wherever you go you ought to – to take me with you! "

" Oh, Lord!" he said, softly. Then reassuringly, " They won't. They sha'n't! " he promised me. " I will make it perfectly clear that I have got to go off on business, something to do with the India Office – anything. I will tell them that I am going somewhere where it is against orders to take – to take *any* kind of wife! That you have got to stay here with them until we all are able to get back to Wales again, together," he added with a very odd note of bitterness in his voice. I expect he was feeling enraged at having so much of his leave taken up by lawyer's business, by anxiety, and suspense.

He went on, " I shall have to stick this out for another day or so – I mean, I shall have to ask you to stick this out. Then, perhaps, we shall soon get tothe end of the " – he paused – " the bother. . . . Shall we be getting on again? "

He rose from the log and put out his hand to help me up. I skipped up without taking it.

As we walked back, he asked, " You aren't *annoyed* with me about anything, are you ? "

" Oh, dear no! " I said, lightly. " Why should I be? You can't help all this – I mean all this botheration as you have called it! I – I can't help it, either, as you know; now. We have just been forced into it. Fate forced us into it."

He dragged off his cap as we walked along, as if he wanted to let the breezes blow on his forehead. Against the sunlit branches his hair was blue-black and glossy as a feather of that magpie's wing, or as the smooth head of the first swallow of Spring.

He shook that head, with the trace of a half-whimsical smile.

" Curious old lady, Fate, isn't she? Not quite a fair old lady, always. Doesn't always seem to see the point of playing the game. That is the thing everybody's got to do, isn't it? " He looked at me hard as if he expected some answer.

I didn't know what he meant me to say. . . .

Funny, funny, moody creature! I thought again.

He seemed as if he wanted to talk to me, and yet as if every word he uttered were reluctantly dragged from him.

I supposed he was thinking of his wife, of the whole of that story of which I suppose I shall never knowmore than scraps. For as we walked along towards that little inn, where we were going to have a late lunch, he wrapped himself once more in that absorption, walking along with his dark head bent, his eyes on the ground.

Then, abruptly, he exclaimed, " Look, there; a daisy or something," and pointed to a dark-green patch among the brown of the dead leaves.

A tiny gem of white gleamed out of it. " Oh! The first violet! " I said, delighted.

He stooped, picked it, handed it to me.

Yes; the first violet. Small as a hailstone of February, pale as a pearl, with that obstinate downward curl of the stem that almost hides its little head from the seeker, it is yet a sight to bring tears to the eyes of any one who loves the woods, the earth, the promise of all young and growing things. It is the herald; it means the coming of the rose; it prophesies carnations, musk, sweet-peas, mignonette, bergamot, honeysuckle, and all the hot and strong delights of Summer. . . . But all their heady sweetness will not drown the memory of its own tiny scent.

That is unique; poignant, wild, and pure.

I sniffed at the little white flower as I would have fastened it into the breast of my blue coat.

Then the idea struck me that perhaps he hadn't meant me to keep it.

I handed it back to Captain Meredith.

He looked at it, as he held it, twirled between his finger and thumb. Then, we passed a pool of rainwater, clear above dark-green moss. He threw the violet in. ... The little white blossom floated above its reflection like a miniature water-lily.

It's too absurd that I should wish I had kept it! There will be plenty of white violets presently – and why should I wish for any memento of that morning in the woods at Saint-Cloud?

Captain Meredith meant to see his people alone the moment that we got back.

" I'll tell them what I'm doing about going over to London, at once, by myself," he planned to me. " Then we'll have dinner – the last evening all together, and that sort of thing. And then I don't care what they say, I'm going to carry them both off to the theatre with us."

We caught an early train back to Paris. But there our usual luck awaited us. Again those well-meaning parents of his had given us the slip. The message that they had left didn't even tell us where they intended to dine.

Captain Meredith frowned, just before he turned to me and said, " Well, what about the inevitable dinner *a deux,* for the third time of asking? "

" Oh, I don't think so," I said, quickly. " I was just going to say that I was rather glad Sir Richard and your mother were out, because I don't really want to go out this evening, Captain Meredith," I told him. " You go out somewhere by yourself. Look up one of your friends; that Major Thornton, or somebody "

" No; I don't think I will," from Captain Meredith. " No."

" Anyhow, you go to a music-hall or somewhere, off by yourself," I urged him. " I – the fact is, I am very tired. I will have dinner by myself, here."

" You can't have it all by yourself – a girl like you – here!" he objected as we stood in the lounge. "Not the thing at all."

" Well, then I will go to bed, I think. I don't feel as if I wanted any dinner. I had heaps of lunch. I won't have anything more."

" Oh, how like a woman! " he said, irritably. " Whenever there is some special reason why she ought to keep herself particularly fit and able to cope with things, she at once starts by knocking off all food. Come along at once."

" Where to? " I asked.

" I am going to take you to Henry's," he said, turning to the entrance. " You can get back early, and you can go to bed immediately afterwards; but you have got to have something."

And before I knew where I was, I was sitting opposite to him again in the wonderful and truly French little restaurant with the wall-flower-brown and creamy coloured decorations.

The head waiter, with a face like Henry Irving and the gestures of some other actor, brought up some dish with a tremendous flourish, and introduced it by some name. . . .

I only remember that Captain Meredith waved hishand at it, flippantly. I don't know what it was. Or what we ate or drank. It was a hurried meal. At the end of it, he put me into a taxi, and let me drive back by myself.

" I say," he said, through the cab-window. " Don't say anything to my people about my going, please. I will see them to-morrow morning myself, bright and early. Good-bye. . . . *Cocker,* Hotel Ritz." CHAPTER XXII

WITHOUT EVEN A MOTHER-IN-LAW !

E2SS than ever had either of us suspected what the next morning was to bring forth!

I had slept a little late. It was nine o'clock when, after I had finished my coffee and rolls, I tapped again at the door of *Belle-mere's* room.

There was no answer.

I tapped again, louder. I raised my voice, " May I come in? " Finally I went in.

I found a scene of desolation indeed!

A hotel bedroom from which the guests had departed.

The empty wardrobe doors stood open. Not a single one of Lady Meredith's pretty grey frocks was hanging from the pegs. From the glass-topped toilette-table there had vanished all her silver-backed brushes, her crystal-stoppered bottles of scent and bay rum and face cream. Even the boughs of eucalyptus, the marigolds and carnations which we had brought her in the day before yesterday had been spirited away!

I gazed round in astonishment. *Belle-mere* had never told me that she intended moving her room!

At that moment the tiny *femme-de-chambre* with the small feet and the gendarme-like tread, stumped into the room and found me standing all forlorn, gazing at the stripped bed.

I said, laboriously, in French, " Mademoiselle, will you say to me the number of the room which Lady Meredith has taken instead of this one? "

" Ah! But Mademoiselle – Madame does not yet know? " cried the little chamber-maid, black eyebrows raised to her hair. " Milady Meredith went this morning! She and my lord Sir Meredith, very early, very early, very early. At six o'clock already I have brought them the chocolate! The Mees also, the maid, is departed! All!"

I gazed at the girl with her blue-black hair and her vivacious face under the white butterfly cap.

" They *went?* " I said. " But where to? "

" But, to England! Very early they had to go to the station," explained the little Frenchwoman. " Last night they told the night-porter that he must find them one, two, taxi-auto to convey themselves and their luggage to the Gare du Nord! "

I gazed at her, incredulously. What was this?

" They have gone to England ? "

" Madame is surprised?" said the little Frenchwoman with an inquisitive look at me. " Madame will grieve that *Madame se Belle-mere* is departed? A lady so sympathetic! So beautiful! So kind! And of a generosity! " She clasped her hands on her breast and rolled her big black eyes to the ceiling with a dramatic abandonment that an Englishwoman, even after months of training at a school of cinema-acting, would find it impossible to attain.

As for me, I stood rooted there, in a room that, though empty, still breathed something of my adopted mother's faint, elusive perfume. I murmured to myself in English, " Why on earth did they go ? What has happened ? "

The chambermaid's eyes descended, while her hands and shoulders rose in a shrug of non-comprehension. Then with another quick gesture, she said, " Hold! I forgot. There is a note, I believe, for *Monsieur le Capitaine!* In a great hurry milady gave it to me. She was already late. She ran down the corridor with her grey travelling-mantle, and her bouquet of eucalyptus and carnations clasped in her arm. She handed to me this note. Here it is." The French girl drew it from behind the bib of her apron.

I took it, looked at the address.

In Lady Meredith's sloping handwriting it was inscribed :

" *To my dear children.* "

I heard myself saying, mechanically, " Thank you; I will give it to Captain Meredith."

Uncertainly I stood for a moment outside what had been Lady Meredith's door. Should I put on my hat and things, go round to the Grand, and send a message up to Captain Meredith?

Then I thought, No, he was certain to come round to the Ritz. Hadn't he said so? "Bright and early" may mean eleven o'clock from a man. But he was in such a hurry to explain to his people that he must, *must* go and see about that business of his in London!

Well! If *he* left, I should be the only one of " the family " remaining here.

And 7 couldn't stay!

What were we going to do?

I waited in the anteroom with its huge marble mantelpiece and its mirrors, its French and English and American papers on wooden holders. And scarcely had I read through an account of some French reprisals for an air-raid than my eyes, wandering towards the open door, saw, crossing the hall, the broad, sloping shoulders in khaki and the back of a black head that seemed as well-known to me now as if I had been brought up with them.

I tossed *Le Matin* down onto the table and ran out into the big, palmy hall.

" George!" I called, breathlessly, scarcely noticing at the moment that I had addressed my supposed husband for the first time by his Christian name. " Oh, George, George, listen to this "

Promptly he wheeled. " Hullo! Good-morning," he said, briskly. Then, still more quickly, " Hullo – I say! What's the matter? "

" Your people! " I gasped.

Instantly anxiety flashed into his face.

" My people ? My mother? " sharply. I knew

at once what he was thinking about: Lady Meredith and her heart. " Is there anything wrong? "

" No, no; not that," I reassured him, incoherently. " They – she – can't be ill, or she wouldn't have been able to go "

" Go where ? " demanded Captain Meredith, standing there by a hall writing-table, staring at me. " Have they gone somewhere ? "

" I should think they had! " I said, still incoherently, but with an intensity. " Do you know what's happened? Your people have gone home. They've gone – Oh! I do think it's dreadful of them. I never, never thought *Belle-mere* would have done such a thing. They've gone without us! They have! They've left us here – all alone – without them "

Captain Meredith checked me with the swiftest little frown; for at that moment the Princess Jinka, all glorious without in sables and Russian violets, and accompanied by the baby aviator, was slowly coming towards the entrance. " *Ah, vilain! tais-toi!* " she was scolding her escort. This time her smiling Highness did not glance at Captain Meredith, but I had a feeling, from the mere set of her head upon her shoulders, that she was pricking up her ears to hear what the imagined " war-bride " was confiding, in that agitated voice, to her young " husband." I suppose the tone of real anguish in which I had exclaimed, " *They've left us here alone, without them!* " sounded hardly *appropriate.*

" Come in here, won't you? " said Captain Meredith, quietly taking me by the arm and leading me back into that anteroom on the right. He shut the door.

" Now," he said. " Sit down. *Where* have they gone to, did you say? "

" Home! " I told him, desperately.

"Home? What, to Wales?"

" Yes; I expect so. To England, anyhow," I said, looking up at him from the armchair. " The maid said they got up with the dawn and went off to catch the boat-train."

" Oh, Lord," said Captain Meredith, in his very quietest tone; and turned quickly away from me. " Oh, *Lord!* "

I said, " They never said a word about going, to me, yesterday! Not even when I asked about those passports. Did they to you ? "

" Rather not," said the young man, quickly. *"Rather* not!"

" They went without a word!" I took up, angrily. " That is – oh, there's this note for you."

For the instant I had forgotten it. Now I handed it to him.

Captain Meredith glanced at the envelope as he stood beside that red velvet chair where I had flung myself down. " Here, I say; this isn't only for me," he added. " This is meant for – for both of us. Why didn't you open it? "

" I? Certainly not, *I'm* not her ' dear child,' " I almost snapped. " *You're* that! "

" She thinks you are," he put in.

" Well, I'm not. And I don't mean to open letters that she means you and your wife to "

" But if I ask you? Ladies first," persisted Captain Meredith.

Impatiently I took the letter from him. I had just opened it when he said, hastily, "Oh, d'you mind? Perhaps I'd better glance through it first, after all."

He took it from me again, and I watched him read it.

With a curious little laugh he handed it back to me. " You'd better read what it says."

I read it.

It said:

" My Dears –

" Your father and I do so want you to have this first little time in Paris all to yourselves; it is a time you will not have again as long as you live "

("Mercifully!" I thought.)

" – but we think you are much too unselfish, and that you feel you ought to be with us. We feel that as long as we are here you will not really consider yourselves ' on your own.' And that perhaps you were a little shy of suggesting that Rose should leave me. So we made up our minds to strike camp, as your father says, quite quietly, and to get through our business with the passports, while you were at Saint-Cloud, without telling you.

" You see, my dears, I shall be able to see plenty of George, I hope, when you come over, as we arranged, in a week's time, and we are all together at the old Bryn once more. But you will have had these days quite alone – and they don't come twice, children, I know that.

" I am sure my darling little Rose and my own Georgie-boy will quite understand, and that I don't have to ask them to forgive me for this little deception.

" With all love and kisses, and hoping that you will go on enjoying yourselves as much as you can,

" from

" Your Mam.

" P. S. – I shall love to be at the Bryn to welcome you."

There was another postscript in Sir Richard's cramped, boyish hand:

" Your mother and I thought we'd have a little honeymoon on our own, too.

" Yours affect'ly, R. M."

I felt ready to burst into tears of pure rage and helplessness after I'd finished reading this letter. I almost threw it back to my companion.

" There! " I cried; " I told you so! "

"What?" took up Captain Meredith with a quick glance of amazement. " You've never told me "

" I told you we ought to have told Lady Meredith everything, at once; that first evening! " I snapped. Indeed, I felt as if all my nerves had gone snap, too. " I knew there would be complications, and here they are! It's your fault! " I told him, as he stood there, blankly composed now, but with his fingers up to his moustache in the little gesture that, I have learned, signifies perturbation. " You wouldn't let me tell her! I'm sure you were quite wrong! It would have been less of a shock "

He began to say something. I think it was " Well, 7 regret it right enough now. No use saying that, though; too late."

But I *would* finish. I persisted, " *Far* less of a shock to have told your mother *then* that I wasn't your wife than it will be – after all this! " I pointed, hopelessly, to that letter in his hand. " After she's got so accustomed to the idea that we *must* be together! After she's written all those – those *things!* Gone away, too; *left* us! Oh, dear!"

" She meant to be – kind and all that," Captain Meredith told me in that blank, muffled voice of his, and blankly he stared out of the anteroom window at the paved courtyard. " She did it, don't you know, to try and – please me."

" Oh, I know," I sighed, impatiently. I was so utterly exasperated that I was even past feeling embarrassed at the unexpected turn events had taken now. It was desperately awkward – but what came first was my rage over the false position in which I couldn't stir a finger, it seemed, to set myself right. Whatever I did, wherever I went – well, I'd no real business to be doing it, or being there! I had to bite my lip to keep from blurting out the sentiment that it was just the people who " meant to be kind " who were responsible for half the mischief and the misery in the world! Such an ungracious thing to say about *Belle-mere,* of all people on earth! Still, it shows my state of mind at the moment. I was furious with her; *and* with her son!

"And now, Captain Meredith," I. said, hitting mypalm impatiently against the red-padded arm of my chair; " now will you please tell me what is to happen? We can't stay on as we are "

I saw he guessed the unspoken end of my sentence – " You at the Grand, and I at the Ritz! "

I went on, desperately, " It would seem odder than ever when – when we came away! "

" Quite," he agreed in that blank voice.

Still desperately, I added, " And it wouldn't be very easy, if I went on to Wales, with you! "

For already during the last two days I'd thought of the difficulties that might lie ahead when we left Paris, supposing that we had to leave it without news of Miss Vera Vaync. Some of those difficulties dashed through my head at express-train speed even in the time that it took me to utter my last sentence. Imagine them. . . .

Any newly-married young couple may be certain of *one* thing in that uncertain career, matrimony; they may be certain of comment and discussion from every one who knows (or who thinks) that they are on a honeymoon. Now *here,* in Paris, there had been nobody, nobody that counts, to watch the make-believe honeymooners that we were, but his father and mother. But *there!* At Llandedwydd! Anybody who has ever lived in a country neighbourhood would know what it was going to be like.

The whole valley would be eyes! *And tongues!*

There would be these people who were calling at the Bryn when I arrived. There'd be the tenants in the cottages and farms all about. The servants. Pritchard, the butler who had been pantry-boy in the time of " old Sir George." The maid who had waited on me when I was ill. There would be the question of this, that, and the other arising at every turn!

Oh, it would be preparing to leave the comparatively comfortable frying-pan for what I felt would be a blazing fire of fresh complications!

Still I'd an alarmed feeling that he had meant to suggest going to Wales.

Already he'd told me, some time in the course of the last two days, " D'you know I'm aching to see the place again? Good old Cader Idris scowling down under a cap of clouds, and the river in flood, and "

He'd pulled up, apologetically, and admitted that Welshmen were the most home-sick idiots in creation, always maundering about the Hen Wlad (the old country) and the blessed mountains that you can't see, four days out of six, for rain. And I had constantly felt that, even while the gay cosmopolitan stir of the Boulevards passed before the young soldier's eyes, his thoughts were back among his own purple hills and brown woods, back in the old stone house that I, a stranger, had felt so welcoming. What must its welcome seem to him, whose childhood and home it meant? The picture of it must be cut deep into his heart, as that outline of the first salmon that " Master George " had ever caught was traced on a slate slab beside the dcorstep of the Bryn. Over that doorstep, Lady Meredith had told me, Sir Richard had carried her in hisarms, as a bride should be carried, into her husband's house. . . .

But, oh, how I hoped that their son would not insist upon returning to that home at once! Not unless he went by himself. Of course he'd have to go. . . .

" You see, there's your – your lawyer-business! " I reminded him. " You've got to get back to London at once. To see about your wife. To find her!"

He nodded, his dark head averted.

" Still, I can't go on to London with you," I added.

" No. Oh, Lord, no. I shouldn't ask you to."

" Then you'll leave me here, while "

" What? Certainly not," he said, firmly, turning

now. " Leave you here ? Alone ? Without even

My mother's maid went, too, didn't she? Well, you can't possibly stay on here, by yourself, in this place. Of course not."

I hesitated. "Can't I?"

" No," he repeated, compressing his lips. " A girl – like you ! Not to be thought of."

I sighed. " Then, what is to be thought of? " I demanded. " What – what *do* you think we had better do next? "

I waited for a moment without receiving any reply. Then Captain Meredith seemed to pull himself together out of a sort of daze. Very quietly he made the only suggestion that seemed to come into his head. He said " We might go out and get a bit of lunch, somewhere, first."

" Lunch? Lunch? " I retorted. " Oh, how like a man! "

I sprang up from my chair so as not to have such miles to look up at him while I vented some of my feelings upon him.

" Lunch! " I repeated, bitterly. " The most awful things may happen – everything can be too topsy- turvey and frightful for words – people can be left stranded in Paris with people's husbands – they can feel perfectly helpless in a – a – a *web* of films and fib- dramas – it will take at least three days to get a letter

through to Wales But all – all – all a man can

think of is something to *eat!* – I've only just had my breakfast, too! " I wound up, defiantly.

Captain Meredith looked down at me, and in his face I saw again something of that boyish kindliness with which he had treated me during our first day together. His voice, too, had its old tone of admission that none of this was my fault. Quite mildly and severely, he protested now. " You can't call a bit of crusty roll and a thimbleful of chocolate ' breakfast.' This beastly French arrangement leaves me too faint and weak to think of anything until I've had a mid-day feed," declared this Briton. " And it will be nearly a quarter to twelve by the time we find some little kind of a place. . . . Run and get on your hat, won't you? Honour bright, you'll feel better afterwards "

Well, I confess I did feel more capable of grappling with the situation after I had done justice to some heartening French soup and a *plat* of golden eggs smothered in green velvet spinach.

Then, over a *marmalade de fomm. es* we sat andtalked, discussing the possibilities of what we might do next. That is to say, I found myself doing most of the talking. Captain Meredith seemed plunged at long intervals in the kind of reverie that bears the stamp of being at one's wits' end!

I found myself saying " Couldn't we wire to your mother Yes, but what?"

And " If I went to stay with the Young Women's Christian Association – even then Lady Meredith would wonder! " Finally, " Ah, but couldn't I leave you in London, Captain Meredith, as soon as we got to Charing Cross? You could stay on there. I could go straight down to the Bryn, to your people. By myself,

as I did before, I could explain to them " Here I

checked myself with a rueful little memory of how difficult it was to " explain " things to his people!

" – I could try," I said, " and explain to them that you had been going to come down with me, but that you had been unavoidably kept in town, on business, or " – glancing at his face – " perhaps you think that wouldn't do either? You think that, too, might seem odd? "

" Very, I'm afraid," he told me with his little nod across the table. " But – by Jove – there doesn't appear to be anything that doesn't seem odd!"

" Very well then, if this isn't any odder than any of the other plans, why not follow it? " I said, eagerly. " Don't let's stay in Paris any longer. Let's pack up and go, at once. Why not? "

" Because there's only one boat-train in war-time," said Captain Meredith, shaking his head at my eagerness. " And that's the one my father and mother took this morning. They'll be on the Channel now, I suppose. We can't go to-day."

Disconsolately, I looked at him. " We sha'n't be able to get off at all until to-morrow morning? "

"If then," returned Captain Meredith. "There's your passport to be *vised.* You'll have to go to that place before three o'clock if you want to get it done to-day."

" That means," I said, slowly, " that I shall have to stay two whole days in Paris, just as I am, at the Ritz, and – and *supposed* to be with you? "

" I see nothing else on earth for it," said Captain Meredith, briefly. There was a little line of worry between his brows as he looked away from me. " What else is there, you see? You don't know anybody in Paris, do you? Any ladies who could put you up while you're waiting? "

I shook my head. " I don't know anybody," I told him, " except Reg – except Captain Penmore. And I don't want to – to trouble him. And I don't suppose he'd know of any ladies "

Here I broke off. I had been suddenly struck by an idea so excellent that I could only wonder why it had not suggested itself to me before this.

" Oh! Wait, wait! " I cried, exultantly, clasping my hands above my coffee-cup, and meeting Captain Meredith's glance with a pleased smile of relief. " I have thought of some one "

Here I caught the eyes upon us of a stout Frenchgentleman at the next table, with a tiny scarlet speck in his button-hole. He had been smiling, sympathetically, upon the pair of us at intervals ever since we had come in. As he had unfastened the table-napkin from about his neck he had continued to beam benignly upon the English couple. Now, as he wedged himself out past our table, he bowed, ceremoniously, saying, to Captain Meredith, " *Monsieur! A la victoire definitive!* "

The young British officer rose and bowed – not at all awkwardly, for a Briton. Then, dropping lightly into the seat beside me again, he said, rather anxiously, taking up the conversation where it had been broken off, " Well? Who is it that you have just remembered that could put you up? "

Delightedly, I told him – the happy thought that it was:

" Phillipa Tracey! Mrs. Tracey and Phillipa! " To my surprise I saw his whole face harden and set at the mere sound of their names.

" Oh! I don't think that would be a very good scheme," he said. " How often have you met – the Traceys? Only twice, wasn't it? "

" Yes – but – but they were so kind to me! " I told him a little excitedly as I put on my gloves. Phillipa – Phillipa was a dear to me!"

I broke off for a moment thinking of Phillipa's extraordinary confidence to me. That, of course, I must not say anything about to this young man for whom Phillipa still cared. . . . But the other I could tell him.

" Do you know," I said, turning to him, " Phillipawas so nice to me that I felt I must tell her everything!"

" Tell her – what? " he asked.

" Why – the whole story: Who I am – that I'm not your wife – everything about it "

" You told Phillipa all that? " he uttered, sharply, aghast.

" No, I didn't," I explained, quickly, " but I was just

going to when Oh, it was the day before that

evening when you came home. I was going to ask Lady Meredith if she would allow me to tell Phillipa all about myself. Of course I didn't feel I could without her permission "

" No; nor without mine," said the young man opposite to me, unexpectedly and very decisively. " If you don't mind, I – I absolutely forbid you to speak to Phillipa Tracey about any of this business until it's settled."

" Forbid!" I echoed, looking up at him with indignation and surprise.

My hand, half in and half out of my white glove, rested on the rim of the table beside me.

" Forbid? " I repeated. " But you haven't any right to forbid me anything."

" No; I know that," said Captain Meredith, more angrily than I had ever yet heard him speak. Tears sprang into my eyes. Tears partly of mortification at the harshness of his tone, partly of disappointment over the difficulties which he seemed going to raise before this excellent way out.

There was an instant's silence. Then, in a less angry tone, but still quite strained, I heard him repeat, " I know I have no right to forbid you anything. But I can at least tell you that it is the last thing in the world I should wish! Do you see ? "

I didn't really see why he shouldn't wish Phillipa told, considering the whole thing would come out, presently.

I said " I believe I promised her I *would* tell her something I had got to tell her ... as soon as I had asked your mother."

" Well, you see, you haven't asked my mother," this dictatorial young man said, finally, but always in the softest tone. " So you can't tell her, can you? "

" Can't I ? " I faltered, feeling as if my only friend had now been taken away from me. " Can't I even go to Passy and ask Phillipa to put me up for two or three days?"

He frowned, hesitated.

" Fact is, Phillipa Tracey is the sort of girl who knows too much," he said, slowly. " She always did; always."

This was no time to defend Phillipa.

I said, in a desperate little voice, " But there's nobody else."

And he, "It's too bad!" Then again, "It's too bad!"

"You won't let me even go to them?" I appealed again.

Suddenly, in an altered voice, he said, " I say, youmust hate me for giving you all these bothers. You must look upon me as the most impertinent nuisance that you've ever met in your little – in your life! . . . Look here." He had been looking, aloofly away, at the door of the restaurant. Now he turned to me. " Go to the Traceys if you like. Yes, perhaps it would be the best plan. One thing I do ask, and that is that you won't give away a word of the whole "

Here he made a little pause that I felt might have been filled up by all the very strongest words in the English language, before he concluded:

" – the whole botheration! You will promise me that, please? "

I was glad to hear his friendly tone again.

But how he varies! How he is one minute one thing, and one minute another; like an April day, or a woman!

I promised what he asked.

" And now I shall go straight off to Passy," I determined, rather falteringly. " And ask the Traceys about it now."

" Well, but hold on. You will have to get your passport seen about first," he muttered.

And so we settled to walk back to the hotel together.

My thoughts, as we turned down the street, were all of Phillipa, with whom I was to take refuge. My disturbed mind was busy with pictures of her.

So that for the moment I thought it was a trick of my imagination that I saw the girl herself just ahead of us, up the Boulevard; a girl with a tall, slim figure in dark blue, with a curious black silk hat of a ratherNapoleonesque shape on her small, proud head. "Look! look! – isn't that Phillipa? " I said, quickly, with a touch on the arm, to my companion. " Look! standing there! She's stopped. Let's catch her up and speak to her now."

He hung back a little.

" I say, are you sure? "

" Yes, yes! " I said.

The girl ahead of us had stopped now at one of those stalls and was buying newspapers from one of those dark-haired, black-shawled, neat-aproned Frenchwomen who seemed to have mobilised themselves into a uniformed army of workers, long before the war.

And I saw a long, slim arm raised to point to a journal hanging higher up the stand. Ah, that was Phil- lipa's gesture! I felt sure it was she!

And now Captain Meredith saw that, too. For he paused in the street. Hastily, he said, " Yes, it is. Well, now, look here. You'll go to her, will you? I don't think I will come. I have got to rush on to Cook's and to Cox's, as a matter of fact. I will pick you up at the Ritz later; or I will telephone. Good-bye."

He saluted and was off before I could reply. And indeed I had to take to my heels and run to catch up with the tall figure in dark blue just before she disappeared into a shop.

" Phillipa! " I said, as I caught her up at last. My black furs were streaming behind me in the quick February wind. I was breathless.

Phillipa turned a surprised face of welcome. " Oh, it's you! " she said. " I was just wondering about you. How d'you do, Mrs. George? " She drew me a little aside out of the way of some people who wanted to pass into the shop. "Are you alone? " she asked, quickly.

" Yes, yes! Of course."

" Oh ? I heard George had arrived back, safely, on Tuesday."

"Yes, yes! He has just gone on to Cook's and Cox's "

Oh! the usual two Meccas of the British in Paris," smiled Phillipa with a little nod. " You going to come shopping with me until he is finished ? "

" Yes, please," I said, eagerly. " I wanted to see you so much! Do, do let me stay with you! – that is, if you don't mind? " CHAPTER XXIII

CONFESSIONS TO THE OTHER GIRL

I SUPPOSE I spoke rather desperately, for she gave me an astonished little look.

Forgetting all about my passport, I spent the rest of the afternoon with her. The oddest, I think, of all the mixed-up and embarrassing afternoons that I have spent since I have been living in the shoes of

the girl whom Oh! how I wish more than ever

that I had never, never, NEVER! met George's wife! That there was no such person

At least, that would make no difference to me, if only I had had the good fortune never to have set eyes on her!

We were presently standing, Phillipa and I, at what seemed the bottom of an enormous gilded tower, looking upward at the spiral *rayons* of the great shop – each with its name in gilded letters, " *Voilettes,* " " *Chapeaux et plumes,* " " *Chemises-de-jour,* " " *Jw- pons,* " and " *Fantasies* " – whatever that last might be.

It can't have meant anything half as " fantastic " and as grotesque as the situation that kept me fidgeting, nervously, at Phillipa's heels as she passed up and down the stairs, going from *rayon* to *rayon,* in her competent, quick manner, making purchases for herself, for Mrs. Tracey, for the flapper sister.

Crowds passed us. All about us was the glitter and colour of wares displayed and the high-pitched French chatter. But again, I heard little of what was around me. I was trying to think how I should propose to Phillipa to billet myself upon them for to-night and the next two nights.

In the handkerchief department I came to myself. Phillipa in that accustomed, efficient way of hers was selecting and ordering a dozen men's handkerchiefs which she was going to have marked, by the exquisite French embroideresses that work for that shop, "M. N."

Vaguely, I remembered that I had heard Mrs. Tracey refer to her future son-in-law as " Monty." So I supposed those handkerchiefs were a gift for Phillipa's fiance.

As the clerk booked the order, Phillipa, with her papers under her arm, turned to me and said " That's all. I wanted to get everything done first before I talked to you, or I should have forgotten something; and I hate forgetting things. But I wanted to tell you -"

Here she slipped her hand into my arm as we walked away from that department, and through the umbrellas, and the perfumery, to the door. " You know, you must have thought me perfectly dreadful the other day, talking to you, about George! " She gave a little laugh. " You will hardly believe it, but I didn't know, then, that they hadn't told you that George was alive! "

" No, no! I know you didn't!" I said absently." Of course you couldn't have. You thought I knew. I didn't know until the evening afterwards, you know, when he came "

" When he came!" repeated the other girl, a little absently also. " How wonderful! "

I didn't say anything. I was remembering that ghastly tete-a-tete with Captain Meredith in my room. How different from the picture of it in Phillipa's mind, probably at the moment!

" Now, shall I take you to your hotel? " added Phil- lipa. " Or – you won't want to come back with me, will you?"

" Oh, yes, I shall! Yes, I shall," I said, feverishly. " I wanted to speak to. ... Is Mrs. Tracey there? "

" No, I am afraid Mother is out for the rest of the day."

" It's you I wanted to see," I said, looking up at her, as we walked along. " At least, of course I shall have to ask Mrs. Tracey, too." I brought out without any further beating about the bush: " I want you to let me come and stay with you."

I saw Phillipa's startled face stop against the background of a big plate-glass shop-window set out with little girls' frocks. I saw that she could scarcely believe she had heard what I had said. " You – to stay with us? Do you mean . . . both of you? "

" No, no, no! " I cried, shaking my head, vigorously. " No, that is just the very thing that I've got to – I mean no. Not Captain Mer – not George. Me – by myself!"

-tf riirt

"But where are the Merediths? Your mother-in- law? Sir Richard?"

" They have gone back to England," I told her.

Phillipa's bewildered voice took up, " And George ? Where is he?"

" He is going back too," I said. " Directly. He's going too."

At this she dropped some of her papers in her astonishment, and there was a little confusion of picking them up. I helped her, and so did the street-seller who had been standing close to the kerb, displaying the toy of the moment: an image of the German Emperor who was flinging up his arms to cry " *Camarade! Ca- marade! "*

"They are going? Leaving you here?" said Phil- lipa with a glance at me as direct and dark as that of George himself.

" Yes; oh, yes! " Then, taking a leaf out of George's book, " Of *course! "*

My poor wavering little " of course " didn't have the same effect upon Phillipa as George's had upon his mother. She looked amazed, aghast, disturbed even. " We can't talk here," she said, quickly. " Come along; I am taking you home."

Arrived at Passy, Phillipa took me, not into the goldfish bowl drawing-room, but straight upstairs, to her own room.

A cheerful place; just like most girls' rooms, except that there were more books about it. French and German books, I recognised, with a swift, absent glance. How clever she was – she could read Nietschze in the original! I – what did I know about *anything?* Nothing!

Before I had seemed to hear her give an order, or to know how she had done it, Phillipa produced a tray, with tea and biscuits. Gently and swiftly, she took away my hat; slipped my shoes off my feet.

I heard myself say " No, thanks; I don't want to lie down," but I found that I was on her bed already with Phillipa's eiderdown tucked comfortably about me, and Phillipa's hot-water bottle at my toes.

" Poor mite! She's worn out – tired to death! " said Phillipa in the tone of one speaking of some child. Then, to me, " Yes, you are; you know you are! You lie there and rest while you tell me about it."

How devoutly I wished at that moment that I hadn't given George my word not to tell this kind, capable girl anything that really mattered.

With an effort I pulled myself together, to use an ordinary afternoon-tea-call tone.

" Oh, there's nothing to tell, Phillipa," I said, turning my head on the fresh-feeling pillow. " It's only, you see, that Sir Richard and Lady Meredith found they wanted to get back to Wales, so they went off, this morning "

"This morning?" took up Phillipa. She was sitting in an American rocking-chair now, with her back to the curtained window. "This morning they went? But, you know, Lady Meredith made an appointmentwith my mother for to-morrow afternoon. She must have changed her mind, rather suddenly."

" Oh, yes! she did," I said, as casually as I could. " And then, you see, *he* has been called away to London, too, on business."

" He ? Do you mean George ? "

" Yes," I said. " He has been suddenly called back to London on business. So, of course, I don't want to be alone in Paris! So – so *dull!* I thought your mother would perhaps be good enough to let me stay here for the next two or three daj's, before I go over, too."

Very directly and with her dark eyes full upon me, Phillipa asked, " Why on earth doesn't George take you with him?"

" Oh! because he can't," I said.

And, under her inquiring gaze, I felt my cheeks turn so hot that I thought they must have singed the pillowcase.

I twisted a little sideways on the bed, and nibbled at the biscuit in my hand.

" He can't take you with him? " said Phillipa, slowly.

" No," I said. " I – er – can't tell you why – exactly but

" Is it because your passport has to be got ready, by any chance? " suggested Phillipa.

" Oh, yes, of course. There is my passport," I said, gladly remembering that.

" And can't George wait two days for that? "

" Oh! it's more than two days – it's three or four," I said, rather feebly.

" I suppose it's because you have some more clothes to fit, isn't it?" said Phillipa with a touch of her mother's irony. Then, as I agreed, " Oh, yes, there are my Jeanne things to try on," she laughed.

" Do I have to think of your excuses for you, Mrs. George? " she said.

Then she rose, moved away from that rocking-chair, and came and sat on the edge of the bed where I was tucked up.

She took my hand.

" Tell me," she said, simply.

And then, quickly, before I could even say " I can't;

there's nothing to tell " she took the words out

of my mouth with:

" Oh, yes, there is. You were going to tell me something of it that day at Suzanne's. Besides ! Do

you think I can't see? Do you think I can't hear? Out in the street just now when you said ' Captain Meredith? '"

" Oh, that was nothing," I protested, weakly. " A slip of the tongue "

"Pooh!" she said; "it's not 'nothing.' There is something the matter. Tell me," she said. " Tell me everything. Don't think about me at all – that's all over. That would never have done! I explained about that. That's finished! But you are just beginning – you and – George," said Phillipa, putting up her little head. " And I want it to be all right for you. What is the trouble? His people seemed so fond of you. Surely, they haven't been making mis "

" Oh, no, no! They are such darlings! " I said, helplessly.

" Then – George? " she said, as if to herself.

Then she turned to me again. " Are you – disappointed, somehow, in George? " she said. " Disillusioned? " And there was a little hostile note in her tone now. It might have been for me; it might have been for him. I felt that if it was for him, it was only fair to take his part and to stand up for him. Hastily I said " Oh! he couldn't possibly have been nicer to me. He's done everything he could. It's not his fault if – if "

" If what?" she said, looking at me, searchingly.

" If he's got to go away – to the India Office, I think he said – and leave me."

" The India Office? " said Phillipa, puzzled. " He's got nothing to do at the India Office! He's got

what Nearly a month's sick leave! You know

there's something behind all that! "

Something? Oh! if I only could have told her what it was! If I could only have confided it all to her! I could say nothing. Feverishly, I drank some more tea as I lay there with Phillipa watching me; looking at me as if she would look down, down into my heart! She said, again, " Don't think of me. Don't think it's me that's asking you questions like this. There isn't really anything of *me* left," she told me. " What there is has been given over to "

She nodded towards her dressing-table.

I had already seen that the place of honour there, onthe right, just beyond the big crystal powder-box, was taken up by a photograph in a big oval silver frame.

To make a diversion I held out my hand towards it. "May I look?" Phillipa handed it to me, and I examined the photograph of the man in uniform who had written " Monty " across the bottom in a cramped, boyish hand, rather like Sir Richard's. He was slightly bald and had a wistful, trusting sort of face, rather like a nice dog's.

" The kindest heart in the world," said Phillipa, with a little half-rueful, half-affectionate glance. " Anybody ought to be proud to give him what she could." And she replaced the framed photograph on her dressing- table.

I felt myself filled, suddenly, by a curious little wonder. Where is her photograph of the man she really loved? Somewhere, I am sure, she has a snapshot of him taken in Wales. Perhaps she even has that same photograph that I – that Lady Meredith sent to his wife. The photograph in the pearl pendant now locked up at the Ritz. Locked in her heart – but where else does Phillipa keep her portrait of George?

Phillipa took up again, " Look here, I am going to talk, quite frankly."

This generally means, from another woman, that one is going to hear unpleasant home truths.

I sighed, apprehensively.

" It is only me," said Phillipa, reassuringly, gravely. " I am really only a girl, like you (though I feel about a million years older)", she added half to herself. " Iknow that this is what they call a ' church-door marriage.' I know he had to leave you; that you had hardly seen each other. That you have everything to begin, since that other evening when he came back from the Front. Is it that that makes it so strange? Is it that you have been – *shy?* "

"Oh! Lady Meredith thought that!" I admitted, with a little despairing sigh. " As if that had *anything* to do with it! "

Phillipa moved quickly on the edge of the bed, as if she had seen some light. in the darkness into which she was peering. She took up the first half of my sentence.

"'Lady Meredith thought that'? Ah! Perhaps that was why she and Sir Richard went away ? To leave you alone with George. To give you and him the chance of getting accustomed to each other? "

" Yes – oh, yes, I believe that was it," I heard myself admit, reluctantly. "Yes?"

" And you refuse this chance ? " took up the girl sitting before me. " You avoid it! Why? "

Desperately, I wished that I had allowed George to forbid me to come near this Phillipa! Indeed, indeed she knew too much – for some one who did not know anything at all. She sat there, a little pale, determined: she, the girl who adored George, questioning the girl who was, presumably, George's most eccentric bride!

" It seems unpardonable, the way I cross-examine you – you, George's wife. But I think I have some right. I gave up a good deal for it," she told me, earnestly, tapping a slim foot upon the rug beside her bed." I wanted him to have happiness. He was born for it, made for it. I want, still, to make sure that he gets it! If I can make sure ! "

The great emerald flashed upon her finger as she moved both slender hands as if they were full of an unseen gift that she wished to press upon some one, beckoning me – me! – to help her.

" He can't be happy unless it's all right about *you."*

" You'll have to forgive me – and to answer me," she said. And turning straight upon me, she demanded, " Don't you like being with him? You *don't?* "

" Oh, of course I do – don't. No, I mean do," I told her, incoherently. " I – I have liked being with him all this time."

" D'you mean since Tuesday? "

" Yes; I've liked being with him – I have, really that's quite true," I said. And meant it.

She gazed at me. " What is it that you don't like about him, then ? "

" Oh, nothing! I mean, there's nothing except things to like about him," I said, Hurriedly. " I see nothing to dislike."

" Not the same thing," she said, quietly. And then, as if it were quite an ordinary question, " His looks – do they please you? You think he's good to look at? "

" Yes, I do. Oh, yes, I do," I admitted. " Though he didn't like one to say so. ..."

" M'm," said Phillipa. " You did say so then. . . . You like him to talk to? "

" Oh, yes! Yes! " I hardly knew what I was saying." And all his little ways He's thoughtful, easy

to get on with? You should find him so "

"Oh, yes, I do! I did "

(For he had been much easier to get on with the first day that we had gone about together; before that time that Lady Meredith had practically driven us out together to solitude *a deux* in the woods at Saint-Cloud.)

But here was Phillipa insisting, " He's been nice to you, you said, all the time? "

" Oh, of *course* he has! He's been charming," I told her, falteringly, but sincerely. " He has been – considering everything – a perfect dear "

" Yet – considering everything – you're not happy, Rose!"

" Anything but! " I breathed, fervently, incautiously. And then of course I wished, frantically, that I had held my tongue.

Her next question was, " Do you think that George is not going to make you happy? "

" Me? Of *course* he isn't," I cried, startled, defensively, raising my rumpled head and flushed face from the pillow. " Of course George isn't going to make me happy. How could he "

" How could he ? " repeated Phillipa's bewildered but searching voice. " I don't say this because I cared for George myself. But I can tell you that nine girls out of ten would be glad to be in your shoes!"

The extraordinary announcement rose to my lips, " They aren't my shoes! " I choked it down in time, and again the heartfelt yearning took me that I could work some spell, and *will* into that room the girl who ought to have been there, in my place, standing that cross-examination of her heart's inmost secrets. She wouldn't have objected. She – Vera Vayne – could have stood up, gaily obtuse, to all Phillipa's questionings. " *Make me happy? Him?* Oh, well, *marriage is a lottery,* when all's said!" I could hear the invincible Cockney cocksureness of something she'd said to me as we went to lunch in the train. " *One man's much the same as another, once a woman's learnt how to handle 'em right. The three F's, eh? ' Flatter, feed, and fondle ' – that's the matter! Nobody wants to be an old maid trailing round on her own forever, neither. That's no life for a girl. I dessay him and me'd a got on first-rate together s'long as I didn't have to see too much o' that classy fam'ly o' his* "

The phantom echoes of young Mrs. Meredith's shouts were broken in upon again by the real tones, the proud, steady, searching, charming voice of Phillipa Tracey.

" Why do you think George could not make you happy, Rose? "

" Oh, *dear!* " I cried, with my hands up to my hair. I felt like tearing it, sticking straws in it. " Phillipa! There's no *idea* of such a thing!"

"'No idea'?" insisted the other girl.' "When he has just married you? When you're so young, so attractive "

"He doesn't think I'm attractive!" I cried. "I mean, he doesn't think anything about that!"

" Oh, yes. He must," said Phillipa. And her dark eyes seemed to search every detail of my appearance. She spoke, gently and impersonally, as if she were describing some picture. " Your feet and hands are exquisite, and you're so prettily made, and your colouring is lovely. All that pink and white, with that goldeny-brown hair! It looks sweet, tossed down on the pillow like that. And your eyes are like love-in-the- mist; so blue. You are one of the little Watteau ladies. You should always have a fan, a nosegay, a knot of sky- blue beckoning ribands, a wreath of tiny blush roses about you. . . . Things that would look absurd on girls like me." She threw a quick, hold-cheap glance at the reflection of her own chiselled features in the glass. " It's not that we think we're beyond those pretty, frivolous things. They're beyond us. . . . Oh, do you know, Rose, how lucky you are to have that small, soft, crushable, eternal-feminine type that men have always coveted? Always it wins them. In the Middle Ages it got fair Rosamond's King Edward. It got Romney and Nelson in the eighteenth century. And now – now, in nineteen sixteen, it has got George."

" No, *no!* " I broke in, feverishly, at last. " If you only knew, it hasn't got George." (One could hardly describe his wife in those terms, could one?) " Certainly 7 haven't!"

A little incredulous smile passed over Phillipa's face. " You mean you actually imagine he's not at all attracted to you? "

"Not at all. I know he's not," I told her. And there was very little " pink and white " now about the face that Phillipa had flattered. It felt scorchingly scarlet.

She watched it. " Even now, you're not in love," she suggested, " with him? "

" Never! There was never supposed to be anything of that sort," I explained, still feverishly. " It's never – never been thought of! It – it doesn't come into it at all "

" Curious sort of marriage," said Phillipa Tracey, dully. I could not check a little hysterical laugh. What worlds away she was from dreaming *how* " curious " was the bond between George and the girl whom she must think was the most oddly-conducted war-bride on record! " Yet I could have sworn the other day," she took up again, half doubtfully now, " I could have said, almost for certain, that you were not in love with anybody *else!* "

" Never! " I declared again, leaning upon my elbow to look her straight in the face. " There are quite enough complications in my life already, I should think, without my falling in *love* with anybody!"

"What complications?" demanded Phillipa, quietly but insistently. "What complications, Rose?"

Hopelessly, I shook my head. It seemed going round and round and round. Not the whole of George's cross-examinings (and those were severe enough) had been one-millionth part as trying to me as was this ordeal by Phillipa.

(Yet some women wish tohave woman judges and lawyers and juries. Thanks!)

She plied me – me, the girl whom she took for her rival – with unanswerable questions. " Don't you think you might soon grow to care for him? – Why not? – *Not* ever ? – Why, then, did you accept him ? – Why did you want to know that day in the hat-shop, what I thought of George? You said you had your picture of him in your mind; has he changed, since first you saw him? – What did you think of him, when you did see him first? – You don't remember? – But when was it? Can't you tell me that? And where, Rose? Where?"

" Oh! " desperately from me; " in Paris! "

" In Paris ? But no! I refused him in London," said the other girl, quickly," and you must have got married less than a week after that. Besides, when you and Ladypleredith came here to lunch you told Mother you hadn't been in Paris since long before the war. Was it then that you met George? "

"Then? No, I should think not," I cried, breathlessly. " Then, I was alone with my own mother. I was perfectly happy then. I'd never even heard of Cap – of him, then, and I'd give anything," I wound up, impetuously and bitterly, " never, never to have heard of him, or of any one to do with him, now!"

Phillipa Tracey looked at me so hard that I had to bury my face in my pillow again. But through the rumpled curls about my burning ears I heard her voice. The grave, detached sweetness had all gone out of it. It rang agitatedly:

" Rose! listen to me. I told you I refused your husband "

Anguished, I muttered, " Oh, *don't! "* but she didqjt seem to hear what I said. She went on :

" I refused him because I cared too much for him. I understood him too well. I knew that I could not have made him happy. But "

The threatening note deepened.

" – but if he is going to be miserable with you, he might just as well have stayed with me! I might have kept him! "

I think that my reply to this startled Phillipa as much as anything that I had said during this nightmare interview of ours, for with a quick movement I sprang up from the pillow, my hair all loose now about my face. I sat bolt upright on the bed clasping my hands round my knees. I looked up at her. In tones of the sincerest and most despairing conviction I returned, " You might have kept him. Oh, why didn't you ? You ought to have married him, Phillipa! You ought! I wish you had! "

She gazed at me, this dark, handsome, spirited girl, as if she could not believe her ears.

Words seemed – at last – to fail her.

" I *do* wish he had stayed with you, Phillipa," I said, miserably. " I mean it. It would have been so much better. He ought never to have married . . . anybody else. It's a perfect tragedy that he did."

To my horror I felt a big lump coining up into my throat as I said it.

" He ought to have married the right girl," I faltered. " He deserved her. Oh, do remember, always, that I said this. He married – Phillipa! Remember that I told you this, at least! – He married quite, quite, *quite* th" wrong woman! " I wound up.

And I felt a bitter, passionate wave of resentment sweeping up within me against that woman, that " Vera" whose entire unsuitableness has not yet dawned upon poor

George's friends. Phillipa was not the only one who felt that he was born, meant to be happy! Phillipa would not be the only one to realise the cruel waste of his absurd tragi-comedy of a story. That wave of sympathetic resentment was almost swamping me

I choked it down as I flung Phillipa's eiderdown aside.

I felt I couldn't bear another minute of this.

I rose to my feet in their blue silk stockings and fumbled for my blue suede shoes with the buckles.

Hastily I said " I am going, now."

" You are not," said Phillipa, also rising, and dominating me with a look. " You can't go now, Rose, until you have told me everything. You see, you've told me one thing that I can see isn't true. About your meeting George first in Paris. Now, you've got to let me know the whole truth. I shall not let you go until then."

She stood there, tall and handsome and straight asa lad, seeming to bar the door of her room against my going.

" I can't," I said, huskily. " Do you suppose I don't wish I could tell you? "

" Ah!" She looked down at me. " You admit, at last, that there is something to tell? "

" Miles," I admitted, miserably and impressively. Miles!"

" Can you at least let me know *"why* you can't tell it to me? "

" Oh, yes," I said, unhappily. " Yes, I can tell you that."

And in three quick words I told her, " I promised George."

Instantly, Phillipa moved away from the door. In a suddenly broken little voice, she said, " All right. I won't ask you any more. I didn't know that. Shall you – shall you ever be able to tell me? I suppose not."

" Oh, but yes! I hope so," I cried. " I think so. Perhaps – even in a few days "

" And you are coming here to stay; for those days? "

But I shook my head. Already I saw the blank impossibility of this.

" I can't now," I said. " If I stayed here with you, I know what would happen. In spite of what I promised George, it would come out. I should tell you in spite of myself. I should feel I should *die* if I didn't – and I mustn't. I did promise him. I'll go."

Phillipa gave a little consenting nod. I wondered – I wondered what interpretation she could have put uponit all; what wild guesses, what surmises not as unusual as the truth, could fill her mind at the moment.

She moved across to the dressing-table, handed me a comb. Then she turned to the chest-of-drawers, took up my hat in one hand, my pins in the other.

" I see, perhaps, that it is better for you not to stay here, then," she said, in a tired but gentle voice. " Shall you be at the Ritz? "

" I suppose so, for the present. I'll telephone you and I'll let you know," I said, heavily. For all my dilemma seemed crowding down upon me once more. " I'll come and see you again, Phillipa, when there is anything that I can tell you."

And with these words I left her.

7

SECTION 7

CHAPTER XXIV

A MAIDEN MEDITATION

OH, what a miserable evening I spent! I used to think that those evenings alone at my club in London were the abomination of desolation; but there at least I was free from all these cares and worries. (Surely I ought to have been frightfully happy then!)

I had meant to make a1 clean breast of the result of my interview with Phillipa to Captain Meredith this same evening. But he hasn't come near me. . . .

There has been no sign of him. Merely the shortest note to tell me that he will call to-morrow morning – a copy of " *The First Hundred Thousand,"* which I suppose he got at Brentano's – an armful of the new papers, *Femina, L'Illustration, Vogue,* for me to look at – and a telephoned inquiry if Mademoiselle White- lands had come in yet; nothing more.

I'm a little surprised. Surely he ought to have come! I think it was casual – unkind of him to leave me like this. His people gone; and I, alone, in Paris! Left to my own resources!

For a moment I had the idea of going out and spending an adventurous evening in Paris by myself.

Why not? My last chance possibly of ever doing such a thing.

I thought I might go up to Montmartre to the Grand Guignol and see the shocker that they had got on there now – " *Horrible Experience "?*

I don't know what it is about; but it cannot be much more " horrible " than the experience that I have been going through to-day!

Or what about my even taking a peep at the *Moulin Rouge,* that I have never seen yet?

Captain Meredith refused to take me there the evening that we went to see " *The Man Who Stayed at Home "* instead.

He said that the *Moulin Rouge* was dull, and absolutely Anglo-Saxon, that it wouldn't amuse me one bit. But there was a little firm tuck-in to his lips as he said it, and I don't believe he was refusing to take me because he thought I should be bored. On the contrary. . . .

It would serve him right if I did go. I mean to say it would show him that I am going to dissociate myself entirely from him, from all of them. That I am going to put an end to the whole impossible situation.

Let him find somebody else to impersonate his missing wife until she chooses to turn up. Or what does he want with any one to impersonate her now that his father and mother are out of the way? He will be in London conducting his business with those lawyers. Seeing detectives or whoever one does have to see when one is set upon bringing back a runaway wife.

Sir Richard and *Belle-mere* – I mean, Lady Meredith – will be safely at Bryn. They won't know that Roseis no longer with George. That Rose simply has gone back to London by herself again. Back to the same old room, probably, at her club; and that she is looking out for some job. Some job duller and less luxuriously set, but without any of these complications that were making me feel as if my hair ought to have turned completely grey!

Yes, that's what I am going to do. He can't force me, after all, to stay, and it can't do any harm to Lady Meredith's heart if she doesn't see what is going on.

In the meantime why should I stick up here in this bedroom, turning over the leaves of the sheaf of picture- papers that Captain Meredith has left for me, just as if they were to amuse some little girl who's been told to be good, and to amuse herself alone while her elders and betters go about their own business?

No; I shall not stay in, walking up and down this room like a trapped animal in a cage, or like Captain Meredith himself walked up and down, up and down, during that grotesque interview when we set eyes upon each other for the first time!

I shall not mope alone here, fretting and fretting over the idea of Lady Meredith. I shall go out, even if it's only to some amusing little restaurant. Not " con- venable " for an English girl alone? Well, I thought, mutinously, I am *supposed* to be a married woman! And I put on my hat and my coat; turned to take up nay furs, my moire hand-bag. . . .

And then I was stopped. I was checked by thethought of that factor which has been so often a check to a woman's bid for independence!

No money!

All the money I had in the world had been the change from a hundred-france note of Lady Meredith's with which I had paid a glove bill at the Louvre. And the last two francs of that had paid my taxi coming away from Passy!

And now there would be my bill at the Ritz to pay, as well as my fare back to England!

There was only one thing to do about that.

I should have to ask Captain Meredith for the money to-morrow when I told him what I had decided to do. That was a horrible thing to have looming in front of me. To ask a man for money!

It is one of the anomalies of our sex that a woman will chatter away for hours to another woman upon the cost of things, quoting prices, adding up shillings, or even reminding her of debts, without turning a hair.

But how she loathes mentioning money to the sex that makes it! It must be torture to her to ask the man of the house for the weekly housekeeping money. Yes, even if most of that money has gone in food for the master of that house!

I believe that if more men realised this fact and met it, there would be many more happy marriages.

Awful to have to apply to Captain Meredith to pay my bills under the circumstances!

Still, not as bad as if it were another kind of man. . . .

For I had always liked his way of settling up in cabs and restaurants. He did it in a way so few men seem to achieve; making it of no importance and yet promptly done. Without any hint of fumbling or fuss, or of keeping his women-folk waiting, or letting them feel self-conscious as they stood there.

I hoped that Miss Vera Vayne (when she came back) would appreciate that trait in him. I hope

Here my meditations were broken in upon by a tap at the door; and by the arrival of that smiling *femme- de-chambre* who is so typically French that she looks as if she ought to wear a scarlet cap of liberty with a tricolour cockade upon her ink-black coiffure. She carried a tray with a delicious little supper with wine. When I, surprised, exclaimed that I had ordered nothing, she beamed upon me and insisted, " *Si, si, si, si, si, si, si!* It was that Monsieur the Capitaine; the – *fiance* of Mademoiselle had commanded that there should be brought up to Mademoiselle this little repast!"

So he had thought of that although he had not come round to take me out to dinner himself?

To do him justice, he would make a duck of a husband in the way of little attentions and forethought.

I hoped Vera would realise how lucky she had been, where another woman (as different from her as filigree gold was different to stage tinsel) had been crossed in love!

Oh, Phillipa! With the tragedy-behind-smfling- stoicism of her girlish face! Poor Phillipa! With my first sip of claret and Vichy water I felt myself gulpingdown again the big lump that had come into my throat when I declared to Phillipa my conviction that George had married the wrong woman.

Another gloomy conviction was forming itself in my mind as I sat there over my solitary little meal.

That woman would never be aware of her luck. Never!

She would always hold her complacently-voiced theory that one man was much the same as another – " That old George, poor young feller! was all right, but for his people, and but for being a bit of a nuisance about his wife keeping on with her profesh! "

Putting aside the half-finished cold chicken on my plate and turning to the sweet, I thought that even though George's wife never grew to care any more than that for her young husband, he would probably grow to care for her. He had been so anxious to know how " affectionately " she had spoken of him. He was probably already quite attracted – why, of course he was! He'd chosen her after all!

A sharp stab seemed to go through my heart at this thought.

It was so terrible to think that the Veras of this world could attain to that, and the Phillipas not! Yes; it seemed to me very likely that George might become very fond of that handsome, common wife of his. I had heard before that men in their love-affairs are absolutely without the sense of class. And isn't this borne out every day for a truth?

If once, in the bluest of moons, a well-bred womanso far forgets the whole of the social order as to elope with her chauffeur, are there any words strong enough to express the outrage which is felt by Society? It doesn't matter if the young man has quite a decent voice, or looks like Apollo in his car. " *Nobody* could *know her – marrying a man who . . . well, my dear, she picked him out of a garage! She must have lost all sense of everything!* "

But that same lady's brother can marry that same chauffeur's sister, and it causes little talk beyond a pleasant stir of amusement!

" *Oh! Do you know old So-and-So's gone and done it! Have you seen his missus? Ripping pretty girl! A lady? Oh, no! Doesn't pretend to be one, but she's awfully taking – she dances, or sings, or something in ' Whatever Next,' I think it was! Anyhow she was on the stage.*"

Ah, how that takes them! The eternal lure of the dancer, the chorus-girl – I don't believe there's a stronger call to men. I believe that Mrs. Tracey was right, and that paint appeals to them. I believe they prefer the Cockney accent: " *Ah think Ah'll jest take a w'iskey-and-soder, dear.*" It's a change! I believe it's a treat to them to loll about in feminine society without having to " mind " what they say; and that they are amused by little theatrical gags and by greenroom gossip and by snappy anecdotes about all the picture-post-card beauties. I believe vulgarity *rests* them, or something!

Yes; I believe it's a mistake for girls of the Phillipaclass to take such trouble about turning themselves out in such exquisite and quiet taste. That's all very well for a man's sister, about whom the one thing needful is that nobody shall notice her. Or, supposing he is " settling down " at the end of his youth, this conqueror – well, no girl can be too frumpy for Caesar's *wife*. . . . But what *attracts* the man? A handful of mauve gossamer, worn over heaving billows of lace at " three- three " a yard, stockings that look like bare ankles, and shoes composed of an Eiffel Tower heel, a brown- paper sole, and eight jewelled straps! Yes, just like those evening shoes that were put out for me that evening at the Bryn.

For *me!* . . .

As I sat there alone in my room, I suddenly surprised myself by hearing myself utter aloud a thoroughly spiteful taunt. Had I, then, come to *hate* Miss Vera Vayne, George's wife? For that unworthy little comment was one that no woman would pronounce about another woman unless she had some reason for detesting her.

I said " Well, I may have been in her shoes all this time, *but she could never have got into mine. Her feet are too large!* "

CHAPTER XXV

" TO CUT THE KNOT "

"yAPTAIN MEREDITH, I shall have to ask

1 . *you* to lend me some money." I said it without beating about the bush the moment that the young man turned up this morning at the Ritz.

Promptly his hand went to the breast of his tunic. As promptly he said " Yes, rather so. Of course; I had thought of that. Tell me if that isn't enough, will you ? I think it will be all right." And he handed over to me, without glancing at it, his treasury note-case; a thin, brown leather one with G. R. M. in sloping gold letters across one corner. That was one of *Belle-mere's* presents to him, I knew.

I took it, found it stuffed with two-hundred and five- hundred franc notes.

" Oh! but of course it's enough," I said, feeling helplessly shy about the whole thing. " It's far too much for – for what I want! "

At that he looked quickly at me.

We were both standing up in that anteroom off the hall, with the mirrors and the enormous vases and the gilding under the lofty ceiling.

It was as if he had caught a hint in my voice of what I meant to do.

" You mean it's enough," he said, quickly, " to just get along with – I mean, settle up here before you go on to the Traceys'? By the way, what about the Traceys?"

So then I told him, frankly and sorrowfully, that the Traceys were out of the question. I couldn't stay there; I couldn't go there again. If I stayed with Phil- lipa I should have to tell her.

"And you won't let me tell her?" I hesitated. I thought that I could perhaps still persuade him.

From the mere shake of his dark head I knew that this was hopeless.

" She – Phillipa guessed there was something rum, I suppose ? " he said. I had to laugh. Without mentioning Phillipa again he brought me back to the question what it was I meant to do.

I told him in a word.

" Go! " I said, looking away from him at the gilding and the cornicing and the background that would soon be as unfamiliar to me again as it had been any time these last three years.

"Go?" he repeated. "Off, on your own, you mean? "

" Yes, I can't stand it any longer!" I said, clearing my throat, clenching my hands. " It's too – it's got too complicated – too tangled. I am just going to cut that knot. I am going! "

He looked at me, blankly, for a moment. Then he said, in an uncertain voice," But, look here! We aren't out of the wood yet, you know. About my wife. Ididn't get any letter this morning. I was going to tell you that."

" Oh, yes! I ought to have asked you. Stupid of me "

" No letter came," he said, again, almost absently. " Awful, the way you simply cannot rely on the post nowadays. Hardly any mails seem to have got through from London this week. So there's no news for me."

I said, shaking my head, " I am sorry; I can't wait for that. I want to go away as soon as I can." I spoke as doggedly as I could. " I must go."

Then I waited for his opposition. I expected him to say " No; look here, impossible. You can't go away before we have got to the end of this business. It isn't fair! You've got to stop on at least until I have heard from Vivie."

Here surprise awaited me. He made absolutely no attempt at objection. As quietly as possible he said " All right."

"'All right'?" I said. "You don't mind my – jacking up, like this? "

He didn't look at me as he replied " I think, perhaps, after all, it's the best plan," . . . and then, quite hastily," You will go as soon as you can, I suppose ? "

" As soon as I can get my passport through," said I. "Of course."

" May I come with you at least for that ? "

" I should be glad if you would," I said.

He came with me. He was very silent during the whole walk to the Consulate, to the funny little upstairs room where marvellously polite French gentlemen interviewed and signed the papers of divers travellers.

We came away, and still he was silent. I was sorry.

It was extraordinary how accustomed one can get to a companion in three or four days. I felt positively as if I were going out for the last time with a friend – a real friend – rather than a mere

Well, I don't quite know what to call him – " Temporarily commissioned husband," perhaps.

" I shall see you off", of course," he said, as we turned into the Place Vendome. " I'll come to the train tomorrow morning. But you'll want to pack now. I'll – get out of your way, this afternoon."

I suddenly felt that I had a million things to say to him. A million things about which to ask him – to ask his opinion about. And yet I didn't know what they were. . . .

I felt that I had come to the end of a pleasant friendship and that I'd wasted so much of it. ...

He didn't seem to feel that. He didn't seem to be thinking about me at all, these last minutes that we were together. They were the last minutes, for who counts that hasty, flurried, uncomfortable, engine- scented moment of parting at a railway-station? I wished he wouldn't come to the Gare du Nord to-morrow. I wished that – instead – he would take me out to lunch again to-day, and make my last days in Paris something that I should like to remember, instead of a mere welter of packing and worries and regrets.

This he never suggested.

8

SECTION 8

He seemed to have nothing more to say to me. Now that his mother had gone and my *ratson d'etre* was at an end, he hadn't even a " thankyou " for me. He was positively hurrying me back to the hotel, hurrying to leave me. All he wanted was to get me off as soon as possible. . . .

Very well.

I let him see me into the hall of the Ritz, and then I turned to nod " good-bye " without even holding out my hand.

Apparently, he hadn't expected me to do so.

" Good-afternoon," he said, in his most casual, his most commonplace tone – the sort of tone that hurts a woman far worse than any curtness. " Good-bye "

CHAPTER XXVI

ENTER A FRESH CHABACTER

HE was off – he was gone No, at that last moment he was intercepted: $; one of the hotel attendants darted forward. With a truly Latin bend in the spine, with his bestl *entente cordiale* smile on, he accosted the young officer, I who, I have noticed, is a favourite with these people.

" Excuse me, Monsieur the Capitaine," he said. I " But justly, an English gentleman desires to speakl with Capitaine Mayraydeet and Mademoiselle."

" Who's this ? " said Captain Meredith, curtly, and *M* rather irritably, as he turned. Yes, evidently he wasl in a hurry to go! " Somebody who wants to speak tol us?"

Even as he spoke a thought struck me. I turned tc Captain Meredith. Hurriedly, and in a not-too-de lighted voice, I said, " I expect I know who this is. thought he would come and call, presently. It was fault for not having written to him. It must be Cap-l tain Penmore! You know – the man in the R. A. M. C., that I told you about? The man I asked you to call or the other day at the hospital ? "

And I looked down the long corridor to see if I coulcfl catch a glimpse of him.

9

SECTION 9

Captain Meredith turned to the attendant and said:

" The gentleman is in uniform with the Croix Rouge?"

" But no, sir. He is not in uniform at all! He is *en civil,"* said the man. Then, touching his sleeve, he added, " He wears something – some decoration here."

" Now, who on earth " began Captain Meredith,

still irritated. He spoke as if every minute more that he had to spend at the Ritz were a fresh annoyance. " Is he in the waiting-room now? "

" Yes; he said he would wait half an hour to see if you and the young lady would be soon of return."

Then he broke off. "Ah! Behold! the gentleman who comes out. He is not waiting. What a chance that he should still find *monsieur et dame.* Hold! Here he is! "

I turned, as did Captain Meredith, to give a quick glance at the figure which was coming out of the anteroom on the left.

It was a tall, slim figure. English, though not of the type of Englishman to which most of our countrymen in the hotel belonged. This was not a soldier. He had a clean-cut face that was just a little too mobile and pretty for a man. His hair curled almost down to the astrachan collar of his coat, and about the sleeve of that very stagily-cut overcoat he wore the " decoration," a khaki band with a scarlet crown, that meant he belonged to group something or other, to be " called up " according as the military authorities thought him requisite for service.

" Never seen him in my life," murmured Captain Meredith, turning with an inquiring lift of his dark brows to me.

I shook my head. Certainly I had never set eyes on this extraordinarily actorish-looking young man before.

" I don't know him either," I said, just as the waiter took a step after him and called " Monsieur, hold! Here are Madame and Monsieur, the Captain."

Just at the door the strange young man turned. Catching sight of me and the khaki-clad form at my side, he swept off his hat, a broad-leafed affair that made him look like something oub of " The Breed of the Treshams."

" Ah! " he exclaimed, dramatically, in a deep-carrying voice. " Have I the pleasure of addressing Captain George Meredith? "

" Yes; but I don't think I know you," said Captain Meredith, a tiny bit stiffly.

" No doubt, no doubt!" said the stranger with the deep voice. Then, " Let me introduce myself. Arthur Harrison – your most obedient servant."

At that instant the name woke no memories in my mind. Evidently none in Captain Meredith's either. He said, while we all stood there, rather uncertain, " I am afraid I don't happen to know you even yet."

" My stage name is, sometimes, Clarence Fitzroy."

Again Captain Meredith shook his dark head.

" And this is Fame! " returned the young man in the Trilby hat and the armlet. " Suffice it to say that there are others to whom that name is, I may say, without boasting, not at all unknown! But sir, I would have a word with you. Ay, I would have speech with you."

" I will go and get the passport," I said, hastily, to Captain Meredith. Again I was just about to slip away to the left, when the stranger held up a long, pale hand with a signet ring on it. " Stay, madam," he broke in. " Tarry awhile. What I have to say concerns you also. Ay, even you."

" Oh, does it ? " I said, gasping a little, without knowing how much harder I should have to gasp in about five minutes. He was certainly an odd figure at the Ritz, this young man who seemed to talk like a cloak- and-dagger melodrama!

Arthur Harrison – Arthur Harrison. Yes, I had heard the name somewhere. I suppose I had seen him act.

Captain Meredith's dark brows drew together, impatiently. He was, I knew, champing his bit to be off. And his thoughts, translated into words, would have been: " This fellow's come here to cadge half-a-crown."

I saw his hand move towards his pocket flap. The stranger, noticing this, too, gave a shake of the head, a gesture of the hand, that immediately brought before me a vision of the footlights, of red plush curtains, slowly parted, and of a girl's voice chanting " Pro- grems? Progrems sixpence?"

I had to suppress a smile while this Mr. Arthur Harrison, catching the eyes upon him of the manager, two hotel attendants, gesticulated with the Trilby hat towards the entrance of the anteroom, and brought out, in a very intense " aside " that quavered a little, " Shall we seek scenes less public for what I have to impart? I bring a letter "

Here, delving with his hand into an inner pocket, he brought out a large, heliotrope coloured envelope.

This he handed to Captain Meredith with the remark, evidently meant to sound easy, but sounding a trifle nervous as well, " I think you know the sweet Roman hand?"

The young soldier took the note, looked at its address.

" Oh, Lord! " said Captain Meredith, very blankly.

Then, briskly, " Oh, good! Yes." He nodded to the theatrical young man. " Yes, I was expecting this. We'll see about this in here, shall we? " He turned to the anteroom door, with an including sort of gesture to Mr. Arthur Harrison. Then, quickly, to me, " I don't think I need bother you about this."

" Pardon me; pardon me," put in the Breed-of-the- Treshams young man, " but this young lady " – another sweep of the hand – "is this (a name to conjure by) MissWhitelands?"

Captain Meredith looked, anxiously, at me. I don't know what he wanted, or thought, I should say. But I promptly replied " Yes! I am – I mean, this is."

" Then " – again the impressive aside – " it concerns you too. Pray accompany us."

In another moment the three of us were at the far end of the anteroom, I sitting in one of those red velvet chairs where I had waited for Captain Meredith themorning his parents left. The two men stood beside a console table in front of an ornate mirror.

In that mirror I saw Captain Meredith's full face reflected; it was the emblem of gloomy outward patience. What lay beyond that I don't know. His hand, on the table, held the unopened envelope.

I guessed – it didn't take much guessing – the meaning of this! It was news of his wife. And this was one of her appalling theatrical " crowd " who had come to bring it. . . . Arthur Harrison – Arthur Harrison. . . . Ah, now I remembered where I had heard the name before! It had slipped out, with so much else of the Vision's confidence, during that fateful interview in the train. " Pore Arthur Harrison " was the young man who had acted with her. Yes, that was it! In some love-scene where she had made him laugh fit to kill himself, so that twenty-seven yards of film had been spoiled! *That* was the one!

He cleared his throat, smiled ingratiatingly but still rather uncertainly, and began, " Well, Captain Meredith – I – I – I should have been here three days ago, to say that which I have to unfold, had it not been for the trouble I had at that French Consulate, waiting, waiting, to get my papers in order. Ye gods! " He turned to me and passed his hand over his hair. " The red tape! The arrogance of the officials! Dressed in a little brief authority, you know, with all the fond, fantastic tricks of power! "

Here he caught sight of himself in that gilt-framed mirror, and it seemed to give him a little more confidence. He moved nearer to it. Captain Meredith, meanwhile, stood like a rock, with that parade- ground face on, only his eyes moving a little now and then, as the other young man continued in a firmer voice.

" I went first, Captain, to your family residence in Wales. Gallant little Wales, ha! What a beautiful country, and the inhabitants how delightful! What character-study there! The same now as in the days of Fluellen and "

" Yes," Captain Meredith cut him short, " you went to Wales ? "

" To the stately pile of your ancestral halls," continued Mr. Arthur Harrison. " There I expected to find you in the bosom of your family, but lo! ' Where was now the merry party ? ' so to speak!

(More gesture.)

" No one but an aged family retainer, who told me that all, all were gone, the dear familiar faces; gone to

Paris! Post-haste I returned to London, and to ."

He pointed to that envelope.

"To the writer of that letter."

It crackled a little as Captain Meredith's hand closed tighter upon it.

" She said – our friend the writer said – that I was to let no grass grow under the wheels of my chariot – that is, my feet – until I had found you, seen you, spoken to you myself," went on Mr. Arthur Harrison, *alias* Mr. Clarence Fitzroy. He drew himself up a little and turned his profile to me. It certainly would have lookedvery well on a coin, but I did wish he would get on with what he had to say, more especially with that part of it which concerned me. I imagined that Miss Vera Vayne, whose ambassador he was, would have sent all sorts of apologies to me. Well might she do so! Her friend, Mr. Arthur Harrison, continued in a would-be appealing tone:

" You know her! You know what she is! the dear girl; a perfect child of nature! All impetuosity! All temperament! ALL "

" All right, all right, let's come to the point, shall we? " broke in Captain Meredith, with his voice and face well under control. But I, as I sat there watching first one and then the other of the men, could see that the young soldier was consumed with a mixture of disgust, impatience, anxiety. Also I felt in some odd way that he was made specially uncomfortable by my sitting there. Yes, I suppose he thought no stranger ought to hear all this. . . . Yet I couldn't get up and go while this other being with the hair described the " temperament" of the bona-fide Mrs. George Meredith. There I had to stay, hands in my lap, listening for the end – quite as embarrassed, really, as the lady's husband.

Captain Meredith said " I don't quite see why "

he moved his hand with the letter in it upon that console table. " Why she couldn't have wired to me. I have been expecting "

" There's too much to explain," cried Mr. Arthur Harrison, eagerly. " It couldn't possibly have gone ina wire. And as for posting on a letter – why! " He raised both his hands and then dropped them again by his sides. " I agreed with her that it was a far, far better thing to meet you – in person."

Captain Meredith looked at him again and said, quietly, " I don't quite see why you should have given yourself all this trouble just to bring me a letter from my wife."

Mr. Arthur Harrison returned his look with a stare that appeared to me to have a little bravado in it.

" Your wife? " he echoed. Then, a little louder, he repeated " Your wife? "

Then he allowed a short pause for effect.

He certainly got it.

For, as he placed a clenched fist on that table and leaned his regular profile and clustering curls towards Captain Meredith, he brought out his next sentence with a dramatic suddenness that must have thrilled any audience.

Yes, I think the method would have thrilled me, even if the words had not been such that for a second I could not believe that I had heard aright.

Yet Mr. Arthur Harrison had uttered, sharply and distinctly enough, " *Your* wife? *My* wife. *My* wife, you mean!"

" What ? " rapped out Captain Meredith.

It was exactly the same tone as of a pistol shot with which he had turned upon me, the other evening in the bedroom when I had confessed, so tremblingly, " You see, they think 7 am your wife!"

With exactly the same X-ray look in his dark-brown eyes, he turned upon this other stranger.

He asked, quietly, " What did you say? " .

" You heard me, Captain. I announce that Vera Vayne was my wife; my lawful wedded wife," repeated the deep, impressive voice of Mr. Arthur Harrison, while I gave myself a surreptitious pinch on the arm – to make sure I was awake. " And if the wish is father to the thought that you cannot believe me, here are the proofs!"

Again he delved into that inner pocket, and precisely at the word " here " he produced more papers. One was a grey-blue slip of printing –

" Her marriage-lines! " he said, huskily.

– the others seemed to be cuttings from old newspapers. " ' *Interesting theatrical wedding; Miss Vera Vayne and Mr. Arthur Clarence Harrison, the well- known* ' Here you are. Proof positive. A quarter column in the *Referee,"* cried the actor, passing one hand over his locks while the other held out the press- cuttings towards Captain Meredith, who was quietly and intently scanning that grey-blue certificate. " Impossible to put that aside! And "

" Right-o!" broke in the very quiet voice of the young soldier. " This " – he put a finger on that license, scanned it for another moment, then handed it back – " this appears to be in order." Then his voice hardened. " Now, if I may ask you a few questions, Mr. Harrison "

But Mr. Arthur Harrison, having got so far in thegrand melodramatic manner, suddenly dropped it. From the long breath that he drew, from the manner in which he whisked out a handkerchief of Nile-green silk and mopped his brow, I began to see that under the stage gestures and the quotations (which no doubt he had rehearsed for this occasion) he had been utterly and painfully nervous. And now, having broken the back of what he had to say, he was grotesquely relieved.

" Whew!" he said, and then in another voice with more than a trace of untrained Cockney in it, " Read her letter first, Captain. Will you?"

Captain Meredith apparently remembered, at this, the existence of – me. He glanced at me with a little lift of the brows that meant " May I? "

Out of a dream I heard myself murmur " Oh, please " He opened the mauve envelope.

10

SECTION 10

CHAPTER XXVII

ON MAUVE WRITING-PAPEB.

WAS it my fancy, or did that letter distribute a strong odour of " Phul-Nana " and face powder as soon as it was opened?

It was a long letter; a sheaf of thick mauve sheets that Captain Meredith had to sort into order as I, sitting there in the big plush arm-chair, watched first him and then the other young man. Mr. Arthur Harrison had folded his arms, and stood with one knee a little bent looking up a little towards the chandelier, just as if he were standing for a photograph. Captain Meredith, taking no further notice of either of us, began to read, quickly, but without haste or fumbling.

What could be the meaning of it ? I pondered. Could that mad lunatic Vera Vayne imagine that just because she had chosen to disown her " lawful wedded husband," Captain Meredith, in this manner she was now entitled to go off and marry whom she liked? Certainly, I

thought she was mad enough. Had she But stop!

Of course she had thought she was free. She had thought she was a war-widow. She had thought she was able to get married again.

But – so quickly? And after having married oneman who was such worlds too good for her Well!

I suppose she might feel more " at home " with this other, this terrible young man. He, Mr. Arthur Harrison, had turned his eyes from the chandelier again and was anxiously watching George's face as, at last, he came to the end of that letter.

Clearing his throat and unfolding his arms again, he said "Well; got it yet?"

Very simply and gently and politely Captain Meredith said " Yes; I think so, thank you."

Then he turned to me as I sat.

" Will you read it ? " he said.

I hesitated. " Oh – but – it's really nothing to do with me, is it Had I better "

" I think so."

So I took the handful of scented mauve sheets.

They were splashed over in that writing that I had seen once before – on the post-card that had been written to me, or rather to " Mrs. George Meredith," at the Bryn. The post-card that had been signed " The Princess Meta." That writing romped from page to page in loops of violet ink; and I had to stare several times at the curly numerals before I discovered which was page 3 and which page 5.

Then for the second time in that room I proceeded to read a letter which had been addressed to my make- believe husband.

It was dated from some rooms in Bloomsbury. And it began:

" Deab. Old Stick,

" Expect this will be a bit of a nasty one for you, but as you'll see, when you come to think things over a bit, you can't blame it all on to me.

" That night in the cab when you were seeing me home after that show with the boys when you put the *fatuU* question to me, you never thought to ask at the same time if I'd been married before "

Here I broke off. The last two words had seemed to spring a mine upon us. " Married *before* / "

With a gasp I glanced from one of the young men standing there to the other. I spoke to the actor.

I asked, feeling extraordinarily concerned about his answer, " Was she – was Miss Vera Vayne married to you, then, *first?* "

With a return of that " Lyceum" manner, he retorted, "Married, to me? Aye; seven long years ago!"

"Oh," I said. *"Then,"* I said, as it gradually dawned upon me, " then she must be *still* married to you?"

Mr. Arthur Harrison folded his arms again, looked down at me, and nodded until his hair shook.

" Just so," he boomed. " Even so! "

I turned from the *tableau* that he was making to the quiet figure of the other of Miss Vera Vayne's husbands.

" If – if he's married to her, you're *not,* I suppose,"I heard myself saying to Captain Meredith, almost as if I were telling him the astounding news. "Of course, you *can't* be, you see! Why – why, you never even were!"

He said, in the most expressionless voice that I have ever heard even from him, " You haven't quite finished that letter, have you ? "

" No " I murmured. I turned to the odorous

sheaf again. It went on

" You may think it funny, but I didn't even think to tell you about my first marriage, it was so long ago, and you know we girls in the Profession are so accustomed to keep on with our maiden names I fair forgot you didn't know I was only Miss on the stage! what with me and Mr. Harrison having quarrelled and seperated, and what with me having heard from Alf his own married brother that he was dead, and believing it. Which I did do, George, and bar larks! I kept that letter from Alf for ages, saying that poor Arthur was out of the way of me teasing him any longer having always had shocking colds in the Autumn as I knew myself, and another letter Alf wrote back saying that Arthur was burried in California after a thick night at the good old Bohemian where he'd gone with the Number Fourteen Company and sending me a picture post-card of no end of mountains with a cross marked for which was his grave.

" It was only when we met, Mr. Harrison and me, in the Lost Property Office in Lime Street Station whichI'd gone back to from the steamer to get my umbrella with the parrot's head that your pal Major Thornton gave me for a wedding-present that you could have knocked me down with a feather!

" And how could I help making it up with him, well it seemed only yesterday that we'd parted and any one would have done the same in my shoes, say what you like, and him the only man that ever really played up to my temperament. It was him that persuaded me not to go over to New York in that boat after all. For what's the use of drawing a salary like a cabinet minister in the movies when you are going to be torpedoed by those Huns as likely as not before you get to Long Island or touch a penny of it? Well George, so I agreed to join forces with him again, seeing that I'm his wife when all's said, and I dare say I can help him with the company he's going to get together next month, that is if this Military Service Act doesn't put a stop to everybody that wants to do a bit of artistic work. Arthur is a wonder for that. I always did get on with him, in spite of him being such a brainy one, until that bust- up when we behaved like kids.

" And as you know, me and you, George, are almost totull strangers. You can't say it wasn't rash, me accepting you the way I did."

Again I stopped in my reading to flash a glance of involuntary comparison at the two young men of whom the Vision wrote. The face of one of them was a blankcovering to whatever he felt at the moment. The other (" the brainy one") was alert, sympathetic, mobile, going from one extreme of expression to the other. (" Making faces," children call it.) For the soldier is trained to conceal all feeling upon occasion. This helps him to do half the world's work to an accompaniment of pretence that he is doing next to nothing.

The actor is trained to express – as much as he can. Thus, doing next to nothing, he is credited, I suppose, with world's work!

The soldier, under gaiety and trivial talk, covers who knows what struggles ?

But under thunderous solemnities the actor covers – emotions that I can't help calling trivial. " What's Hecuba to him? "

And to think that the woman who wrote this letter had cared nothing for the sort of young Briton who refers to his element, war's gravest perils, as " things getting lively " or " unhealthy." She had *preferred* the other, the mummer who talked of " temperaments "!

People with the one taste will never, I suppose, understand people with the other. I don't *want* to!

I went on with the letter.

" Still I must say George that it was a fair knockout for me a week or so later when I came across that bit in the paper about your Regiment and about Captain G. R. Meredith, reported killed, was alive and well. Talk about *laugh!* "

Dazed, I could imagine the Vision's hyena-like screech at this juncture.

" Talk about *laugh!!* Here am I, I thought, with two husbands and me thinking I hadn't got one. I must be a mascot, enough to bring luck to any young man. They simply can't bear to die, once they've seen my fair young face. Then I thought well, here's this poor kiddie that I sent off down to Wales, playing understudy for me as the war-widow. There she is let in for a different scene than what she ever rehearsed for – "

I looked up at Captain Meredith, and there was triumph in my face, I know. He just nodded. I read on.

" – ever rehearsed for. I hadn't the face to come myself, I sent Arthur tearing down to Llandedwydd to explain for me. Talk about seeing life! Then when he found that the whole family including young Mrs. G. had just bunked over to gay Paree to fall on your neck, I thought the sooner he came along too and put you wise about what had happened and no harm done, the better.

" Well now George hoping that you are in the best of health and spirits I will draw to a close, hoping that you will not bear any grudge. In a few years time, most likely, you would have realised that this wouldhave been a case of ' marry at Hastings and repent at St. Leonards ' as it says in that saucy sketch. " So with all that's good, old dear, " Hoping to remain,

" Yours affectionately,

"Viv.

" P. S. – ' For old times sake, let us forget and forgive,' and look here, George, if "

Here it breaks off. " It must go on to another page, I think," I heard myself saying in a small, dazed voice. And I held out my hand for the last page.

It Whs H long letter; a sheaf of thick mauve sheets that Captain Meredith had to sort into order CHAPTER XXVIII

LOSS AND GAIN

BUT that last page wasn't handed to me. Hurriedly, Captain Meredith muttered something about there being " nothing particular " in that.

He took the rest of the letter and tucked it away inside his coat. And then – then came something that surprised me; for he turned upon Mr. Arthur Harrison, and in his face and voice as he spoke there was some expression at last.

" Now, sir! " he rapped out, " I hope you see what a dashed muddle you and your wife might have been making of things? I hope you see the very unpleasant position that this young lady," with a swift, dark glance upon me, " might have found herself in ? "

" Might " was good! " *Might* " was very good! Considering the complicated awkwardnesses for which I've been let in, and his share in keeping me fettered by them! Yet here he was saying quite violent things to Miss Vera Vayne's husband about the " impossible inconvenience " and " things taken for granted " from which Miss Whitelands had suffered. . . .

I sat there wondering at him while he turned and rent the bewildered-looking actor, all on my behalf. Ialso wondered at Captain Meredith's tone. It was so *very* angry. Too angry. So angry, in fact, that *it didn't ring quite true!*

He wound up – " To say nothing of my own people! Supposing your wife had picked out a fellow-passenger who would actually have*fallen in* with that preposterous plan of hers! Which, naturally, Miss Whitelands never *did!* "

Here the other young man's jaw dropped. " Never – did? " He looked towards me as much as to say " Then how is that she's sitting here at the Ritz with all of you?"

" When Miss Whitelands went on to my mother's house," pursued Captain Meredith, " she went for the express purpose of explaining to them the whole idiotic thing as it happened."

" D – did she " stammered Mr. Arthur Harrison,

still looking at me. " She told them? "

" Yes, *indeed I* did," I began with fervour.

" Certainly," said Captain Meredith, emphatically.

I wondered if the husband of that other girl would say " And did they believe her? "

But he hadn't time. Quickly, and very firmly, Captain Meredith explained that his father and mother had thereupon begged Miss Whitelands to stay on with them as their adopted daughter – " as you see, she *has,"* he concluded. Adding, " Her name hasn't been altered; it's down on the hotel register as Whitelands. And I'd like you – if you don't mind – to tell all this to your wife, Mr. Harrison." Then, before the young actorcould speak again, " I am very angry with *her."* Indeed, his voice shook. " Very angry."

Here Mr. Arthur Harrison dropped the theatrical manner that he seems to put on and off like a wrap, for which the weather is not quite right. He thrust his hands in his pockets, he flushed, and, presently, he blurted out in that other voice, the Cockney and more human one, " Come, Captain, I don't think you've any real right to be that. My girl was square with you. She thought I was dead all right. We'd parted by mutual consent, and, as for me " – he turned to me with his confidence – " as for me, I hadn't stopped regretting it for a day."

He spoke, warmly.

" Yes! She thought I was dead. Hadn't I changed my name to Fitzroy on purpose so as to give the girl a chance, thinking" – he reddened, more deeply – " thinking she was fed with me and that I'd better disappear? Not *her* fault for thinking she was free to marry again. Galsworthy would do justice to that subject, ha! And as for this other business " – again turning to me – " about the young lady "

" She – Miss Vayne – behaved unpardonably!" snapped Captain Meredith.

Quite hotly, the actor took this up," She did nothing of the kind, if you'll ex-cuse me!"

I began to feel rather nervous.

" It's *my wife* you're speaking about," added Mr. Arthur Harrison, rebukefully. " And I can't have it, see? If I'd been speaking about *your* wife, Captain,*you* wouldn't have it. You shouldn't have said that."

Oh, dear! Would this end in a violent quarrel between the two young men? Here, in this high and ornate anteroom, would they fly at each other's throats? But I need not have been afraid.

Captain Meredith answered in a voice that was changed and pleasant. " No, I oughtn't to have said it. I'm sorry."

Mollified at once, Mr. Arthur Harrison said " Oh, I'm sure that's very handsome of you. By Gad, sir, I – I wish Bernard Shaw had heard you say that. I sometimes think he is scarcely fair to the military profession, eh ? Very generous of you. I dare say you only passed that other remark because you're naturally feeling a bit – overwhelmed "

" Rather so," from Captain Meredith. He turned aside and began doing something jerky to a tassel of one of the heavy curtains.

" I understand – don't I know how I should feel in your place," said the young actor, with real feeling this time. It's obvious how he cares for that flamboyant, heart-sprinkled wife of his. " I know. Can't be helped, but there it is." This he said, quite simply. " After all – my gain's your loss, Captain."

" Quite," agreed Captain Meredith, hurriedly, " quite."

A pause.

I didn't know what I could say. . . .-

Then –

" Cue, and exit!" remarked Mr. Arthur Harrison, airily. He picked up the broad-leafed hat from the console-table. " That's all, I think. Except' all's well that ends well,' as the Bard has it. And, as my Vivie says at the end of her letter "

" Yes, yes; I'll write to her," broke in Captain Meredith, still more hurriedly. " This is the address, is it? Ill write."

" And so will I," I put in. " Oh, and I've some things to send her " – I had just remembered those forced lend- ings the bag, the clothes – " I'll send them as soon as we – I – get back to England."

And then I have a bewildered impression of leave- taking; a gleam of teeth, an *empresse* bow from the actor – some muttered regret from Captain Meredith about " war-time – not allowed even to ask him to have a vermouth " – more smiles, and, finally, before Captain Meredith saw our friend into the hall, a ceremonious: " Convey my salutations, please, to Sir Richard and Lady Meredith and tell them how extremely sorry I am to have missed them "

" Oh, thanks, awfully, I will tell them as soon as they come in to tea "

This, with the last two words, very distinct, floated back to me in Captain Meredith's voice from the hall. So he was allowing Mr. Arthur Harrison to go off under the impression that Lady Meredith and Sir Richard were still in Paris – still here!

Just as I was thinking this Captain Meredith came in again from the hall. And for the next five minutesthat young man, whom I've *always* – save once – seen so self-possessed, so well-balanced, went completely mad!

I can't express it any other way.

For he came in, *dancing.*

He did, really!

Dancing a two-step – in spite of the little jerk of his limp – down the length of the anteroom, and singing the tune as he danced.

" *When the Angelus is ringing –*

Tum-ty – tum-ty – tum-ty – turn –

Turn, turn, turn "

He pulled up opposite to me where I'd risen from my chair in bewilderment, and for a moment I thought he was going to drag me, as his partner, into that mad prance. He was holding out both hands to me!

In a reckless, exultant voice he demanded: " Won't you shake hands with me? Please! *Somebody's* got to! " So, rather uncertainly, I put out one hand. He took it in both of his, clutched it tight, drew a long breath, and let my hand go again.

" That's better! " he exclaimed. " I say. I *say,* Miss Whitelands "

" Yes ? " I hesitated, feeling glad that we had the room to ourselves. Any one coming in would have thought it a most extraordinary scene; the young British officer looking and talking as excitedly as if he had just come from a pre-war lunch – the English girl, staring at him as if she were a temperance lecturer! I laughed a little awkwardly, as I said "What is it?"

" It's – *reprieve!* " he declared, unexpectedly. " By Jove, *yes!* " And then he went off into uncontrollable fits of laughter. How like his father's hearty, enjoying laugh! ... I watched him, shaking with mirth beside that mirror where he had stood so rock-like during that interview with Miss Vera's husband. Still laughing, the young soldier caught at one of the dark-red curtains; he buried his face, his black head in it. At last, gasping and shaking himself, he emerged; pulled himself together.

" I say, you must think I've gone off my head!" he apologised. " So I had, a little. Rather rotten of me " He tugged his belt straight, then gave another short, delighted laugh and broke out, joyously, once more:

" Did you hear me strafing that priceless – that Mr. Harrison, as solemn as a judge?" he chuckled. " Worse than having to keep grave in church, when you

feel you'll break loose in a minute Never mind.

I'll be sane again directly. . . . Do you mind shaking hands with me again, Miss Whitelands? It might steady me. Thanks. Now I really am composed. Look!"

I looked at him and it seemed to me that I had never seen his face before. So altered! So much younger! So gay! It seemed as if some burden had dropped from those shoulders of his. And I began to guess now how heavy that burden had been. That marriage in haste, of a boy whose vanity and heart were hurt and sore; that absurd hot-headed marriage pique! Why, Ireally believe he had repented letting himself in for it even before he had left the bride at the registry-office door! It had been no marriage! no, but there had been the prospect of chains of steel. These had clanked to the ground with the hearing of this afternoon's news. He was free – and the knowledge had fairly turned his head. I could see that, and I could guess how much more there was behind his bubbling-over gaiety of relief.

A reprieve? Ah! Hadn't I said to myself that this young man couldn't possibly ever have cared for that girl?

I *knew* it!

Now, more soberly, but still with those black diamonds of twinkles sparkling in his eyes, Captain Meredith said " Look here. You and I have got something to settle now, at once."

" No; not at once. Wait."

For there had come to me even as I stood there the first clear thought I had had since I had read that epoch-making letter.

Phillipa must be told the whole truth! Phillipa, who adored him! must be told that George was not married after all.

I found myself almost running to the door. " There's something I have got to see about," I said, and in spite of his quick, limping stride after me, in spite of his persisted " This is really something I want to say very much," I shook my head.

" I will hear it afterwards," I said agitatedly. " You don't know how important this other is! "

I shook my head again in his face, blank and eager. " I will see you again about it later," I promised him. Anything to get rid of him for the moment! " But you go now. I want to go and telephone to some one."

I saw the impatience give way to anxiety, consternation, on Captain Meredith's face. Then came again the parade-ground expressionlessness that covers . . . goodness knows what.

" I will call for you, then," he said. " How soon may I come? Will you have lunch with me, presently? "

" No, no! I sha'n't be finished by then. I mean – no, thank you.

" Please meet me later – this evening."

He spoke, hurriedly, " Can't you meet me before then? Please. I will come at three, shall I?"

" No; I sha'n't be done by then. Five o'clock, perhaps," I said.

" Four," he urged. " I shall be here at four. I shall be waiting for you at four."

" I can't promise," I said, and I ran to the telephone.

It was luck that I managed to get the Passy number at once. It was luck that Phillipa herself should come to the telephone, answering my faltering, breathless request with her clear, self-possessed " Yes. This is Miss Tracey speaking now. Who is it? "

Then, more quickly, came her " Who is it ? Mrs. George Meredith? "

"No – no That is It's me – Rose! I

want to see you, Phillipa, at once," I called. " I said I would as soon as there was something to tell you. Well – can you hear? There IS. Tell me where we can meet."

A few more breathless seconds of arrangement, and than I hung up the receiver and flew to get on my outdoor things.

Phillipa was too busy, she had said, to give me more than half an hour. Her cousin Harry Tracey had just got leave. . . . They were arranging a " tamasha " of some sort for that evening. . . . She had countless commissions to do. . . . She would take a cab for her shoppings, and I could drive about with her.

Her cab called for me. I got in, breathless with agitation, with emotions that I could not classify, and we drove – we drove

Goodness knows where. . . . Up and down some of the boulevards, I suppose. Trees and shops slid past us, unnoticed by me as I talked, and Phillipa said, every now and then, to the man, " Go back. . . . Drive as far as the Arc de Triomphe and back again. . . . And again, please. ..."

Goodness knows what happened to her commissions for that evening's party!

For I think the first two sentences that I uttered, clutching her slender hand as it lay beside her on the seat of the cab, were quite enough to drive out of either of our heads any thought beyond the matter in hand.

"It's all right. He's free! George is free! ..."

Phillipa's voice broke in, clear and cool as a jet of spring water.

" Rose, don't be so excited. Please don't talk so fast. I can't understand you. I didn't understand what you said."

" You can understand this at least," I told her, trembling with eagerness to make her see at once: " George isn't married!"

Here I surprised a suspicion in her eyes, the only thing that could have calmed me. " I am perfectly well. I am not mad! " I said, more quietly. " Don't think I am out of my mind, as Sir Richard and Lady Meredith always did. Presently, George will tell you himself that what I say is perfectly true. He isn't married – he's free! "

" Can you mean," asked Phillipa in a slow, stunned voice, " that you are going to try to divorce him ? "

"Divorce him?" I said, impatiently now. "How can one divorce a person, Phillipa, if one isn't married to him?"

And it was then that the other girl turned and began to shower questions upon me as she had showered them yesterday in the bedroom.

Only then – then I had not been able to answer them. But now, I could look her straight in the face, and give back, for everything she said, the undefended truth.

" What – why – was George hoaxing us all this time? "

"No!"

" What has he been doing then ? Do his people know "

"Not yet!"

" Why – why did he give out that he was married? "

" Because he thought he was. He did go to that registry office. But he didn't know that his wife had got one husband already! "

" One – husband – already," repeated Phillips, slowly. Then, sharply, " You were married all the time ? You – to another man ? "

" No, no " I began. But I got no further. She

hadn't heard. For suddenly a strange light seemed to break over Phillipa's face. And catching me by the arm as we sat, she cried, not as a question but as a challenge, " You weren't, ever! *You weren't married!* And you said you'd met him in Paris first . . . Rose ... I think I see it. ... Tell me, quickly. . . . No! I've guessed. Of course. I understand. You aren't the girl George did marry, at all. Not the girl he went to the registry office with, I mean. You aren't the film-actress ? You're not Vera Vayne? . . . You're . . . some one who's got nothing to do with them all? *Isn't that it?* "

I nodded, hard, to every question. Relief and surprise seemed to flow in upon me. " That's it, that's it!" (Oh, what a comfort!) "Phillipa! You're the only person who's ever guessed by themselves, like this "

" Because people don't use their eyes. They go by circumstantial evidence or whatever they call it; theydon't trouble to look at people for themselves. Oh, didn't I know? Didn't I see? " cried Phillipa, breathlessly. " Didn't I see you were just – a child? Couldn't I realise that you weren't the sort of girl to whom any of that applied that I had heard about George's wife! *You* had never been on the stage, bless them! I knew that! He had never met *you* at a night club for the first time, as Major Thornton told me. Oh! I have been there to supper with a party, once – just to see," declared Phillipa, hurriedly, with a funny little reminiscent laugh. " I saw what they were like – those girls! All screech and decolletage. *That* wasn't you. I knew it – I've been puzzling over it ever since I saw you. And now tell me from the very beginning."

And with fresh surprise, I began.

I, sitting there beside her, in the open cab began telling her the story as I had told it first to Nurse Phyllis; then to Lady Meredith and Sir Richard; then to Reggie Penmore at the hospital. And, finally, to George himself. . . . The story of Miss Rose Whitelands " as " Miss Vera Vayne.

The surprise was that it was so much easier to tell Phillipa than it had been to tell any of those other people.

She didn't contradict me. She didn't interrupt me: " Why didn't you so-and-so ? But look here! Couldn't , jou have this-that-and-the-other? " She saw. With every little nod of her dark head in the black silk Napoleon hat, this other girl made me feel that she understood. She followed me: her quick mind received pictures from what I was saying of what had actually been. I felt that even as I talked, she was reconstructing for herself that scene in the railway-carriage – those scenes at the Bryn. And, later, that harassing interview with George himself in my room at the Ritz.

She said, with utter sympathy, " I wonder you weren't worn to a shadow by all this, you poor little thing! "

" They wouldn't believe me. None of them believe " I enlarged. " *You* believe me at once."

" Of course I do," said Phillipa, quietly. " If you had set out to invent a story like that you'd have taken care to make it sound so much more what people call ' probable.' Turn once again, please " – this to the *cocker. " As* for me, you know, Rose, I never can make out why (in a world where most things are so – so impossibly arranged) people consider some things more extraordinary than others. . . . Even George, you say, didn't believe for ages that you were perfectly genuine "

And she turned upon me again with questions about George and everything that he had said and done since the Thursday evening when he had arrived to find his family entertaining the utter stranger that I had been to him.

" Oh! if I could have seen George's face then," exclaimed Phillipa with an odd little laugh. " Turned out to shop, and dine, and do theatres, and stroll about the wilds of Saint-Cloud with a girl he'd never even taken in to dinner in his life. . . . What did he call you? 'Rose'?"

" Yes, once or twice, when his people were there," I told her.

" What a reversal of the usual plan! ' Miss White- lands ' when they weren't there, I suppose ? "

" Yes – I think so," I said. " At least, I think he hasn't said anything but ' you' to me since the first part of the time."

" Oh," said Phillipa, and smiled again, oddly. " And you say he was not such friends with you the last part of the time? He seemed bored with the whole thing? – I don't believe that," she said, musingly.

" He did," I maintained. " He simply wanted – and I don't wonder at it! – to get me packed off as soon as he could. He's been avoiding me ever since the Merediths left. He truly has. Any one could have seen it."

" Possibly," said Phillipa, with a dryness that I couldn't fathom. And then to my relief she dropped the subject and mooted another.

" This other girl of George's. The first – the real one. The one he married. You saw her. Tell me some more about her. . . . She was, I suppose, awful ? "

I hesitated. I felt a queer reluctance to say so of Miss Vera Vayne. . . . Perhaps I had a mental glimpse of her as Mr. Arthur Harrison had seen his wife. I felt that she was not really so bad after all ... quite likable, in her way.

" Well," I said, slowly, " of course she *did* wear purple mice "

" Purple *mice? "* put in the startled voice of Phillipa. "Mice?"

" Embroidered," I explained, " all up the insteps of her stockings. But – but she was *kind, I* think "

i

; Oh! She'd ' a heart of gold,' I'm sure: it always seems to go with the type," Phillipa said. " Voice – impossible, I suppose?"

"Quite."

"And face?"

" I – I can't describe her," I protested. Then, impulsively, " If I could only show you what she was like – if *only* you could have seen her too ! "

Never before, I think, has any spoken wish of mine been so promptly granted.

For it was at this moment that the arm of coincidence – long and slim, and deft as Phillipa's own (I imagine) – was once more stretched out to put a finger into this story of mine – of ours.

Oh! it was almost too good to be true that I should have been able, that same afternoon, to show Phillipa Tracey, so exactly and so adequately, just what George's so-called wife had been like!

We had got out of the cab then, I think, for Phillipa had said " What am I to do? It's so late. They were expecting me home for lunch, with all the thing's, and it's three now! I shall have to take a taxi." We were standing on the pavement, looking up and down the street in vain for a taxi, *libre,* when suddenly I caught sight behind me of " IT." The joyous – the unique opportunity!

I scarcely saw the huge gilt letters " Cinema " above. It was the poster that took my eyes! " The PrincessWho Wanted To Know! " with a highly-coloured representation of a vision – *the* Vision in red velvet, with two thick plaits of hair hanging down over a sumptuous bosom. A stage crown and a smile like the open keyboard of a piano – a communicative smile I knew! Surely, I could not be mistaken?

Again I clutched Phillipa's arm.

" There she is! There she is! " I cried.

My friend looked at me as if I had taken leave of my senses.

"Who – what?"

" George's wife! " I told her. " The girl who isn't George's wife! I know it's her. It's her celebrated part. . . . You must see her! "

Phillipa's dark, quick eyes were scanning everything that went by us on the boulevard. She thought, I suppose, that I meant somebody who was merely like Miss "Vera Vayne. But before she could say again " Which one? " I had dragged her inside that picture palace with its *Gaumont* and *Pathe* advertisements. I had paid for two seats with one of the hundred-franc notes that Captain Meredith had handed to me this morning.

The two of us were wedged together in the dark, stuffy, red-plush-seated cavern. Very good seats too. We could not have had a more excellent view of that which presently flashed before our eyes on the screen.

It came almost at once.

We only had to sit out, I think, the end of some drama concerning Max and the Linaburgher cheese. Then – then it came!

First the title, " *La Princesse qui voulait tout savoir,"* with beneath it, in large capital letters, " LA PRINCESSE -META – Mile. Vera Vayne."

"Now! Now!" I said to Phillipa. " In these important and long films they have the heroine first, all by herself, to show you. It's coming now! Yes! Look, this is she! "

Yes, that was she – *thirty-five times life size!* The enormous face that grinned at us off the screen! The coiffure, of which each individual hair stood out thick as a trellis-wire! The mouth – that cavern set with the miles-stones into which had been magnified Mrs. Arthur Harrison's excellent teeth! The smile that made abysmal creases in her immense cheeks! The eyes, rolling like headlights upon Miss Vera Vayne's adoring public! There was her whole battery of charms, in apotheosis, looking as did the faces of the giant ladies to the aghast eyes of Gulliver!

Phillipa and I, feeling like insects, sat there and regarded the image until that moving map of light and shade had flickered, with a final Gargantuan grimace, off the screen.

We waited for nothing more – not even for the love- scene with " pore Arthur Harrison."

We hurried out. In a stifled voice Phillipa asked me: " My dear, my dear, was she like *that? "*

" All – all but the size," I managed to gasp out. For now reaction had come upon us both, as it came upon Captain Meredith after his interview with the Beauty-Queen's husband. Helplessly, we laughed as weThere she is! 'J'here she is!" 1 c-ried

got into the taxi that was to drop me at the Ritz again on the way to Passy.

" I must thank you, Rose," said Phillipa, with a sigh at last. "I enjoyed that! I don't know when I've laughed so much. I feel as if I must be what the Scots call ' fey ' "

" Oh, don't! Doesn't that mean when a person is gay and excited just before something frightful is going to happen to them? " I said, apprehensively. " It can't be that in your case, Phillipa. For everything is going to be quite all right now, isn't it? I mean, about – George? "

" Oh! All right for him; yes, I should think so," retorted Phillipa, lightly, tears of laughter still wet upon her lashes. " He's well out of his marriage with the Cinema Star! . . . Why *do* they, Rose ? The men of our class, with voices and ways like George's? They're *always* marrying them. Are they *all* sorry, afterwards ? Still, perhaps, he'll regret her yet! "

" *What?* "

" Ah, you never know what a man will regret, provided it's well out of his reach forever . . . will you get out here? Then you'll telephone to me, child, will you? about when you'll come and see me to-morrow. . . .. Good-bye!"

" Wait, wait " I stopped the driver. I stood

there with one hand on the door of the cab. " One thing, Phillipa, before you go. You *are* happy, aren't you? You are very happy because you – he'll be able to marry you now? "

She leaned out of the window towards me. She spoke, quite flippantly. " What *are* you talking nonsense about? "

"'Nonsense'? Why ! But "

" But it is, you know," Phillipa said, clearly. " Nothing is altered between George and me. I'm doing the best for all of us. The man I'm going to marry is the man who cares for me. Married or not, George isn't that. Couldn't be. I am just as little of George's sort of girl now as I was before. Less, my dear. Less."

Opening my eyes, I cried "What? After all this, you mean you won't have him? "

" He won't ask me," said Phillipa, sitting back in the cab with that curious little smile of hers. " You'll see."

And then she was off.

11

SECTION 11

CHAPTER XXIX

FATE AND THE PUPPETS

HE (Captain Meredith) was already waiting for me at the Ritz when I got back, although it was not quite ten minutes to four. Evidently he was anxious to get " over and done with " whatever it was he still wanted to talk to me about. I'd decided already what it must be. Something to do with his mother. Some arrangement about how she was to be told. I thought to myself, " And *Belle-mere* doesn't like Phillipa! Oh, but she must – she will! "

I noticed that all the laughter and high spirits had left her son again. He was grave; he was anxious. He came up to me at once and said, quietly, " Did you telephone? "

" What? " I said, a little bewildered. For, in the excitement of my last interview with Phillipa, I had quite forgotten how I had had to summon her.

" Oh, yes," I said. " I telephoned."

" You got Captain Penmore all right, then? " he said, in an odd, strained voice.

I looked at him, astonished,' as we stood there in the hall, that has been the *decor* for what seems an endless quantity of meetings and partings between us; of talks and arrangements for what is to be done next.

Well, I thought, here was the end of all of them r. t last.

" But I didn't go to telephone to Captain Penmore," I said. " Of course I ought to, I suppose – to let him know at once. I have meant to write to him for such a long time. ... It was Phillipa I rang up. I must tell you about that "

" No, no! Never mind telling me that now," said Captain Meredith, and his voice was suddenly eager again. " I made sure you had 'phoned up this fellow – this friend of yours, Penmore."

"No," I said, ruefully. "I'm afraid I forgot all about him!"

"What?" said Captain Meredith, quickly. "He isn't such a very great friend of yours, then ? "

" Great friend! Oh, no. I mean – Oh, yes. He is a very old friend," I said. " I am very fond of him, really."

Captain Meredith asked " Do you mind telling me what you mean by ' *really '? "*

I laughed a little, doubtfully. Reggie's face seemed very shadowy and out-of-date and indistinct beside all the extraordinary things that occupied the immediate foreground of my mind.

I said " Oh! I mean I do like him. He has always tried to be very kind."

Captain Meredith turned away for a moment, and as he did so I think I caught an extraordinary irrelevant remark. It sounded like " Poor chap! Then, here's his finish! " I couldn't think what he meant.

Then he turned to me again and just as I was going to say " But about Phillipa," he broke in, " Well, now about this thing I want to talk to you about. Can you come out with me at once! now ? "

"Out? Whereto?"

" To buy something," answered the young man, whose face had now cleared, almost unrecognisably. " I want to buy a wedding-present for – you know? " The line of even white teeth flashed right across his oval, pale face in a delighted grin as he said " A belated wedding- present for Mrs. Arthur Harrison! "

" Oh! " I said, lamely.

" Just to show there's no ill-will, by Jove! " he went on, taking out his cigarette case. I had been told that he keeps a reserve supply of notes there; and I believe he would gleefully have taken every penny he had in the world to squander in some thank-offering. It was so obviously a thank-offering that he was preparing to lay before the " Vision's " showy boots, in all gratitude to her because their path and his lay for the future far, far apart!

" What shall I get her? " he asked me like a school- hoy. " You must come and help me choose, you know. As a sort of wind up! "

Such an appropriate " wind up! " I, who had taken her place for so long, I, the " relief-chum," choosing some memento to mark the occasion that the place was no longer to fill. I wondered what gift he thought of buying. Jewelry, I suppose, something large and *glittery.* . . ...

" Yes, and then I can tell you that other thing as we go," he planned, cheerily. " Come along! "

When one goes out to buy wedding-presents one does not usually pick out for one's shopping-centre a gigantic square, towering monuments, and with sun-swept spaces with fountains that play freely to the wide heavens, and without any shops. Such as the Place de la Concorde.

For it was to that Place de la Concorde that Captain Meredith piloted me as soon as we came out once more into the breezy, gay afternoon.

After so much excitement I was now, rather unreasonably, depressed. I felt then as if some bleak, depressing draught had been let in upon me from somewhere. Everybody knows these moments of reaction after the crowded hours!

Certainly things had been happening at a terrific rate for the last six weeks of my life! They had been bound to come to an end some time. Well, this was it. A happier end than I had prophesied, seeing that two people (George and Phillipa) were going to be left very happy!

Anyhow, it was the beginning of the end. This was the last shopping that I was to do in Paris. This meant " Good-bye."

" *Adieu, charmant pays de France!* "

There have been plenty of other girls who, since the day of Mary Queen of Scots, have said that with a sigh. It was quite natural that I should be depressed.

Perhaps the place, too, helped? The Place de laConcorde. Wide open spaces, combined with huge buildings, are supposed sometimes to have this effect upon one.

They make one, I think, feel of no account. As we crossed the wide pavement leading away from the rue de Rivoli, I felt that the pair of us – the tall young soldier in khaki and the girl in the short, wide *militaire-blue* costume – were two quite unimportant scraps of humanity ! Puppets in the hands of fate, taking their way across the immense stage of life. You see, I was deep in the mood that every one of us has sometimes. The " nothing-matters " mood, dovetailing with the mood that prompts one to think, " And now nothing exciting will ever happen again."

Captain Meredith took a cigarette out of his case and lighted it as we walked along. He was taking us in the direction of the river.

For a moment he was silent. He was thinking again.

I glanced at his intent young profile as he walked along, lightly, in spite of his slight limp, beside me. Walked in step with me as he had done so often during these weeks that we had been together. No, no! Not weeks! It was only days. Quite a few days that we had gone about Paris together – the curiously assorted couple that we had been.

For, just think of us once again, and for the very last time in this capacity –

He – the husband of another girl!

I – the reluctant impostor, who had been forced into playing that other girl's part!

Here was the end of it all.

He smoked for a few yards more in silence. Then he flung aside the cigarette.

His quiet voice, that I seem always to have known, came to me above the clatter of taxis and the purr of motors.

" You told me before that you had no friends of your own in Paris, didn't you? No ladies."

I shook my head. " None at all, except the Trace "

" Leave them out of it," he said, quickly, " if you don't mind. We will also leave out that pal of yours, Captain Penmore."

" Oh, yes! Let's," I agreed. I felt a bright blush beginning in the centres of my cheeks and spreading outwards.

This, I suppose, is shame over the manner in which I have treated poor Reggie Penmore. I must write to him. I simply must.

Captain Meredith then surprised me, as we came to the river, by suggesting that we should go over and see the captured German cannon that the French have set up as war trophies, in the great square of Les Invalides.

" My father and mother went, you know, that time we were in the Luxemburg Gardens," he told me. " I don't want to miss it. Shall we go? "

"But what about buying that wedding-present?" I asked.

" Can't that wait until to-morrow morning? The guns first, I think, then I can talk as we go along." i

But as we went across the Pont Alexandre he seemed to have nothing more to say; and just as I was going to begin " Well, what is it ? " he began. It was then that I remembered something. He had not called me by my name for what seemed a long time.

Now he used it.

" Miss Whitelands "

"Yes?"

Then he began again, which was not his way.

" Miss Whitelands, I hope "

Then another stop.

I was obliged to say " What do you hope? "

His answer was rather odd! " I hope you won't think I don't know any better. I *do* know better, of course."

" Do tell me what you're going to say!" I half laughed, looking at him as he twirled that inseparable little leather-bound cane in his hand. " What do you ' know better '? "

" I know perfectly well what I ought to do," he returned. And now he seemed to have got his " start," for he went on, quite briskly, " If this were peace-time still, I could do it. The correct thing. The conventional thing, don't you know." He broke off for a second to whistle below his breath a bar of that swinging tune

" *When the Angelus is ring – ing "* as we walked along.

Then again he took up the brisk, matter-of-fact tone.

" After having wired to my people when to expect you at the Bryn "

Oh, so he imagined I would go to the Bryn again? – Ah, to explain the situation in person to his mother, I supposed.

" – I should find out for you, at once, one of those places that they have here in Paris, I believe," he went on. " Homes for Stranded British Ladies Abroad, or something of that sort. Some bleak billet that's all Hymnal Companions and cups of Lipton's tea! I should hand you over to the Blameless Lady Superintendent in charge of the show, about ten minutes from now."

" Thank you, Captain Meredith," I said, rather defiantly. " You seem quite sure that I should *go?"*

Of this remark the young man took no notice. He went on: " You'd stay like a good little nun in this abode of sanctity until you had to catch your boat- train. I shouldn't see you at all. I shouldn't come on to England until a boat or so later than yours. Then I'd go home. But not to the Bryn."

" Not? " I said. I believe we had crossed the bridge by this time, but I was too surprised at that moment to see where we were walking. " Why not to the Bryn? "

" Most incorrect," he retorted. I looked up at him, and caught another flash of those black diamonds in the eyes beneath the peak of his soft cap. He spokegravely, but with the effect of another of those bursts of wild gaiety behind the gravity. He said, irrelevantly, " When people are busy doing the Correct Thing, they seem to lay the most enormous stress upon *roofs* and *doors*. It's always ' Not under my roof ' or ' I shall not darken his doors.' You must have noticed it, Miss Whitelands, in books ? "

" I don't know what you're talking about; do get on with what you were going to say," I urged. But I saw that this he would do or not just as he chose. His high spirits were rising again. I thought of what I'd heard Lady Meredith say to her husband: " You utter schoolboy!"

Her son went on, " Well, I should stay with my aunt on the other side of the valley, so as not to be ' under the same roof' with you. But the morning after my arrival I'd borrow her hair trunk of a cob and ride over to see you. I suppose you'd come to me in the hall – my people seem to live and do everything in that hall. Dare say you've noticed. So I'd ask you if you'd come into that little snuggery of Mam's, on the left. You know her little room? "

" Oh, yes," I said. I smiled, a little sadly, as I remembered that it was in there that Lady Meredith had asked me to stay on as her adopted daughter.

" When I got you in there," said her son, " the first thing I should say would be "

His hand went to his breast-pocket.

" The first thing I should say would be ' Do you mind reading *that'? "*

And pausing in his walk, he handed to me the scented mauve envelope that had brought such a bombshell of news into the Ritz that afternoon.

Puzzled, I asked " Do you want me to read it now? Again? "

" Yes, please."

" But – I've seen it "

" You didn't see one sheet – the last – that I kept back this morning," quietly. "Don't you want to?"

By this time I was simply bursting to, of course. So I said, with some reserve, " No."

" Yes, you do," he laughed, mischievously, as he twirled the little cane. " You know you do. Anyhow, I *want* you to. So please do."

" Most incorrect! " I rebuked him. " You talked just now about the Correct Thing. Well, I was brought up to believe it was bad manners to read a letter when one was walking about the streets! "

" Right-o! We'll wait till we get to the Invalides." Then, cheerfully, he took out the last page and held it in his hand, putting the rest of Vera Vayne's letter back in his pocket. " We can sit down there, and let you read it at your leisure."

I was tingling with suspense when we reached the great square of the Invalides. Under the grey pointed roof at the further end of it the statue of Napoleon looked down upon an odd scene, an odd crowd. The square is bordered by cloisters decorated by frescoes after Raphael. By the immense doors of those cloisters there are trophies of cannon set up on end; the cannon of seventeen hundred and eighty-five, with ornate mouldings, with ornaments of dolphins and laurel wreaths and stars and suns. In sharp, arresting contrast to these ceremonious and decorative weapons of a by-gone age was the park of German guns captured in battles of nineteen fifteen.

These were set up at the further end of the Square. Jack Johnsons, machine guns, pip-squeaks, painted field-grey and of a deadly utilitarianness, there was no moulding of laurel leaves upon these things, just as there is no ornament of chivalry or honour about war as waged by their makers. Grimy, shattered, coated with mud and clay and rust, these guns had still stood for the perils of war. They had roared with the voice of death as surely as had those nobler cannon of two centuries ago, but they were as securely out of action now.

Only a slender rope divided them from the crowds that came to stare at them. I watched that crowd of tourists. Frenchwomen, children, with a generous sprinkling of wounded soldiers, French and Belgians, passing slowly by and gazing at the sinister, silenced horrors that had mown down so many comrades, so many friends of their own. I saw one blue-coated soldier, whose eyes were bandaged and who was led by a comrade in khaki, put out his hand, feel for the muzzle of one of the guns. Then the blinded fighter thrust his fist down its empty throat. I heard him say, with a short, savage laugh, " Useless, now! A useless mouth!"

I turned to Captain Meredith to see if he had heard it. Curiously enough, he was taking very little notice of what was going on all around us. He was smiling at me.

" Here's this," he said, quietly, as he held out that last sheet of the letter that he wanted me to read.

Sitting on a wooden bench that was set at the bottom of the cloisters on the right, with the moving crowds below me, and with Captain Meredith standing just above me and watching me, I read what has often been described as the most important part of a woman's letter – the postscript.

This particular postscript was certainly the most astonishing part of all Miss Vera Vayne's long, curly screed to the man who had imagined himself, all this time, to be her husband:

– " and if you take my advice, George, you'll just up and marry that pretty kid that I put up to pass herself off as your widow. Being in my profession does give you an eye for who would be good in what part, and I tell you she's just born, what I can see of it, to play Mrs. George Meredith. She isn't engaged, because I asked her in the train, not without she has gone and met somebody since I shoved her out on to the Camrys platform. And look at the easy way out of it, and you that were determined to *get* married as you as good as told me! Well! Here you are. Advice is cheap, I know, but I've a presentiment that if you takethis you'll not be sorry. It's the best thing you can do.

" From

" Yours,

" Vrv."

I sat staring at the perfumed mauve paper with its violet writing that showed every capital letter looping the loop. I was too surprised Not that

" Viv " should have written what she had. No, that was just like her. But that he should have given it to me to read!

Well, I suppose I ought to have got accustomed to that dazed feeling by now. But I haven't Perhaps it takes an even longer apprenticeship before one is hardened to these shocks! I could think of nothing to say.

Why had he shown it to me? It was not like *him!*

Raising my eyes, I saw that the late afternoon skies were blushing from primrose to apricot. Beneath them there was the blur of the moving patchwork crowds, the parked bristling guns, the tall building at the end, dominated by the Napoleon statue. Then nearer to me, against this blurred background, I saw the clear, pale oval of the young British officer's face. He put one booted foot up upon the end of the bench, leaned an elbow upon his knee, and in that attitude looked earnestly down upon me.

"Well?" he said.

"Well " I faltered. Then, pulling myself togethcr, for it was no use making an absurd situation absurdcr still by seeming to be embarrassed by it, I laughed a little and said " What perfectly ridiculous things she always does say, doesn't she ? "

" No, not always," said Captain Meredith, seriously. " Not there." He nodded at the sheet in my hand. " Everything she wrote there is just plain horse sense. It *is* the best thing I can do."

" Wh – what is? " I gasped.

" Taking her advice," he said, steadily. " Look here, do you think you could stick it? "

I was now utterly at sea again.

" Stick ? " I repeated. " Stick *what? "*

" Me," said Captain Meredith, very softly and simply. " *Will* you marry me? "

There was quite a long pause before I even gasped again. It was a proposal, then? From him – to me?

12

SECTION 12

CHAPTER XXX

NOW, I've read and heard of lots of different ways of taking them. I had experienced one way myself; the uncomfortable " *this-is-too-sudden- and-you-must-give-me-time-to-think-it-over"* answer that I had bestowed upon poor Reggie; the answer that had better be " No " at once – it's seldom a success if it's badgered into " Yes! "

But I don't think I've ever dreamt of a proposal of marriage being received in quite the way with which I turned upon Captain Meredith in the cloisters of Les Invalides.

For as soon as I'd made quite sure of what he'd said, and that he was actually serious in saying it, I turned upon him as violently as I have seen Lady Meredith's Blue Persian kitten turn upon his own bull-terrier Straf.

" You want me to marry you ? " I said, glaring at him and feeling hot waves of anger surge up all inside my chest. " You think I'm *that* sort of girl? "

" Sort of girl ? " he said, in a startled voice, looking at me. It was his turn to repeat things now. "What sort of girl?"

" Why! the sort that you could ask to marry you after you'd known her three days "

" Well, but look here ! They haven't been three *ordinary days* "

I took no notice. " And just because it was ' *the easy way out of it* ' as your wife – I mean as Mrs. Arthur Harrison *says* in that letter of hers! " I cast an incendiary glance at it in his hand. " You married her at a minute's notice, I understand, just because another girl turned you down "

Here the thought of " another girl " filled me with fresh spirit. Phillipa cared for him. He could do as he liked with the infatuated Phillipa. But I would tell him, first, exactly the sort of young man he appeared to me.

" You – you're heartless with women! You – you don't mind how you hurt their feelings. You have been an outrageous flirt, always. Princesses wouldn't smile

at you like that, if you hadn't been " All this

sounded rather beside the mark, once it was uttered; but what I *meant* was so lucid, so sensible. " And to me you've always been as horrid as you could "

All this time, he, gazing earnestly upon me, was trying to break into my talk. I waved his interruptions aside. I hastened on.

" The first evening you told me I was an adventuress! – Yes, I know you didn't *say* so. Men think everything is all right as long as they ' never say ' some actual word. As if words matter!" I stormed on. " You treated me as an impostor "

" Yes, but afterwards "

" Afterwards you insisted upon my *being* the imposter! For three whole days I had to *allow your* people to think that my memory had come back, and that I knew I was ' Mrs. George.' Oh! It's been too terrible, all this time! "

" Hasn't it! " he agreed, with feeling; he!

" You don't know," I snapped. " You can't."

"Oh? You think I was having an easy time then, do you?" he took up, quite violently. He laughed, curtly. Then he said " It was a hundred million times more rotten for me than it could ever have been for you, little lady. By Jove, yes! "

" You don't know," I persisted. " You didn't even say ' thank you' to me for all I'd done for you. As

soon as your people went But never mind that

now. And now, when the whole complication has come to an end at last, you put the last straw to it. You actually ask me to be Mrs. George for *good,"* I wound up, with another boiling wave of anger. " Not only that, but you think I will!"

" No! " he said. Putting down his foot from the edge of my bench, he stood straight, looking away across the glowing sky: " I hadn't the cheek to *think* you *rctiltl.* But I *hope* you *may."*

" Oh!" I cried in a frenzy of irritation at this. " The way men seem to think things don't mean the same thing when they do! It's maddening." I twisted round more towards him on the bench. " You thought I would," I repeated, hotly, " or hoped I might (it's the same thing!) just because you knew I was out of work when your wife – I mean the Vision – I mean Mrs. Harrison met me. You knew I had to take up girl-clerking in the city, or nurscry-governessing at the Sutcliffe- Smythes'. And you thought I'd think that this was easier! You thought I'd take up this! Don't look so surprised at me, Captain Meredith," I wound up, with an angry tap of my foot on the pavement.

" Surely you see why I'm furious ? Wouldn't any girl be right in looking upon a proposal of that sort as an *insult?* "

I expected he, too, would flare up into temper at this. I paused a second awaiting the outburst. The answer came in Captain Meredith's readiest, softest tone. v

" Yes. Oh, yes. Rather so. She would."

Now is anything on earth so utterly disconcerting as finding oneself whole-heartedly agreed with just when one has made ready for an indignant denial. Isn't it the most effectual method of spiking an enemy's guns, rendering them silent as these others, these German guns in the square below us?

So, feeling suddenly foolish, I returned, in the wan tone of anti-climax, " Ver – very well, then! Wh – what have you got to say? "

" Plenty, if I can only get it in. I am going to sit down by you, if I may."

And he sat down beside me on the bench, planting his brown-booted feet firmly in front of him, and digging with that cane of his at a little crack in the pavement between his feet. Then, without looking at me, staring intently at the end of the cane, he broke into quick, soft talk. . . .

He was in the middle of it all before I could quite catch what it was all about. But the first words that were clear to my bewildered brain were – " speeding up."

" Training! Munitions! Everything. It's a case of hustle," he was saying. " We used to give a fellow two and three years at Sandhurst before we thought he knew enough to come in out of the rain. But now, it's six weeks O. T. C. and up with him into the firing- line, what? The same with everything else. Can't be taken at the old pace." (Prod.) " Not now." (Prod.) " No time for the dear old leisurely ways. In this war there's no such thing as exceeding the speed limit, even

in " Here he flashed a bright, dark glance at me

and looked back at his cane again. " Even in one's courtship."

" So you seemed to think!" I retorted, feeling my self-possession coming back to me. " So you seemed to think before you went out last time."

" Yes, I made a bad break then," he agreed, in that disconcerting way. " I don't pretend that I didn't make a very bad break." (Prod.) " Not much excuse for me either. I was sore and hurt ... I was an *ass* " (three emphatic prods). "But to go back to what I was talking about. The way I've taken you like this, all in a rush. I have to. I told you I knew what I ought to do. Now I'm telling you why I can't. It might be a case of *now,* or "

He looked towards the grim array of the guns that can do no more mischief.

" Or *never,"* he wound up. " I'm due back again in a week, you know. You – you owe me just a hearing."

At these words, so simply spoken, I seemed to feel a change within myself. Those hot waves of anger seemed to be receding, leaving ground which appeared to me an unexplored tract of my mind. . . . He was " due back " in a week; back to face the muzzles of guns that looked just like these grey-painted, vindictive mouths before us; only – those guns would not be " useless mouths." Back to face bursting shell and sniper's rifle, a hundred hourly perils.

I looked, quickly, at him. I looked as if I had not seen him before. There he sat beside me, leaning a little forward. His slim, brown hands clasped the cane that dug into that crack in the pavement. His dark head, with the soft peaked khaki cap, was tilted a little sideways to glance back at me.

I have always admitted that I found Captain Meredith extremely good-looking.

And how much more he had than just " looks "!

How typical he was of his age and caste and kind ; the flower of Britain, the nation's best, the cream that is at the top! I looked at him in his youth and strength, his easy grace, his unthought-about smartness. . . .

The thought came to me, " Fancy offering *that* – to a bullet!"

It held me silent.

He went on speaking, taking up his subject at another point. " It makes people much franker – war, and the feeling that if you don't *say* what you've got to sayyou may not have time to get it into people's minds any other way. Now, look here. About these war marriages. Lots of people are against them. I was myself at the start. But not since I've realised what this particular war means." He gazed, soberly, at those guns.

He began, again: " In my room at home there's a big framed group of a lot of fellows I was with at Sandhurst. It's a group for Musketry Instruction. There are thirty-two of us there. I was thinking about it the other night, do you know? Thinking over what had become of all those fellows, going over their names. Thirty of them – thirty! – have been outed in this show. Some at Mons, the others later on, down to the other day at Loos. Good chaps, all of 'em. There are only two of that original class left. One other chap – and me."

" Yes," I said, through a lump in my throat. I remembered that framed photograph in " George's room," the room that had been mine at the Bryn. I remembered the cluster of boyish faces; bright with the joy of life, decently-bred, of clean, sporting instincts, trained in a gallant tradition

" Only two left – to carry on," said George, simply. " One feels that it's rather a pity. That sort – wiped out first. Other people, without any particular code, or standard, or notion of doing anything for their country; cranks, conscientious objectors, and what nots – and the unfit – those are left going to be responsible for the ... next lot. Pity."

He paused to acknowledge the salute of a *pottu* whopassed our seat, wearing a blue tin helmet that gave him an oddly ancient Roman look, and leading a little black-bloused boy by the hand. George looked at the little boy. It was the same look that I'd seen on his face as he had saluted those kilted babies in the Luxemburg gardens.

" You see what I mean," said George, looking now full at me.

"Oh, yes, I see," I said. Then, hastily, "But – but "

U *I* TJ.,1.

But' ? Yes, I know what you mean." He

suddenly ceased to prod with that cane. He laid it across his riding-breeched knee as he sat back a little and regarded me. " You mean that sort of proposal would be – well, not an insult, of course. A compliment even. But a cold-blooded sort of way of asking a girl to marry one, if that were the only reason one had. By Jove, yes." The even white line of his teeth' showed under the jet-black finger marks of his moustache as he concluded. " It's not the reason, though."

Full of wonder, I asked " What – what other reason is there then, since it's not You say it's not *because* it's the easiest way out ? "

" Of course not," smiled the young man beside me. Adding one word to explain his reason:

" *Dear!* "

This – well, naturally, this struck me dumb again. I felt nil the pink glow of the sunset flushing my cheeks. I felt my blood singing in my ears, and, overwhelmedand confused with surprise as I sat there, I heard him going on talking to me, softly, persuasively.

" Can't you see now, what I mean when I said that the last three days were immeasurably worse for me than for you ? " he said, close to me. " Before I came I knew I'd made a fool of myself by getting married like that. But I didn't know the exact brand of fool it was until I came here. Met *you!* Saw *you* with my people! Watched you take the place my wife should take ! Went about all over the place with *you* as if it was you I'd married . . . and knew, knew it must all come to an end, and that it was all my own doing that I couldn't even make a beginning. Knew that you'd have to go out of my life instead of staying, Rose, Rose! – where you belonged. Now, don't you think," he ended this rapid little outburst, " don't you think *that* was a rather special little Hades of my own ? "

What could I say to this? " Captain Meredith "

" You called me by my name, once," he reminded me, quickly. " In the hall one morning you called me 'George'!"

I shook my head, bewildered, utterly at a loss. I could feel my heart beating absurdly fast, beneath my *militaire-blue* coat.

I murmured: " But you couldn't f – feel like that about me in that minute of time!"

He gave a short laugh, flicking that cane against his boot now. " Couldn't I, you little blue-eyed witch? The only ' couldn't' in it was that I couldn't say so. Mightn't. Mightn't even keep one white violet overfrom what would have been the morning of my life in the woods with you ! Yet – all the time "

He gave an immense sigh. " I daren't see you, after that, since I hadn't the right. ... I had to keep away from you. Daren't look at you. That's over, thank God! It's gorgeous luck; I've never deserved it,

but " He would have taken my hand. I drew it

away. I stammered " It's too absurd! "

" Isn't it? But it's true for all that, Rose! "

" You wouldn't believe that what 7 said was true "

" Ah! Now you're getting your own back, are you? It's only fair, I suppose," he said, with his dark eyes laughing straight into my bewildered blue ones. " Go on."

I couldn't, the big square and the grey buildings and the guns and the crowds seemed to fade away from me. I saw nothing but his bright face, mischievous and tender. I forgot everything else. And now he had my hand. He was holding it on the bench beside my skirt. He gave it an exultant little tightening of his clasp. And he said, boldly, challengingly, " Ah! You know I care, Rose, you know it now. You can't say you don't believe. And, listen "

" No I – I won't" . . . I guessed what he

meant, what his next challenge would be. " Listen," he persisted, gaily. " You aren't indifferent to me! "

I say I had guessed what the sense of his next remark would be. I hadn't guessed the exact word he would use.

"Indifferent. ..."

That was the word that reminded one of something. Something I'd heard of him before ever I saw him; before I knew that he was still alive.

" *The man isn't born who could be indifferent to George; certainly not the woman!* "

The words fitted a picture in my mind; the scene was a hat shop where two girls sat on a couch and ignored Suzanne's latest *modes,* talking eagerly, softly together. It was the tall, dark, handsome girl in blue who had said those words; the girl I had been with when she questioned me; and to-day, only to-day!

And the memory came to me with a sudden bracing shock.

Of course! Of course . . .

I snatched my hand away from George's clasp.

I looked him full in the face. " Now *you* listen." My voice was suddenly fire again. " I've got something to talk to *you* about. It's about "

I brought the name out, clearly, still looking him in the face as I did so.

" It's about Phillipa Tracey." CHAPTER XXXI

INFATUATION

GEORGE lifted his head. " Phillipa Tracey? Phillipa again? (sharply). What about her? She hasn't got anything to do with this."

"Hasn't she indeed? She has! She has!" I protested, with a sudden rush of memories sweeping over me as I sat there sideways on the bench to face him: memories of everything that Phillipa had said.

" I must tell you. She talked to me ... so much! We're such friends now," I tried to explain to the young man, all incoherently and higgledy-piggledy. " The second time I saw her we had a long talk . . . Even then I saw it all "

" All what? " George's dark brows knitted, a trace of red crept up his cheek. " What did you see, Rose? "

" Everything. The whole truth," I said, still more earnestly. And clasping my hands in my lap I brought

out with utter conviction: " She Phillipa *She*

is the girl you ought to marry! "

He gave his little laugh again; put his hand up to his moustache. He said, quite composedly now, " My dear child, the humiliating truth is that it was Phillipa who refused to marry me."

" Yes, I dare say. I mean, of course. But it isn't a bit humiliating, if you only knew. If you only understood !" I said, emphatically, as he turned a little away again. " Only I don't believe a man ever understands *anything.* Except things like Battalion Orders, and X-rays, and finding where they are by the compass, and all that. You never understand *us!* "

"No?" said George, quite gently.

His face was still turned away from me, but I caught a tiny alteration in the curve of his smooth cheek.

" Don't laugh," I begged. " Don't; it's serious. I've got to tell you "

And, still more incoherently, I got out as much as I could of how Phillipa had talked to me first at *Suzanne's;* about George's disapproval of her; their wrangles, and what that had led to; his proposal, her refusal, the feeling that I knew she had for

He tried to stop me. More than once he tried to stop me, putting a hand on my sleeve, saying " Look here, this hasn't got any bearing on things now, you know. I don't think we need talk about this, need we? . . ." and " I don't think I want to hear "

" You must hear, whether you want to or not. You shall hear."

I meant it, this explanation had to be made *here,* in these cloisters, and *now,* before the sun had stopped setting! This I felt – and all the more because

Well, I can't explain it. But it was there, right at the back of my mind. " It" was an unexpected, a cowardly weakening. It was a wish that I needn'tsay anything more at all about this Phillipa Tracey.

Could it be? Was this the meaning of so many things? My sympathy with Phillipa, who cared for him? My sudden jealousy, yes, *jealousy* of the girl I thought he'd married? My lonely depression and brooding of the last days – not all because I was leaving *Belle-mere?* My resentment against George himself – was it really a groping anger against myself because, unconsciously, but with every moment, I was growing to care, too much, for a man who might not and who did not think of me. . . .

And now – Oh, Heaven! It seemed he *did?* Or thought he did. ... As Phillipa had said of herself, " I might keep him "

But that was *too* selfish. . . . Here was the happiness of two people at stake; two people I liked so much and who had been so nice to me in their different ways. It must be all a mistake that one of them actually thought he was in love with me! Besides, I couldn't want him to be. I *couldn't.*

" I *must* tell you all this," I brought out, desperately. " It's no use two people being made unhappy for life just because nobody would speak out sensibly, like in some old ballad! Three people, perhaps. Because I'm sure that this Major that Phillipa is engaged to can't be happy with her if she's always breaking her heart because he isn't *you!* She "

" I say, my dear little girl, do – do shut up, won't you? Please? " said George, very gently and nicelybut hurriedly. He took my hand again as he said " It's quite a thing of the past now, d'you see? Phillipa is going to be married (and a good thing too) to somebody probably far better suited to her than I should ever have been "

" Nobody's better suited to *anybody* than the person a person wants ! "

" No, no " – George shook his head at my violent interruption. " When she told me that we shouldn't hit it off later, she and I, she was perfectly right. I see that now. Perfectly. We shouldn't have. And now she'll settle down with this gunnei – a Major is he? – and "

" She won't anything of the kind." I pleaded, anxiously, the cause of the other girl. " She wouldn't settle down with an angel from heaven if there was the faintest ghost of a chance of your – *your* proposing again ! " Here I took breath.

" You may think I don't know," said I to the young man, " but I *do.* I may not be any good at reading maps. Hardly any woman is. But," I said, " but I *can* guess what another girl means when she's in the middle of saying ' No,' and that's what no man can do."

And I gave a convinced little nod at the man in question.

" You try her," I said. " You go to her and try. You tell her ' Look here; I love you, I want you!' Say you ' didn't mean what you said before.' You say that, Captain Meredith, and see whether I am not right!"

He cleared his throat. He took up that everlasting little cane and again began prodding that eternal crack in the pavement. Exasperated by impatience, I fidgeted at his side. I should have liked to have taken the stick from him and given him a little hit with it!

Then, just as I thought he was never going to speak again, he took up, quite quickly, " Even if you happened to be right, Rose Mind, I don't admit that

I think you *are* "

(No. Men *never* "admit.")

" But even if it were true, it couldn't make any

difference." (Prod.)

"No difference? You mean, because she's engaged? But it isn't as if she were *married* to this Major," I explained to him. " She would break it off with him in one second (why, do you know she scarcely even *looked* at her trousseau-hats?) if there were the slightest chance of you, of her first love coming back to her. You're the person she really wants to marry."

" It cuts both ways. She (prod) is not the person 7 want to marry."

" But " I said, staring at him, " you were so

madly in love with her. When Phillipa refused you, after (as you thought) flirting with you, you felt that your life was all over. You just married the first girl you thought would be ' consistent' because you were sore and hurt by a girl you couldn't understand. You felt that nothing would ever matter again. You know you did."

" I did," agreed George Meredith. And now he

spoke in the preoccupied voice of our first time together.

By Jove, yes! So I did." And his thoughts seemed to stray off down a lane of recollection. Then he gave himself a little shake, and sat straight up beside me on the bench.

" It's all *bhas* – over," he told me. " It reminds me of some verses I used to like once . . . funny thing to quote verse now, isn't it? I haven't thought of it since about the first time I was badly in love "

"Oh!" I said (deeply interested, as a girl can't help being when a man does actually begin to let her into this part of his autobiography). " *When* were you first in love ? "

" Oh About the age one usually *is, I* suppose,"

this man said, simply. " I must have been eighteen or so. Nine years, . . . By Jove, yes! But I remember those verses. Something about

' 7 *had died for this, last year, to know you loved me* '

and there's another bit

' *Live and let live, and so will I.*

Love and let love, as I will do.
But, sweet, for me no more with you,
Not while I live, not till I die!
Good-night good-bye.'"

The deadly soft and gentle voice stopped speaking.

Sadly, my own voice sounded in my own ears. " Is
that really and truly how you feel towards Phillips now?"

" Really and truly," said George, half whimsically, nodding at me. " That expresses it exactly."

A chill took me to hear him; a mixture of wonderment and sorrow over all the loves that haven't lasted.

Are there many of these? Did these, too, have their wonderful thrilling beginnings and their talk of " forever " and their gay, insolent certainty that never before had two lovers been so made for each other? How pitiful that such passionate dreams had to die just as the rose-glow of the sunset above us was fading away out of the sky, leaving it to the gentle, monotonous dove grey that comes before the dark. . . .

I gave a little shiver.

" Dearest! You're cold! " said George, quickly.

He took hold of my black furs and drew them closer about my throat. And, close to me himself, he said, softly, " I should never feel like that verse about *you,* though. Not about *you,* Rose!"

I drew away from him. " It is a little cold," I said, shakily. " We have been sitting here rather a long time. Let's walk about now, shall we ? "

In the slow Spring dusk we walked through the cloisters, passed the captured German *Taube,* to the other side of the square. We paused beside the trophy that is set up there, the French " *avion "* that can show the riddling of four hundred enemy bullets, and that is now surmounted by a framed announcement: a verseabout the " *coq gaulois "* arising to chase the accursed German hawk.

I turned to it. Anything to put away for another moment that other too-poignant subject.

" How different nations are in their ways of showing their feelings," I mused, as if quite lightly. " Imagine our. putting up sentimental verses over any of our English aeroplanes!"

" Yes; but imagine the French descending to any of our recruiting-poster methods, what? " said the young British officer beside me, drily – ' *Is YOUR best boy in khaki?* ' and the rest. That was a show-up! "

Then his manner altered again. He tucked a slim brown hand inside my arm, drew me close beside him as we stood there before that battered triumphant eagle made of canvas and stays and spars. He bent his handsome head down and muttered, teasingly, coaxingly, " Your best boy is in khaki all right, isn't he? "

"No. Don't!" I protested, unsteadily. "You oughtn't to be saying that to *me."*

And I thought, bitterly, " Must I spend my life in some other girl's shoes? At first it was 'Vivie' whose place I took *pro tern.* Now here I am listening to the things he will be saying, presently, to Phillipa!"

The young man beside me, still holding my arm as we walked along with our faces turned riverwards, persisted in his love-making.

" Why not ? Why must I not; m'm ? Aren't you the girl I care for ? "

" I don't see how – how I *can*

" How ' be bothered," he retorted. " You just are. It's like those new note-cases for holding paper money. You've got the note with the straight bands over it, *here.* And you turn it over and it's got the criss-cross bands over it, *there.* I can't tell you how it works, but it does, don't you know." His voice grew more impatient. " Look here. You're *mine."*

" You must have said that to other girls."

" What difference would that make ? "

"W – wouldn't it?"

" You know it wouldn't; and doesn't. Ah! you know that; you don't even care, now. This is different from any of the – from anything else, Rose! "

" No, no H – How do you know? "

" I'll *show* you, if you let me." Passionately, the silk-soft voice, that was yet so utterly and forcefully masculine, pleaded with me as we walked along. " Rose! You *must."*

" No."

" Little – devil! . . . Ah, my sweet one! I've often wondered if I should ever know the feeling that's kept my father all these years at my mother's little feet. This is it, is it? By Jove, yes! Yes! I've got to have you."

I shook my head, feeling all unstrung, but certain on one point.

" He had made mistakes before. I was not going to be another ' break.' I would not take anything that might mean bitter, fruitless' regrets."

At the stone entrance to Les Invalides I stared *dog*gedly away from him at the lacey spire of the Eiffel Tower; a grey, translucent dragon-fly shape hovered beyond it in the sky; a flying *avion!* the " falcon of France," her speed and safety. At that moment I felt myself repulsing an attack by the strongest force with which a woman ever has to contend; the will-to-yield. I said – gaining ground (I felt) with each word – " Captain Meredith, you think these things about me now, perhaps! That's because you haven't seen *her* "

" Not *seen* her ? "

" Not for a long time. You have forgotten," I told him, " how beautiful she is "

" Yes; as beautiful as a statue. *You're* a live

rose "

-" And how clever she is-

" Who wants a woman to be clever, good God ? "

" Nobody, I know; but if they love her they forgive her, they don't *notice* it! " I urged. " And you've forgotten how much you cared for her once "

He made it sound the cruellest word in the world.

" Once! "

" But you haven't seen her since I've told you what she said. That'll make all the difference," I heard myself positively gabbling at his side. " Now that you know she's not a bit ' a statue' – not to you, not to you! Now that you've heard how she *said* she cared for you so much that "

Gently, but definitely, George interrupted me. (I fancy this was somewhere in the middle of the Place de la Concorde again, the Place that we had crossed – when? Centuries ago. Before I knew anything – *anything!)* Well, he broke in. " I say, darling, that's enough, please. We won't talk about it. Please stop. It's not a bit of good, you know."

" You don't know. You can't know until you have tried. If you would only go there – see her once," I insisted – " see for yourself "

" ' *Breathe upon Love's ashes, it may be flame iciH leap.*' "

George quoted, ironically, smiling down upon my uplifted, pleading face. " My dear little girl, I tell you that sort of thing has never been a success yet. By Jove, no! Always a wash-out. Always! What's over is over. By Jove, yes! Might as well try and put a chicken back into the shell. I know that. I don't see why I should even try."

"Not – to please me?" I said huskily. I felt that with a few more minutes of this I should disgrace myself utterly and break down. " To please me, George! "

Silence for a second as we walked along.

Then George said, quite briskly, " Nothing else satisfy you? Very well then. To please you."

" You mean you'll go ? " I took up quite brightly. But I confess that, to my utter shame, my heart sank. Growing, growing at the back of my mind was the knowledge that, in spite of all my pleading, I was terrified to let him go. " To please me " I realised

how utterly it would not " please " *me* if Captain GeorgeMeredith, late Miss Vera Vayne's husband, and more lately still the suitor for my own hand, were to fall into the arms of his first sweetheart. At least, not his *first* sweetheart. She, whoever she had been, would possibly be knitting waistcoats for sons in the Flying Corps at this moment. But, as he knew himself, what girl would worry for a moment.

Sitting beside George in that ramshackle French taxi, I grew more and more certain that I was preparing to put away from me with my own hand what I was beginning to look upon (perfectly ridiculously) as my own happiness.

I couldn't even pluck up enough spirit to refuse to let him take mj hand again. He did so. Not only that, but he stripped off my white glove, tucked it into his pocket, and then sat with my palm held against his cheek.

I let him.

It was for the only time, I told myself!

Confusedly, I remembered Phillipa's saying that George was one of these " ultra-masculine men who show the touch of feminine finish." He did, he did. Mentally ; for hadn't he quoted verse like a woman or an artist? Physically; for wasn't the cheek below my palm as smooth and as fine in texture as that of another girl? Yet no one could for one instant hint that anything about the young soldier, mental or physical, was effeminate. He was virile! I felt that his mind was a man's mind; with all the depths that *we* shall never fathom, all the preoccupations in which we have nopart, all the acuteness and the coarseness of grain and the delicacies and the obtuseness that each in turn take M by surprise, all the little differences of code and humour and phrase that – well! *Make* all the difference. And the rest of him showed the strength and grace of a thoroughbred; he was steel under velvet.

Any woman might be proud to belong to him; Phil- lipa or *any* woman!

And the taxi was jolting us on towards Passy – and her.

Smoothing his cheek against my hand, he broke out suddenly, joyously, like a schoolboy. " I say, *darling, isn't* it topping that we've managed to meet each other? Rose, d'you know what?"

"What? "I sighed.

" It sounds awful neck to say it, but it's true. You are."

"lam what?"

He laughed, tenderly and triumphantly, as he said:

" You are going to be so awfully in love with me! "

" I'm not. I'm *not!"* violently. And now I did snatch my hand away. " I'm *never* "

" Oh, aren't you. You wait! Yes, you are."

" *Indeed* I'm "

Here a jolt of the taxi flung me suddenly against George, just as the other bouncing cab had flung me on to Phillipa's lap the first time that she and I had met.

He put out an arm to steady me, holding me for a second.

For a second, as we were whirled round a corner inthe dusk where the Paris lights gleamed dim as do the lights of London, I thought that he was going to take things for granted.

I stiffened against his arm.

Instantly he released me, giving a little odd but reassuring laugh.

" Oh, no; I wasn't going to kiss you," he said, quietly. " Not here; not now."

Adding, firmly, " But very soon! "

A little breathlessly I said " Wait until you have seen the Traceys."

" Not if the blessed people are not at home," retorted George. " Supposing they're out? "

It was at this minute that I remembered the Traceys' " tamasha " and Harry's leave. They were all going out somewhere to spend the evening. . . .

Sternly I had to repress a thrill of hope. " It's quite early," I told myself. " They can't have gone out yet."

They hadn't gone out.

The neat *bonne* who opened the door to us said that madame was at home – that she was receiving

"George! Ye Gods! it's George and the bride!" exclaimed a breezy voice over the bannisters.

(So Phillipa had not told her mother the news yet, that George did not yet own a bride?)

" Let 'em all come. The more the merrier. They can eat off the same plate "

There was the twinkle of Mrs. Tracey's slim feet and ankles downstairs as she ran to meet us. " Nice of you to bring him, my dear " – to me. " George, I am delighted. You ruffian! Handsomer than ever! Quite the young wounded hero. How's the leg getting on, doing you all right? You know the old proverb – *'A lame man always limps Ms way into the ladies' hearts!'* – of course, you do, villain! " And she lifted her short, firm-chinned face and bestowed a hearty kiss upon the young man who followed me in.

"You don't mind, do you, Mrs. George? A flower or so growing out of the ruin," she rattled on in her inconsequent way. " The one advantage of growing grey and fat and harsh with years is that one may say and do as one chooses to any attractive young man who comes to the house! Remember my words a hundred years hence. In the meantime, come and have supper with us."

" Supper, Auntie Tracey ? " protested George as we all went upstairs. " I thought we might get here in time for ' husband's tea '! "

" Yes; but we are having supper to-day in the middle of the afternoon, to give us time to pick up some other people we know, before going on to Montmartre. Why didn't you bring your mother with you, George? It lends a zest to the dullest show for me, to watch Meg Meredith being shocked! "

" She's off somewhere with my father," said George behind my shoulder.

At another time I should have smiled over this vague excuse. " Somewhere " in England!

" Now, Mrs. George, brides first! " Mrs. Tracey went on as we reached the top of the stairs. " We are feeding in the studio. No room for Harry's legs in that cubby-hole, the other place."

The studio took up the whole of the top floor. It was a long, brown-papered, top-lighted room that I had not seen before, though I suppose Lady Meredith was taken to it by our hostess while I was having that first talk of mine with Phillipa: *("Did George never say anything to you about me? "*)

And here in the studio, with its gleam of a white- decked table and pink-shaded lights, we found what seemed a crowd of khaki gathered about Phillipa.

I instantly realised that this was what a woman would call " Phillipa's day." In the cab this morning she had looked tired, older than her age. This

evening

How had she pulled herself together? How had excitement caused her to glow as if illumined from within?

Her eyes were laughing jewels. Her slim, white throat gleamed from the ruffle of an all-black frock, a lovely thing from Jeanne's. She wore one great scarlet carnation at her waist. Another was placed as if it had just dropped carelessly on to the hem of her out- - jtanding skirt.

t I saw George's odd, surprised glance at her as she ' jpeld out her hand to him in a laughing greeting of absolute self-possession. Beautiful, she looked. Beautiful. At the sight of her beauty I became like the poor Queen of Sheba when she was shown what she could never hope to rival, and " there was no more spirit in her."

Oh! it was all very well for George to put on that conventional mask again. I knew he must capitulate. He must take his affections back from whence they had strayed for so short a time. Back to lay before those slim, arched feet (inherited from her mother) of Phil- lipa's.

Well, I should have had one afternoon of George all to myself. One glimpse of what his love-making migh be. One taxi-drive with my hand held where it woul have wished to linger. That is more than some girl get of the man with whom they have become absolutely hopelessly infatuated.

These other two, I felt certain, would make it up tha very evening.

13

SECTION 13

CHAPTER XXXII

Phillipa's Good-night

IHAT evening is such a confused blur to me now I I scarcely remember in order how things happened. I know Phillipa took me up to her own jjlagain, to lay aside my furs and tidy my hair, it must have been before supper, then? She id my face in her hands, looked at me and kissed nice, very lightly on the cheek. Then she said ady here knows anything, yet." Then she looked . at me, so hard that I could not face her eyes. I . my own away. I felt myself shaking. Still look- lard at me, but speaking very gently, Phillipa said haven't *you* anything more to tell me since this hoon?"

heard myself give a great quivering sigh as I said I, Phillipa! No. I don't think I have anything you."

lecause, of course, I thought that I had better leave fhat now to George.

think I said " He will tell you everything there is," I think she said " He won't have to. *Because I*

how could she?)

we were going out I said " Oh! Phillipa, you look so lovely to-night, lovelier even than I thought you could ! No wonder people make love to you! "

And she said, lightly, " You little, sweet silly! If I were a man I would marry you myself."

But at table it was at Phillipa that the men looked. I don't know even how many there were of them. George sat next to her. One of the others was a young French officer who had been brought in by Harry TraceyiHhe long-legged cousin. There was a loud-voiced, Indian Army man who hailed " Old Meredith " with a shout of surprise.

(I noticed that he called him " Merry-dith " in the English manner instead of putting the emphasis on the last syllable but one, which is the unvarying Welsh Way.) Then there was a gunner, but not PhiBipa's gunner with the " kindest old heart in the world.' the *fiance. I* know I felt an added queer and unre able pang to hear that he was still " sitting tight at Salonika."

(How glad I am now that he was not there at party!)

There were no introductions, I think, but I gatt that Phillipa was right; that I was still " Mrs. George " as far as the people there were concerned, and there would be scarcely time for any explanation during the hurried feasting that this, was to be.

Sitting there, bewildered, by the side of the gunner and opposite to George! I heard much laughter and a good deal of talk, most of it (as usual) from Mrs. Tracey. At one moment I realisedthat she was talking cynically (also as usual) about marriage.

" A hopeless institution – quite hopeless," I think she called it. " It is based on something that is wrong in its essence. . . . No – it doesn't matter Maudie hearing," this was the silent flapper, " because she won't believe until she tries, and then it will be too late. . . . Based on an utterly false idea, my dear friends. . . . It means trying to make something permanent that was never intended to be more than a delightful phase."

Her brown eyes snapped, more audaciously than ever as she added: " Shortens even the natural length of the phase! Like sniffing and sniffing at a bit of mignonette till there's no scent left! "

And then I think she went on to say something about the whole arrangement being like having a nice dinner off a leg of good hot roast Welsh mutton, and then sitting for the rest of one's life at the table before the cold joint.

" Or worse, the congealing joint," she said.

Let me see Was all this before or after that the

French officer said? Oh, it must have been before.

Yes, because the I. A. man with the boisterous voice gave a shout of laughter and burst in, " Oh! I say. Come! that's a bit off, saying a thing like that, Auntie Tracey, to a party like this! Here's old Merry-dith on his honeymoon!!! and Phillipa engaged! And me just thinking of taking the plunge myself! Cold mutton – oh! I say! Well, I suppose it's better than having no dinner at all – Ha, ha! and having to keep

yourself going with simpkin pegs at the side-board, what?"

" Much better," came George's " deadly-soft" voice from the other side of the table.

And then the voice of Phillipa, who so seldom said anything before her mother, quite decidedly broke in, " Oh, yes! much better. It's starting with something all right anyhow, if it is a marriage with a right sort of reason."

I saw her mother's surprised glance at her.

" Don't let's call it mutton," Phillipa added, challeng- ingly. " Let's say it's like ordering a new frock that you have got to wear and wear, every day. A frock that would have to last out your time. If it's a good frock, if it's decently cut, and of the best material – well! You don't mind so much, even when it *does* go out of fashion; even if it *does* show it is old and done for now. You can still tell at a glance – ' *It may be a rag note, but it has been a good frock.'* And you feel kindly to it. You respect it to the last thread! "

" Bravo, Phillipa! Hurray! That's right, you stick up for matrimony!" vociferated the India Army officer, clapping his hands. ' It may have been a rag once, but never you mind, I will respect it now!' (Ha! ha!) Very sensible. Just what I feel myself! "

The echoes of his voice were still making the welkin ring when George spoke again in the quiet tone that is always more forceful than a shout. At that moment it sounded clearer and more direct.

" Thank you, Phillipa," he said, with a friendly littlenod to the white-and-black-and-scarlet beauty beside him. " That was very sweet of you, Phillipa. Thank you for cheering up my little girl over there. She was beginning to look quite scared! "

Then he looked across the glitter and the flowers of the table and smiled straight into my eyes.

I think it was then – Yes! I'm sure it must have been *then* that I knew. A miracle had happened. He had seen Phillipa again in all her loveliness. And still – still he turned to me. " My little girl," he said, in a tone I couldn't mistake. It was true, it was true.

" Mine after all? " I thought, dazed, and I went on feverishly eating up the gunner's roll for him not knowing what I was doing, not knowing what was being said. Somebody noticed the flowers – a war-economy, cunningly imitated blossoms of calico from the Galeries Xiafayette – no, no; that was at the beginning. It was after what George had said that the French officer gave a sudden movement that set a row of full-sized medals clanking across his chest.

" *EcoutezI"* he exclaimed, his dark head turned towards the curtained windows. " I have heard "

We all paused.

" Distant fire – firing," he said. " Guns."

" Guns ? My dear chap, you've guns on the brain, naturally," returned young Harry Tracey, who was carving cold bird at the side-board – a black oaken Brittany coffer. " I expect lots of us will go on hearing those at times a couple of years after peace has been signed. . . . Look here, Auntie Ethel" – theleggy boy turned to Mrs. Tracey, who, I could see, put him in the place of a son she would have adored. " Look here, is red ink all you're going to stand us to drink? Four – five fellows from ' the fly-blown Front,' and one of them a gay bridegroom, dash it all. Aren't we going to have a thimbleful of Boy ? "

" Oh, well, you go and buttle in the cellar then," said Mrs. Tracey. Her nephew went, to return with a couple of fat gilt-collared bottles. With an imitation of the theatrical head-waiter at Henry's, he passed round the table, pouring out the whispering wine into the daintily-cut French glasses.

" Well! Here's the usual toast," announced Mrs. Tracey, from her end of the table. " Success to our Arms!"

The Indian Army man added the tag –

" *Our Arms for your defence –*

Your arms our recompense!

Fall in! "

We raised our glasses. I caught Phillipa's dark eyes smiling at me above the golden wine. She nodded to me, vivid and lovely as that blood-red carnation below her breast. She leant forward, calling in her clear voice her addition to the toast.

" *Here's Luck – to the Bride!* "

They were the last words she ever spoke.

For they were drowned, the words of her gay andchivalrous toast, in the deafening hideous explosion, the " crash!" the shrill shattering of glass, the sudden noisy overturning of chairs which meant that battle, murder, sudden death had made their way into that cheerful, laughing, unsuspecting war-time party that thought itself so far, for the moment, from all thought of war.

Did you ever see, some years ago, a play – a grimly prophetic play – called " An Englishman's Home " ? It foretold trouble with Germany; consequently many people called it hysterical and far-fetched. But there was one scene in it of which even those superior people praised the acting. It was where Gerald du Maurier, as the young footballer who shirked military training, is shot where he stands on his own dining-table, peering out at the fighting. " They've kicked off over there!" he is calling excitedly when he is hit. With a jerk his voice breaks right off. He drops without a cry; drops, inert, killed on the spot.

It was exactly so that Phillipa Tracey fell back into George's arms.

An air-raid: a Fokker over Paris!

That had been the secret of the distant firing that the young Frenchman's quick ears had caught.

A bomb dropped at random: a bomb that brought about two casualties only, as far as we have heard. Through the studio-roof it was hurled, killing one woman, wounding one British officer.

For George's shoulder, as he sprang forward, was almost cut through by a triangle of falling glass from that sky-light. And Phillipa was killed by a blow on the head from a splinter; struck down in her beauty and killed on the instant in the arms of the man whom she had never ceased to love.

" It's the best way."

This thought came to me in the midst of the tense horror afterwards: in the midst of her mother's tearless collapse and of her sister's sobs, and of the silent boding fury of those fighting men who had seen their countrywoman fall.

For the life of me I could not help feeling that Phillipa herself would say it was better so. It was then, even then, that she would have asked to take leave of life.

Don't you see, she had known the very heights of it!

She had cared so much for her man that – she could even give him up. She could be friendly and sweet to the girl whom he had chosen. She could live through the most poignant of her hours with a smile on her lips to the last.

Never, never now would she have to know the descent from those heights. There would be no reaction for her. No relapse into everyday, petty, unemotional, trivial existence. No agony of jealousy – which might have come? No heartache. No knowledge of marriage without love.

Am I so wrong in thinking that Phillipa was well out of it all?

What I shall see of her forever will be the quiet, restful pose of that little, proud, dark head among flowers; and the smile, half-whimsical, half-triumphing, that lurked still about the dark-fringed lids, about the chiselled lips whose last words has been " *Luck to the Bride."* CHAPTER XXXIII

The Bride's Home-bringing

IT was a month after all this that I travelled down to Wales by the train that I took at the very beginning of my story: the 10:30 from Euston to Llandedwydd, via Camrys.

George Meredith, a little pale still from his weeks of being nursed at Passy, sat in the corner-seat beside me, looking out with a happy smile as the flat, broad fields and sluggish canals of the Midlands gave place to the jagged rocky hills and dales, the stone-fences, the tint green pastures and the rushing clear waters of Wales.

" This is pretty good, darling, isn't it? " said my husband, taking up my hand that lay in his own, and giving a little bite to the finger that wore his new wedding-ring.

For, after all this make-believe of marriage that had been nothing but fibs and difficulties and hopeless yearning, we were really married now. We had been married early that very morning before we started. Married in a grimy little Bloomsbury church, with Mrs. Tracey, who had come over from France with us, to give me away.

George had the license in his pocket now, to show his mother.

" That'll explain almost anything," he said, cheerfully, to me, with his cheek against mine as we looked out of the window together at the flying Spring landscape under the pennon of racing white smoke. " She never *did* approve of that registry office. We'll tell her what we told poor old Auntie Tracey. Say that you didn't feel that it was all *pukka,* that you didn't feel properly married to me until you'd gone to church and said all those things about obeying me."

This was startling. " D'you mean, George, that we're *not* to tell her we never even met each other until "

" T, ssh," said George, solemnly, clapping my hand over my mouth.

I pulled my head aside, remonstrating. " Yes, but "

" It will take you at least a fortnight to tell her that story," said George, reflectively, " *with* the whole of the additional Paris chapters. Still, I dare say my aunt on the other side of the valley will put me up for a fortnight."

" You mean *you'd* go away while it was going on, at the Bryn?"

" Rather. Couldn't stand any more ' explanation.' Having to help you to write to that unfortunate R. A. M. C. fellow about your engagement to me was quite enough. By Jove, yes! Poor chap "

" Oh, well, never mind *him," I* said, rather callously, I am afraid. " I have thought of a splendid plan for Reggie Penmore. I shall ask him to stay with us '

" Topping for him," put in George's more expressionless voice. " Ripping plan."

" and I'll introduce him to Nurse Phyllis. They

would get on so beautifully. They've the same sort of "

" Oh, well, never mind *them,"* George laughed. People in love have a way of hating to let the conversation stray away from themselves and the other person. I've noticed it even in myself. " I'm just telling you, Rose, that if you're going to involve me again, I'll go."

" And leave *me? "*

" Ah, you think that would be too hard a thing for me to do, what? " he said, coolly.

Then suddenly the coolness vanished.

Quickly, as the train dashed past woods all freshly greening over, he made a little snatch at me. He clasped me with his strong arm, pulling my furs away from my neck. He put his face close, and kept it there for a second as if brooding over me, without touching me, murmuring " What's this scenty stuff that you've got about you, child? "

" Some of that that you bought me in Paris. That time ages ago. That lovely big bottle of scent called ' *Quand Vote went.'* The first thing you ever gave me. I shall try never to – to use that all up, George."

" You darling, you darling. *Oh,* you sweet," he whispered again, impetuously. " Ah. To think that

I needn't ever again " he broke off, to crowd a

dozen swift hot kisses into the curve of my bare throatbefore he let me go as suddenly as he had caught me. I was breathless. He spoke, coolly, again. " I don't think that I'll have to leave you after all, perhaps."

" Don't, ever," I begged him, shakily. And I put my lips to his coat-lapel, just by the badge. " How *could I* live without you ? "

Thank Heaven that there will be no more " leaving," no return to the Front for Captain George Meredith. That wound he received from the flying glass on the night of the raid will keep him on light duty at home until the end of the war. . . .

Meantime here was our journey's end. Here was the funny little coal-box of a station, and here the car, waiting on the rocky road. Here was Sir Richard, in his beloved shaggy Norfolk, hastening to meet us. In the lengthening Spring evening we sped up the drive where that foam of white snow-drops had melted into a dancing yellow sea of daffodils. Up, to the Bryn, where windows glowed rosily, doors were flung wide. There, within, were the flying skirts and meadow-sweet hair of *Belle-mdre.* Behind her was Pritchard, with (I suspected) a background of every maid servant in the place. And behold. As we pulled up before the mounting-block and the slab cut with the outline of George's first saddle, lo and behold, from somewhere at the back of the house, there dashed through the gloaming a shapely, white four-legged form, leaping into the air with the *abandon* of the Welsh Dragon himself, rending that air with shrieks of exultant welcome thatdrowned anything that any mere human might wish,;? to say.

" Down, Straf. Down," shouted George, laughing1? and clearing his throat and shaking away something that j sparkled on his own lashes at the sight of the delight of this " dumb friend " as some people would have called him. " Down, Straf, old man "

Down? Any one who knows his kind would-guess that Straf would not " down," that, in fact, he upped, per- ' sistently and gleefully. First upon George as he came out of the car, then upon me, then again upon the beloved master; coming near to hurting that wounded H shoulder. So that at last Sir Richard had to make a grab at him and, catching him by his studded collar, dragged him away from the travellers.

" Hully, Mam; hullo, everybody," sang out George, I as naturally as if he had only just come back from I school. Even I could only just catch the excited little I quiver that threaded his voice.

" Now, then, hold on a minute, please, all of you," he said as he was surrounded. " Stand back a second: I've got to bring my wife in, you know."

" Oh, George, don't – you mustn't lift me. My darling, you'll hurt your shoulder."

But he caught me up, as easily as if I had been a I"I child, with his other arm.

So, leaning against his breast, I was carried as a bride has to be carried – over the threshold into her husbands home.

THE END

Breinigsville, PA USA
24 October 2010
247926BV00001B/70/P

9 781150 002106